MEDICINE GAME

DELBY POWLESS

Cover art by Vision Artworks
Learn more at visionartworks.ca

CONTENTS

CHAPTER ONE

BE A GOOD BOY

The first things you notice are clouds of dust. Then, if you squint, you can see lacrosse players. Eighteen men running, breathing heavily, sweating. Intent on crisscrossing the field, jockeying for position, their minds in another world. Two stoic goalies, their minds very much in the present, bracing for the next assault. Generations have pounded around this field, killing a lot of the grass in the process but making the white rubber ball easier to spot among the slashing sticks. Easier to control, easier to flick past the opposing goaltender, especially when you are in the flow of the game. This game can heal your spirit and lift you to new heights at the same time. Watching the game can excite you and also calm you. Native Americans believe when lacrosse is played the Creator smiles and grants them good health, a good mind, and a strong heart. That's why they call it the "Medicine Game."

Even the youngest of children are riveted by the game – in the crowd a six-year-old boy and his four-year-old brother sit mesmerized. No fidgeting or complaining. When James, the sturdy four year old, coughs because of the dust drifting through the air, he does his best to stifle it. He doesn't want to miss any part of the game while his father is playing. Next to James, his brother Tommy pats the younger boy's shoulder approvingly. For a kid, James always tries his best to not disturb anyone during the game action.

The game is lacrosse, but to the people of the Sparrow Lake Nation, it's more than a game – it's a way of life. Today, the stands are packed to near capacity for the 1992 local men's league championship game. The mild September weather makes it easy on young and old alike to enjoy the game.

The game is tied. Regulation time is running out. For a split-second the players remain still, and then comes a flurry of action. The face-off goes in the home team's favor, and all of a sudden, James and Tommy's father has the ball. Beau Henry smoothly shifts around the other players, avoiding their slashing sticks. He shows quick athletic strides and slick control of his lacrosse stick as he moves closer to the opposing goal. When he reaches it, a heartbeat ahead of the pack, there is no hesitation. He shoots.

The goalie lunges hastily, but the ball ricochets violently off his stick in the wrong direction, streaking past him and into the goal. Time expires. Half of the crowd groans; the other half launches into celebration. The league championship trophy awaits the victors for pictures to be taken. The photos will be blurry because of the excitement, but the images will still capture the sheer joy and intense emotion the people feel about the game.

The home team, Beau's team, explodes in cheers, patting him on the head in celebration. He beams broadly, white teeth dazzling against his deep, polished bronze skin. On the sidelines, the collected families applaud and whistle. Marian hugs her two sons, long black braids swooping forward to join the embrace. She is a tall, lean woman with the same polished bronze complexion as her husband. Her face is smooth-skinned with a bright smile and dark brown eyes that snap fire when she is angry. Right now, though, she is laughing and smiling with the infectious excitement that has spread throughout the crowd.

The hero of the moment breaks away from his teammates to watch his family's reaction. Marian claps her hands together in celebration of the winning goal as Beau points to his family with a broad smile. His two sons are almost falling off the old bleachers with excitement, and Marian hauls them back by their shirts. Every spectator in the stands seems to be yelling and cheering, showing their approval. Beau Henry continues to smile until he sees Hazel Blackwater. She is a tall, older woman with long, white hair in a single braid down her back. Hazel has kind, sad eyes, and she looks directly at Beau with a slight smile on her face. He can't hold her gaze and quickly turns his head.

Beau Henry's eyes focus on his family again. He thinks how beautiful Marian is and how lucky he is to have two happy, healthy boys. His number one priority is his family and enjoying their lives together. Yes, there's the game and his work, but nothing can match the feeling of accomplishment. Not just scoring a game-winning goal, but also being part of something larger than himself. He is happier than he has been in a long time. *If only this moment could last forever*, he thinks. The proud, loving father and his adoring family.

Beau grins at the wide-eyed expressions on his sons' faces and jogs over to the official collecting the lacrosse ball out of the opponent's net.

Beau asks the ref for the ball, and with a nod the official hands it to him. He makes his way over to his little family on the sidelines. The boys are thrilled when he produces the game-winning ball, tossing it to Tommy with a flip of the wrist. Tommy reaches out to catch it, running his hand gently over the smooth, white surface. The ball is battle-scarred with dirt, but Tommy manages to clean it on his jeans, polishing the rubber ball until it almost glows. Tommy lets James, who is awestruck, hold the trophy for a while, but takes it back for safe keeping for the ride home.

Marian waves to her husband, pleased with his thoughtful gesture. She feels proud of being married to him, someone who helps to build skyscrapers by day and plays lacrosse in his spare time, skilled in both his work and his hobby. Working with iron and climbing steel has given Beau muscles that she loves to trace with her hands. When he takes his shirt off to chop wood or swim in the lake, Rez women loudly catcall him. He loves it, and Marian puts up with it, secure in the knowledge that he loves his family above all else. He has never strayed from her, not even during the mood swings of her first pregnancy.

Marian Henry is not obsessive about her feelings and tends to be immensely practical. Over the almost seven years they've been married, she has taken Beau's measure precisely. He is physically strong and athletic, very skilled with iron and steel work, but not as adept with books. She knows his intelligence to be more of the hard-nosed kind and books just don't speak to him like they do to her. She does the household accounting and tries to make sure they get by financially. He is fun-loving and spontaneous with a few rough edges. He isn't always realistic and often doesn't think ahead. Accordingly, Marian does her best to plot their family's future and channel his sense of play into useful activities. Weighing Beau's pros and cons, though, she finds that the balance sheet is decidedly on the plus side.

With the celebration on the field over, the players head for the locker room. The field is empty only for a moment before being flooded with chattering young kids who always bring their lacrosse sticks to the game. They watched the men intently during the game, clutching their own sticks tightly, and now their moment has come. The young boys take quick advantage, firing balls at the lacrosse net while the field is open for them to use. Tommy is one of them, using his newly acquired lacrosse ball to work on his technique. The kids take turns eluding phantom defenders before firing their own game winning shots into the twine. Some pause to revel in the imagined victories, others immediately run to retrieve so they can shoot again. Slowly the numbers dwindle as the sun fades away until only Tommy is left on the field. He continues shooting at the net from different positions, over and over again while Marian and James sit in the stands watching him. Beau emerges from the locker room with his lacrosse stick and equipment bag in hand. He glances around, puts his gear down, and jogs over to Tommy to play catch. Tommy works hard to impress his father, trying to make sure every time he passes the ball to Beau that it goes accurately to his father's lacrosse stick so that the older man doesn't have to move to catch the ball. Even at six years old, Tommy is aware that his father is watching him. He tries his best to ensure his passes are perfect. Tommy feels nervous and pleased at the same time.

Marian calls over, "You guys ready to go yet?" Beau and Tommy make their way to Marian and James, then on to the parking lot where the family piles into a Ford pick-up truck. They ride home bouncing on the long dirt road that leads back to the Sparrow Lake houses. James dozes off in his car seat and Tommy sits on Marian's lap for the short ride back. The talk revolves all around the game and the loudness of the crowd. Laughter fills the truck cab as James wakes up just before they arrive home and says, "I score goals, too!"

Their wooden ranch style house has been passed down in Beau's family for two generations, last belonging to his Great-Uncle Ralph, who generously gave it to the eighteen-year-old couple as a wedding present before he passed away. The home has three bedrooms and a single shared bath, old windows, and an attic full of odds and ends. The front porch is welcoming, and Marian loves the big, cleared yard that her boys to play in.

Overall, the house remains cozy throughout most seasons. Marian has worked hard to make it a snug nest, and Beau has spent many evenings and weekends improving the insulation and carrying out various home improvement projects. Handmade quilts keep them warm. A wood-burning stove adds needed heat during upstate New York winters, and careful accounting on Marian's part has given them a full-size deep freezer in the garage. This extra space is invaluable for storing deer meat.

James has fallen asleep again and Beau carries him into the house. Tommy is too wound up to stop talking.

"You were awesome, Dad! You smoked those guys!" he chirps enthusiastically, looking up at his father with hero worship. Beau grins. Even from a child, praise is sweet.

"Thanks, buddy. Were you paying attention?" he asks, teasing his son.

Marian cracks up at the surprised look on Tommy's face. "Paying attention? He was practically on the field with you!"

"Well, there were times today when I suppose we could have used another good player."

Tommy's mouth drops open at hearing his fondest wish expressed. The six year old is obsessed with lacrosse. Not just because his father plays but because it is everywhere on the Rez. In driveways, on front lawns, back yards, on a real playing field if you are lucky. Even looking at newspaper cut-outs of favorite lacrosse players can occupy hours of time. But to score a goal, in a real game, to win a championship, that is almost beyond imagination. The boys think and talk about the game constantly.

Laying his youngest down on his bed, Beau ruffles Tommy's hair. It is slightly curly, like Beau's, but his eyes are like Marian's – large and tilted over high cheekbones. They are deeply expressive. He remains clutching his newest, most prized possession – the white lacrosse ball.

"Maybe someday we'll play on the same team? But you'll have to work hard to be a good player. Time for bed now; go get your pajamas on."

Excited by thoughts of lacrosse fame, Tommy sprints off to his room to don his Spiderman pajamas. Beau laughs softly and undresses the sleeping James, who doesn't wake up as he is tucked into pajamas and under the covers. He brushes a kiss over James' forehead and the boy doesn't stir. From the beginning, James has been a stoic, calm child who slept through the night even at only a few months of age. Tommy, on the other hand, is sensitive and prone to nightmares that send him crawling into his parents' bed for comfort. Beau loves them both, but privately agrees with Marian that James is much less exhausting.

"Are they in bed?" asks Marian as Beau comes back out into their kitchen.

"I put James down, but Tommy is just getting changed."

He leans in and kisses her. There is heat in it. He loves to win, and except when she is nagging at him, he adores his clever, loving wife.

"Call the babysitter," he whispers in her ear. "We should go out for a bit tonight."

Blushing a little, Marian dials one of their nearest neighbors, "Is Jen still able to watch the boys for us tonight? Good. Thank you so much." She hangs up the phone and turns back to her husband.

"Her dad is bringing her over now," she says, stealing a kiss of her own.

Tommy walks into the kitchen in his pajamas and freezes, eyes wide. "Who's coming over?" he asks.

"Jen. She's going to watch the two of you while Daddy and I go out with our friends," replies Marian, wondering if she has time to do her make-up.

Instantly, Tommy clings to her leg, wrapping around her like a black bear swarming up a tree. He buries his face against her hip, squeezing his eyes shut.

"I don't want you guys to leave! Can't you stay home with me? I don't want you to go."

Beau crouches down next to Tommy and gently pries him off Marian. She mouths her thanks at him and heads toward the bathroom.

"It's okay, buddy. Mommy and Daddy are just going to go out with their friends for a little while, okay? We'll be back before you know it."

Tommy opens his eyes wide, studying his father's face. In the background, Marian comes out of the bathroom and seeing that she still has a little time, goes into the bedroom to change her outfit.

"It's okay," repeats Beau, smoothing Tommy's hair. Tommy can see the impatience in his father's eyes. He wants his parents to stay but he feels overwhelmed by the desire to please his father.

"Okay," he whispers. He can't bear to disappoint his hero.

There's a polite knock on the door, and Jen lets herself in. Few of the houses on the Rez are ever locked.

Jen is a petite girl with waist-length black hair, a narrow face, and slanted eyes. Her mother, Eliza, died almost ten years ago. Those who remember Eliza never fail to exclaim at how much Jen resembles her. At twelve years old, Jen has the promise of extraordinary, elegant beauty.

Her eyes, however, are curiously flat, unanimated. Not dull but emotionless. When she speaks, her face moves and forms expressions, but the eyes never change. Other children avoid Jen. They think there is something spooky about her that seems oblivious to adults.

Marian strolls out of the bedroom wearing a slightly newer and somewhat tighter pair of jeans. She has on a red blouse that perfectly contrasts her dark hair, which she wears loose, hanging to her waist. She grabs Beau's arm and leans down to address Tommy.

"Now, you be a good boy for Jen, okay?" she encourages.

Tommy nods silently, reaching up for a last hug and kiss.

"Love you," she says, a little surprised at his scared, abandoned expression. There is real sadness in his eyes. Marian thinks him too young to look that way, but she feels hopeful that he'll grow out of it.

"Love you, too, Mom," Tommy replies automatically.

Beau helps Marian out the door, boosting her into the truck with a playful hand on her rear. She slaps at him and laughs. She puts on her seatbelt, fussing with it so that it doesn't crease her blouse. Beau doesn't bother with his seatbelt. They pull out of the driveway and head toward their favorite local bar. They know that when they arrive, members of Beau's lacrosse team will have the celebration well underway. Beau looks forward to being the star of the show. The center of attention. He loves a good party.

Tommy watches them leave with his nose pressed against the window. Darkness envelops his sight as the headlights disappear down the road. He doesn't want to turn around. Tommy feels like crying and running at the same time. His body flinches and freezes when he hears Jen speak.

"Come here, Tommy," Jen softly orders, reaching for his hand. Numbly he follows her to the living room. After all, he promised to be a good boy, and it wasn't as if this hadn't happened before.

When she touches him, it is the only time he has ever seen her eyes change expression. The distant, frozen stare disappears. In its place is a burning rage and fury. It reminds him of the time that Jen was given a puppy. Her uncle's dog had a litter of six almost purebred huskies, adorable bundles of fur with bright blue eyes and fluffy tails. Generously, he had given her the pick of the litter, a yappy little male with a dark gray mask and white feet.

Jen had smiled and thanked her uncle. The puppy yapped and licked her face.

Later, Marian brought Tommy over to see the puppy. Tommy walked into the back yard and heard awful crying sounds. Instinctively, Tommy had hid behind the woodshed. Alone, he'd snuck into the woods to see the source of that horrible noise.

Jen was hurting the puppy. The soft, white fur was matted with blood. There was only one blue eye now. She had tied it to a tree so that it couldn't crawl away.

Tommy was frightened, but didn't make a sound. Carefully, he crept back out of the woods and tore back to the house where Marian was. He never said a word about what he had seen. The next day he heard his father say that Jen's puppy had gotten loose and gone missing. Both parents sighed and agreed that it is so sad for a little girl to lose her pet.

Tommy suspects that the puppy was dead long before anyone noticed it was missing. He had nightmares that night. He has bad dreams all the time.

Standing him next to the couch, Jen grabs his pajama pants and pulls them down, letting them pool at his ankles. She then reaches out and touches the child where he knows she is not supposed to touch him.

He holds still. He knows by now that if he moves, she will hurt him.

"I guess you'll have to do. I'll make you into a man yet," she sighs. Rubbing him harder, she pushes him down on the couch and lies on top of him. His head is buried somewhere under her shoulder, and his legs end partway down her bony shins. Tommy begins to whimper. He knows what comes next.

"Be quiet," Jen growls, sounding less human now, more like the predator she is. Her hands, acting like searching snakes, tighten around his neck as she begins to squeeze. Tommy is having trouble keeping his eyes open as he struggles for air. His face begins to bloat, turning a reddish purple as he fights to breathe.

The boy tries to pull Jen's hands off his neck, but his childlike strength and small hands are useless. "Stop please," the little boy manages to plead. Jen slowly releases her grip just before Tommy passes out. He tilts his head to the side to get some air, gasping. He knows to suck air as silently as possible. Jen has told Tommy before if he is quiet and does not tell anybody what she does, then she will not hurt James. Tommy will do anything to keep his little brother safe.

Just as Tommy fills his lungs with a complete breath, Jen lunges for his throat again and applies even more pressure. It seems to Tommy that he can't breathe at all now and his vision is slowly fading. As his eyes flood with tears, Tommy has only one thought. *I want my dad.*

Chapter Two
PLEASE BE OKAY

Heavy snow falls on the Sparrow Lake Nation. Six inches already rest on the ground from an earlier snowfall. By morning, a fresh foot of the white stuff will be there for people to shovel out of their driveways and complain about. Lacrosse season is definitely over for the year.

Beau and Marian both wake-up suddenly to the sound of a child's scream and then some high-pitched sobbing.

"I'll get it," mumbles Marian, getting out of bed and wrapping an old robe around herself to keep off the chill. She sees her breath hanging ghostlike in the air, a white vapor cloud threatening to suffocate her, she imagines, and it sends a shiver down between her shoulder blades. They've done a lot to insulate this old wooden house, but the cold is never banished completely. It seems like there is always more work to do, always another project to be undertaken to "fix things up."

Groggily, Marian heads toward Tommy's room, expecting to deal with another one of his nightmares. Instead, when she opens his door, she sees that he is just barely stirring out of sleep. It is James who is crying, and the realization snaps her completely awake. James does not cry often.

"What, Mommy?" murmurs Tommy, looking up at her uneasily.

"Shhh, nothing. I'm sorry I woke you, honey."

She quickens her pace to James' room and opens the door, flipping on the light to hopefully help chase away whatever nightmares are bothering him. She cannot remember her youngest ever having had bad dreams before.

Her four- almost five-year-old son sits in the middle of his bed, sobbing and clutching his left leg.

"It hurts, Mommy!" James' face is red from exertion and the obvious pain he is in. "It hurts bad! Make it stop!"

She sits down next to her little boy and pulls him tight against her, soothing the upset child as best she can. She examines the leg as much as he will let her, but it looks normal. As she manipulates it gently James cries harder, jerking away from her.

"What is it?" asks Beau from the doorway. Tommy pushes past him and crawls into bed with his little brother, snuggling up to him and trying to comfort him. Empathetic tears are standing out in his own eyes as he pats his little brother consolingly.

"I'm not sure," Marian replies to Beau. "I'm going to take him to the doctor as soon as it's light. He was complaining about his leg earlier, but it didn't bother him nearly this much. I can't see anything wrong with it."

"Did you fall, James? Did someone hit you? How did you hurt your leg?" asks Beau, crouching down next to the bed. In the dim light of the single ceiling bulb, Marian can see the faint creases on her husband's face that will someday become worry lines.

James continues crying too hard to answer, but Tommy shakes his head. He keeps a close eye on his brother, and he knows that James didn't fall. Tommy would never let anyone lay a finger on him.

"No one touched him. I always take care of James."

Marian looks at the two of them, feeling helpless.

Beau stands, picking up his younger son. All four troop back into the master bedroom and get into the big bed, cuddling under the thick quilts. Marian wraps herself around her youngest child, stroking his hair until he sobs himself into an uneasy sleep.

Twice during the night, James wakes up crying with the pain in his leg flaring to new heights. None of them get much sleep. By morning, both parents are red-eyed and yawning as they bundle the boys up in their snow pants, coats, boots, and mitts. Marian swallows a hasty cup of coffee and makes one for Beau, who is busy shoveling a path for the truck, but neither boy will eat anything. This is not unusual for Tommy, a picky eater at the best of times, but to see her sturdy little fireplug, James, refuse even his favorite sugary cereal, feels like a knife driven into her heart. She leaves a message on Beau's work answering machine that her husband will be absent today. Construction slows down in winter, so this is unlikely to be a problem.

The sound of James' low moans of pain punctuates the entirety of the lengthy drive to town. The whole experience puts all of them on edge. When Beau reaches automatically for the radio looking for distraction, Marian snaps at him. "Don't turn that stupid thing on. The last thing we need right now is more noise." His eyes darken, and his jaw tightens as he glares at his wife who gives it right back to him. It is the same stare down they've been having since they were both fourteen and young Rez teens getting into trouble. Having had years of practice, they are masters at it.

James is in a world of his own, whimpering and scared. Tommy sobs silently, tears and snot running down his face. Marian locates an old, balled-up tissue in her pocket and quickly swabs his face clean. She glares over Tommy's head at Beau, who simply ignores her.

They manage to put their animosity behind them once they reach the hospital, and Beau stays with Tommy as Marian gets James checked in. Tommy and Beau chill out in the waiting room, which is getting more crowded and chaotic by the second.

Tommy is bored and worried. The waiting room has no toys, and the magazines are old and falling apart. Beau squints at an old *Reader's Digest*, but he puts it down after a brief glance at a story about a family who survived a bear attack. He is not illiterate by a long stretch, but he doesn't have any real interest in reading or continuing his formal education. He has always been more of a blue collar guy.

Tommy picks up the *Reader's Digest* and begins trying to wade through the bear story. It has cool pictures – snarling grizzly bears scooping salmon out of a wide river. The waiting room is cold, crowded, and smells bad. Two babies are crying, an old man is hacking up a lung, and by the smell of it, someone has vomited nearby recently.

A loud scream comes from the rooms behind them, momentarily silencing the waiting area. Tommy recognizes his brother's voice and bursts into tears.

"Christ," mumbles Beau, putting his face in his hands.

Marian comes back out to them, tears streaming from her eyes, although she fiercely wipes them away.

"They're drawing some blood," she explains to Beau. "They won't let me stay."

She looks at Tommy's tear-streaked face and goes to the restroom to get some toilet paper to wipe his eyes. She takes a minute to splash her face and regain her composure. When she reenters the waiting room, she cleans Tommy up and reads him the grizzly bear story. She locates one about wolves and reads him that too. Beau listens with half an ear, getting up to bring Marian another cup of coffee. She shoots him a grateful look.

The hours blur together and it is the worst sort of agony – what seems like an endless, punishing wait the Henrys are helpless to do anything about. The waiting room has emptied, filled, and emptied again. All three family members are hungry, but no one dares leave. They have been told that the results of the blood test will take some time and that they could go home. That they would get a phone call. Occasionally, Beau sits with his eyes closed but not sleeping. Tommy's feet are off the ground when he's seated and he jiggles those feet constantly. Marian doesn't have the energy to tell him to stop. Her heart feels too big for her chest; she imagines the organ's beating getting louder and louder. Finally, James emerges with a nurse holding his hand. Marian squeezes her little boy as the family packs up to head home.

Several days later, they receive a phone call from the hospital. They find themselves in the same waiting room. James is taken to an examination room by a friendly nurse who leans down to talk to the small boy as they walk.

"How old are you, dear?" the woman in white asks gently.

James looks around with eyes as big as saucers. "I'm four."

"You're big for your age, aren't you?" the nurse says as she slips her hand into his.

"Yeah," James pipes up. "I'm gonna play lacrosse like my daddy."

It is like an endless loop of the same bad movie playing over and over for the Henrys as they wait. Babies crying and bad smells.

"Mr. and Mrs. Henry?" calls a nurse suddenly. Both young parents are on their feet almost before the words are out of the woman's mouth. A doctor stands there with the nurse. Both of them have long faces. Marian knows there isn't much good news in their profession. She has never seen a doctor look so grim, and her heart flutters erratically in anticipation. Tommy's hand is clutched in his father's, which is clammy with nervous sweat.

"James is resting now; we've given him something to help with the pain and let him sleep," explains the doctor in a business-like fashion, leading them to a large window. James lays tucked into the middle of an enormous hospital bed. Marian thinks he looks so lonely and so small. An IV is fastened to his arm and other machines display vital information about his condition.

Tommy kneels on a chair next to the window just outside of James' room and puts his face against the glass, trying to see James breathing, to sense if his brother is getting better. He is in the hospital and that's where people go to get well. How long could it possibly take? James' eyes are closed, so there are no more tears, but he still looks pale.

"This is your other son?" asks the doctor impatiently, gesturing at Tommy. Marian wonders why the man is being a bit rude.

"Yes, Tommy," she replies, thinking that the doctor asks questions with pretty obvious answers.

"I think it might be best if Tommy waits out here," says the doctor, shooting the adults a meaningful look. They catch on.

"Tommy, stay here. We'll be right back," promises Marian with forced cheer.

"Okay," he whispers without turning, keeping an eye on James. He wonders how long it will take before James feels better again. Maybe they will be able to play tonight. He resolves to play whatever James wants – even if it's a dumb baby game.

The doctor leads the couple to a separate waiting area and makes Marian sit down before he gives them the news.

"We have run several blood tests on James, and we have also done something we call a bone marrow aspiration and biopsy. All of the results from these tests tell us with some certainty that he has a kind of cancer called leukemia. It starts in the bone marrow and can move into the bloodstream and ultimately other parts of the body if not treated. Over time, those leukemia cells crowd out normal blood cells so that they can't do their jobs. Ultimately the blood becomes unbalanced with too many white blood cells and not enough red."

Marian's face crumples as she begins to sob. Hearing the word "cancer" flips a switch in her, releasing all the emotions that Marian has been trying to keep in check ever since this nightmare began. Once the "C" word is used, Marian doesn't hear anything else. A feeling of panic overwhelms her and a million thoughts crowd her mind, all fighting for space, making each of them incomplete and unbalanced. All Marian can think is that she has nowhere to turn. Her baby's life is in danger! How could that be? He is so young and they have done everything they could to raise healthy children. Beau pulls her against him and hugs her, whispering words of reassurance; his own eyes are bright with tears. Beau's first reaction is to be angry. To look for someone or something to lash out against. But all he can do is hold his wife. Somehow this doesn't seem like his life. It's too unreal. He shakes his head, hoping to wake up. The doctor continues.

"We've caught it fairly early, which is positive. It is treatable, and there is a good chance of him having a full recovery — if we begin chemotherapy treatment immediately. I have set up his first session starting tomorrow. We'll need to keep James in the hospital while we are doing the initial series of treatments to monitor him and make sure he progresses the way we want him to. It would be helpful if you could spend as much time with him here as you can. That would help keep James feeling as positive as possible."

Tommy hears his mother crying and looks up from his post. Through the doorway he sees Marian sobbing into her hands and Beau's face contorted with anguish. Tears run down his father's face even though he trying to be strong for his wife.

The looks on their faces convince him that James is very sick. Without further thought, Tommy climbs down out of the chair and opens the door to James' room. His father has drilled it into his head that he is to always look after his brother so Tommy wants to do anything he can for his younger sibling. James remains unconscious from the pain medication, so Tommy climbs into bed with him, cuddling up next to him. Careful to avoid the IV, he puts an arm around James.

"I love you," he whispers into his brother's ear. "Please be okay."

After a lengthy discussion about what to expect over the coming months, the doctor, Marian, and Beau find Tommy asleep next to James, worn out from the long ordeal. Beau carefully scoops his oldest son up and carries him back to the truck. Marian does not follow. She stays with James and will await Beau bringing her an overnight bag.

James' stay in hospital becomes an extended one — a different kind of medicine game. One about the life and possible death of a child. It is an odd and disjointed time in the Henry household. Tommy feels a bit like an only child. Marian stays at the hospital throughout most of the days and nights. Beau stays away at work, sometimes overnight, so Tommy is left with several babysitters, including Jen.

CHAPTER THREE

SPARROW LAKE

Sparrow Lake is not a large community. Just over ten thousand people call it home, and everyone knows their neighbor's business. It was once known as "Sparrow Lake Reservation," but some people didn't seem to like that "R" word. Though the signs now says, "Sparrow Lake Nation," most of the people who live there simply call it "the Rez."

Everybody knows the Henrys are facing massive medical bills because of James' treatments. Marian and Beau constantly worry about money. As the family accountant, Marian soon realizes they are involved in a financial nightmare as well. In casual conversation, nurses at the hospital have told Marian some of the costs involved in treating a child with leukemia. Marian cried on the way home that day. Life is expensive but life is so precious was all she could tell herself while trying to keep her bloodshot eyes on the road.

Every once in while there are moments when it seems natural that the community comes together to support each other. The crisis the Henrys face is one of those times. Even though James is still in the hospital battling cancer, his smiling face appears everywhere in Sparrow Lake. His cheerful, childish grin beams down from posters in coffee shops, gas stations, and telephone poles. The message on the poster is clear: "Help the Henrys bring James home!"

So, it is a tremendous relief when Laurie, Beau's sister, says she is organizing a dinner fundraiser. It's a meal designed to help with the monstrous medical bills that never seem to end. Laurie has a good heart, and so do many of the people in the community. That's why at four o'clock on a Friday afternoon there is a long line-up of people at the Sparrow Lake Community Hall. Everyone waits patiently to help the Henrys but also to partake in a good meal and see some friends at the same time. The smell of food is overwhelming and everywhere. No one needs any convincing to put down their ten dollars for a meal that includes roast beef, Indian Tacos, mashed potatoes, corn on the cob, ham and scones, and corn soup. If you've got room, there's even apple pie for dessert.

All the food is donated and people have volunteered their time to help serve and cook. Marian is among those helping to make sure there is a continuous flow of good food to satisfy the hungry crowd, and even Beau is helping serve everyone. When Marian takes a minute to catch her breath, Laurie stops by to give her some moral support. "Did you think you had so many friends?"

Marian pauses for a minute while looking around, gazing at the happy crowd. "I've been to a few of these meals in my lifetime but never imagined that we would need one. I don't know about having this many friends, but there sure are a lot of hungry people here. With all those bills, you go around with a tight feeling in your chest most of the time. I think I can breathe a bit better now."

Laurie touches Marian on the arm when she notices a concerned look on her face. "What's that look for then? What's wrong?"

With a sad smile, Marian says, "I was thinking that we just might get through this after all. I love James so much. I want to see him grow up." Then she gets a little choked up. "I just want him home." All Laurie can offer her is a hug. Marian and Laurie hang onto each other for a long time.

IT'S EARLY EVENING, not quite dark but the light has started fading fast. Tommy and Weasel are throwing the lacrosse ball back and forth in the Henry's front yard. They are practicing behind the back passes. Neither boy is very good at it, but they've seen the big boys do it, so it's a cool thing to try. It's cold outside and the snow can make running difficult, but the boys have been at it long enough to have an area packed down. Many play hockey on the Rez in the wintertime but it seems lacrosse is never completely out of season. Just throwing the ball around a bit seems to put many things back in perspective, even for six year olds.

Weasel is one of Tommy's best friends. With his red hair, he doesn't look much like anyone else on the Rez. He's a scrappy little guy who spends a lot of time at the Henry house and elsewhere, rarely at his own place. He doesn't have much of a home life. There is no father around and his constantly working mother doesn't have much time to spend with him. Weasel flips the ball behind his back but it goes nowhere near Tommy.

"Why does James have to be at the hospital so long? Can't they just make him better and let him come home?"

Tommy isn't sure himself why it's taking so long but he doesn't want Weasel to know that he doesn't know. "I think it's because the luke-kemia is in his blood and they have to make sure everything is cleaned up before he gets out. That takes a long time because the blood is so slippery." Tommy's backhand pass comes close to Weasel but he drops it.

Weasel nods his head as he digs the ball out of the snow. "Fucking luke-kemia better not come near me or I'll kick its ass." Though only six years old, Weasel is well versed in cuss words. He just makes sure he doesn't say them when adults are around or he knows that might mean a whooping from his mom.

Tommy smiles at Weasel's words. He doesn't get to laugh much these days and somehow Weasel is always funny, even when he doesn't mean to be.

CHAPTER FOUR

MARIAN'S DILEMMA

Day after day sitting in James' hospital room, nursing cold cups of bad coffee, Marian has no choice but to continuously reassess her life. A steady anger has been building up in her. This is not how she'd envisioned life going. This is not what she deserves.

The uncertain balance that is Marian's life finally tips on a cold February night, shortly after Valentine's Day.

This year, with James fighting for his life in the hospital, there is no mention of chocolates or fancy dates. Instead, the young parents are struggling. To pay their bills, to keep getting up every morning, struggling to even talk to each other. Driving back and forth to the hospital is still cheaper than staying in a hotel room, but barely. Exhausted by her long visits at James' bedside, Marian drives home in the dark at the end of every day and tries to wrestle the family bills into submission. Beau is no help. He seems lost and stunned by what has happened to his little family. He copes the only way he seems to know. Too often, he heads down to the bar and sits at the long counter, telling his troubles to the seemingly sympathetic bartender or any other friendly, listening ear he can latch onto. Everyone seems to understand the sorrow of coping with a seriously ill child. No one is dumb enough to ask Beau what he is doing at the bar instead of tending to his other son or helping his wife. They don't ask him why he is spending money he doesn't have. Beau has been known to answer with his fists and so no one asks those loaded questions. When he stumbles home at night, truck weaving unsteadily along the road, Marian ignores him. Sometimes she coldly wonders if fate has given her another child to take care of as some sort of punishment. She knows that's not what she needs, but she doesn't have the energy to confront him. At least, not until the whole thing blows up that February night.

Marian is deeply, dreamlessly asleep with Beau snoring beside her. Alcohol oozes out of his pores, and despite the cold, she lies as far away from him on the bed as possible. The alcohol smell turns her stomach. A crashing noise of metal crunching from outside the house jolts her awake just in time to glimpse Beau running out the door, still wearing his T-shirt and jeans. Groggily, she tries to figure out what is going on.

An angry yell from outside startles her, and she throws back the covers, running to the door. For an instant, she doesn't understand. Then, she spots their truck. A car has rear-ended it, and though the crash was loud it looks like most of the damage was done to the smaller car. The offending vehicle sits behind the pickup, driver's door open with the faint yellow interior light barely illuminating a second scene.

Figures move wildly in the driveway, Beau beating the living shit out of the offending driver, both of them wrestling on the ground in a flurry of flying fists and dirty snow. Despite lots of alcohol and little exercise over the past several months, Beau's rage gives him the edge over the other man. Finally, he has an enemy that he can fight with his bare hands, and he is wasting no time throttling the man who represents everything going wrong in Beau's life. The intruder is covered in blood from a shattered nose, and Marian doesn't recognize him.

She screams Beau's name, and it brings him back to an intoxicated version of reality. He looks down at the man lying beneath him. The beaten man is wheezing; blood seeps from his mouth and nose. Some teeth are missing, and in Beau's rage he vaguely recollects knocking them out. He hopes the sonofabitch swallowed them.

Beau stands, staggering. The other man whimpers, rolling over to his hands and knees, spitting and drooling blood into the snow. Painfully, he tries to crawl toward his car. Beau helps him with a swift kick to the ass.

"Get the fuck outta here!" he snarls.

The man pulls himself into his vehicle, and with a last angry scowl at Beau, drives away as fast as possible, trying to wipe the blood out of his eyes and spraying a rooster tail of slushy snow behind the car.

Recovering from her shock, Marian slips on a pair of boots and comes out to the driveway to check on the damage. Beau has a scratch above his eye, though the truck has fared somewhat worse. He breathes heavily, still fired up, but lets her lead him back into the warmth of the house, mumbling cuss words under his breath.

Tommy peers around the doorway to his bedroom, eyes the size of saucers. Marian ignores him for the moment.

"What the hell was that all about?" she demands, dark eyes snapping. Beau shrugs. Even through the haze he recognizes those eyes.

"Ahh, he was mouthing off at the bar last night, so I threw him around a little bit. Guess he was pissed about it, so he came here and rammed my truck," he slurs, scuffing his red feet on their living room rug. He had run out the door without his shoes, and his feet are now freezing cold and wet.

Briefly, Marian remains speechless with her mouth hanging open. Then her brain engages and her rage overwhelms the room.

"So, now you got people coming here to fight with you? What if just me and Tommy were home? What if he tried to hurt us?" she demands with her chin thrust forward in defiance. Beau waves her off dismissively, trying to ignore her words. Marian is incensed, feeling actively sabotaged. She walks over to Beau and stands face to face with him, a deliberate invasion of his personal space, all of the pent-up frustration of the last few weeks spewing out of her at once.

"Why are you going out drinking anyways? We barely have any money in the bank, you've got a sick son in the hospital who is fighting for his life, and one at home you should be looking after! You shouldn't be acting like an idiot!" she screams, tears standing out in her eyes.

"What do you want me to do, huh? Nothing I can do will help James! Every time I see him, he's crying and in pain – and I can't do anything! You think you're the only one who feels… fucking helpless!?" he yells. Marian's jaw clenches. Bitterly, she recalls the few visits that Beau has paid to the children's cancer ward. She has spent almost every day watching her son cry and struggle. Her soul feels shriveled up from the misery of it.

"Maybe getting drunk and starting fights is the way I deal with it. I might go out and party a little bit, but at least I come home to my family," he finishes. Tears well up in his eyes and his nose is running.

Marian is rigid with anger. She pokes her finger in Beau's chest.

"I'm warning you, one time. Find a better way to deal with it – or you won't have a family to come home to. I'm serious and I'm not telling you again!" she hisses, whirling away from his shocked expression. She knows that she can't sleep here tonight. If she has to look at Beau's drunk, stupid face and hear his pathetic excuses one more time, she is going to kill him. She doesn't want to do that. She can't do that. She is a responsible adult with two children to look after.

She storms into Tommy's room. After listening to part of his parent's fight, the boy has retreated to bed where he pretends to be asleep. Marian opens his closet, snatching a duffel bag, and begins to pack it with the clothes from the worn dresser next to his bed.

"What are you doing, Mom?" Tommy asks warily.

She glances at him. He has his father's facial expressions. It's not his fault but the sight makes her wince. She turns back to her task, forcing calm into her voice.

"Just packing a few things. We're going to stay with Gramma for a while."

Tommy is stunned, but he obediently gets out of bed and puts on the clothes that his mother lays out for him.

Marian grabs a few things from the master bedroom, toothbrushes from the bathroom, and zips the bag shut. They go out into the living room to reach the entryway, and Beau is sitting on the worn plaid couch. His mouth hangs open, and an empty beer bottle rests on the coffee table next to him. Marian's mouth tightens but she doesn't say anything. Her stomach is in knots but she knows leaving is the right thing to do. Silently, they put their coats and boots on, and Marian leads Tommy out the door. They take her beat up Pontiac sedan, which doesn't run very well at the best of times but usually manages to get the job done even on these snowy roads. Wisely, Tommy doesn't say anything about the state of the yard — the bloodstains and the dented bumper on his father's vehicle. Even at six, he is learning when and how to keep his mouth shut.

As Marian carefully follows the ruts in the road to her mother's house, she glances over at her son. His dark brown eyes seem to belong to a much older person. He stares back at her, and tentatively pats her arm, comforting her.

"It's okay, Mom."

Tears blur her eyes, and she slows down until she can see properly again.

"Thanks, Tommy."

CHAPTER FIVE

WAHIÉNTHA

The sun shines brightly. Blue skies with just a couple of skinny clouds on the horizon. It's a bit too bright for Beau Henry, his sunglasses resting down on his nose. Aviator-style glasses that he bought in the city. Everyone says he looks like a tanned Michael Landon with the shades on and his curly black hair.

Beau is driving his pick-up, one hand on the wheel, one hand fiddling with the radio dial. Suddenly, there's an old country tune wailing away. Not just any song but one of Beau's favorites, Charley Pride's version of "Kaw-Liga." As Beau starts to sing along, he's not thinking about his upcoming visit with Hazel Blackwater. He's trying to put that out of his mind. He's just concentrating on the words of the song. Beau likes to sing the high notes and does the whoops with enthusiasm. A thought occurs to him while he's listening to Charley put his heart and soul into the music. Maybe Beau has a few things in common with Kaw-Liga. Like not being able to say what he feels.

His head is pounding a little bit from the night before, but the headache isn't too bad. He's had worse, even at work sometimes when walking the high steel. Mixing a hangover and work isn't a good idea, but sometimes you just get carried away. The boys like to work hard and party hard. His teeth are brushed and the taste of mint mouthwash is making his mouth water a little. Beau isn't driving very fast. He's not anxious to get to where he's going. His heart is pounding right along with his head.

He makes a right hand turn off the main road down a gravel laneway. A couple of minutes along, there's a small house on the left. Beau pulls over. The truck has a standard transmission and Beau pushes the clutch in as he comes to a stop. When he turns the ignition off, Charley Pride and the pounding drums get shut down in midflight. Beau sits there for a minute gazing at the large German shepherd sitting by the front door. *Damn, that dog is big.* Beau has a tight feeling in his stomach. Nerves. That's a laugh.

You can work hundreds of feet in the air but you're sweating now?

Beau Henry has never been much of a talker. He'd rather do almost anything than flap his gums. *Don't tell me how to do it, show me.* That's the way his father taught him to learn. You have to get your hands dirty. Not going to get anywhere in this life unless you know how to do for yourself. And after a hard day's work, there's no harm in having a drink or two.

Except maybe there is some harm in it. Marian sure doesn't have the patience for it anymore. She has told him to get his act together or else. Beau doesn't want to go down the "or else" road. If he's being honest with himself, Beau is starting to feel a little tired of feeling tired after the night before. That's why he's here. To talk to Hazel. Hazel Blackwater. Wahién-tha. Her Mohawk name means "she makes the fruits fall." She is one tough lady. Beau knows she's been through a lot in her life. She's told him a little bit. Hazel also wants to help Beau. She has told him that too. He doesn't know how she senses the good in him but somehow she can see it in him. She's told him so.

Beau closes his truck door quietly and starts up the front walkway. The little yard is neat and well-cared for. That dog watches him all the while. No barking, just those piercing brown eyes following his movements, the ears standing tall, and his mouth open a little just so you can see his teeth and the red tongue hanging out. No one would bother Hazel anyway, but with a dog like that, it's definitely not worth the trouble.

When he reaches the door, the dog stands up and walks around behind him. That makes Beau even more nervous as he moves to knock. Before his knuckles hit wood, the front door swings open.

Hazel is standing there with a little dog in her arms. Looks like one of those Shih Tzus. Beau doesn't like yappy little dogs. He'd rather take his chances with the shepherd. Hazel motions Beau in using her free hand. The white-haired woman has a smile on her face while the little dog growls. "It's alright. Leo doesn't bite anymore. We have had some long talks and he sees the error of his ways."

Beau takes the sunglasses off and steps through the doorway, the guard dog right on his heels. Hazel puts Leo down and both the little dog and shepherd lie down by the woodstove.

"I need you to help me with something," Hazel says in a voice that reminds Beau of one of the teachers he had in school. Miss Duncan was a kind woman. She was one of the few teachers Beau ever felt comfortable around. Most of them seemed to be bent on disciplining the kids. The strap in the principal's office. Beau started to hate school after his first few visits to that office. What was the point?

"Can you undo the lids to these jars of paint?"

Hazel has some small paint bottles sitting on a side table with a partially finished painting resting on an easel. There is a window right there that looks out onto a back field with some trees in the distance. It's then that Beau notices several paintings on the walls. A couple are landscapes but one is of a young man. There is a serious expression on his face and his hair is shortly cropped around his ears. Something is familiar about the face but Beau is sure he doesn't know the person. Beau easily twists the tops off the paint bottles while Hazel moves to put on a sweater.

"Sometimes I feel cold even when it's warm. That must be part of getting old. Let's go out back for a walk."

Hazel knows Beau feels better when he is moving. She picks up a sketch pad and both of them walk to the back door. "Sorn, come on." The big dog gets up quickly and moves into the heeling position at Hazel's side. "You go out first, Beau, then me and Sorn."

The grass grows long in the field with a few small trees starting to spring up. The area stretches out far enough that it might have been cut for hay at one time, but not anymore. It's a spot full of quiet nature, some bird sounds with no wind. It's a very private spot. Hazel's outdoor office if there could be such a thing.

"We haven't talked for a while," Hazel remarks. It seems like a statement but it's really a question. Beau knows she is waiting for him to talk, to share something of himself, but he is preoccupied with watching Sorn whose brown eyes never waver from him.

"I'm sorry about that. Been busy you know, at the hospital and away for work."

Beau wants to say more but the words stick in his throat. He could really use a drink of water, but instead he just swallows hard.

"Yes. How is James doing? I like that little boy, so full of energy and so smart. When do you get to bring him home?"

Beau matches his stride to Hazel's as they walk towards the tree line.

"I think we can bring him home in the next few days. We'll still have to take him back to the hospital for chemo, but the doctors say it will help if he can get back into some kind of a normal routine."

There are a few loose hairs blowing into Hazel's face as the wind picks up a little bit. She brushes them to the side and tucks the stragglers behind her ear.

"It has to be one of the best gifts a man can have. His family. So precious. What do you think about that, Beau? Your family I mean."

He remains silent. Beau doesn't know how to answer. He knew she would ask him questions like this and having to think of answers makes him uncomfortable. Does he love Marian and the boys? Of course, he does. That's why he's here talking to this woman who looks at him like she has known him for years. He is embarrassed to talk about his feelings. This woman always intimidates him a little. Sometimes a lot.

Hazel probes further. "You, more than most people, would know about balance in life. The work you do, how mistakes get made and how costly they can be. One error in judgment and you can lose everything you have."

Beau is a Mohawk iron worker, a rare breed of men known for their expertise in extremely dangerous work. Balance is of the utmost importance hundreds of feet in the air, walking on a steel beam with no safety line. A wrong step, lose your balance just once, and you may never have the opportunity to make that mistake again.

Hazel extends both arms wide, palms down. As she talks, she makes a tightrope balancing gesture. "There are many truths in life. Some are bigger and better than others. There are times when you may begin to lose that balance. How do you steady yourself again?"

Sometimes it sounds to Beau like Wahiéntha speaks in riddles. Beau doesn't like puzzles or mysteries, but he slowly feels himself beginning to understand this one. There is only one choice. His family is the most important thing to him in this world. That means some of his other things in his life, the smaller things, have to go away. Beau stares at Hazel and then at the ground. Eventually some words struggle to come out.

"I just don't want to let everybody down. I want to be a better husband and dad. I just don't know if I can."

Hazel and Beau have now reached the trees and just a few feet into the woods there is a small creek. The soothing sound of the moving water causes Beau to take a deep breath and close his eyes. He wishes he was somewhere else. Hazel is looking into the distance as she speaks very slowly, as if she is listening so she can repeat words that are being given to her.

"I think sometimes the Creator intends for us to take baby steps. When we do that, we show our intent to follow the right path. It could be as simple as that for you."

Hazel sits on a fallen tree with her sketch pad on her knees. She pulls a pencil out of one of her baggy sweater pockets and begins to draw. Beau sits down beside her and they rest in silence. Beau can hear the pencil scratching over the art paper but his eyes are focused on the water flowing in front of them. Sorn has forgotten about Beau for the moment and sniffs around for squirrels.

Beau feels uncomfortable with the silence. "If I stop drinking, I'll probably lose a lot of my friends. I'll lose the only life I've known."

Hazel doesn't take her eyes off her art, "What will you lose if you don't."

TOMMY IS RUNNING ALONG THE SIDE OF THE ROAD but he is slowing down. His legs are bleeding from the berry bush scratches, and he feels himself growing tired. He hears the crashes in the bushes not far behind. Why did his parents leave him alone? How was he supposed to be safe on his own?

Shouts ring out now, voices getting closer to him. He can't run anymore and his own heavy legs trip him up. Falling into the gravel at the side of the road, he glances behind him and sees that a girl with long hair has almost caught up to him. She is laughing and her eyes are dancing with pleasure. He recognizes Jen as she reaches for him. Her hands are huge and her breath reaches him in hot waves. Tommy can feel her hands tighten on his arm as he tries to pull it away. He's too small, though, and not strong enough. He can't get away. He is supposed to look after himself, but he isn't the big boy his father says he is. He needs help. Tears drip down his dirt-smeared cheeks as he rolls over in the road. There are other shapes behind Jen coming closer. Tommy can hear them laughing but can't see their faces. He wants to ask them for help but his lips won't move. He has no voice. His body is rigid, frozen with fear. It's so cold.

Jen's voice is low pitched and menacing. "Are you ever going to grow up? Why do I always have to do this? You ran away, and that's not being a good boy."

She touches him where she always does. Where she isn't supposed to but she doesn't care. He can't tell anyone. Tommy is too afraid. Jen's body seems huge as she sprawls on him in the dirt. She whispers in his ear, "You know what will happen if you tell anyone don't you? James is getting to be a big boy now."

Her body seems so heavy that he can't breathe. Tommy closes his eyes. Just then a squeal of delight makes his eyelids flutter open. James is on top of him, laughing and hugging him.

"Tommy! Wake up. I'm home. They don't need me at the hospital. Let's go play outside."

Tommy is lying in his bed. The warm sunshine streams through the window and chases the nightmare chill out of his body. He sees Beau and Marian smiling, standing in the doorway to the bedroom.

"Get up, sleepyhead. Go play with your brother."

CHAPTER SIX

BROTHERS

Eight-year-old Tommy's stomach is growling and gurgling as the bus jolts along the bumpy road towards home. Since Marian has insisted that Beau share the chore of packing the school lunches, noon time meals have become decidedly more interesting. Beau tends to use anything he can find from the fridge and cupboards: bags of stale chips, half-eaten leftovers, crackers, and chocolate bars. By the time Tommy and James get home, they are starving, and usually can be found eating straight out of the peanut butter jar with a spoon. Tommy, who was once a picky eater, will now scarf down just about anything.

Marian rolls her eyes, but she always makes sure to have large dinners on those days. Since James' illness, she has learned to adapt to the family that has been given to her to love. It's taken Marian some time to understand that life doesn't always play by the rules. On the bright side, family life has settled down quite a bit. Beau seems to be trying harder. Marian hasn't talked to her husband much about their marriage since the night Beau beat the shit out of that guy in their driveway. He knows and she knows and that's probably enough said.

Another thing that Marian has decided to tackle is going back to school. She always loved children and books. She spends considerable time with both Tommy and James on their homework. It felt like a natural next step that she study to become an educational assistant, with the goal of helping in the schools on the Rez. Marian knows that sometimes children just need a little extra push in order to get engaged in school. Sometimes they need a little fun to learn. She knows that and wants to help.

Returning to school has given her an intellectual outlet, but it has meant a lot of changes in the family routine. For now, Beau continues with his skilled steel work. With a large portion of their savings, he is hoping to buy a rundown building in Sparrow Lake, fix it up, and turn it into a family business. It will mean regular hours and being his own boss, not having to go on month-long trips to different parts of the country to build skyscrapers in distant cities. The chemotherapy treatments for James have been long and grueling, not to mention expensive, but his illness has retreated enough that he is home and attending school.

Tommy is lost in a daydream, resting his knees up against the back of the school bus seat in front of him. In his mind, he is at McDonald's, ordering everything on the menu. Thoughtfully, he gives all the Happy Meals to his little brother, who is standing next to him, miraculously restored to robust health. The many chemo treatments in reality have left James a frail shadow of his former sturdy self.

A cruel snicker interrupts his daydream, and Tommy looks over to James, who is sitting across the aisle. James' skin is flushed, and he has pulled his hat down as far as it will go. It doesn't matter, of course – you can still see that he doesn't have much hair. The two boys, both a year older than Tommy, sit in the seat behind James, teasing him.

"Must be cool to be a skinhead, nowadays," says one, jostling the other. His buddy laughs.

"Think I'm gonna go home and shave my head – be cool like this guy." He reaches forward and flicks James' baseball cap.

James adjusts his cap and stares straight ahead, trying to ignore his tormenters. Tommy can see tears starting to well up in his eyes. Both Henry boys have been instructed, time and again, to keep their hands to themselves. Fighting is strictly forbidden, both by school and bus rules, but this kind of teasing often flies under the radar.

One of the older boys leans forward in a seemingly friendly manner. "Seriously, what do you think, Baldy? Should we shave our heads too?" When James doesn't reply right away, the bully leans forward and pokes his shoulder. "Hey, I'm talking to you, Baldy."

Stubbornly, James tenses and stares straight ahead, determined to endure.

Irritated, one of the bullies grabs James' cap off his head, running his grubby hand over the younger child's scalp. The second bully reaches out to feel it too. They both laugh at the younger boy.

Driven past endurance, James turns around in the seat, bright red with embarrassment and anger. "Give it back!"

The bully opens his mouth to taunt James again but before he can utter a word a fist slams him in the mouth. It's Tommy, who then hauls the older boy out of the seat by his shirt and begins to furiously beat the smirk off his face. Although the instruction not to fight is clearly in his mind, he just couldn't take it anymore. The excuses and explanations can come later.

The bus driver glances back and his eyes go wide when he sees the ruckus. *Not another fight.* He curses under his breath and signals to pull over, wondering for the thousandth time why he took this job. Didn't he get enough trouble from his own kids? Why did he have to go asking for more driving this daycare on wheels?

"Knock it off! You guys, quit that right now!" he yells over his shoulder, at the same time checking traffic. Tommy is past hearing though, lost in his rage. He drops the crying bully and lunges for the second, who is cringing back against the inside of the seat. *Not so brave now, is he? He seems to have lost his desire to continue the bullying game now there are some consequences.* Teeth bared, Tommy grabs the boy's face and slams his head against the window, making a satisfying crunching sound with his skull as the kid cries for Tommy to stop.

The bully takes a shuddering breath and sniffles, snot running from his nose. He whines, "Leave me alone. You're not supposed to fight on the bus."

Tommy doesn't care about consequences. He only knows that no one picks on his brother. He is so focused on his latest victim that he fails to notice the first bully getting up off the floor. James has been watching carefully though, and flings himself on the boy, keeping him away from Tommy. Even the slight weight of a six-year-old cancer survivor is enough to send the first bully crashing down on the bus seat pinning him against a window.

The driver finally manages to pull over and hurries up the aisle toward the little knot of rioting children. Those in the seats around the four boys are yelling and cheering on the combatants throwing imaginary punches of their own everywhere. The bus driver's normally red face is starting to turn to an unhealthy, ugly shade of purple.

The driver's yelling produces little effect on the fighters, so he grabs James first, peeling him off the one boy. *Gutsy little kid*, the driver thinks for a second, before depositing James in an empty seat. Tommy continues wailing on the other bully, and breaking them apart proves difficult. Even when he manages to drag Tommy off the other boy, giving him a bear hug around the torso to carry him away, Tommy steadies himself by grabbing onto a bus seat with each hand and lashes out with his feet at the other boy, booting his head against the window. Blood smears on the glass.

"You two are off the bus. Right now. Grab your stuff," orders the driver. Tommy nods, satisfied that the two wannabe bullies have been taught a lesson. Tommy grabs both of their backpacks, and he and James are escorted off the bus. As they step out the door, Tommy takes the hat belonging to James and places it on his little brother's head. They are not far from home, and so they begin walking. As the bus pulls away, Tommy notices one of the bullies wiping away blood from his nose and tears from his eyes. The boy looks at Tommy and is met with a cold, angry stare. Tommy calmly lifts his right hand and flips him the bird. James joins him in a cheerful show of brotherly solidarity.

"That was awesome," smiles James. "I hate those guys!" He wipes his hand across his face, hiding the traces of tears. Tommy notices, but says nothing. He shifts both backpacks onto his shoulders.

"Yeah, but Dad said no more fighting. I'm gonna get in shit," he grimly predicts, trudging down the laneway to the house. James looks at him, startled but with his mental wheels turning.

Before Tommy can say anything, James takes off at a full run toward the house. Tommy follows at a walk, dragging his feet. He wishes the walk would take longer, postponing the inevitable. Mom will scold and ground them; Dad will yell. He's not sure which he dreads more.

James reaches the house and bursts into the kitchen, yelling for his father. Beau is in the living room and Marian is working on dinner. Seeing her son's face, she wisely returns to peeling potatoes. Beau can handle this one.

"What is it? Are you okay?" he asks, checking his son for injuries. Since the leukemia diagnosis, good health doesn't seem like such a given. It's taught Beau to wear a seatbelt for the first time in his life and not to resent tying off with the safety lines while working on skyscrapers.

"Tommy got in a fight. These guys behind me were teasing me and they took my hat and called me Baldy," begins James, almost out of breath.

Tommy walks as slow as he can up the long laneway. His dad is gonna be pissed. While he might not resemble his father in some ways, he shares Beau's quick, volcanic temper. Both Marian and Beau are determined to make sure that Tommy's temper doesn't get him into precisely this kind of trouble by grounding him every time he loses it.

Reluctantly and with a deep sigh, Tommy pushes the door open. He kicks his shoes off and dumps the backpacks by the kitchen table. Marian always makes sure that they do their homework promptly. Feet dragging, he decides to get the worst over with, and skulks into the living room to talk to his father.

Beau and James are on the couch, talking intently. Both of them glance up as Tommy walks in. Before his older son can give his side of the story, Beau gently cuts him off. Standing, he comes over to Tommy and examines his face for injuries. There is what looks like the beginning of a shiner around Tommy's left eye, but he is otherwise in one piece. Beau pulls him into an embrace.

"Thank you for protecting your brother," he whispers.

From the couch, James smiles. He has repaid his brother's good deed with one of his own.

CHAPTER SEVEN

BRAGGING RIGHTS

I t's summer and the lacrosse playing is easy. At least for the six twelve-year-old boys assembled in the Lucas family back yard for today's show-down. Ben's dad, Larry, is meticulous with the grass, using his riding lawn mower to keep it about two inches long, except for where the boys play lacrosse which is now mostly just dirt. So, most of the summer it's three-on-three time using the smaller four-by-four goals that are normally reserved for indoor box lacrosse. Redheaded Weasel is the goalie for Shane Smoke and Ben Lucas. While his talent as a goalkeeper is suspect, his mouth is always on the move.

"You guys ain't got shit. Can't get nothing by me." Weasel does a little dance and twirls his stick while giving a high-pitched laugh that makes him sound demented. The other guys aren't convinced the auburn-haired mouthpiece isn't a lunatic. But they need six guys, so he's in. Jordy Baker stands in the other net with Tommy and Andy Flint running the field. They are using a tennis ball instead of the real thing for a couple of reasons. The most important concern is safety. The adults insist on the guys using tennis balls or "no game." Real lacrosse balls can cause concussions and broken bones and that's just to the players in the field. Forget about it if you're a goaltender with no padding. The other reason? Tennis balls usually mean no broken windows. That goes a long way with Mr. Lucas.

While it's a friendly match, there is no love lost among the competitors. Ben lunges past Tommy and whips a shot at the net. Jordy is quick enough to deflect it with his stick. A smirk appears on his face.

"Ohhh, what a save! Wooo!" whoops Jordy with all the cheerful obnoxiousness he can muster. Even his teammates, Tommy and Andy, roll their eyes.

Weasel hoots, "What a save? What a jackass!"

The ball dribbles past the net and Shane and Andy chase after it. Shane scoops it up and loops back around to shoot on Jordy again. Andy pushes after him, slashing with his stick to knock the ball away from Shane. A mis-judged hack clips Shane's hand.

"Awww, fuck!" yelps Shane, shaking his hand. "Watch your fucking stick, asshole!"

"What, can't handle someone playing tough D on ya?" taunts Andy, still reaching for the ball.

Shane glares at him and takes out his rage on Jordy, cranking the tennis ball hard at the goal. It goes in, but his stick follow-through whacks Andy's forearm.

"Ouch! Shit!" he yells. Shane is satisfied. Now they are even.

"Where the fuck was the D in there?" Shane taunts Andy, rubbing in the fact he scored while Andy was guarding him.

Jordy pulls the ball out of the net and flips it to Tommy. "9-9, next goal wins!" he reminds the other players. The talent on the two teams is pretty much even, but Tommy and Andy play very well together.

Tommy gets the ball quickly and dashes toward Weasel's goal. Weasel mutters to himself as he watches the players approach. "Let's go, bitches. No more goals, I'm shutting the door."

Before Tommy reaches the net, he passes the ball to Andy and then runs and sets a pick on Shane, just like you might see in basketball. Ben switches to cover Andy, but as he is doing that, Tommy makes a break for the goal again, Shane right at his heels. Next to the goal, Andy throws a pinpoint pass right into Tommy's stick, and Tommy fakes Weasel out, get-ting him to dive to one side. With noticeable ease, he hurls the ball into the empty side of the net that Weasel just vacated.

"Shit! No fucking way," exclaims Weasel, slamming his stick on the ground.

"Crease!" insists Shane. He's claiming Tommy shot from inside the goalie's crease, a violation that would disallow the goal. The only problem is there are no referees in the Lucas back yard. No one officiating is usually a recipe for some mayhem.

Tommy's teammate Andy shakes his head laughing and walking toward Shane. "Yeah right – you got beat."

"He was in the fucking crease," Shane reiterates, knuckles whitening on his stick.

"So you lost. Learn how to play some D and you won't get beat all the time," Andy retorts with a laugh.

"Fuck you!" yells Shane, and he lunges with his stick to slash Andy's arm.

"Fucker!" snarls Andy, and then slashes him back even harder.

Shane throws down his stick and grabs for Andy. Andy drops his stick and swings a right hook into Shane's cheek. They fall over in a pile of thrashing limbs and cussing. Even though Andy is getting the worst of the wrestling match and is on the bottom, he is still reaching up to punch Shane's face.

Concerned, Jordy runs out of his net intent on pulling Shane off of his teammate Andy and breaking up the fight.

"C'mon, Shane, quit being a dick just because you got beat."

The other goalie, Weasel, comes out of his net. He loves a good fight.

"Get the fuck outta there, Jordy! Let 'em go," yells Weasel, getting up in Jordy's face. He stands shorter than any of the other boys, a cocky little shit, and he is quite likely the mouthiest kid on the entire Rez to boot.

"Shut up, Weasel, you red-headed fuck!" Jordy snaps.

Weasel's jaw clenches and a murderous glow lights up his eyes. "It's auburn, motherfucker. Get it straight!" he howls, lunging at Jordy. Jordy dodges the charge and pulls him into a headlock, dropping them both to the ground. Weasel lands on his back and begins punching the back of Jordy's head. Next to them, Andy has flipped Shane onto his back and is attempting to rub his opponent's face into the dirt.

On the sidelines, Tommy and Ben toss the tennis ball back and forth casually, watching the combatants roll around on the ground.

"Should we break 'em up?"

"Nah, they'll get tired."

Later, when things have calmed down, all six players troop inside Ben's house for cold drinks and a couple of icepacks for their assorted injuries.

This is a regular occurrence at the Lucas household. The six best friends spend the summer months off from school playing backyard lacrosse and oftentimes the intensity of these games leads to a few spirited bouts. Though they are all friends and the games are only for bragging rights amongst each other, it seems that all of them would rather lose an organized game to a team from another town than a backyard battle against each other.

If you were to drive around Sparrow Lake on a summer day you would spot all kinds of kids playing lacrosse in their yards. Lacrosse is the norm here, as natural as walking and breathing. Though the employment rate on the Rez isn't the greatest and nice houses with fancy cars are rarities, one thing the people of Sparrow Lake draw great pride from is how well they can play lacrosse. Lacrosse players from the Sparrow Lake Nation are good. Damn good.

CHAPTER EIGHT

A BOTTOMLESS WELL

Spaghetti is an all-time favorite around the Henry household. Marian makes it at least once a week and never has a problem getting the boys to clean up their plates. The same can't be said of pickled beets. Tommy and James both hate that vegetable impersonator, and if Marian tries to get them to eat beets at any meal, no matter what else is on the menu, the boys treat all the food on the plate like it has been contaminated with some kind of poison. Tonight, there's not a vegetable in sight, just the way twelve-year-old Tommy likes it.

"You know, Tommy, most kids would be thrilled to death to have their dad coaching the lacrosse team. It's your father's way of showing that he's interested in what you're up to. It doesn't hurt that he's been playing the game a long time and he's pretty good at it. Half the kids in Sparrow Lake would love to have their dads spend time with them like that. Think just how lucky you are." Marian glares at Tommy through the steam coming off the pot of boiling water.

"I know, Mom, but sometimes I just wish he'd just chill, you know… just let everybody have fun and play like we do in our backyard games." Tommy doesn't like the feeling he gets when he knows his dad's eyes are burning holes in the back of his jersey as he's running down the field. Beau might have mellowed in some parts of his life but lacrosse is definitely not one of them. *If anything,* Tommy reflects grimly, *it seems he has channeled all his internal rage into this single narrow pursuit.*

"Mom, it don't matter how good I play. Dad always thinks I should do better."

Tommy is a good lacrosse player, sometimes exceptional, but he gets the feeling he'll never come close to matching Beau's unrealistic expectations.

Marian dumps the whole package of spaghetti into the hot water. She used to try and get away with using three quarters of a package, saving some for another meal, but the boys' appetites only continue increasing and that conservation measure doesn't make sense any more. Everybody always wants seconds.

"Tommy, you just need to be more patient with him. He loves you and sees so much potential in you – he just wants you to do good," Marian says as she stirs the pasta to keep it from sticking. She hopes Tommy can understand what she's trying to explain. As Marian sees it, she's dealing with two peas in a pod. The problem with Beau and Tommy is they are too much alike.

Tommy mulls over his mother's comments. He likes playing lacrosse and being around his friends, but sometimes his dad can take the fun out of it. So, not much is going to change, which means Tommy doesn't have much to look forward to. He watches Marian stirring the spaghetti sauce on the stove top. Well, maybe there is one thing.

⌐O-⌐O▲O-⌐O-

TOMMY PASSES THE BALL TO ANDY, who dodges his current defender, which causes a panicked sprint by the rest of the opposing team to chase after him. He waits until the last second before lobbing the ball back to Tommy, who now stands undefended. Tommy reaches, catching the ball, and fires a shot past the stunned goal keeper. The goalie reacts quickly, but the ball has already long gone by, buried into the net, top shelf.

Tommy grins, his teammates slapping him on the back and congratulating him on making it look so easy. Now the score is 8-7, one point behind the opposing team. There's a chance for them to get the W.

Beau calls to the referee for a timeout and brings the boys in for a quick meeting and a quick rest. They have exactly thirty-two seconds left to tie the score and force the game into overtime.

"Okay, guys. We shouldn't be in this situation, but we can still win the game," cautions Beau. "Just 32 seconds left: win this face-off, get possession, and then we'll call another timeout to set up a play and tie it. Shane, you get the face-off. Ben and Tommy on the wings," he instructs, briskly clapping his hands together. "Let's go, boys! We need the ball here."

They jog back to the field and take up their positions as instructed. Shane has amazing reflexes, and he wins the face-off sending the ball in Tommy's direction. He lunges for it, but an opposing player shoves in and slashes Tommy's stick so that the ball sails past them. Shane's opponent from the face-off scoops the ball up and sprints toward their goal.

In disgust, Beau throws his ball cap on the ground.

"Come on, Tommy! Get it back – now!" he commands, face reddening.

Tommy and Shane run after the player, trying to pull even with him and slash his stick to make him drop the ball. He is just a bit faster than them, and by the time they catch up, he passes to a teammate. They are playing keep away, not even bothering to try and score. Why should they? All they need to do to win is keep Tommy's team from scoring and let the clock run out.

It feels like an eternity before the ref's whistle blows marking the end of the game. It brings some relief – the fiasco is over – but Tommy knows that he's going to be hearing about this for the whole ride home and probably longer.

The players walk off the field, and Beau glares at them. Mostly at Tommy. "Dammit, Tommy, that was your ball!" he growls, and Tommy's shoulders hunch with tension. Every one of Beau's words is like a punch to the gut.

After the game, they go out for fast food. It's a tradition. Parents pick up the rest of the team, but Beau carpools Tommy, Ben, and Weasel. His crew cab truck can easily fit them, the coolers, and the mountain of gear that goes along with the sport. The four of them have a preferred dining spot near every lacrosse field they travel to for games.

Today it is McDonald's. Everyone orders and Beau pays. He sends them to the condiment station to grab ketchup and napkins and pick out a table while he waits for the food. They are happily shoving each other back and forth, goofing around with no indication that having lost the game is bothering any of them. Beau's jaw tightens. He was pissed off at the end of the game and he is still pissed off. *What will it take to make these boys understand that losing is no laughing matter? Losing is not acceptable, especially if you're from Sparrow Lake.* Beau knows this nonchalant, "it's okay we can win another day" attitude is exactly the thing that costs them games in the first place. These kids just don't seem to get it.

The food arrives, and Beau carries both trays of food to the table. The four sit by a window, watching cars go through the drive-through. There is lots of happy chatter with their mouths full.

"Man, we should've won that game. That team wasn't as good as us," rehashes Weasel, happily stuffing chicken nuggets into his already crowded mouth. He's not really upset – he is consoled by the plum sauce and freshly deep-fried chicken in front of him.

"We play them again in a couple weeks," Tommy reminds everybody. "We'll crush 'em next game," he finishes defiantly, scarfing down the rest of his burger.

"We shoulda killed 'em *this* game," grunts Beau in disgust. "Could have at least tied them if you'd hustled for that last ground ball... and slow down on that burger. You eat so god damn much it's no wonder you can't run," he accuses Tommy, glaring at him from across the small table.

"I missed one ground ball at the end," protests Tommy. "I scored three goals." He and Andy score most of the goals for the team, and Tommy feels that to ask more from him is unreasonable.

"If you weren't so damn lazy, you woulda scored five, and we woulda won," snaps Beau.

The boys all fall silent, and Tommy stares at his dad. Beau glares back.

Tommy shoves away from the table, blindly stumbling toward the restroom. After he leaves, no one says a word. Beau calmly picks up his burger and begins eating again. Ben and Weasel shoot each other nervous glances. Eventually they start to pick tentatively at their food again, nibbling. Weasel kicks Ben under the table, and when he deems it okay, Ben politely excuses himself.

Beau doesn't bother to check on his son, but he doesn't keep Ben at the table either.

Reaching the refuge of the restroom, Tommy shoves open the door. The room is empty, and he is finally away from judgmental eyes. He stands by the sink, muttering under his heaving breath. The muttering becomes louder and he gets angrier as the seconds tick on. He knows where this is going. His anger feeds on itself.

"Fuck you!" he snarls, punching the air and imagining Beau's hateful face mouthing off at him. "Fuck you, you fucking asshole! You goddamned prick! It's never good enough!"

Punching the air doesn't come close to taking the edge off his anger. Tommy grabs one of the stall doors and slams it shut bouncing it off the metal frame. He does it over and over again, until the door latch is bent at right angles. He wishes he had a baseball bat to smash everything in the room.

Gasping, Tommy looks for something else to destroy… and Ben walks in. There is no judgment in his eyes.

"You okay, man?" he asks kindly, putting a hand on Tommy's heaving shoulder. Tommy closes his eyes and grinds his teeth.

"You okay?" repeats Ben.

"Yeah, I'm all right," mumbles Tommy, abruptly shrugging off Ben's hand.

Ben goes into the second stall to give Tommy some privacy. He knows when Tommy's pissed you have to give him some space. Tommy stands at the sink, looking at himself. His face is so distorted with anger he doesn't recognize himself. He runs some water into the sink and splashes his face, slowing the pace of his breathing, trying to calm down. He knows, dimly, that he can't keep going on like this. There is a bottomless well of anger in him, and when it spills over, bad things happen. Maybe he isn't good enough. Maybe he never will be.

THE HUNTING RIFLE has been standing in the hallway for a few days now. Ever since Beau got home from his weekend hunting trip. More venison for the Henry freezer and some to go over to Hazel Blackwater's. Marian is usually on Beau's case to put the rifle away as soon as he gets home, but for some reason, maybe schoolwork combined with keeping the household going, she hasn't paid any attention to the gun this time around. Tommy lets his hands glide over the varnished stock. He has used the gun before but only in the company of his father. It's a 30-06, and he knows it packs a large recoil because it almost knocked him down when he pulled the trigger. He can remember Beau laughing at him when Tommy staggered, barely able to keep his balance.

The anger Tommy felt earlier in the day has left him completely drained. He feels strangely hopeful as he grabs the rifle with both hands and slowly walks to his room, closing the door quietly behind him. The door is a tight fit in the frame so Tommy has to give it an extra push for the latch bolt to catch.

Tommy cocks the rifle and sits on his bed with the butt end of the gun on the floor. The thoughts are racing through his mind faster than he can keep track. There seems to be no room for them all in his head. Hate starts to bubble up, consuming him. Tommy starts to feel uncomfortably hot as he thinks about the last time he saw Jen and how much he hates her. He hates himself for the problems with his father. He slips his shoe off and positions his toe so that it just fits in the trigger guard. Tommy finds that if he sits up straight, he is tall enough to just squeeze the barrel behind his front teeth. Wrapping his hands around the top of the barrel a tear rolls down Tommy's cheek but he doesn't realize he is crying. He just wants to feel better. He wants the constant pain, anger, and sadness to go away.

Tommy holds his breath as his toe jerks the trigger. The click of the firing pin landing on the empty chamber echoes throughout the bedroom. Tommy quickly wipes his tears away. He can hear James and Marian talking in the kitchen.

Tommy quietly places the gun back where he got it and retreats back to his room. Tommy closes his eyes, hoping to fall asleep.

HAZEL BLACKWATER SITS IN HER CHAIR in front of the easel, staring out the window into the distance. The landscape she sees has nothing to do with what the image on the canvas. The painting remains unfinished and only vague shapes are present. At first glance it appears to be a self-portrait with the outline of a woman with long, white hair on the right-hand side of the picture. But there is no face.

"You see, Leo, you are making good progress. Not biting people is a gigantic first step. Now you must learn that you don't need to bark ALL the time. Sorn is here and he watches everything that goes on. If you need to bark, he will surely let you know when it's time."

The little brown and white dog, Leo, is sitting at Hazel's feet. He is staring intently at her and would prefer to be in Hazel's lap but that's not allowed when she is painting.

"Sometimes progress isn't pleasant. It means letting go of familiar things. Now let's take you, for instance. You like to bark. You are good at it, but much of the time you bark when it is unnecessary. Do you feel that? That maybe it's hard on you doing that when you don't really need to do it? You could be conserving your energy instead."

On the left-hand side of the canvas there are other shapes. A young woman's profile appears next to a building with many windows, but again, the images are not fully formed. The painting has a layered, double exposure effect, with multiple images struggling to be seen at the same time. There is something resembling a white mist rising along the bottom of the painting.

It is a late spring day and Hazel has a small fire going to take the edge off the moist chill in the air. She removes the painting from the easel and walks over to the woodstove. She carefully folds it in half, and then in quarters, opens the woodstove door, and shoves the painting into the fire.

"Sometimes, Leo, you just have to start over. You need to stop what you are doing. Rethink everything and start with a fresh canvas. The important thing is not to get angry... don't carry any anger or grudges. Don't lash out. Don't make any rash decisions. No one can make it better for you except yourself. Change is hard. But change can be good. It is also inevitable. Remember that."

CHAPTER NINE

A GOOD START

Switching his bulky headset to "Live," Hank Thomas smiles and begins his spiel. He has a deep, echoing voice that is custom-made for radio. His wife jokes that he has the perfect face for it too.

"Hi, folks, I'm Hank Thomas, your voice of Hoganton Hawks lacrosse. Joined, of course, by former Hoganton Hawk and All-American Midfielder Robbie Redbird. Great to have you back with us for another year of Hoganton lacrosse, Robbie," enthuses Hank, grinning at the man in the booth with him. They are high overhead of the bleachers and green field, watching the players jog around in warm up drills. Parents and diehard fans are gathering in the bleachers, holding homemade signs and wearing school colors.

"Thanks a lot, Hank," smoothly replies Robbie. "Looking forward to another good season of competitive lacrosse from the Hawks." Hank had given him a list of questions an hour before the show, so Robbie knows the script.

"Well, Robbie – what do you think we're going to see this year from the Hoganton Hawks? Looks like Coach Tim Blair has quite a talented squad on his hands heading into the season. Do you think they're primed to take a solid run at the State Title?"

Robbie knows the script and is a good color commentator, but sometimes he can wander a bit off track. So, Hank has devised a method for keeping Robbie focused. Even though Robbie has his own notes, Hank has written up some cue cards that he uses when Robbie gets into some extended analysis. And it's a good thing too. Just as Hank poses his question to Redbird a strong gust of wind kicks up sending Robbie's papers flying into the breeze, scattering them high in the air above the gathered crowd.

"Uh, definitely, Hank." Robbie is a little flustered but his partner backs him up.

Hank flips over the first cue card. It says, "Offense. Flint, Henry, McCrae, Smoke."

Robbie regains his confidence with the prompt and does what he does best. "This senior class is a really special group, and I think we can expect big things. You've got Andy Flint who was an All-American last season as a junior, and Tommy Henry who was All-State last year returning. Add in first year starter Sophomore Steve McCrae and they make up a very solid attack unit. They will run the offense and make up an extremely dynamic scoring trio that is expected to put up big numbers for the Hawks. The ball will be in the offensive end a lot this season since they have a great face-off man as well in senior Shane Smoke, who will be counted on at both ends of the field."

Hank jumps in to give Robbie a momentary breather. "Outstanding offense, Robbie, but how about the defenders? Will they be able to hold up their end?" Hank flips over the next cue card. It spells out "Defense. Wilson, Lucas, Clarke" and adds the words "State Title?" with a question mark. Robbie is on a roll and doesn't really need the help now, but he gives Hank a big smile and a vigorous thumbs up before continuing.

"On the defensive end, senior defensemen Troy Wilson and Ben Lucas will give opposing offenses fits as they are great take away defenders who play a rock-solid physical game. Then you've got the senior goaltender, Devin Clarke, who was named All-State last season as a junior, but who may be one of the best high school goal keepers in the country right now. When you look at this team, they have all the tools to take a serious run at a State Title," concludes Robbie.

Hank smoothly steps in without missing a beat. "Of course, the Hoganton Hawks have not made it back to the State Finals since their lone state championship win twenty-two years ago when they were led by local legend Scott Davis. Since then, the Hawks have only been to the State Semifinals twice, losing both times to the Orrtown Wildcats. Hopefully bringing some added luck for his old team, Scott Davis is actually here today. He will drop the ball for the ceremonial opening face-off to launch the Hawk's lacrosse season. Let's hope that with this impressive line-up we'll see the Hoganton Hawks in this year's State Final. With that said, it's time for a word from one of our major sponsors. This game is brought to you in large part by Carla's Pizza. Family owned and operated for over twenty years. Carla's Pizza, Sparrow Lake's original pizza joint."

Hank reaches forward and kills the sound. They have a couple of minutes before game time. He digs out a thermos from his backpack and pours himself some scalding coffee, offering it to Robbie with a gesture toward a cup dispenser. The younger man smiles.

"Is it any better than the crap at the concession?"

"My wife says so, but that's debatable," retorts Hank, dropping a pair of sugar cubes into the steaming liquid.

Far beneath the booth, Weasel and Jordy sit in the stands. Weasel's gingery orange hair bobs in the brisk breeze. Both boys are sporting the Hoganton red and black colors.

"This is our year, man," gloats Weasel, hunching into his sweatshirt. "We got the squad to take States. We're stacked this year: got Andy and Tommy, Shane on face-offs, Ben and Troy on D, Clarkie between the pipes. We're set!"

Jordy nods agreeably. One of the great things about Weasel is that he can talk enough for several people. There is never any pressure to hold up your end of the conversation.

Weasel opens his mouth to continue, but the loudspeaker drowns him out.

"Here to drop the ball for the ceremonial first face-off is the captain of the Hoganton Hawks 1981 State Championship team: Scott Davis!"

Cheers ring out throughout the Hoganton side of the bleachers, stretching part-way into the other side of the stands. It is a home game, and the locals have turned out in high numbers to support their boys. The visiting Fenora Falcons fans are seriously outnumbered.

Local media crews rush forward as Scott Davis steps onto the grass. He is a handsome, clean-cut Mohawk man with a wide smile and broad shoulders, clearly still in excellent shape despite being more than two decades past his championship game. He good-naturedly waves the media back, walking forward to meet Tommy Henry and the Fenora Falcon captain at the face-off "X." He vigorously shakes hands with both boys, pausing and smiling for some pictures. Tommy and the other team captain assume their face-off stance as Scott carefully places the ball between their sticks. There are more pictures. Finally, Davis, followed by the reporters, walk off the field so the game can get underway.

The loudspeaker booms.

"And we are just moments away from the kick-off of another sensational season of Hoganton Hawks lacrosse as they take on the visiting Fenora Falcons!"

Davis climbs the bleachers, pausing to shake hands with a couple of school officials and smile at a pretty girl seated just below Weasel and Jordy.

"What d'ya think, Scott?" belts out Weasel. "They got the team to take 'er all this year?"

Davis' handsome face turns sour. "They're alright, but I'll believe it when I see it," he replies, climbing the stands to find his buddies. Weasel pokes Jordy with an exceptionally sharp, bony elbow.

"That guy's a fucking dick," he says in lowered tones, indicating Davis with a jerk of his head. "He's only here to cut 'em up and hope they get beat."

Jordy nods. "Yeah, I know."

Scott Davis sits down with a group of men also in their late thirties – guys he played with two decades ago. They are comfortable around each other, united in their disgust with the younger generation. The guy on his left offers him a cup of coffee and Scott produces a flask, pouring himself a stiff shot into the coffee. He passes the flask around and they all sip, watching the young players.

"These guys ain't shit compared to the team we had," begins Davis, and the others grunt and nod. It is an old theme with them.

"If we'd gone head to head with these guys, we woulda killed 'em. Only reason they win is because all the teams they play are shit." He downs his cup of coffee in a gloomy salute to the mediocrity of the current generation. His buddies pour him another as the game starts. Shit or not, they all still lean forward with anticipation when the action starts.

Shane Smoke takes the opening face-off and wins the ball cleanly. He passes the ball to sophomore midfielder Quinn Harris who runs downfield, passing the ball to Andy. Andy cradles the ball while running and passes to Steve McCrae, who dumps it right away to Tommy. While Tommy is catching the pass, Shane sets a pick on the defender guarding Andy. Andy cuts through the middle of the attacking zone with his stick in the air, begging for the ball. Tommy sees him and fires a pass at Andy. Andy catches the ball and drills it into the net before the goalie can even react.

"And just like that the Hawks go up 1-0 on a goal by Andy Flint off a pass from Tommy Henry. Good way to start the year with a first shot, first goal for the All-American Attack-man Andy Flint," enthuses Hank. *God*, he loves lacrosse. That's why he calls the Hawks games for free.

"The Hawks won the face-off, swung the ball around the offensive end, and Tommy Henry found Andy Flint cutting through the middle to get the season underway. Flint and Henry play so well together, they know where the other one is without even having to look. That's years of playing lacrosse together. It's like they can read each other's minds," remarks Robbie.

In the stands beneath them, Weasel and Jordy are cheering for their buddies, giving them a standing ovation.

"Those my boys!" yells Weasel, his narrow face split by the broadest grin. "My boys! Oh yeah, we're going to States this year, baby!" He does a mercifully short victory dance and then Jordy pulls him down before the people behind him start protesting the blocked view.

The players line up for the next face-off... and Shane wins it again. The loose ball is tipped to Troy, who cradles it in his six-foot-long defenseman stick and takes off on a fast break toward the Fenora Falcons' net. A Fenora defender comes sprinting forward to intercept, and Troy quickly passes to Tommy. Tommy barely has the ball before he winds up and rips a scorching sidearm shot at the net, hard and high. The goalie has no chance of moving fast enough to stop it. The second goal of the season, and the Hawks are up, 2-0. Tommy takes a breath just to feel good and soak up the moment. Right now he can't imagine any better feeling than being part of a team and putting a good pounding on Fenora. For some reason he can hear Weasel's shrill voice cutting through the crowd noise.

"The Sparrow Lake Sniper Tommy Henry! Way to fire that rock, kid!"

That brings a smile to Tommy's face. That little bastard knows just what to say to make Tommy laugh.

"Troy Wilson scoops up the ground ball with the long pole, uses his wheels to start the fast break, draws a defender to him, moves the ball to Tommy Henry. Henry winds up and fires a laser past the Fenora goaltender to make it 2-0," Hank recounts for the people listening in on the radio. The predominantly Hawks' crowd is practically rocking the stands with their approval.

"Tommy Henry has got a cannon for a shot. I'm glad he didn't hit the keeper with that one," adds Robbie cheerfully. Lacrosse is a dangerous sport, and over the years, the two of them have seen some godawful injuries. Both are glad that the current rules insist on so much protective gear, but there are observers who think goaltenders are lunatics for jumping in front of some of the shots they face.

"Looks like sophomore Quinn Harris will give Shane Smoke a break and attempt to win a face-off," narrates Hank as Quinn trots to the face-off "X." Quinn fumbles the face-off and Fenora gets the ball. Fenora grimly runs the ball into the Hawks end, passing back and forth to try and evade the hovering Hawks. They move the ball around until finally they get close enough for a decent shot. Devin Clarke, or Clarkie as he is affectionately known to his friends and fans, makes an unbelievable stop.

"WHOAAA!! Great save by goalie Devin Clarke!! A nice stick save stonewalls Fenora, keeping them off the board," yells Hank.

Clarke passes the ball to Ben Lucas, who fires a long pass to Andy, who has run up to the midfield line to catch the ball. Andy dodges his defender and runs towards the net when he passes to Steve McCrae, who is alone with the goaltender. Steve makes several stick fakes that completely confuse the Fenora goalie and McCrae whips the ball into the net for yet another Hawks marker. It is starting to look like a rout for the hometown boys.

"Bullet pass from Ben Lucas all the way up to Andy Flint who blows by his defender, draws the slide to him, and hits Steve McCrae sneaking from behind the cage. McCrae finishes a one-on-one with the keeper to make it 3-0! Oh boy, the Hawks look good, don't they Robbie?" Hank gloats.

"Oh, they sure do. That play all started with a big save by Devin Clarke. The man is so stingy. Then Ben Lucas, rather than run and clear the ball out of the defensive end, just fires a rocket pass to a streaking Andy Flint. The stick control that these guys are demonstrating is really impressive," Robbie agrees loyally.

However, not everyone is as impressed. Up in the stands, one of the old lacrosse players has had enough of Fenora's incompetence. Even whiskey doesn't make this game enticing for Scott Davis.

"Ahh, Fenora is brutal," growls Davis in disgust, shaking his head as the play continues. "This game ain't worth watching, I'm getting the hell outta here." He heads for the road just short of halftime. Maybe a few more drinks will chase the images of today's game out of his mind. "Remember 1981, boys? That was a real game. This shit is playground ball. Not wasting my time." The other guys nod at Davis and wave as he leaves, but they all stick around. Even one-sided lacrosse is better than no lacrosse for them.

"As we get ready to start the second half of play, it's the Hoganton Hawks with a substantial 9-1 lead over the visiting Fenora Falcons.

Hoganton starts the second half with many of the starters on the bench. Looks like Coach Blair is gonna give several of the younger guys on the team some playing time this half with a comfortable lead."

"Yeah, nothing wrong with pulling some of the starters to get a look at some of the younger guys in game action. Need to know what they're capable of," agrees Robbie, settling into a more comfortable position.

"One of those younger guys is sophomore James Henry, younger brother of team captain Tommy Henry. He'll take over on the lefty attack spot usually occupied by Andy Flint."

The ball is won by the Hawks and is passed over to James who is chased down by a defender and stripped of the ball.

"Ohhh, James Henry gets stripped of the ball and the Falcons take possession. Not how you want your first shift of the season to go!" says Hank.

Down in the stands, Weasel agrees.

"Ahhh man, James has gotta step it up if he wants some playing time this year." Jordy nods. Tommy may have a bad temper, but it seems to give him a ferocious inner drive that mellow James seems to lack. James is a consistent player; Tommy is hit or miss, flashes of brilliance combined with really boneheaded decisions when pissed off. Brothers from the same family but not peas in a pod.

The Falcons pass the ball around the Hawks' end of the field when a Falcons player makes a dodge on his defender and goes to the net. Ben Lucas sees the Fenora player has an opening for a shot but double-teams the ball carrier and delivers a crushing body check.

"Ohh! Big hit by Ben Lucas as he read the play perfectly and slid over to help his defensive partner, laying a huge hit on a Fenora player!" cheers Hank.

Ben then picks up the ball and throws it to Quinn Harris who is on a fast break. James cuts into the middle of the field and Quinn passes it to him. James catches the ball, hesitates for just the briefest second while his eyes search out the sweet spot, shoots, and scores.

"James Henry makes up for the turnover earlier by capitalizing on a fast break that was started off by a bone rattling hit from defenseman Ben Lucas," says Hank approvingly.

As the final whistle goes the scoreboard shows 15-4 for the Hoganton Hawks.

In the locker room Head Coach Tim Blair talks to his team, analyzing the win. He is pumped over their high-scoring victory. He is the good cop in this pairing of coaches, and almost everything he has to say is positive. He is solidly built through his arms and chest even though the years retired from competitive sports have caught up with him in his heavy midsection. He claps his hands together for attention and the boys stop the chatter.

"Okay, guys, good start to the season. More than good. Decisive. You showed what we can do when everyone is thinking. When everyone shows up to play. Starters played well and we controlled the play just like we needed to. Offensively, I liked the way we moved the ball. We are not a selfish offense. We move the ball and keep it hot. That is what makes us tough to defend against. Good job on ground balls and defensively; great job keeping them out of the scoring areas. We protected the front of our net and when we did have breakdowns, outstanding job bailing 'em out Clarkie. Coach Jenkins, anything to add?" he asks the thin man leaning against the locker room wall. Jenkins has been scowling throughout the assessment.

Assistant Coach Adam Jenkins' grew up on Sparrow Lake, but never seemed to have anything good to say about its lacrosse players or anybody else from the Rez for that matter. He came off like he thought everybody on the Rez was beneath him, and his sourness is like a dash of cold water on the celebratory atmosphere.

"Too many breakdowns defensively, and on offense we have to cut out all the freestyle bullshit. The backhands and hotdogging crap won't work against better teams. Stop forcing the play with those crazy passes! We need ball control. Short passes. Short runs and pass. And our groundballs could be a lot better. We will be doing more conditioning throughout the season. In my opinion, we got outworked at times today. So be ready to work at Monday's practice," he grimly warns. The boys quietly groan. Coach Jenkins can make any win feel like a brutal loss.

Coach Blair sees their shoulders slump and he quickly brings them in for a last cheer.

"Okay, bring it in. 1-0, that's just the beginning. We've got a lot of talent in this room, but we've got to stay committed to our ultimate goal this season. We all know what that is. Tommy?" he smiles at the team captain.

Tommy knows the drill.

"Hawks on three! One! Two! Three!"

"Hawks!" they all yell, and the unpleasantness in the room turns into excitement. There will be partying tonight. Coach Jenkins wonders if the effects of it will be worn off by Monday practice. If it hasn't, he has a plan to make them forget about the good times in a hurry.

CHAPTER TEN

REZ KIDS

Tommy loads his lacrosse gear into the Dodge double cab pick-up truck, waiting on James who is still in the locker room.

He hears a familiar rattle and turns around to see Jordy's beater Chevy Cavalier approaching, bouncing along on worn-out shocks. Weasel is riding shotgun, using a pair of scissors to nonchalantly cut up a chunk of weed. They pull up next to Tommy, Jordy rolling down the window to talk.

"What happened?" jokes Weasel. "Only a few goals tonight – do I gotta come outta retirement and show you guys what's up?"

Tommy grins. Weasel always make him chuckle even when he comes out with the dumbest lines. For Weasel, the cheesy humor is just part of who he is. Tommy wouldn't have it any other way.

"Don't gimme that shit – you know you ain't got no game left!"

"I'd kick your ass," Weasel retorts confidently. "If I started playing again, I'd be tearing shit up. Take your spot and have you riding the pines."

"Shit, you peaked at twelve. Maybe before," snorts Jordy.

Tommy shakes his head. He likes chirping with Weasel. Just like the game on the lacrosse field Tommy knows where Weasel's wit is going and makes sure the pass is there to meet him. "I'm sure you would, Weasel. Please don't come out of retirement – don't want you taking my spot."

"What's up tonight? We hittin' the club? Jordy said he's good to drive," Weasel smirks, slapping Jordy's shoulder.

Tommy plays it straight. "Sounds good to me. Let me guess... we're taking my truck?"

"Oh, you know it. The ladies love your truck, and I do want the ladies to be happy," Weasel says with a grin. "I'll round the boys up. Meet us at Ben's later?"

"Sure," replies Tommy, catching sight of his girlfriend, Jessica. She is walking toward him, a sexy smile on her full lips. Leaning in, she kisses him, accompanied by catcalls from Weasel and Jordy.

"I told you, man, they love your truck!" hoots Weasel.

"Good game," Jessica congratulates Tommy, beaming a big, broad smile at him.

"Hey, Jess! When you hooking me up with your sister Amy?" demands Weasel.

She turns around and leans against the truck. "Oh, Weasel, I love my sister. I would never do anything like that to her!"

The other boys laugh at the line. They like to see anyone give Weasel a few chirps.

"Oh, come on, you know I'm a nice guy. Put in a good word for me?"

"Okay, but I think she might be better off with a nice guy like Jordy," Jessica retorts, flipping her shoulder-length curly brown hair. Her younger sister Amy has the same dark chocolate curls and athletic figure.

"You tell him, Jess," encourages Jordy. "You let Amy know she can call me anytime."

"You fucker," growls Weasel, smiling in spite of himself. "You ain't getting none of this weed now. All right, I see how it is. Catch you kids later. Out," he calls as the Chevy rolls away, bouncing over the potholes.

James finally makes an appearance, tossing his lacrosse gear in the bed of the truck next to Tommy's and closes the tonneau cover and tailgate. His hair is still wet from the shower.

"Nice job out there; you played good," Jessica tells him.

James smiles shyly. "Thanks."

Jessica has a serious look on her face as she asks Tommy, "So, what are you doing tonight?"

"I guess I'm going out with the boys. You girls coming out too?"

"Yeah, maybe we'll see you," she replies.

James rolls his eyes and piles into the truck, shutting the door to give them a little privacy.

Jessica smiles exposing her cute dimples, grabs Tommy's collar, and pulls him in for a quick, heated kiss. He takes the opportunity to grab her exceptionally firm ass, already wishing that he'd planned to spend the evening with her and not clubbing with Weasel and the other guys. What the hell was he thinking?

From inside the truck, James gives a strategic, polite cough. The young couple lose the embrace on cue.

"I gotta get James home," Tommy explains lamely with a little blush.

"I gotta get going too. Amy's waiting for me," Jessica replies.

Tommy steals one last quick kiss before climbing into the cab of the truck.

Jessica waves to both boys as they pull out of the parking lot. She is never sure what Tommy is all about. Maybe that's part of the problem with them. One day he is so sure about things and the next day it seems nothing is certain at all. Tommy is being recruited by colleges to play lacrosse and the future of their relationship can feel a bit uncertain. Despite that uncertainty existing, they have always been faithful and committed to each other since they started dating over a year ago.

EVEN HEADING OUT TO THE CLUB, it seems all the guys can talk about is lacrosse. Jordy is behind the wheel, Tommy on the passenger's side, and Ben, Shane, and Andy are crammed into the back seat. Weasel and Troy are even less fortunate – they're in the covered truck bed, trying to avoid getting their clothes dirty.

"You guys looked good in the game today," reflects Jordy. He is a good-natured designated driver. Jordy has seen the negative effects of boozing and getting behind the wheel. His father Harry had many impaired driving charges before finally being involved in a pretty serious single-car accident while driving drunk. Harry is lucky to be alive but spent some time in the hospital and a few years in prison because of it. Jordy missed his dad in those years and made a promise to his mom to never drink and drive. Jordy rarely drinks as it is and is content with driving for his friends. But he does indulge in the cannabis with Weasel from time to time.

"Yeah, younger guys looked good too," absently replies Tommy, wondering if Jessica and her friends will be at the first club. As far as he is concerned, other women might as well not exist. Jessica's sporty girl-next-door appeal and relaxed attitude is enough to make him forget every high-maintenance girl he ever considered. She is all he ever thought he wanted. It's still a struggle, though. Tommy sometimes feels completely in love with Jessica and other times he feels completely empty. He never can tell if it's something with the relationship or just him.

"Some of the sophomores ain't bad," Andy agrees grudgingly. "We're gonna need 'em to play good if we wanna take this fucking thing."

"I thought we played good today, too. And all Jenkins does is give us shit after the game. Probably run the piss out of us on Monday," Ben predicts gloomily. "It's only his first year, and I'm already sick of that fucking guy."

This is a generally-held sentiment; everyone in the cab agrees.

"Yeah, he ain't nothing like Coach Blair," Tommy agrees, checking his reflection in the truck's mirror.

Andy hits the nail on the head with the major difference between the two coaches. "Coach Blair is the fucking man. He lets us play the way we learned in the back yard. Coaching Rez kids is different, and Coach Blair knows it. He lets us do our thing – and that's what makes us tough to stop. Defenses don't know what the hell we're gonna do 'cause most of the time we don't even know!" he finishes, chuckling.

The others agree. They were holding lacrosse sticks in their hands as babies in their cribs and learning the game since they were old enough to walk. The majority of their city teammates have logged probably half the number of lacrosse years that the Rez kids have.

"Get off your phone, Shane – you're always on that fucking thing," complains Jordy, signaling to turn left. Shane is texting away happily, screen lighting up his face and the back of the cab.

"What, what? Got something going on here," he leers.

"Yeah, you always got something going on, you ol' fucking whore," retorts Ben, not without a note of jealousy in his voice.

"Nothing wrong with options – your mom ain't always available," jokes Shane. Before Ben can retaliate, they pull into the parking lot. It's crowded with cars, and they are lucky to find any parking at all, even on the distant perimeter. Jordy turns off the ignition, pockets the keys, and they all climb out of the truck, adjusting their shirts and brushing themselves off. Andy opens the back of the truck to let out Weasel and Troy, who are unfazed and only slightly coated with dirt. Looking around they dust themselves off.

"Ahh yeah, let's get after it, boys!" cheers Weasel. He is wearing a bright green shirt that, if anything, makes his hair appear even more orange. The whole ensemble practically glows.

"Everyone got their ID?" inquires Jordy, ever the responsible one. After patting pockets and checking wallets, everyone is set to go, and so they strut up to the entrance, which is guarded by a pair of towering bouncers. The fake IDs are not too patently bogus, and business is business, so the boys are soon inside with beers in hand.

CHAPTER ELEVEN

TROUBLE JUST SEEMS TO FOLLOW

The music is deafening, the room hot and humid, and the dance floor crowded. The only empty spot is at the bar, so the boys line up and sip their beers, scanning the crowd.

"Does your brother want an ID?" yells Jordy in Tommy's ear. "I could hook him up if he wants," he offers. Tommy shakes his head.

"I don't think he does. He seems to like just hanging out with his buddies on the Rez." For some reason, knowing that puts Tommy at ease. The leukemia might be long gone, but James still treats the Rez as his safe place, the place where he can just chill with his buddies. Tommy likes that James is not into partying that much. He knows that if James were out with them, he would probably be overly protective of his little brother. With Tommy's temper, that could spell trouble.

"Damn, there's some hot women in here tonight!" yells Andy, grinning at a busty brunette on the dance floor with her eyes closed as she grinds along to the music. She is falling out of her low-cut top, and it is truly awe-inspiring.

"Too bad none of them want you," teases Ben.

"Fuck off," Andy says dismissively, ordering his next beer.

"I'm a go score me some strange," announces Weasel, grabbing his next beer and heading out across the dance floor with Shane as his wing-man.

"Not enjoying that view," laughs Ben.

"Twenty bucks says they get mistaken for a couple," Jordy jokes, quickly losing sight of Weasel's skinny five-foot-five frame in a room full of men and women taller than him.

Tommy orders a round of shots for the remaining guys, excluding Jordy who nurses a Coke.

"Here we go, boys. Here's to the Hawks going after the State Title!" They all toss them back, and Jordy raises his glass to participate in the toast.

A pair of pretty college-aged girls walk by, smiling at the line-up of athletic boys at the bar.

"Glad we came here tonight instead of hanging out at a Rez bar. Hey ladies, how are ya?" inquires Ben suavely, following after the pair like a faithful hound.

Weasel reappears. Fumes rise off of him, his fists clenched, and his face a crimson red.

"Fucking Shane!" he snaps. "Again!"

"What?" Andy asks through laughter, guessing the punch line because this scenario is all too familiar.

"I was dancing with this hot girl on the dance floor, and she's got her tits right in my face. Asked her if she wanted a drink and she says yes. We go to the bar, I buy her a drink, we're laughing and flirting, getting a good conversation going, and then fucking Shane walks in and jacks it up. He's all like, 'How you doing?' all up in her face, then she's like, 'Aww, my friends are probably looking for me. Thanks for the drink.' Fucking Shane!"

"I don't call him the world's biggest cock blocker for nothing," laughs Troy, slapping Weasel's shoulder in sympathy. They've all lost prospects due to Shane's bumbling intrusions.

"Fuck, he always does that shit," mourns Weasel, staring into his drink. "Why do we even bring him? He never has any fucking money – spends his whole night bumming beers – and then to top it all off, he throws a fucking wrench in everybody's game! Fuck," he finishes, gulping his drink.

"Yeah, he'll hit on anything with a pulse, man. Oh well, just put up with him like the rest of us do," Andy advises.

"Ta hell with that," Weasel sternly disagrees. "He pulls that shit again, I'm gonna fucking drop him. God, the tits on that girl!"

"He'd probably kick your ass," Jordy laughs. Shane outweighs Weasel by a good fifty pounds, but then most people do. Weasel probably tops the scale at 140 pounds, and it is mostly skin and bone. And attitude. Don't forget attitude.

"Fuck that noise!" insists Weasel. "I'll fucking speedbag the prick! Give me a fucking shot; I'm hitting that floor!" he snaps, tossing back a shot before swaggering out onto the dance floor.

"I would pay to see that fight," remarks Ben.

"Shane's a lot stronger, but that Weasel's a tough little fucker," agrees Tommy. "My money's on Weasel."

"You got red hair and grow up on the Rez, you'd better be fucking tough – or at least able to take a punch," observes Andy. Weasel's one of the most exotic of the Rez kids; the genes of his absentee Irish father combined with his Mohawk mother to produce a wiry redhead with pale copper skin that sunburns at the drop of a hat. Weasel has been teased by the other kids endlessly from day one.

"I've seen that little fucker take a lot of punches and still be swinging. He can handle himself alright," Tommy says, reflecting on the number of fights he's seen Weasel involved in. Usually Weasel instigates things, but he is very seldom the first to tap out. He does not care about getting hurt and is full of rage – sometimes that's enough to get him a win over larger opponents. Tommy appreciates and worries about the rage part at the same time. He recognizes it in himself.

"Watch my drink," Jordy asks Tommy, and Tommy nods as their "DD" heads over to the can located on the far side of the club. The bathrooms are predictably disgusting, but Jordy tries not to touch anything and finishes up quickly. Pushing his way out the door, he spots Weasel burning up the dance floor with a partner about the same height as him. She is a sexy white girl with long, blonde hair wearing a tight, black mini that shows off her killer curves. Jordy admires her from afar and wonders why the hell a girl like that is dancing with Weasel.

Jordy is about to leave them to it, but just as he turns to go, he spots trouble. A tall guy wearing a collared designer shirt with gelled-up hair walks over to Weasel and deliberately spills his drink on him. Outraged, Weasel turns.

"What the fuck?" he demands, voice shrill. His hot dance partner has stopped moving and starts watching the scene in horror.

"Oops," apologizes the arrogant prick, smiling insincerely.

Before Weasel can explode, a bouncer has a hold of him, pulling the redhead out the door.

"You're fucking outta here!" he snaps, ignoring Weasel's protests. Jordy knows something is up and follows them out the back door. Weasel attracts violence like a light attracts bugs.

Behind the club, the bulky bouncer drags Weasel behind a series of dumpsters, shoving him to the ground. Weasel's face is red with fury and his ruined green shirt clings to him with sticky remains of the drink.

"What the fuck – he didn't do nothing!" protests Jordy, setting himself next to Weasel. "Some other guy threw a drink on him! He didn't do anything – you don't have to push him like that!"

The bouncer gives Jordy a stiff straight arm to the chest. "Shut the fuck up! You wanna get involved in this too, huh?"

"Involved in what? You're a bouncer – aren't you supposed to be working?" Jordy demands. He has a feeling this is not going to turn out good. With a sinking feeling, Jordy spots four other dudes making their way out of the club and heading toward them. One of them is the asshole who spilled his drink on Weasel. It dawns on Jordy that he has crashed a spontaneous Weasel beating. The bouncer takes off his employee T-shirt and grins.

"I'm not working now."

"Why the hell you always come here, anyway?" demands one of the guys, a little unsteady on his feet. His question is squarely directed at Weasel who raises his narrow little head, sneering defiantly.

"If you guys knew how to fuck your women right, I wouldn't have to come here!"

Jordy's jaw drops. He knows that the two of them are quite possibly about to take an ass kicking, but he still admires Weasel's suicidal nerve.

The bouncer is really pissed now.

"That's it, you little fuck!" he snarls.

Three of the guys grab Jordy, shoving him up against the building as Weasel bolts through the parking lot, chased by the bouncer and the drink-spiller. He has pretty good wheels and manages to turn the lot into an obstacle course of cars and parking blocks, keeping distance between himself and his lumbering pursuers. As he streaks by the parking lot entrance, a car pulls in and Tommy's girlfriend Jessica spots Weasel running behind an SUV.

"Oh my god, that's Weasel and Jordy!" exclaims Jessica, who is riding shotgun. Amy, her sister, is driving, and two of their friends are in the back. Three of the girls seem stunned, but Jessica unsnaps her seatbelt and bolts into the club. The single bouncer at the door doesn't bother checking her ID because she's been there many times before – a frequent flyer.

Meanwhile, Jordy takes a beating from his remaining two captors – the third guy now trying to help the other two catch Weasel, who is as evasive as all hell. There is a reason he has that nickname.

"You dick heads only fight five on two?" Weasel yells, hiding behind a pickup truck. "That's how you work – five on two? I'll fight any of you one on one, you gutless fucks!" he shrieks.

"You're gonna get it, you little shit!" snarls the bouncer, who is seriously out of breath.

Jordy finally wriggles loose from one of the two guys holding him and takes the opportunity to start punching. He gets in a few shots, but one of them trips him, and he is thrown to the ground. He's lucky that none of them are wearing steel-toed boots, but the kicks are still capable of breaking ribs. Jordy partially uncurls to try and catch his breath and he sees one of the guys grin, winding up to kick him in the face. He braces for the impact.

But instead a fist sails into the guy's face with a fleshy smack, spraying blood everywhere from a broken nose. The guy howls, dropping to his knees to clutch his wounded face.

Troy shakes the soreness out of his hand as he runs to help Weasel, who has finally been cornered by the bouncer. Jordy catches his breath and prepares for his second attacker when Andy arrives and takes the honors.

"Motherfucker!" he yells, happily punching the guy in the jaw. He watches with satisfaction as the bully drops to his knees. Jordy lets Andy whale on the dude for a while before taking over. He has a lot of rage to work out on this asshole.

Weasel is being dragged out of his defensive corner at the far end of the parking lot, but it is taking all three guys to do it. He is a whirlwind of fists and kicks, flailing viciously, and still yelling insults. Tommy, Troy, and Shane are running toward Weasel, hoping to get there in time before Weasel gets totally fucked up. The bouncer already has him on the ground.

Back inside the club, Ben realizes that he hasn't seen any of his boys in quite some time – Jessica had missed him when she had warned the others about the fight. He heads toward the exit, but gets side-tracked by the food stand – pizza, dollar a slice. He grabs three slices, pays, and heads out the back door to see if the guys are gathered at the truck.

Ben walks out of the exit carrying a paper plate piled with the fast food and nearly drops everything when Jordy's latest punching bag screams. He stares at the scene, totally confused.

"What the fuck?" he mutters, but still taking a bite of his pizza at the same time. That shit is only good when it's hot, and it looks like the parking lot rumble is under control for the most part.

"I'm gonna enjoy this," sneers the bouncer.

"That's what your mom said before I fucked her in the ass!" yells Weasel breathlessly, half-crushed, but still undaunted. The bouncer's face reddens, and he cocks his fist back for a punch. Tommy crashes into him from behind before he can land his punch onto Weasel. The other two guys take off running as Troy, Shane, and Andy arrive, and they chase them all the way to the perimeter of the parking lot.

"Fucking chickenshits!" yells Andy after the fleeing men.

Tommy is raining down rights on the bouncer's face. Every smack of fist into flesh gives Tommy a sense of satisfaction. He hates a bully, and while Weasel is annoying, he is still his buddy. Weasel pushes Tommy to the side and begins punching the bouncer. Tommy reluctantly lets the little guy take over. Tommy breathes quickly in shallow gasps as he watches.

"Five on two, huh? Five on two, motherfucker? How you like it now, bitch?" the redhead snarls, while throwing rights and lefts.

Andy pulls him away, with a note of regret in his voice. "Okay, Weasel, let's go – we better get outta here, the fucking cops might be showing up."

Weasel gives the bouncer a last kick in the ribs before heading back to the truck with Andy, Troy, and Tommy. "There's one to remember me by. I don't fuck around. Remember that next time you dicks try to jump somebody."

Jordy appears, bruised and cut from his beating but wearing a smile on his face. The two guys who jumped him are both bloodied and disoriented, trying to get back up to their feet.

Ben rolls up, still eating his pizza. "You guys got 'er?" he asks jokingly. "What the fuck happened?"

"I don't know, but you're giving me one of those," Weasel insists, grabbing a slice. Ben graciously allows him.

"Me too," insists Jordy, grabbing the remaining untouched slice. Ben rolls his eyes and continues chowing down on his piece. He knows he shoulda bought more, damn moochers.

"Everybody okay?" asks Jordy.

"Yup, but we need to get out of here," replies Tommy, breathing heavily as they run to the truck.

Jordy hops into the driver's seat as the rest of them pile in while Weasel and Shane duck in the back under the cab cover. Tommy takes a quick second to grab a case of beer out of the truck bed and put it in the cab with them. Jordy drives cautiously through town making sure to go under the speed limit. When they pass the sign that reads "Sparrow Lake Nation," Tommy passes out the beers and they crack them open.

"So what the fuck happened?" asks Ben curiously, having missed all of the fight except for the mopping up at the end. None of them are entirely sure.

"Weasel must have been dancing with somebody's girl?" ventures Jordy, shrugging. "I don't really know – just looked like we were gonna take a shit kicking."

"Guess we won't be going back there for a while. One of those guys worked there," remarks Troy.

"Guess it's Rez bars for a while," sighs Tommy. He is most upset that he didn't get to spend any time with Jessica, who came running into the bar to tell him about the fight. Andy hands him an empty, so Tommy passes him a full one. He slides down the window and waits for a road sign to come up, winging the empty bottle at it. It misses.

"Haha, strike one, bitch!" teases Ben.

In spite of himself, Tommy laughs. Despite the brawl and the blood there is no place else he'd rather be.

"Shut the fuck up and eat your pizza."

"Don't mind if I do," Ben replies placidly, chewing thoughtfully.

Troy grins and hands Tommy another empty bottle. Tommy takes careful aim at the next road sign and the others smirk. They know what's coming. Just as Tommy winds up, Jordy taps the brakes and the truck jerks. Tommy throws the bottle awkwardly out the window, totally missing the sign.

"Jordy, you fucker, that one doesn't count!" he snaps and the others crack up.

"Fuck that; strike two!" bellows Andy, doing his best umpire impression.

"Strike two," agrees Ben, finishing the last of his crust.

"You're a buncha assholes," mumbles Tommy, draining the last of his beer. Somehow this group of deadbeats is like one big family. Looking out for each other and making sure nothing really bad happens. Unless it's to do with Tommy and road signs. Another road side target comes up on the right and he aims as carefully as possible. He still misses, and Jordy pulls over, all of them dying laughing. Tommy gets out and goes around to the tailgate, opening it. Weasel jumps out.

"What, you go zero for three again?" he grins.

"Shut the hell up," growls Tommy, and Weasel cheerfully pats his shoulder, ushering him into the back of the truck to join Shane and closing the tailgate. Weasel trots around to the passenger's side and hops in, grabbing a beer. He opens it and takes a long drink.

"Just got a text from Clarkie; after party's at his house," calls Andy from the backseat.

"Well let's go," cheerfully insists Troy, and they all agree. Jordy takes a left and begins heading to Clarkie's. The night is looking up.

Ben hands Weasel an empty bottle, and Weasel winds up dramatically, letting fly at the next road sign. He hits it dead-on, and the bottle shatters with a satisfying crash.

"That's how it's done, bitches!" Weasel yells, and inside the truck bed, Tommy resigns himself to a night of riding around in the back of his own truck.

CHAPTER TWELVE

BOYS BEING BOYS

Clarkie's house has everything that the truckload of high school guys are looking for – beer, weed, girls, and no parental supervision. A big bonfire crackles in the fire pit, and clumps of kids stand around the yard, chatting and chugging beers.

Predictably, Weasel's story of the fight at the club has only gotten better in the re-telling. At Clarkie's, he is bragging to a group of girls, waving around his joint and drink to make his point.

"Yeah, those fools got what they deserved. My boys had to come help me out a little bit, but I had 'em right where I wanted 'em," he gestures confidently. Shane, Troy, and Andy stand with them next to the bonfire, and Weasel's rendition cracks them up.

"Shit!" exclaims Troy. "When I got there, you were in the fetal position!"

"I was okay," Weasel asserts confidently. "I was just waiting for them to tire themselves out. That's how you fight a bunch of big guys all at once."

"I think you woulda been waiting for a while," teases Andy.

"What the fuck?" snaps Weasel. "You guys smoke my weed and then start giving me shit? The fuck?" he insists, and the guys laugh him off but stop kidding him. Weasel's temper is not improved by the ribbing, but he cheers up when one of the girls leans in and whispers something to him, coyly rubbing up against him.

The host of the party, Devin Clarke, comes up to Jordy, who is one of the only sober, trustworthy people left.

"Hey man," Clarkie says apologetically. "We're running low. Think you could take a run to the bootlegger for us?"

"Yeah, sure," he agrees, and begins walking around the party with his hat, drumming up donations.

"Let's go! Who wants to keep drinking? Buck up! Get off your fucking wallets! Chip ins, chip ins," he calls out as crumpled up bills begin filling the hat. Everyone is in a good mood, and the hat fills quickly. Jordy takes off for the truck with Tommy's keys and Weasel runs up, tugging a plush-figured girl behind him.

"We'll go for a ride too," he grins, and Jordy rolls his eyes.

"Hop in," he sighs, and starts the engine. Weasel's always had a thing for the thick girls. The two passengers hop in the back seat and begin removing key items of clothing. Jordy tries to keep his eyes on the road – the sight of Weasel's scrawny, pale ass would undoubtedly blind him if he caught sight of it by accident.

Back at the party, Tommy has reunited with Jessica, who figured the boys would head to Clarkie's after the debacle at the club.

"Thanks for helping us at the bar tonight," Tommy gives her a hug. "Who knows what woulda happened if you hadn't seen what was going on in the parking lot."

"No problem. I'm just glad that Weasel and Jordy are all right. Well, Jordy anyway," she amends, and they both chuckle.

"Yeah, some pretty crazy things can happen hanging out with that Weasel," he admits. Weasel has gotten him into more stupid situations than Tommy cares to recall. Some pretty hilarious ones as well.

"Maybe you should stop hanging out with him so much," suggests Jessica, surprising Tommy. Her thinly-veiled worry at first seems charming to him.

"You trying to tell me who I can and can't hang out with?" he says lightly, smiling. She smiles back. Jessica senses this isn't going in the right direction.

"Maybe," she says, half-seriously. "I like Weasel, but I know he attracts trouble. That's something you don't need, Tommy. Seems like you can do just fine in that department all on your own," Jessica raises her eyebrows and bats her eyelashes. Tommy knows she's trying to soften the advice. Jessica is sensible most of the time and usually pretty level-headed, though she does have her moments when she can let loose. Tommy has been on the receiving end a few times, but mainly, they have a lot of respect for each other. Tommy doesn't want to get into an argument right now.

"You just don't know Weasel like I do. He's a good dude, and he's been my boy since we were kids. Hanging with him just makes me laugh. So maybe you should let me make my own decisions about who I spend my time with." Tommy knows that might sound a little harsh but it is the honest truth.

Jessica is too smart to push Tommy towards anything all at one time. There is always next time.

"How come Jordy and Weasel don't play lacrosse with you guys on the Hawks?" she asks, changing the subject. "I remember them being pretty good when they were kids."

"Yeah, they were good, and they still like playing. Only problem is they hate practicing lacrosse more than they like playing it."

"Yeah, I have trouble picturing Weasel following rules – or exercising," she agrees. Tommy chuckles.

"I don't know, he got some exercise tonight – sounds like he did about three laps around that parking lot.

THE FRIENDLY BOOTLEGGER gives Jordy a small discount in honor of the lacrosse win. Jordy thanks him and stacks the cases of beer, carrying them back to the truck. He loads them into the bed and closes the tailgate. He climbs into the front seat and chuckles. The girl's pink and black thong is draped on the passenger-side seat next to him. That didn't take long.

Weasel's ruffled head pops up and he grins.

"Emily says to take the long way back," he orders, and from somewhere beneath him, Emily giggles.

"Okay," agrees Jordy, rolling his eyes. Emily is clearly enjoying herself, and who is he to ruin a lady's fun? Within a mile, Weasel has her up on all fours, braced against the opposite door. Her denim skirt rides up around her waist and her full brown breasts bounce with each thrust. Weasel continuously nails her with the enthusiasm and finesse of a jackrabbit, and it's working for Emily, who is moaning enthusiastically.

Weasel stops to cool off for a moment – it wouldn't do to finish before the lady did – and calls to Jordy. "Hey, Jordy, get ready – you're next!"

Straight-faced, Jordy turns around to look at them. "No way, man, you ain't fucking doing that to me!"

Emily and Weasel bust out laughing.

"What are you laughing at?" Weasel says to her jokingly as he gets back to work.

BY THE TIME JORDY MAKES IT BACK TO HIS HOUSE, it is 6:00 in the morning and the sun is barely up. His eyelids feel like they weigh roughly a thousand pounds each, and all he can think about is his bed. He could only imagine how the others felt – he isn't hungover or stoned on pot and still feels like shit.

His mother Shelby is sitting at the kitchen table when he comes in. A cup of coffee rests on the table in front of her, and their Rottweiler dog, Cash (named after his dad's favorite country singer Johnny Cash) is curled up at her feet.

"Hey, Jordy," she greets him, yawning.

"Hey, Mom. What are you doing up so early?" he asks uneasily. He knows that it wasn't on his account – he'd told her where he was going and would be home in the morning. She trusts him.

"Your dad didn't come home again last night. I can never sleep well when I'm here by myself," she explains. Jordy's heart sinks. Usually his dad made it home for a late dinner – he likes his wife's cooking. Not showing up for dinner means he's already drinking and doesn't want to bother with eating.

"You hungry?" Shelby asks, getting up from the table. "There's some leftover spaghetti." She hugs him, and he knows that she was unconsciously checking his breath for booze. He lets her – there is nothing to find. He rarely drinks, knowing the shit that she'd dealt with because of his dad. Jordy sometimes indulges in alcohol when he feels he has something to celebrate. But that's not often.

"No thanks, Mom. I'm pretty tired – I just wanna go to sleep," he yawns, shuffling toward his bedroom. He freezes as a familiar sound comes from outside – his father's truck has just pulled into the driveway.

Shelby Baker stands over by the table where she can't be seen from the kitchen window. Her thin lips press together with determination.

Harry Baker walks into the kitchen, still wearing his dirty work boots. He is startled to see his wife and son up at this hour, but he smiles and sits down at the table.

"Hungry?" asks Shelby softly, and he sports a big, sloppy drunk smile.

"I'm starving!" he exclaims. She smiles and dumps all the spaghetti onto a plate, microwaving it. When the microwave bings, she takes it out, stirs it, and sprinkles some parmesan cheese on top. She brings it over to the table... only to lean down and place it in front of the astonished Cash. Cash wastes no time questioning the motives of his human caregiver, and he begins scarfing down the noodles and sauce.

Shelby strides out of the kitchen and into the master bedroom, closing the door firmly behind her.

Harry sits at the table with a dumbfounded expression on his face. He watches Cash devour the plate of spaghetti. Jordy stands frozen in the hallway, watching the scene.

At last, Harry shrugs and gives an uncertain laugh. He hefts himself up from the table and stumbles into the living room, lying down on the couch. Within seconds he begins snoring, and Jordy drags himself to his bedroom. Despite being exhausted, he has trouble falling asleep.

Out in the kitchen, Cash is still nosing the fast disappearing plate of spaghetti around the floor, lovingly polishing off every last trace of sauce with his tongue. He wanders into Jordy's room, curling up against his feet. For Cash, this has already been a very good day and it's still early. He falls asleep almost immediately.

CHAPTER THIRTEEN

THE MORNING AFTER

B en's mom, Brenda, is a veteran mother of teenage boys, having gone through it all before with Ben's two older brothers. So she doesn't scold or lecture, she just counts the bodies spread out across her basement family room. She comes up short.

"Six? Ben, where's Jordy?"

Ben peers at her out of bleary eyes.

"He went home. He took Tommy's truck."

She nods, briskly clapping her hands together. There are groans of genuine anguish from around the room.

"Okay. Get this room cleaned up. Ben and Shane, you two vacuum upstairs and downstairs. Tommy and Andy, you two sweep and mop the kitchen. Troy and Weasel are on dish duty. Larry and I are going to watch Kimberly's (Ben's younger cousin) softball game. This house better be clean when we get back," she orders, going upstairs to join her husband and head out the door.

Slowly, the boys stagger up from their various sleeping positions. Mrs. Lucas is a nice lady, but you do not fuck with her. They begin straightening up the room, folding blankets, and putting pillows back. Tommy is the first to gain some aspect of alertness.

"I got first shower!" he yells, galloping up the stairs. With six people in line, getting in first means getting hot water. The others hash out an order of showers, the last unlucky few deciding it makes more sense to shower at their respective homes.

Weasel is the only one who is too cheerful to surrender to a hangover. He has Emily's thong in his pocket, a head full of sweet memories, and a crumpled piece of paper with her phone number scribbled on it.

Standing at the sink with Troy, Weasel whistles and dries while Troy scrubs. Few things stick to a pot like mac and cheese – and this was, of course, what they'd decided to eat for their post-party snack.

Beau Henry walks into this scene of the boys cleaning the house and is more than a little taken aback. Everywhere, boys are cleaning; Shane is obsessively vacuuming, going over the same spots twice and three times for in-depth cleaning; Andy is mopping the kitchen floor and Tommy is wiping down the fridge with a rag. Beau admires Brenda's enterprise – had she decided to start a cleaning service she'd be well on her way to retirement he figures.

"Hey guys," he greets them, and they all look up, returning the greeting in various ways ranging from nods and waves to Weasel's fist bump with Beau. Weasel just assumes people like him until they don't, and he treats everyone with a casual respect, especially his elders.

"Sorry, Tommy, I've got to pull you away from this fun. We're having dinner at Gram's."

With relief, Tommy tosses his rag on the counter. He follows his father over to the door and puts his shoes on.

"Hey Beau – do you think I could get a lift with you guys? Just drop me off at my house?" asks Weasel, joining them at the door.

"Yeah sure, but we have to leave now," replies Beau.

"What the hell? Where you going?" demands Troy in outrage. "You gotta help with these dishes!"

Weasel shrugs innocently. "Sorry, man, I need a ride."

Beau stifles a smile as he ushers the two boys out the door. Troy glares at the pot that he's been vainly scrubbing for the last few minutes. "Fuck sakes!"

Weasel hops into the backseat of Beau Henry's pickup truck. Tommy climbs in the passenger side with a sigh of relief. He is still shaking off his hangover, and various parts of him are still throbbing from the fight at the bar. Even while rubbing his scabbed knuckles he is thinking about some of the sweet punches he threw. It was all worth it. Every second of it.

"Where's your truck?" Beau asks Tommy.

"Jordy took it to his place. I'll go get it after dinner," explains Tommy.

As Beau slowly brings the truck up to speed, Weasel just can't keep quiet.

"So, what did ya think of the Hawks' game, Beau? They looked pretty good, huh? Think they can go all the way this year?"

Beau smiles. "They've definitely got the talent," he says, looking over at Tommy. "I think if they put as much effort into lacrosse as they do into their social life, they wouldn't lose a game."

Tommy smiles absently, staring out the window at nothing in particular. This was a familiar rant of his dad's, but Beau had mellowed – he no longer yells it. Now that he no longer yells and fumes about it, Tommy hears some of what he was saying. He has to admit, there have been times when even Beau possibly had a point.

"Maybe you should start playing again, Weasel – they might be able to use you," the older man teases. The ribbing went right over Weasel's head, who took it as a serious suggestion.

"Nah, I wouldn't be able to put up with someone telling me what to do. I'd have a real problem with Coach's yelling at me and stuff. I don't respond well to authority figures," he finishes.

"Did your teachers write that on your report cards?" Beau asks, pulling into Weasel's driveway.

"Every single one!" he replies cheerfully. "Thanks for the ride! See ya later!" he calls out. Beau starts chuckling the moment Weasel goes into the house.

"Doesn't respond well to authority figures – ha! You remember when I coached you guys the first year you played – you guys were only five?"

Tommy vaguely remembers this and nods.

Beau continues as they drive toward his parent's house. "The first practice, I told all of you guys to get on the goal line and you all did – except Weasel. He looked me right in the eye and said, 'No!' He was the smallest kid out there – just this little runt with orange hair. I said it again: 'Get on the goal line.' He calmly took off his lacrosse glove, smiled, gave me the finger, and replied, 'I said no!' I was trying so hard not to laugh, and I said, 'Okay.' Who I am I argue with a five year old?"

Tommy smiles. Some things never change. Welcome to Weasel's world.

JOYCE HENRY'S HOUSE IS STUFFED TO THE RAFTERS WITH FAMILY, just the way she likes it. Cousins spill out all over the porch. Aunts and uncles file through the kitchen grabbing platefuls of food, and presiding over it all is Gram Henry – a gray-haired woman with a large wooden spoon. The utensil is more than a symbol of cooking excellence. It has a storied history. Once upon a time the spoon used to come into contact with some kids' behinds, helping her children shape up as she saw it. It's hard to say which is more terrifying – the thought of being whacked by the spoon or missing out on the feast. Gram Henry's cooking is legendary.

Grampa Henry is already installed on his favorite chair in the living room, tucking into a dinner of roast beef, mashed potatoes, and creamed peas. The corn on the cob is too hard on his dentures, and he leaves it for the young folks. Three of Beau's sisters are present, and they've all brought their families. Beau kisses the forehead of his newest niece, a sleeping baby in her mother's proud arms. Beau and Tommy thread their way into the kitchen, load up their plates, and head toward the living room. Beau's younger brother is sitting in there with Gram and Grampa Henry – the rest of the family dispersed around the house, mainly focused in the kitchen. An aging TV buzzes with a baseball game – spring always means baseball in this household.

Grampa Henry looks up from his peas and beams at Tommy. He is un-abashedly proud of his grandsons – he thinks both Tommy and James are excellent lacrosse players, just like their father was in his youth. James is perched on the edge of the couch and Tommy plunks down next to him.

"That was a good game the other day. You didn't give Fenora much of a chance, did ya? What you end up with, Tommy? Three goals and a few assists?" If pushed, Grampa Henry could likely recount each and every as-sist. He watches every game like a hawk.

"Yeah," smiles Tommy politely, before digging into his potatoes.

"And you got a goal too, huh, James?"

"Yeah, I got one," replies James, wondering if there'll ever be a day when he is the one with three goals. It's not that he wants Tommy to play bad – on the contrary – but it would be nice to be able to brag too.

"Oh, that's good. I'm glad my grand boys are doing so well," beams Gram, patting James.

"You should come to our next game, Gram," suggests James.

She sighs, and her face clouds. "I'd go, but I'm not allowed in that place."

One of the aunts sticks her head into the living room. "You're the only one who thinks you're not allowed to go there! You can go to the games if you want!" she insists, rolling her eyes in exasperation. One of Tommy and James' younger cousins looks up from his plate.

"Why wouldn't you be allowed there, Gram?" he asks.

"'Cause I cause too much ruckus," she says playfully.

Beau smiles. "Oh man, I'll never forget that. It was one of my club lacrosse games, about fifteen years ago. Mom and Dad were in the stands, and I got in a scrap on the field and got booted out. As I was walking off the field, some woman was giving me the business and yelling things at me. I didn't pay her much attention, but she was yelling a lot. I got to the locker room and all of a sudden, I heard the crowd hollering – I figured that the guys were tussling on the field again so I ran out to see what was going on. I look out and everyone is heading toward the stands – even the players. I look up in the stands and Ma had that loudmouth woman in a headlock, feeding her uppercuts. Half of the crowd was cheering and the other half was trying to peel her off of that woman."

Gram Henry looks distinctly pleased with herself and she whispers to one of her granddaughters sitting beside her. "I gave that ole gal so many rights, she was begging for a left. Week later I got a letter in the mail saying I can't go back to that place anymore. I haven't got a letter saying I can go back, so I ain't been back. Quit spilling gravy on my couch!" she orders the two boys, who are dying laughing.

"Careful, she's got a mean right!" wisecracks Beau, which sets everyone off again.

CHAPTER FOURTEEN
HENRY'S HARDWARE

Beau taps on his wristwatch and gives Tommy a death stare.

"I have to go help my dad with some errands and then James and I have to work at the hardware store, so I can't," Tommy is holding the phone away from his ear while Beau glares at him. The older man can hear Jessica's high-pitched voice from where he is standing.

"We need to spend some time together or else what's the point? Maybe you don't want to go out anymore. Maybe you've got somebody else?" Tommy can practically hear the tears in her voice and finds himself feeling a little queasy.

"We'll have to talk later. I know that. I promise. I just can't now. There isn't anyone else, Jess, come on. I have to go. Sorry, my dad is waiting." Tommy lets his breath out slowly, trying to calm himself as he puts the phone down. Maybe relationships aren't worth the trouble. Maybe it's better just to hook up once in a while. It would be easy and it wouldn't be half the work. If some of his friends can do it, why can't he? Shane does it all the time.

Beau raises his eyebrows but doesn't say anything. He can't counsel anyone about relationships, and besides he counts on the boys to put in a few hours every week at Henry's Hardware so he can take care of some chores away from the business. Having the store, his store, has been a dream of his for a long time and he is desperate for it all to work out.

The building needed some fixing up, but the location is perfect: smack dab in the middle of Sparrow Lake's little downtown. It used to be a general store way back when, but for most people it's only been an empty storefront for as long as they can remember. There are big display windows on either side of the main door, and with a couple fresh coats of paint there is a welcoming feeling about the place. The new sign that Beau has splurged on proudly boasts "Henry's Hardware – If we don't have it, you don't need it!"

The old building had just been biding its' time on the street waiting for a reason to come back to life. That's where Beau Henry decided to step in. He is not ordinarily a dreamer, but in this one instance his imagination has been fired up. He has been seized with a vision that he cannot let pass. Working high steel paid a good buck, but the travel and unstructured lifestyle had gotten old long ago.

So the Henrys took the leap and bought the building. The price was right. Beau is good with his hands, and with growing up on a farm and working construction jobs most of his life, the hardware business seems to come pretty natural to him. And people trust him to give them good advice. They like to talk with Beau. He's a local guy just like them. Everybody's comfortable. People don't want to drive off the Rez if they can buy stuff in their community. All of these things add up to a business plan that seems custom-made to succeed. Marian helps Beau with the numbers. In fact, she will stay on top of the finances weekly to make sure nothing goes off the rails. It may be Beau's business, but Marian is too smart not to pay close attention. People ask for favors and sometimes favors aren't good for business. If Beau can't be hard-assed, Marian can. She is the not-so-silent partner.

THERE ARE NO DOGS OUTSIDE HAZEL'S HOUSE when they arrive, which is unusual. Beau's truck is loaded down with firewood and venison. Some meat from his hunting trip is destined for Hazel's freezer. Aside from tenderloin and steaks, Beau always includes some deer pepperettes. Hazel has her special recipes and is always thrilled to get what she calls the most organic meat available.

The boys are out of the truck first. James and Tommy head for the front door to check in with Hazel. Normally the big dog, Sorn, is out front, but not today. James knocks and that sets off a chorus of barking and toenails scratching on the wooden floors. The door opens and two canine heads poke out. Then Hazel opens the door widely and says, "Boys, sit!"

Tommy and James are taken aback for a minute before they realize she is talking to the dogs. The barking stops and Sorn and Leo sit, eyeballing the visitors. Both dogs pant with excitement. Beau comes up to stand behind his two sons. "Hazel, you've got those dogs trained better than some

K-9 units. That Leo there, I thought he was a lost cause but you got him under control."

"Leo is a fast learner. Quicker than some people I know. Plus, he didn't have the best start in life so it may be that he appreciates what he has now." Hazel is talking to Beau but looking at the boys.

Beau glances at the black and tan Sorn before starting back to the truck. "James, you come with me and help stack the wood. Tommy, take the meat in for Hazel. Put it in the freezer."

Hazel has her deep freeze in the back porch and Tommy has to make two trips to bring all the meat in. The dogs are sniffing at his heels and trying to get a whiff of the venison, but Tommy doesn't think twice about it. Just dogs being dogs. Walking through the living room Tommy notices several paintings on the wall. One of a young boy catches his eye, so he stops to examine it closely. The child is perhaps eight years old with a roughly done buzz cut, real short on the sides, the hair just a touch longer on the top of his head.

While the child isn't alone in the painting, his expression makes him seem lonely – his eyes in a far off gaze. There are other young faces in the background looking on. They are laughing. It's an odd painting. It resembles a photograph. It resembles a memory. A picture of the mind. There isn't any fear in boy's eyes, but his expression betrays a look of surprise. Tommy has never seen anything quite like it and it puzzles him. Why would anyone have something like it hanging on their walls?

Tommy realizes Hazel is watching him as he puts the meat in the freezer. She is wearing a long, dark skirt, dark top, and large, silver earrings. Her thick hair in its usual single braid. Tommy feels like he is somehow being tested. A visual examination that doesn't use words.

"Is that painting of a real person?" Tommy asks, feeling a bit uncomfortable under Hazel's penetrating gaze. As he poses the question, he watches the woman's eyes soften into a smile.

"He is a real person. To me at least." Hazel moves over to rearrange a few things in the freezer to make room for the venison. The two of them are standing beside the freezer in front of a window that looks out on a dull day with no sunshine, no signs of life in Hazel's neighborhood.

"He was my partner in crime so to speak. Someone I love dearly but haven't seen for a long, long time. I keep a good mind about him and hope to see him again sometime." Hazel's hands are resting on the cold packages of meat in the freezer while she stares motionless out the window. "Sometime you and I will talk about him and how bad things can happen to good people. And what that means for the rest of us."

Tommy hasn't spent much time with Hazel Blackwater but has never before heard her talk so softly and wistfully. Tommy's eyes have become shiny, a little watery, and he squints as if the sun is shining right in his face even though it is an overcast day. He feels emotion bubbling up in his chest. "Sometimes bad things happen to good people, and I don't think there is a thing anyone can do about that. No one can protect everybody all the time, and even if you cry for help, sometimes there isn't anyone listening."

Hazel's smile drops off her face like falling through a trapdoor. "I wasn't always this way, Tommy. I was young like you once, with my whole life in front of me. But my life changed in one day when I was a child. I know about bad things happening to good people." Just as she finishes there is a loud bang from outside, someone slamming the truck's tailgate shut. The wood must be stacked.

Tommy isn't sure what to make of Hazel. He has never thought much about her life, about where she comes from. He only knows Beau does a lot for her so she must mean a lot to him.

JAMES STANDS BEHIND THE COUNTER manning the till at Henry's Hardware. Tommy stocks shelves and helps customers find what they're looking for. Business is good and time goes by quickly. Beau pays them a fair wage, and both guys are glad to earn some spending money.

A forty-something, heavy-set woman brings her purchases up to the cash register – a doorknob and screws, a screwdriver, and a roll of duct tape. Tommy begins to stack a display of tools at the front of the store, but James is waiting to ring her up.

"You all set?" inquires James pleasantly.

"Yes, thank you," she murmurs, rummaging through her purse for her wallet.

"$29.89," he says, helpfully bagging her purchases. She hands him some bills and studies James' face thoughtfully as the change is made. A Hawks poster hanging by the door seems to jog her memory.

"You beat that team pretty bad the other day. You got a goal, right?" she asks.

James puffs up his chest a little and smiles. "Thanks, yeah, I got one."

"Think of how many goals you'd get if you didn't let them take the ball from you all the time. I can tell you don't work hard enough in practice. When I was a bowler I used to work hard in practice and would always win my division," the woman's conversation sounds a bit like a lecture to James.

"Thanks, I'll keep that in mind," he says automatically, wishing the woman would just take her bag and go.

"You'll have to play a lot better when you guys go up against the better teams this year," she warns, wagging her finger at him.

"There you go, ma'am, you're all set," James replies, desperately handing her the bag. The woman sniffs and has one more piece of advice.

"Just remember what I said. I know you young people don't listen very well." With that, she slowly walks out of the store giving Tommy a long look before exiting.

Tommy comes up to the till and pats his brother's shoulder. "You should probably get used to that. Around here, everybody's a lacrosse expert – especially the people who've never played before."

"No shit," mutters James, shaking his head. He tries to not let it bother him, but what does an old woman know about playing lacrosse?

"She said she used to win her division for bowling, so apparently that makes her an expert in lacrosse."

Tommy's face distorts with a surprised look and he asks, "I wonder what division that was?" He takes a sip of his Gatorade.

James, still annoyed by the woman's comments, remarks, "By the looks of it, I'd say the super-heavyweight division."

Tommy busts out laughing and spits blue liquid out all over the floor. "Damn it, you should have to clean that up," chuckles Tommy as he goes to find a mop. They both clean and stock shelves until closing. No one else drops by to give them anymore free tips on how to be better lacrosse players, so they lock up and head home for supper.

CHAPTER FIFTEEN

FUCKED UP DREAMS

Tommy is just about ready to go to bed when he gets a call on his cell phone. The name on the incoming call says it's Ben, so Tommy answers it.

"Hey, come get me. I need a ride home. I'm at Nikki's."

Tommy knows what that's all about. That means he's cheating on his girlfriend Brooke again and needs a ride home before he gets caught.

"Yeah, be right there," Tommy answers as he grabs his keys and heads out the door to his truck.

As Tommy drives to pick up Ben, he wonders why Ben keeps putting himself in this situation. It makes Tommy think about Jessica for a minute. Does he want to be like Ben? The sneaking around doesn't appeal to Tommy, but there is a certain freedom to how Ben makes it work. At least as long as he doesn't get caught. Ben and Brooke have been together for close to three years, and she's the kind of girl most guys would not want to lose. She is pretty, smart, and loyal to him. The only thing is she is not a partier like Ben, so most times she's not with him when he is out with the boys and picking up other girls. In a small place like Sparrow Lake, word travels fast, so she has heard stories of his cheating but has never actually caught him and has always remained loyal to him. Tommy arrives at Nikki's and Ben comes running to the truck wearing a black hooded sweatshirt. Nikki is a good-looking girl, but she is part of the crew that many girls on the Rez have dubbed the "Skank Squad" because of the number of guys they hook up with. Ben jumps in the truck and Tommy glances over at him with a laugh.

"So, Nikki huh?"

"What? What?" Ben says smiling as he flips the hood of his sweatshirt down.

"Looks like she was sucking on your neck quite a bit," Tommy says.

Ben pulls down the passenger-side visor and spots a big hickey on the side of his neck. "Fuck! That fucking bitch! She's been trying to get me to break up with Brooke. She probably did this shit on purpose." Pointing at a water bottle in the cupholder, Ben continues, "Can I use that?"

"Go ahead."

Ben grabs the water bottle and takes off the plastic lid. He pushes the lid onto the suck mark and twists it in an effort to get the hickey to fade as best he can.

"I gotta quit doing this shit. I don't even know why I do it. Brooke is hotter and does everything I like. I just get fucking horny and wanna fuck something and she ain't always around."

"Ahh, well, shit happens. Why you need me to give you a ride home? How did you get there?" questions Tommy.

"I was just sitting at home by myself watching TV and Nikki texts me saying she was almost to my place. And her parents were gone so we could go to her place. After we were done, I had a text on my phone from Brooke saying she is at my house and wants to know where I am. I couldn't have Nikki drop me off. So, if she does ask you, say you needed to talk and we rode around and I just got buzzed. Speaking of which, pull over here," instructs Ben.

Tommy drives his truck into an empty laneway leading into the bush. They are now out of sight from the road and the boys get out of the truck. Ben knows he can't smoke weed in the truck because Tommy's dad Beau is like a bloodhound and would really lay into Tommy if he suspected his son of getting high. Ben pulls a joint out of his pocket and lights it up, taking a couple drags. Tommy notices Ben's fingernails chewed right down to the nubs – a gross habit that Tommy does also, just not a bad as Ben.

"Sure you don't want any?"

"Naw, man, I just had supper, and I get the munchies way too fucking bad when I'm buzzed," laughs Tommy.

"Yeah, no shit. I remember the last time you blazed and ate all the food we had in the house," laughs Ben.

"Why do you smoke weed so much?" questions Tommy.

"Honestly, if I go to sleep and I'm not buzzed, I'll have really fucked up dreams for some reason," explains Ben.

Tommy stares at the red glow from the joint as Ben takes a drag. "Why do you think that is?"

Ben finishes his joint out and puts the roach in a little plastic baggie. "No idea. What are you a fucking psychiatrist all of a sudden?"

The boys get back in the truck and drive to Ben's house. He pulls his hood up over his head trying to hide the hickey as best he can. He may have some explaining to do, but Ben is a smooth talker and can be very persuasive. It's made all the easier because his girlfriend Brooke really wants to believe him.

LAYING IN HIS BED and staring at the ceiling, Tommy begins to feel uneasy and annoyed that he can't fall asleep. This is nothing new to him; he's had trouble falling asleep for as long as he can remember. But he knows how tired he's going to be tomorrow if he can't get some rest. He starts to think he should have taken up Ben's offer to smoke.

He closes his eyes, blocking out the bright red numerals of his clock that read 3:14 AM. He gets a little drowsy and his mind begins to drift… and all of a sudden, Jen is there in the room with him.

"I'm going to make a man out of you. You should thank me," she growls, knife-sharp face distorted with hatred. She grabs him, claws like a bear and sharp teeth that open wide as she lunges at his face. He feels her bite his cheek, hot breath against his eye, and he screams, lashing out.

Then they're on the edge of a cliff and suddenly he's falling into space. She is still tangled around his small boy body, grabbing for him, digging her claws in.

He hits the carpeted bedroom floor with a thump, the quilt tangled around him. Tommy feels so disoriented that he doesn't even recognize his room – he is expecting to see the room he had when he was six years old. The walls are covered with posters of female models, athletes, and Hawks memorabilia.

When he figures out where he is, he gasps, fear crowded out by an overwhelming fury. It makes him shake with adrenaline, and Tommy winces, punching his pillow. It doesn't help enough, so he unleashes a flurry of punches on the mattress and pillow, cursing under his breath, saying every curse word he can think of. He tries to keep it quiet, but the rage strangles his good sense.

A bare patch of wall beckons, and he punches, driving his fist through the drywall and barely missing the stud. His anger slowly drains and he feels a little better. Then he realizes that there is a huge hole in his bedroom wall – and that he can see light under his door. His parents are awake and have switched on their bedside lamp.

Quickly he darts to the closet and pulls out a spare poster. He thumbtacks it in place over the gaping hole and grabs his lacrosse stick and a ball. When Beau opens his door, he discovers his oldest son practicing stick handling.

"What was that noise?" Beau asks with concern. Tommy looks like hell – sweaty, red-eyed, and desperately trying to look calm. Tommy's terrible at lying. The quilt and sheets are lying next to the bed in a tangled heap.

"Sorry, Dad. I was messing around with my stick and the ball hit my dresser kind of hard," he explains, not able to meet Beau's eyes.

"Can't sleep again?" he remarks gently.

"Yeah," replies Tommy, darting an embarrassed look up at his father.

"Okay, but I've told you enough times about lacrosse balls in the house. Put it away and try to get some sleep. Good night," he adds, flicking off the light and closing the door softly behind him. He knows that something has been bothering his son. He's tried to get it out of him, but Tommy firmly clams up every time.

Beau passes by James' room – light snoring can be heard. James is a deep sleeper and would probably snooze through a tornado. Marian is already drifting back into sleep by the time he climbs into bed. Troubled thoughts keep Beau up for an hour or more, tossing and turning. He's worried about Tommy and preoccupied with the hardware store. He wouldn't mind a beer every now and then. It seems the urge to have a drink hits him out of nowhere once in a while. Beau rolls onto his back. What is it Hazel says about going back to the old life? "You have everything to lose and nothing to gain. What kind of a gambler takes those odds?" He closes his eyes tightly and works on keeping his mind blank. Eventually Marian's rhythmic breathing fades away and Beau slips into a light sleep.

In the dim light from the moon, Tommy sits on the edge of his bed, his head in his hands. The bedroom walls are covered with posters – behind every single one of them is a hole.

CHAPTER SIXTEEN

PLAYING WITH FIRE

There is no sign of Andy in the locker room as the Hawks start to suit up for their away game against the Williamton Indians. It is a Saturday afternoon match in Williamton, which is a twenty-minute drive from Sparrow Lake. Hoganton High School does not supply a team bus to away games this close so players are responsible for finding their own way to the game.

"Where's Andy?" Tommy asks Ben tentatively. He is afraid he already knows the answer.

Ben shrugs. "I ain't seen him today. Last night he said he was going out for a couple with Weasel."

"Great," groans Tommy, envisioning Andy passed out somewhere. "Call him and see where the hell he is."

"He'd better be on his way, that's all I can say," mumbles Ben, but he grabs his cell phone and dips out the side door to buzz Andy. He can only imagine what Coach Jenkins might say. Something like this would play right into his impression of players from the Rez.

"Where are you at?" he demands when Andy picks up. "We're going out for warm up soon."

"Almost there," replies Andy, speaking slowly and forming his words carefully. His head is pounding like a sonofabitch.

"Seriously?"

"Yep, I'm just at the store picking up a few things. Keep the side door open." He hangs up just as Weasel comes sprinting out of the convenience store, carrying a plastic bag stuffed with necessities. He tosses the aid package to Andy in the backseat as Jordy revs the engine.

"You gonna be able to perform today?" Weasel asks Andy, who's slumped in the back seat.

"Yeah, I'll be alright, man" replies Andy, wondering why he did this to himself again.

Weasel smiles, shaking his head, "Well, open your fucking eyes up then. I could blindfold you with my shoelace right now."

As they speed over to the playing field, Andy gulps down some painkillers with one of the bottles of Gatorade. He jams some gum in his mouth and slips the rest of the pack into his pocket as they arrive, running over to the side door.

He slumps down next to Tommy and begins changing into his gear as fast as possible.

"Coach been in here yet?" he asks anxiously, his words a bit garbled by the huge mouthful of gum.

"Not yet; I don't think anyone will say anything about you being late. But keep chewing that gum and stay away from the coaches – you smell like a bar," Tommy warns. The Hawks aren't even on the field yet and Tommy has a feeling shit is about to hit the fan. It could be one of those days. *Fuck!*

"Okay."

The Hawks jog out onto the field for a light pregame warm-up. Coach Blair's sons, Keegan and Konner, are draped in Hawks red and black jerseys and work as the team's ball boys; they have set up a standard passing drill with a long line of lacrosse balls.

The Hawks begin their half lap warm-up jog, and Andy tries to look as inconspicuous as possible. His attempt at keeping a low profile is pretty feeble though because, as they begin the passing drill, Andy keeps fumbling passes, dropping one ball after another.

"How is he?" Ben asks grimly, leaning over so only Tommy can hear him.

Tommy shakes his head. "Looks pretty fucking hungover."

"He's usually alright once he sweats it out a little bit," asserts Ben, but neither of them feel any better about it. Andy does not look good at all.

"Hope so," Tommy replies lightly. He'd like to put his foot up Weasel's scrawny ass for taking Andy out drinking the night before a game. There is no such thing as one or two drinks when you're out with Weasel. Overboard. He always goes overboard. It's like the little man doesn't know any other way. Maybe Weasel can handle it, but Andy is a casualty in this case. And maybe more than just Andy. Tommy can feel it coming.

"Aww, for fuck sakes!" Ben groans as he nods for Tommy to look to his right. Tommy glances over and feels a dagger stick into the pit of his stomach. Tommy's prediction is coming true. Two officials make their way onto the field; one of them is Carson Long. Not only are the Hoganton Hawks playing in Williamton, an all-white town that is never very welcoming to the Native American players on the Hawks, but they now have to deal with the worst referee in the state. Every time Carson Long is an official at a Hawks game it is a continual parade to the penalty area for Hoganton. Not to say Long is prejudiced against Natives, but he sure seems to favor any team playing against Hoganton and his presence always puts the Hawks players on edge to say the least. Some of the Hawks think Long should just put on the opposing team's jersey and ditch the black and white stripes.

Andy manages to get through the warm up without setting off any alarms and the two teams take their places on the field for the opening face-off. The starting attack unit of Andy, Tommy, and the Irish-American sophomore Steve McCrae meet for a quick huddle. They give each other some quick fist bumps as they notice some Williamton fans making their way to their seats. Two of the high-school aged kids stand out because they are wearing Williamton white and blue jerseys with their faces painted and wearing what looks to be Halloween-themed Native American headdresses.

"Look at these fucking clowns," says Tommy, grinding his teeth. One of the guys wearing a headdress notices the three Hawks players glaring at him, so he smiles, raises his hand to his mouth, and pats it while making a mocking Indian war hoot.

Of the three Hawks players, Steve is probably the most pissed off at the gesture and says to his two teammates, "What a fucking idiot! Let's just win this game and get outta this shithole town." The other two boys agree with their teammate, but they know this is going to be a tough game to get through.

Hank Thomas and Robbie Redbird are in their usual broadcast positions, high above the playing field. Today Hank has brought reinforcements. There are a dozen doughnuts occupying a prime spot on the table among the microphones and cables.

"Here we go, folks! The opening face-off between the Hoganton Hawks and the Williamton Indians. Shane Smoke picks the ball up cleanly and has a fast break for the Hawks. He passes to Andy Flint and Flint bobbles it. The ball is loose in… and WHOOOAA! Flint takes a big hit from a Williamton defender. The Indians control the ball and they clear it out of their zone and into Hoganton territory!" he exclaims, a down note in his voice. He hates it when the Hawks play poorly.

"Andy Flint bobbled the pass from Shane Smoke and he paid the price for it. Not often you see Flint just drop a pass," says Robbie charitably. Even from the stands, he can see that there is something wrong with Flint – his reflexes are way off. Knowing what he knows of lacrosse players, Robbie is thinking that a big night out has something to do with Flint's sluggish play. However, that's an insight Redbird isn't going to share with the audience.

As Williamton takes control of the ball and heads to the attacking end, the teenagers in the crowd begin giving it to Andy for his early mistake. "What's the matter, Flint, little too much firewater last night?" Tommy can see the rage in Andy's eyes and walks over to try calming him down.

"Come on, man. Lotta game left. Don't let them get to ya," he says in an attempt to encourage Andy and keep his mind off the dumbasses in the crowd.

"The Indians work the ball around the perimeter and fire a pass inside. A quick shot and a goal. Ben Lucas looked a little frustrated on that play and gave the Williamton player a late hit that is going to put the Hawks a man down," remarks Hank, reaching for the doughnuts. He will have to eat quick bites of his chocolate glazed between announcing the plays, but he's a professional. You have to do what you have to do to get the job done.

The Hawks are a much better team than their opponents – on paper. The Williamton Indians might not be as talented, but they are more disciplined. This is a clear advantage today. By the fourth quarter, the Hawks are barely in the lead, and their fans in disbelief.

"It's been a penalty filled affair with the Hoganton Hawks receiving quite a number of penalties, many deserved, and a few that maybe shouldn't have been called. We're late in the fourth quarter with the Hawks clinging to a 7-5 lead," Hank reports. He never thought he could be so disgusted with the Hawks leading. They might be up by a couple of goals but the whole team has seemed a bit off today. Hank knows they have more talent than they are showing.

"They have been playing a lot of man down throughout the game, and you can see the emotions getting a little out of hand for the Hawks. Coach Tim Blair has been on the refs all day about some of these soft penalties the Hawks have received. Even with the penalty calls aside, the

Hawks' potent offense is not clicking today. When they have been at even strength, they have been throwing the ball away and turning it over with some uncharacteristic sloppy play. The Hoganton attack unit of Flint, Henry, and McCrae have one goal each – three goals from that group is not up to their usual standard. The scoring has come from the Hawk midfield with Shane Smoke and sophomore Quinn Harris scoring two each," Robbie summarizes the game for the people listening in on the Sparrow Lake radio station. It's good to see that the midfield can pick up the slack, but Redbird is disappointed in the performance of the others.

"The Hawks have possession with eight minutes left to play. They could really use a goal here to get some separation in this game," notes Hank. With the undisciplined way the Hawks are playing, their two-goal lead could vanish fast if Williamton steps up – or gets lucky.

Shane Smoke drives from the midfield with the ball and takes a shot that goes wide of the net and out of play. Tommy sprints to the endline, as does a Williamton defenseman. It looks as though Tommy is closest to where the ball went out, but referee Carson Long points the other way and calls, "White ball." Tommy's jaw clenches as he gets right up in the ref's smug face.

"Are you kidding? I was closer, it should be red ball!" he insists.

"You know, I don't like red," the ref remarks, while giving a taunting smile. Tommy can't believe what he just heard.

"What did you say?"

"You heard me," Long replies matter-of-factly before smiling and running up the field.

With the ref's gift, Williamton clear the ball into the Hawks' end of the field. Tommy leans over to Andy, who is wishing that the game was already over so he could puke and find someplace quiet to sleep the rest of his hangover off.

"It's time to give that cocksucker a fly-by," Tommy growls, and Andy's eyes light up at the thought of making someone else miserable. Tommy tells Andy what the ref just said to him.

"Fucking right, fuck him."

At the Hawks' end of the field, Clarkie makes a nice save and the Hawks' are able to clear the ball out of their end. The ball makes its way to Tommy, and Andy cuts toward the Indians' net, running in front of referee Long. Tommy winds up and fires a rocket pass towards Andy who deliberately moves his stick missing the ball completely. It is totally believable – Andy has been missing passes all game. Too late, the referee turns to get out of the way but the ball nails him hard in the back. The warm glow of satisfied vengeance spreads through Tommy. He hopes he broke one of his fucking ribs.

The ball is loose on the field, and a Williamton player picks it up in the confusion as the referee drops to his knees, gasping in pain. In the stands, Weasel and Jordy are clapping and yelling. They know exactly what just went down – and they heartily approve.

"Yeah! That's what you get!" Weasel hoots. "What you doing on your knees, Stripes? Nobody's got their dick out!"

Above them Hank and Robbie give each other a look and a nervous look. They know exactly what Tommy and Andy have done but given the track record Carson Long has in his officiating of the Hawks, the broadcasting duo doesn't disagree with it too much.

"Play is stopped after an official was nailed by a pass from the stick of Tommy Henry. They are giving him some time to recover; meanwhile, it's Williamton's ball in their defensive end, so we are going to take a quick commercial break," updates Hank. He and Robbie switch off their headsets while the general time out continues.

"Bad positioning by the ref," says Robbie with a straight face. The refs don't wear protective gear, but not very much can protect you from the impact of a lacrosse ball as it is. Tommy could have seriously injured the man – and it's still possible he has. The ref is white-faced with pain and may have a trip to the ER in his near future.

"Any other ref and I would feel sorry for him," says Hank.

"Couldn't have happened to a nicer guy," laughs Robbie as he reaches for one of Hank's Boston Cream doughnuts. He loves the custard filling.

The ref wobbles to his feet, shrugging off would-be helpers. He is insisting on returning to the game and he is pissed, his lips tight in anger. The Hawks haven't been on the right side of any calls before the incident and they definitely aren't going to get the benefit of any now.

When play resumes, Tommy tries to takes the ball away from a Williamton player with a good check. Carson Long calls him on it, throwing a flag.

"No fucking way!" exclaims Tommy. The opposing player has dropped the ball and Tommy picks it up, still disbelieving. The ref throws up a second flag and blows his whistle, running toward the two players.

"Nine red holding!" bellows the ref. "Nine red unsportsmanlike conduct!"

Tommy jogs toward the penalty area as Coach Blair explodes. He has been watching his team deteriorate, and Tommy is one of the ringleaders.

"You're killing us, Henry!" snarls Coach Blair. "You're sitting!" he orders, pulling Tommy out of the game. Tommy slumps sullenly on the bench, glaring defiantly at the injured ref. Coach Blair sees the direction of his gaze, figures out the rest of the story, and erupts like a volcano.

"Was it really worth it? What about your team, Henry? You're the captain! You're supposed to be a leader! If you're that selfish, maybe you shouldn't be playing the game. Who cares about the rest of the team, let's just worry about you, huh, Tommy?"

Coach Blair isn't given to emotional outbursts very often. This time, though, he wants to make sure that Tommy knows just how badly he has fucked over the team.

In the stands Beau Henry is trying to contain his emotions, clenching his teeth as his wife Marian glances at him. Their eyes meet and thoughts are shared without words. They both know where Tommy gets it from.

"Tommy Henry has taken two penalties with 5:24 left to play in the game and with his team trying to hold onto a two-goal lead," Hank reports grimly.

"Two untimely penalties, and that unsportsmanlike foul is just plain foolish. Coach Blair is really laying into Henry on the sideline, as he should. Henry has put his defense in a terrible situation: putting them a man down in a tight game. The Hawks' defense is going to have to try to bail him out of this one," Robbie shakes his head, wiping some custard from the corner of his mouth.

The ecstatic Indians score a goal while on the man up advantage and call for a time out. After a brief discussion, they re-take the field and win the face-off in a giddy display of nerves. They don't care how they win — they have a real chance now, and they tighten up their game. They're playing with some extra jump. The Hawks scramble after them, desperately trying to hold the lead. They let a Williamton player get a shot at the net, but Clarkie makes a fantastic save, scooping the ball to his defense.

"Devin Clarke makes another great save, keeping his team in the lead as the Hawks' defense manages to hold the Indians to one goal during the man up advantage. The Hawks now have the ball in the offensive end and are back to even strength. Andy Flint gets the ball behind the cage and dodges towards the goal. He's got a step on his defender and fires a shot far side." Hank has a sip of coffee as Robbie takes over. It's a goal and the Hoganton sideline lets out sigh of relief.

As soon as Andy scores he positions himself right in front of the head-dress wearing jackasses in the crowd who have been heckling him merci-lessly all game and simply raises both his arms and smiles. That drives the crowd into a frenzy with some of the spectators screaming obscenities at Andy, but he doesn't even hear what they are saying now. He's just stands there smiling as he gives his victory salute.

"Big clutch goal by Flint, putting the Hawks up 8-6 with two minutes left to play in the game. If they can win the next face-off, they should be able to run out the clock and escape with a win," suggests Robbie.

On the next face-off, Shane Smoke wins it, and the Hoganton Hawks run out the clock, winning the game 8-6 by simply keeping the ball away from Williamton. Even the loyal fans feel lukewarm about this game, and the cheers are ragged and subdued.

"Well, the Hawks narrowly get past the Williamton Indians," sums up Hank in a disappointed tone that makes his feelings clear.

"A very sloppy and undisciplined game by the Hawks. They'll have to play much better if they plan on taking a serious run at the State Title," Rob-bie warns, switching off his mic. Hank does the same, giving an uneasy nod.

"What a shit show!"

Even Coach Blair is angry about this one, his face red and stormy. He seldom raises his voice at the boys, but today he lays into them as soon as they get into the locker room, emphasizing over and over that they are a team, not individuals. Selfish penalties cost everyone.

"I don't know what the hell that was out there today. But I better not fucking see it again!" blasts Coach Blair.

Coach Jenkins doesn't bother reiterating; he just shakes his head at Tommy and leaves. But he is smiling as he exits. Jenkins is happy to see them get a blast. Might straighten some of them out. Especially the Henry kid. The shock value of the usually calm Coach Blair's rage is too good an act to follow.

Afterwards, the boys shower and Andy pukes… in the toilet – thank-fully not in the showers.

ON THE RIDE HOME WITH HIS TWO SONS, Coach Blair is boiling with anger, which slowly subsides to a low simmer of steady disgust as he pulls into the driveway. Sarah Blair has a meal waiting for the three of them: pork tenderloin, applesauce, salad, and baked potatoes.

"Hey guys, how'd the game go?" she asks brightly, ushering her husband over to his seat. He is exhausted but still ticked off. Tim Blair takes things to heart. He views his teams as extensions of himself. If the team screws up on the field, then Tim Blair has screwed up.

"Won 8-6," replies Konner.

"8-6? Williamton must be pretty good this year. Tim?" she asks for confirmation. Her husband shakes his head as he sits down to eat. Nervously, she tucks her long black hair behind her ear. She doesn't like to see him get upset – it's not good for him. She shoves the salad bowl toward him, and he dutifully takes some. Whether he will eat it remains to be seen.

"Not really, we just played awful," he replies, picking up his fork and making a stab at his pork. She's roasted it with rosemary, garlic, and apple slices – the smell should be enough to make even an extremely grumpy man sit up and pay attention.

Six-year-old Keegan pipes up. "Mom, you should have seen Dad yelling at the refs. He was really mad," finishes her youngest in an admiring tone that clearly indicates he thinks his father's performance was awesome.

"Dad was really mad at Tommy; he was yelling and his face was turning all red. He even benched Tommy," adds Konner, reaching for the butter.

"Your dad – yelling at a lacrosse game? No way," she lightly retorts. Inwardly her heart sinks. A big man like Tim should not be getting this worked up over anything.

"How come you benched Tommy?" Konner asks his father. "He's a good player."

Tim Blair shakes his head. "Tommy was doing more bad than good today, buddy. He put himself ahead of the team and was hurting everyone – we can't have that. Don't ever put yourself before your team – you hear me?"

"Yeah, Dad, I won't," replies Konner, surprised by his father's serious tone.

The boys finish their food quickly.

"You guys go put your sticks away and come back for dessert in half an hour," Sarah commands, and her two boys gallop off, leaving their dinner plates on the counter by the sink. Tim can see the militant look in his wife's brown eyes and sighs, readying himself.

"What did I tell you about getting all riled up at the games?" she demands, intensity lowering her voice.

"I know," he sighs, fidgeting with his utensils.

"You've got to calm down when you're coaching. It's just a game. You don't have to be yelling all the time," she insists, worry projecting from her like a beacon. She's been trying to calm him down for almost a decade. Coach Blair was diagnosed three years ago as being a Type 2 Diabetic and takes blood pressure medication, but that won't help if he doesn't change his behavior.

"Yeah, I know," replies Tim, guilt-ridden over the anxious way she wrings her hands. "Sometimes that's the only way to get the message through to these guys. They're good kids, but sometimes they need to hear it a bit louder than usual."

Sarah stands to clear their plates, but first she steps over next to him and bends down for a hug and a kiss. She doesn't want to be a nag, but she worries.

"I know how much you care about the guys you coach. But you've been doing this for a long time, and you're not a young man anymore. Plus, your boys are watching everything you do and say on the sidelines. You're their hero."

"I know. I'll try not to get so fired up all the time. Maybe it's time to think about giving it up."

Her face softens. She knows that is not about to happen. Coaching is something he loves. "Where have I heard that before?" she replies wryly, but she is still smiling. He pulls her down for another quick kiss and a hug before they take the dishes to the kitchen sink. She notes without surprise that he hasn't touched his salad.

CHAPTER SEVENTEEN

FIGURING SHIT OUT

own bars are not such a good idea after the recent bouncer episode with Weasel, so the lacrosse players head to one of the Rez's local watering holes just outside the Sparrow Lake Nation. It has a pub atmosphere, chatty and sociable, with less of the meat market aspect of a club. There, the current Hawks run into some former Hawks, Aaron and Mike Crowe, cousins who were captains of the Hawks when Tommy was a sophomore. The older guys are glad to see the younger players and invite them over.

"Can I get three beers for these guys?" Aaron asks the bartender. He nods, flips off the caps, and slides the bottles across the stained wood of the bar to Tommy, Ben, and Troy. Jordy is already nursing his usual soft drink.

"Pretty close game for a while today, huh?" remarks Aaron to Tommy, ex-captain to current captain. Tommy feels embarrassed, wondering who all saw him get his ass chewed out by Coach.

"Yeah, took us a while to get shit figured out," mutters Tommy, taking a long look at his beer. He's been dwelling on what Coach Blair had to say today. He's been thinking about the team's shitty performance on the field and how embarrassing it was even if they didn't think much of it at the time. Tommy is thinking maybe he should leave the booze alone for a while. Tone down the partying. Set more of an example for himself and his teammates. James and the younger guys too. Who the fuck is he kidding? Tommy grabs the beer bottle and takes a couple long gulps.

"What happened today? Thought you guys were gonna blow it. Andy looked like he was still boozed from last night," Mike remarks, his mouth curving up at the side in sarcasm.

"He was hungover as all hell," says Ben. "Puked after the game. Just barely missed the showers."

Aaron chuckles. "Yeah, I remember Mike having a few games like that."

"Fuck you, you were the worst one for that!" snaps Mike, laughing at Aaron.

"Erroneous!" corrects Aaron. "Ahhh, I may have dropped a pass… or two… or three. Coach tear you a new one after the game?" he asks sympathetically.

Tommy nods. "Yeah, mostly to me for the dumb penalties at the end."

"Oh, I remember getting bitched out like that," smiles Aaron, lost in nostalgic thought.

"Face get all red and veins popping out of his neck?" asks Mike, doing a remarkably accurate impression of an enraged Coach Blair.

They all crack up as Aaron and Mike's good-natured humor makes Tommy feel a bit better about the game today. It helps knowing somebody else has been there before.

Troy Wilson takes a long swallow of his beer and decides this is the right time and place for his big announcement. He's nervous but proud at the same time. "Just want to let you guys know my girl and I are going to have a kid. I'm gonna be a dad. Found out a week ago."

"No shit," drawls Aaron happily. "That's definitely cause for some celebration. Round of SoCo shots," he says to the bartender.

The guys take turns giving Troy handshakes and bro hugs.

"How's everybody taking it?" asks Tommy.

Troy smiles. "Her parents were a little rattled at first, but everybody seems to be okay with it. My Uncle Randy got me a spot on his crew, so as soon as school is over, gonna start ironworking."

"Hittin' the iron, huh, kid? Good man. Here's to you and your little one," says Aaron as the guys lift their glasses in a hearty cheers and toss back their shots of Southern Comfort. Tommy closes his eyes and licks the sweet taste from his lips as he feels the burn at the back of his throat. He's starting to get a little more comfortable now, already starting to put the game behind him. Yeah, it was close, but they won, so maybe everybody should just relax. That's exactly what Tommy intends to do.

"Andy going again tonight, huh?" remarks Mike, jerking his chin toward the door. Andy has just made his entrance, accompanied by a trio of sexy native girls with Weasel bringing up the rear and getting an eyeful. One of them, named Tara, stays attached to Andy's arm, while the other two lookers drift away to mingle. The couple slides onto an available pair of bar stools at the far end of the bar. Andy's girl has blonde streaks in her long brunette hair, and her dainty hands are emphasized with an elongated French manicure. Her trim body is blatantly displayed in tight blue jeans and a low cut red shirt, and from the tightness of the material, the boys are pretty sure she isn't wearing a bra. Turning to talk to Andy, she shows the front of her dress and this is confirmed – her erect nipples are on prominent display. Weasel has been standing there with raised eyebrows but then joins Tommy and the others. For a change he doesn't seem to have anything to say. His expression of total appreciation says it all.

Just then, Jessica walks in behind Tommy and notices the direction of his gaze. She doesn't take kindly to the stares and jealously socks his shoulder. He winces, turning to greet her. He is about to smile until he sees the look on her face. So much for him relaxing.

"I see the Skank Squad made an appearance," she acidly remarks, placing herself in front of Tommy and purposely blocking his view of the girl. "Don't sit on anything after they do or you'll probably get crabs." Jessica is a gorgeous girl usually but now her face is like a thundercloud just before the storm hits.

"Hey, c'mon now, everybody loves the lacrosse-titutes!" protests Mike, and the boys laugh. Jessica is still broadcasting storm warnings.

"I don't," she snaps. "They're fucking sluts and anyone who hangs around with them is trash too."

"Well you're in the minority on that one – just kidding, just kidding!" declares Aaron, throwing his hands up defensively. Tommy is still sneaking peeks at Andy's girl. He knows he is living dangerously but damn she is hot.

Andy and Tara are blissfully unaware of this discussion and more concerned with each other, flirting, talking in low tones with a bit of touching going on. Tara seems to be teasing him with little glimpses of more and more cleavage, daring Andy to go there. "Be a risk taker, Andy; go ahead make a move," her eyes seem to say.

Just as Andy is about to put his arm around her, someone plunks down next to Tara on the conveniently empty bar stool. It's Erica Burns, or more commonly known as E. She is tall and lean, but looks as strong as many of the guys in the bar in her white wife-beater top showing off the definition in her arms along with a tattoo sleeve on her right arm. Shoulder-length, jet-black hair with piercing dark brown eyes a little glazed from tonight's consumption of booze, she's evidently on the prowl.

Mike elbows Weasel. "Oh look, Weasel, your old lady E trying to cut Andy's grass," he teases.

Weasel squirms. "Fuck you, man — that was a long time ago!" he protests. He was E's last boyfriend before she declared her preference for women.

"What happened, not good enough in the sack?" grinned Aaron. "It's probably a good thing, she looks like too much for you to handle, kid."

"Fuck you guys! I ain't talking this shit." Weasel slips away, plugging his fingers in his ears.

At the other end of the bar, E is attempting to put the moves on Tara. She has had a few drinks and gets aggressive with a little alcohol. With her attitude, not much usually gets in her way.

"What are you drinking? I wanna buy you a drink," she slurs.

"I'm okay, Andy just got me one," replies Tara patiently. She is not about to piss off a notoriously explosive woman much bigger than her.

"I been noticing you a lot lately. How about you gimme your number?" suggests E, eyes flickering down to Tara's pencil eraser nipples. This is too much for Andy, who interjects.

"Come on, E, we're talking here. Can't you leave us alone for a bit?" he protests. E's eyes darken with menace.

"Fuck off, Andy, I wasn't talking to you!" she snaps, warningly. Andy's cock has been making all of his decisions for the last half hour, and he's not about to let it stop calling the shots.

"How about you shut the fuck up and piss off," he says nastily.

"How about I fuck you up right now, you little punk!" E snaps, standing to her full height. The Dr. Martens boots her tight jeans are tucked into have her eye to eye with Andy.

Tara hops down off her stool and teeters between them. E's eyes swivel from Andy to Tara's chest.

"All right, all right, I'm okay, E, maybe we can talk later or something, okay?" she coaxes, placing her hand softly on E's shoulder. E considers it, and then nods.

"You're lucky, boy," she growls at Andy before walking away.

Tara and Andy get back on their respective bar stools and Andy orders shots. Tara loves tequila. Andy loves what Tara loves.

The night takes on a life of its own, and the laughter becomes louder, people are stumbling while dancing, and Jordy is one of the only sober people in the whole bar. The lacrosse game had been pretty pathetic, but it was still a win. Many of the players don't have to buy their own drinks, and the lacrosse-titutes are making their rounds. In other words, situation normal.

Tommy and Jessica haven't been doing much talking but both of them have been pounding back the drinks. Jessica because she's pissed at Tommy and his appreciation of the Skank Squad. Tommy because he's still thinking about Coach Blair, but also in self-defense. He knows how Jessica can get sometimes and in a lot of ways he's not looking forward to the rest of the night.

After closing, most of the crowd hangs around outside, reluctant to call it a night. There's a grease truck right outside the bar catering to bar patrons who've finally realized that they've missed a meal somewhere along the line. Always hungry, Weasel orders an extra-large order of fries and stands at the condiment bar, drowning them in ketchup. Enough of the red sauce for any three ordinary people. Behind him, Tara and Andy are sucking each other's faces off, his hands on her ass. But Tara's eyes are on the chip stand menu and she wants fries – tequila makes her horny and hungry.

She breaks off from the kiss and stares at Weasel's fries. There is more ketchup than fries at this point.

Tara is perplexed. "What's with all the ketchup, Weasel?" she asks.

He winks. "It's how I keep my sexy figure," he explains as he sticks a drooping fry into his mouth.

She laughs, holding onto Andy for balance as he orders Tara some fries and they wait.

A few more drinks over the course of the evening have fired up E even more and she is determined not to waste what's left of the night. E wants to take Tara home and teach her what she's been missing.

"Hey, girl, I wanna talk to you," E whispers, gently tugging Tara to the side.

"Fuck, E, leave her alone!" snaps Weasel.

E's eyes narrow. "Shut up and gimme some fries," she demands.

"Fuck off. Get your own damn fries," protests the outraged Weasel.

"I said gimme some!" she insists, reaching for them.

"Fuck you!" snaps Weasel, pulling them away and hunching protectively over them. E leans forward and reaches, slapping the bottom of the food container. The fries fly up onto Weasel's shirt. There is a moment of silence and disbelief.

"What the fuck!?" he roars, staring down at his now ketchup covered t-shirt. Without considering the consequences, he throws what's left of his fries all over E's white, wife-beater shirt.

E stares in horror at her ruined top, quickly evaluating the mess of her plans for the evening now that Tara apparently won't be coming home with her, and decides to salvage at least part of the night. She hauls off and kicks Weasel square in the nuts with her size ten boots.

Weasel drops with a squeal of agony, clutching his sack. Around him, every man is instinctively wincing and protecting his own groin. E don't fuck around – judging from the sounds he's making Weasel might never be a father.

"Awwww fuck! Awwww fuck! Shit, goddammit, you fucking bitch!" he whimpers as he's curled up in the fetal position on the ground. She leans over him.

"Want some more, you little fuck?" she sneers. Before Weasel can say anything stupid, Aaron eases between them.

"Come on, E, I think you got him good enough already," he chuckles, gently steering her away. She smacks his hand away and stomps off, obviously having had enough frustration for one night. Salvaged something, though. Happy to have nailed Weasel and teach him a lesson.

"Fuck you, ya fucking asshole," whimpers Weasel on the ground, trying to catch his breath, eyes squeezed shut. The crowd around him is dying laughing.

"Get that man some ice for his balls!" cracks Mike, not unsympathetically.

"Fuck you," manages Weasel.

CHAPTER EIGHTEEN

FAR TOO COMMON

Ben hosts the after party at his house. It's close enough to the bar for even the drunkest of the partiers to make it there. Vehicles fill the driveway and line the roadside. They gather around the bonfire, but most of them are wasted enough to require something to sit on. They sprawl on a picnic table, lawn chairs, and a couple sit on logs that didn't make it into the fire. Jessica is still standing next to Tommy, but she is propped up by him, eyes drifting shut every now and then. She wishes she had gone home hours ago, but she is not willing to leave his side, not after she saw how he looked at those sluts.

Weasel sits spread-legged in an old lawn chair, nursing a beer and tallying up his grievances. There are a lot. As usual.

"Here man," interrupts Ben, passing him a bag of ice.

"Thanks," replies Weasel, reaching into his pants. He pulls out a bag of melted ice cubes and swaps it for the fresh one. He tosses the bag of water next to him on the ground.

"Man, this fucking hurts," he complains, still outraged that a woman he let have his cock could want to kick him in the nuts. He believes there is no justice or loyalty in the world.

"I honestly thought you could take her, Weasel." teases Ben. Weasel groans and shuts his eyes.

"Fuck off, just fuck off," he mutters. He takes another pull of his luke-warm beer and contemplates the fire. As he does, Jessica's hot sister Amy walks by, and that makes Weasel wonder if his dick will ever work again. If it doesn't, he firmly believes that a lot of women will be absolutely heart-broken.

Amy stops next to Jessica and Tommy. "How wasted are you?" she asks Jessica, and Jessica mumbles something, waving her off. "You've gotta slow down – you've been drinking way too much lately."

"She's all right, Amy. I'm lookin' after her," insists Tommy, slurring his words. Amy glares at them both.

"Screw you, Tommy – she only drinks so much because she hangs out with you and your drunk ass friends. You're both wasted; I'm taking the two of you home," she insists, tugging on her sister's arm.

"Okay, Mom," mocks Jessica, but she follows her sister. Tommy straggles along behind them, yawning and wondering what time it is.

"Just shut up and get in the car. And don't puke in it," orders Amy, tucking her sister into the backseat with Tommy taking a seat next to her. Jessica falls asleep instantly, and immediately launches into a small snore.

James turns up at the party – he, Quinn, and some of the younger kids showed up after the bar closed, wanting to see what was going on. Jordy – still the lone sober wolf – is prodding the fire with a stick, idly waiting for entertainment.

"Hey, what's up, James?" he greets Tommy's younger brother. "Having a few tonight?"

"Nah, not tonight. We were just hanging out at Quinn's and thought we'd come see what you guys were up to."

"You missed some funny shit at the bar," grins Jordy.

"Fuck you, Jordy, that shit wasn't funny," protests Weasel, still icing his nuts.

"And that's why I fucking hate lacrosse players," insists someone loudly. Jordy, Weasel, and James stop bantering and stare across the fire. A new group of guys has shown up – relative strangers who have never been seen at a lacrosse party before.

"Fucking lacrosse players," snaps one of them, a big guy with long scraggly hair.

The guy's name is Tyler Cole. He's a local legend and not in a good way. Cole is a few years older than the rest of the guys at the party. At one point he was the best hockey player in the area; he had some real potential to play pro and he knew it. Tyler also let everyone else know it. Years ago, he was telling anyone that would listen how he's going to make millions playing in the National Hockey League. He quit high school and left the Rez as a sixteen year old to play Junior A hockey in Canada so he could be seen by as many pro scouts as possible. Unfortunately, two years later he came back to the Rez with a major concussion and drinking and drug problems. Apparently, or so the local story goes, in only his second game he got in a fight and took a severe pounding to the head that left him unable to play for a month. He returned too quickly from that injury, trying to get back in the game, but a few more stiff body checks that bounced his head off the boards left him with post-concussion syndrome. Doctors told him he had to quit playing hockey or risk more damage to his brain. When Tyler came back to Sparrow Lake, he had no high school education and no future. He began stealing anything that wasn't nailed down to finance his drunken, drug-riddled benders. This kind of story about a talented athlete living out his days boozing on the Rez has become a far too common story in Sparrow Lake.

Tyler sneers at James, singling him out as the youngest and smallest. "You got a problem?"

James shrugs peaceably. "Nah, man."

"You lacrosse guys think you're fucking hot shit. You punks ain't nothing – especially your brother. If he was here, I'd kick his fucking ass," says Tyler, fists clenching.

"Whatever," says James. It's useless to argue with some people, and James is happy-go-lucky by nature.

"Think that's funny?" snaps Tyler, coming towards James. He reaches out and shoves James hard. James is thrown against Quinn, who catches and steadies him, both of them surprised. Before Tyler can follow it up, Jordy is between them, pointing the stick he had been using to stir the fire right at Tyler's face. He holds it level with Tyler's eye line, the end smoldering slightly.

"Don't you ever fucking touch him," he orders, voice coldly threatening. Beside him, Weasel slides up. By the extension of their friendship with Tommy, James is their little brother too. Weasel loves a scrap even if he isn't feeling one hundred percent.

"If it isn't fucking Salt n' Pepper," sneers Tyler, trying to ignore the stick. Jordy's skin flushes – the Rez kids have teased him about his deep brown skin as long as Weasel's been teased about his pale skin and red hair. It's part of why the two boys are so close.

"What the fuck you gonna do, Pepper?" sneers Tyler, full of bravado. "I'll shove that stick right up your ass."

"You'll have to pull it out of your fucking eye first," Jordy says calmly, keeping the stick level.

Ben has noticed the situation and hurries over before things escalate even more. He doesn't want this kind of shit breaking out at his place.

"I think it's time for you guys to leave," he announces firmly.

Cole has a few parting words before vacating. "Hey, Henry, remember what I said about your brother. Fucking guy isn't as good a lacrosse player as people say he is. He's a loser. Tell him I said so."

With that and accompanied by a few laughs from his crew, Tyler and his boys nonchalantly walk off. James shakes his head in disbelief, palms sweating. Quinn is equally stunned.

"Who the hell was that?" James asks.

Weasel rolls his eyes, wincing as he sits back down. "Fucking Tyler Cole. He always used to walk around the Rez like he was tough as nails. Tommy beat the shit outta him last summer when he touched Jessica – guess he's still pissed about it," explains Weasel. "Will one of you get me some more ice?"

"Good thing Tyler's not a girl – you mighta gotten your ass beat again," teases Ben, heading toward the house on an ice run.

Weasel throws his skinny arms up in disgust. "Fuck! She kicked me in the balls! What the fuck could I do?"

"Keep telling yourself that," prods Jordy. Weasel shakes his head.

"Don't tell Tommy about that guy pushing me," James states. He has seen his brother get into too many fights defending him and worries some day Tommy might get the worst of it.

AMY TURNS THE CAR INTO THE DRIVEWAY at their house. She's not taking Tommy home because he's staying the night. Amy puts the car in park, turns off the engine, gets out, and slams the door as she walks into the house.

Tommy and Jessica get out of the car and make their way to the front door. Seemingly out of nowhere Jessica gives Tommy a nasty look. The night is obviously coming back into focus for her. "Have fun staring at all those sluts at the bar tonight?"

"I wasn't staring at anybody," Tommy says, already knowing where this is going.

"You wanna be with those whores, huh? You do, don't you?" she says accusingly, pushing him at the same time.

"Knock it off. This is getting old," Tommy huffs. All he wants to do is go to sleep.

"Fuck you," Jessica grunts, and out nowhere she punches him in the side of the head.

This is not the first time Jessica has punched Tommy, and though he does his best to ignore it, it pisses him off something awful. Jessica is a tough girl and knows how to throw a punch, and though it does hurt, Tommy does his best to let on it doesn't bother him. Jessica seems to only get angrier when her punch doesn't seem to have any obvious effect on him. She winds up and throws another jab, but Tommy ducks, and crouches so her fist bounces off the top of his head, likely hurting Jessica's hand more than anything. Tommy grits his teeth, doing his best to control his temper. Jessica can see Tommy getting mad, and that seems to make her happy in a weird way. She begins to smile.

"What... does that bother you? What you gonna do about it?" she taunts as she sticks her face out, daring him to hit her back. "Go ahead, see what the fuck happens," she purrs as her smile gets bigger, taunting him more.

Jessica gives Tommy an open-handed slap in the face before she turns to walk away. "Wouldn't happen if you weren't looking at those sluts all night. Like I said earlier, if that's the kind of slut you want then you can't think much of yourself. Something is wrong with you. You better think about that." Jessica stops in the open door with her drunk, wavering gaze fixed on Tommy. "Think I'm fucked up? You're way more screwed up than anybody I know." Then she slams the door behind her.

Tommy takes a few deep breaths, trying to calm down, and waits a while before entering the house. He wants to give Jessica time to pass out before he goes in and lies down beside her. It's not the first time this has happened and likely won't be the last. It's the first time though that she has said something isn't right with him. That's new. And to Tommy it feels like piling on. First that racist prick Carson Long, then Coach Blair tearing him a new one, and now Jessica punching him. They'll wake up tomorrow, and if she remembers she'll apologize and that will be it. From her point of view. Tommy thinks he loves Jessica, and he knew what he was getting into when he started dating her. People told him stories about how much she used to beat up her ex-boyfriend when they would drink. Tommy has seen so much drinking and fighting since he was a kid, he assumes that's just how relationships work. Something is different now, though. Like things are building to a point where something has to give. Tommy hasn't felt quite like that before. He's pissed at the world, but he doesn't know what to do or where to go to handle it. So, Tommy does the only thing he knows how to do. He walks in the house, goes to Jessica's room, and sees she is sound asleep. Tommy lies down beside her.

At first, he struggles to fall asleep. His insomnia can be bad even when he's had a few beers. But tonight, after some tossing and turning, Tommy does close his eyes and sleep. And he dreams of Hazel – Hazel Blackwater.

HARRY BAKER SNEAKS INTO HIS OWN HOUSE AT DAYBREAK, crossing his fingers that Shelby and Jordy are still asleep.

Tiptoeing through the living room, he trips over the suitcases sitting by the couch, catching himself just barely before sprawling on the floor. The lights are on, and Cash, the Rottweiler whines anxiously somewhere beyond the living room. It sounds like he is following someone around in the master bedroom.

Shelby appears carrying a backpack. Cash tags along at her heels, making quiet whimpers as she angrily dumps the bag by the door. She is wearing a jacket over her clothes, and her hair is pulled back into a ponytail, loose strands straggling across her face.

"What's going on?" asks Harry, trying not to understand.

"I'm sick of this shit!" she says, teary-eyed. "I'm leaving!"

He spreads his arms wide. "Well, I'm sick of this shit too. Pack my bags – I'm coming with ya!"

Emotional and exhausted, Shelby starts giggling at his smart-ass remark. He is absurd; she is absurd. The whole situation is absurd. She collapses onto the couch next to him and cries and laughs as he hugs her.

"What, no spaghetti?" he asks, setting her off again.

"Shut up and go to bed," she manages, pushing him away before finally catching her breath.

"You too," he insists, and they stumble down the hallway to the bedroom, falling into bed and going to sleep. Cash happily installs himself at the foot of the bed.

LATE SUNDAY EVENING as the sun is going down, Jordy and Weasel cruise through the Hoganton mall parking lot in Jordy's shit-box of a Chevy Cavalier. Weasel leans out of the passenger's side window, examining the vehicles still crowding the parking lot. He gives them the same fond attention he usually reserves for hot women – and just in the same way, he's looking for an easy score.

He spots her – a black Chevy pick-up with shiny chrome rims.

"Yeah, yeah, stop right here. Stop," he orders Jordy, and Jordy complies, heart racing. This is one way to earn some spending money – God knows neither he nor Weasel are going to get any at home.

Weasel hops out of the car and glances around to see if anyone's watching him, and Jordy slowly drives off. Weasel saunters toward the pick-up and cozies up to the driver's door.

"Now I know you wanna come home with me, girl," he murmurs, pulling out a screwdriver out of his pants. With a practiced movement, he slams the screwdriver into the keyhole, popping the lock open. He opens the door and the alarm begins to blare, echoing across the parking lot. He shushes the truck like a small child, while at the same time breaking the column and shoving the screwdriver into the ignition and turning it sharply to the right. The truck starts up, and the alarm abruptly cuts off. He puts on his seatbelt and pats the dashboard affectionately.

"See? I knew we'd be good for each other," he insists, pulling out of the parking spot and heading toward the exit. Jordy has been hanging around waiting for him, but when he sees that everything is on track, he drives back toward the Rez.

Weasel drives like an old lady – five miles below the speed limit, stopping for every stop sign and red light. He is on the outskirts of town when he spots a police cruiser in his rear-view mirror.

"Shit, I hope that's not for us," he mutters. As if the cop heard him, the cruiser's lights come on and a siren wails at him. Weasel obediently pulls over, and the cop stops behind him. The cop gets out of the cruiser and walks toward Weasel.

Weasel waits until the cop is almost to the truck before he floors it. The cop is pissed, and soon two cruisers are chasing Weasel out past the Hoganton town limits. He makes it back to the Rez with the cops still in hot pursuit, their cherries still blazing. He turns down a dirt road and kicks the truck into high gear. When the cruisers slow down, unable to see through the clouds of dust and dirt that the truck kicks up, Weasel vanishes down a laneway leading back into the bush. He puts the Chevy in park and quickly pops the stereo out. Jumping out with the stereo, he dives into the brush like his namesake, crouching and running south. He stays undercover but keeps moving along the tree line. By the time the cops find the truck and figure out that he's gone, they attempt to track him with no success.

Two fields away, Weasel leans his back against a tree and catches his breath. He spits and pulls out his cell phone to dial Jordy. This new hobby can be lucrative when it pans out. If you don't have too many complications. The cops are always around when you don't need them.

"Yo, come get me. I'm on Thompson road by the old fishing spot. Had to ditch it."

Jordy pulls up a few minutes later, and Weasel hops in.

"You blew it! Fuck, those rims were nice!" mourns Jordy.

Weasel nods. "Big Phil woulda paid up the ass for those. Oh well, maybe he'll give us a few bucks for this stereo."

CHAPTER NINETEEN

INSIDE JOB

Tommy sits in his truck with the engine idling. The radio is playing Bruce Springsteen's "Waitin' on a Sunny Day." It's a song that Tommy can relate to – like he's always waiting for something. Something that never comes.

Right now, Tommy is thinking about his Hazel dream, trying to remember as much of it as possible. In the dream it is a sunny day. He is in a large field. All around him people are having a good time, families chatting and eating together. There is an especially large group of people close to him, everyone laughing. When the laughing subsides, a white-haired woman from the group materializes next to Tommy. It is Hazel Blackwater who seems happy to see him. Hazel is accompanied by a much shorter woman with closely-cropped, mostly gray hair. The woman's face looks strangely bird-like with close set eyes, a beak-like nose, and a permanently surprised expression on her face. Tommy remembers trying to speak, to ask Hazel where he is, but he can't form the words. That doesn't matter, though, because Hazel knows what he's thinking anyway.

"It's alright, Tommy. There's no need to be worried. We are in a safe place where we can talk. Nothing can harm us here. This is a place where things can be made better. Where the bad things that have happened to us can be healed. You could call it the place where your healing journey begins. Give me your hand."

Tommy remembers reaching for Hazel's outstretched hand and the other woman looking surprised. Things get dark as she takes Tommy by the hand. "How can I be expected to walk you out of the darkness and into the light if I don't know the way?" she asks. Then nothing. End of dream.

Tommy's truck is parked outside a house. Hazel's house. Thinking about the dream is disturbing and comforting at the same time. He knows it is an invitation. He is clutching a small package wrapped in red fabric – a gift for Hazel. It is almost dusk and in the failing light he can see into the illuminated window. Hazel apparently has company. They have finished eating but the table hasn't been cleared. Hazel talks to her unseen guest while at the same time rearranging her paints and cleaning up her painting area.

Tommy wants to go in, but his legs seem weak and he can't bring himself to get out of the truck. He is still dwelling on how Coach Blair roasted him during the game. "If you're that selfish, maybe you shouldn't be playing the game."

He is worried about what Jessica drunkenly blasted him with. "Something's wrong with you. You better think about that."

There are voices in his head that he can't seem to shut up. Criticism that cuts him deep. Voices that make him feel worthless.

Then another voice, a calm, measured one, jolts him back to reality. "You can sit there wasting gas or you can come in and have a cup of tea."

Hazel is standing there talking to Tommy through the open driver's window. He kills his engine and gets out of the truck. "Come in and meet my old friend. I've told her so much about you."

It's rare to see Hazel without the dogs by her side. As she leads him back to the house Tommy realizes he has never met anyone quite like this woman.

When Hazel opens the front door, the dogs are lying on the floor next to Hazel's guest who sits contentedly in the old rocking chair. Tommy is stunned to see it is the other woman from his dream. She doesn't look exactly the same but similar enough for him to know it's her.

"Tommy, this is my oldest and best friend, Jean. Jean Hemlock. Jean, this is Tommy Henry."

Jean gets up out of the rocking chair. The dogs, Sorn and Leo, get to their feet as well. She crosses the floor and warmly folds him into a strong hug.

HAZEL GENTLY OPENS THE LITTLE PACKAGE wrapped in red cloth. It is filled with loose tobacco that Beau instructed Tommy to take with him. They are standing at an old fire pit area in the back of Hazel's house that Tommy hasn't paid any attention to in previous visits. Standing there in front of the small fire, Hazel takes a small bit of tobacco and gives a pinch each to Tommy and Jean while taking some herself.

"We should each give thanks to the Creator for bringing us together in good health."

Slowly each one opens the hand with the tobacco and lets the herb leisurely drift into the fire. Tommy's mind drifts back to recent events that have been making him feel so empty.

Tommy, Hazel, and Jean are sitting at the kitchen table now. It's full on dark outside and Hazel just has a couple of lights on, turned low.

"Tommy, I think you have some feelings that you don't know what to do with. Feelings that I suspect control you sometimes instead of the other way around. So here is where we find ourselves. We can take my life experience, and what I've learned, and your life experience, and what you know, and combine them to good use. If we can do that, we might be able to calm things down in your life. Let me use a sports analogy. You might not know it to look at me, but I'm a sports fan. I know you are. I love many sports, especially lacrosse, and if we learn anything from the Creator's game, we know that our goal should always be to 'slow the game down' and learn from it. In this case, the game is life. We need to take our time and see things in our lives as they really are; to be able to accept some things and see through others which are merely distractions so we can think more clearly, be more balanced."

Tommy takes a deep breath and feels himself relaxing a little. He has been feeling more and more tense with a sick knot in his stomach because he doesn't know where all this is going and what Hazel expects of him. When he hears her talk about calming things down, he realizes he isn't in control right now. And that's okay. He's not expected to be.

Hazel reaches out and takes Jean's hand. "Jean knows my story because it's her story too. She has lived through many of the same things that I experienced. You see, Jean was my good friend when I went away. We were both sent to the Martindale Indian School. Our experience at that school would ultimately shape the lives we have now. For a large part of my life I thought that school, and the people in charge, had destroyed me. It took me a long time to realize I was stronger than that and I needed to take my life back and make it mine. Boarding school was meant to take something away, but in some ways for me it was a gift. Not a gift that should ever have been given, but nonetheless, it can't be taken back now. It may be difficult to understand, but it made me strong and it gave me the desire to help others. You might also have been given hard gifts to understand.

That's what we can try to figure out. Together."

Hazel stops and blows on her tea. She takes a sip.

"What are you thinking, Tommy?" Hazel's kind eyes beg for a response.

Tommy doesn't know Hazel's story. He can't imagine what she went through. He really doesn't know her, and he knows even less about Indian boarding schools.

"I'd like to hear your story and how it might help me. I'm tired of being angry and feeling like I'm fucking things up."

As soon as the words are out of his mouth, he knows he shouldn't have used that kind of language. His heart starts to race and the thought crosses his mind that his time with Hazel is over before it has begun.

Hazel is smiling. It's as if she has only heard what he meant to say, not what he actually said.

"How do you begin to tell a life story? Well, you just have to start. Sometimes it's hard to talk about and sometimes easier. For a long time, I didn't want to talk about it. I didn't want anyone to know that I was one of those boarding school children. There was a stigma. You know what that is? It's like a black mark on your forehead that tells people you are less than human. I was ashamed. And that led me to some destructive habits. My life has been a long one, so there's too much to tell in one sitting. So, we'll do this in stages. And we don't want to go fast either. I can't speed through what has been such an emotional thing for me. I can only distance myself so far from my own life. It's still my experience, and I learn something new every time I talk about what happened to me. It's kind of like there are hidden messages but you don't find them all at one time. Everything has to be just right and then, bang, something drops in your lap that you have never thought about before. But I can say this: life is about purpose. Finding your own purpose. A good one. A satisfying one that carries you to the end of your life. A life that you can feel happy about even if you have a bad start. There are hidden messages in your life too, Tommy. We just have to find them. It's really an inside job for both of us. An exploration of the inside of ourselves. So, let me tell you about my journey to happiness. Happiness was a foreign word for me for the longest time."

At this point Jean puts her hands on the table and pushes herself up. "Well said, my friend. Tommy, I have heard Hazel's story many times. I lived through what she is about to tell you. But it is a very personal thing, something that only you two should share. So, no offense to Wahiéntha, but I will leave you both now. Let me take the dogs out. Or is it them taking me out?" She smiles and walks out the door with the dogs following her.

IT'S RAINING OUTSIDE so the team is practicing in the gym. The players gather around Coach Blair and Coach Jenkins, waiting for their instructions.

"Since it's raining pretty hard outside and we can't rip up our only practice and game field, we're gonna be in here today. Gonna do a little stick work and some six-on-six, but it's mostly gonna be conditioning today. Coach Jenkins?"

Coach Jenkins blows his whistle and starts right in on them. It's a good cop, bad cop scenario with Jenkins relishing his role as the bad cop. Shrilling his whistle, he points. "Let's go! Jog around the outside to get warmed up. I know you need the conditioning; we looked slow and lazy last game! We need to get in better shape if you expect to win anything!" he barks, and the boys reluctantly start jogging. For the most part, they are natural athletes, and they've seldom seen the inside of a gym or seriously trained for lacrosse.

The Hoganton High School Principal walks into the gym and eyeballs the boys warming up. Coach Blair makes a beeline over to him. He has to take the opportunity to push his pet peeve… one that should be a high priority but the Coach can't seem to make anyone see it that way. Principal Mason seems to look even more fatigued than usual when he sees the Coach approaching.

"What do we gotta do to get a new field? We've been using that same old field for practice and games since I played here. All the other schools in the area are upgrading to turf fields. We have to do the same sometime soon if we wanna compete," insists Coach Blair without remorse. That's the Coach's best attribute and his worst failing. He doesn't like small talk. Straight talk, shoot from the hip, call it what you will, you always know where you stand with Coach Blair. But from a political standpoint, the Coach doesn't know how to play.

Principal Mason sighs and has no immediate response. Mason has hooded eyelids that give him a drowsy look. It also means you can't see his eyes well enough to know what he's thinking.

"Tim, you know I've been on this. I have asked for funding for a new field from the town of Hoganton and even from the Sparrow Lake Council. Not once, not twice, but multiple times. The funding just isn't there. At least that's what they say. I understand your concern. I'm going to keep trying. That's all I can say," he promises, but there is little hope being offered in his voice. Lacrosse may be the lifeblood of several communities, but it has not even a fraction of the funding that high school basketball and football have.

"Let's go! Get on the line! Sprints! Midline back! Endline back! Let's go!" yells Coach Jenkins. He is enjoying this practice and wants to make the most of his time in charge of the troops. Jenkins is of the firm opinion that most of the players lack backbone and are not in good enough shape to play on a team that he is coaching. If he gets a chance, if Coach Blair will give him a long enough leash, he might be able to make these players into a team. Coach Jenkins secretly believes that, even though he is the assistant coach, he is the better of the two coaches. If you were to say that to the players they would laugh you out of the room. Coach Jenkins keeps the same disgusted scowl on his face. The boys go through the paces half-heartedly, with even less enthusiasm than they can usually muster for a practice. They think Jenkins is a dipshit.

"Well, we need to get something soon," says Coach Blair firmly, staring at Mason. "These kids do a good job at this school competing against bigger schools that have more money and better facilities. They could do even more if they got some of the financial support that the big boys get. They've got heart. They've got the skill, but they need some help. It's about time that happened. Past time."

Mason is blinking rapidly while listening to Coach Blair. He has heard it all before, feels somewhat badly about not being able to get anything done, but he doesn't know what else to do. "I agree with you, Tim. I'm going to keep looking for funding to try get us a new field. You know if I had a championship banner to hang my request on that would go a long way to making it happen," reminds Principal Mason patiently. Bouncing the new stadium ball back into Coach Blair's court is never a bad idea, that way he has to take some of the responsibility for making a new facility happen. They've used these lines on each other before. Tim Blair is a hell of a good man and an excellent coach, but his scope can be a little narrow at times. The man doesn't always think big picture.

Andy and Ben are bent over and sucking wind from the work out that Coach Jenkins is putting them through. The sour-faced man never misses an opportunity to tell them what a bunch of lazy, little punks they are.

"I hate this shit. I can't stand Jenkins," gasps Andy, wishing he could spit, but his mouth is too dry.

"I know. Me neither," Ben agrees.

"One of these days I'm gonna shove that whistle right up his fucking ass," vows Andy.

"My uncle played in his team in high school. Said he sucked, could barely catch. But let's just get this shit over with," Ben grunts in disgust.

Jenkins blows his whistle. "You girls done chit chatting over here?" he asks sweetly, walking towards Andy. "What's the matter superstar, can't handle a little running?" Andy does his best not to let it bother him as he catches his breath. Jenkins is now standing right in Andy's face and keeps up the badgering with a smug smile on his face. "You gonna be okay, Flint? Anything I can do to help you get through this?"

Andy looks at Jenkins with straight face and says, "Sure could use a hug."

Ben hears the remark and busts out laughing. Andy does a bad job trying to hold back a smile as Jenkins is ready to explode in anger. He blows his whistle and shouts, "Superstar just got everybody five extra sprints."

The rest of the team groans as Ben and Andy choke with laughter. Ben can't stop smiling as he shakes his head at Andy, "Fuck you're an asshole," he manages to get out. Andy just gives Ben a quick smile. Another loud whistle and the boys obediently go for the next sprint.

CHAPTER TWENTY

HAWKS ON THREE

Waking up early, Tim Blair is most often a spring-out-of-bed-right-away kind of guy. Grab the bull by the horns and get things underway. Not this morning. That's unusual, doubly so because it's a playoff game day. He feels a little lazy, not tired but reflective. So, he stays in bed for a few minutes, staring at the ceiling. Sarah continues sleeping soundly on her side, and as usual, there hasn't been any commotion from the boys' room.

Blair's mind preoccupies itself with today's game against Dennville. But not just the game. You know he actually thinks this could be his last season coaching. He's trying to get comfortable with that idea. Lacrosse has been his life: playing, coaching, and always talking about the game. The best friends he's made and the great people he's met have come from lacrosse. Sarah could be right, though. Again. Perhaps he needs to take it easy. Retire from the game. Take it down a notch. Just teach high school phys-ed and go home at the end of the day. Could he actually see himself at a game as a spectator? Sitting in the stands and watching? That would be tough. He's a man of action and responsibility. He can't picture himself as one of those people who just sit on their ass and play armchair quarterback while eating a hotdog. He has heard those kinds of critics his whole life as a player and as a coach. He doesn't care much for those type of people. He still wants to come up with game plans, plot strategy, and find ways to motivate young, talented, sometimes distracted players. His heart is still in it. It makes him feel good. That's the problem. He would miss the kids. He needs to give it some more thought, he decides. Besides he's got the rest of the season to roll this concept around in his head. Time to get cracking. He knows he can't forget about it. Sarah won't let him.

Coach Blair rolls over and kisses his wife on her bare shoulder. He slowly gets out of bed, his joints cracking. Things are always a little creaky first thing in the morning. Whoever said getting old is for the birds sure had that one right. He had promised himself that he would do some stretching every morning but something always gets in the way of that. The time spent lounging in bed thinking about the future means he's got to get a move on. Right now, he has to get Konner and Keegan up and at 'em. It's a big day. For some reason, the Coach has a good feeling about the future. Back on the road to a championship. Blair believes in omens, feelings, and today seems like it's going to be a good one. He can feel it in his bones. His boys can win this one.

His wife Sarah has a few last words for him before he heads out the door. "Tim, I know it's a big game. Just take it easy on the sideline, please."

Tim Blair and his wife Sarah love each other in a wholehearted way. High school sweethearts. True companions and accepting of each other's faults. Soul mates. Two young boys and their whole lives ahead of them. All Tim can do is smile and say, "I'll try. I'll try. Love you."

IT'S A GOOD-SIZED CROWD at Hoganton Field. The stands are almost full with a constant buzz coming from the spectators. An air of anticipation lingers over everything – a little more tension than a regular season game. During the season there is always another game, a chance to get back on track. You made a mistake? Have an off day? There is always next game. Not now. Lose and you go home. Better luck next year.

Coach Blair rides this wave of thoughts and emotions as he stands quietly on the sidelines. He's checked out the playing field and everything seems in good shape. The sun is out, but there are a few dark clouds lurking on the horizon. The forecast calls for possible rain showers but the threat of getting wet doesn't seem to bother the spectators. The crowd stirs, getting more and more lively with a good number of vocal Mustangs fans in attendance. Blair tries to collect his thoughts because he wants to give his players a little extra motivation before the game starts. He doesn't want them to be cocky, to take a win for granted. He doesn't want anyone to lose their cool and take a penalty that could make the difference between moving on and the end of the season. *Let's just do all the right things*, he thinks. *Can that be so hard?*

He's wearing his red windbreaker with "Hawks" lettered in black with white outline on the chest. Maybe it's foolish, but he is really proud of that jacket and what it represents. Tim Blair remembers playing Division 3 lacrosse in his heyday and what it meant to be part of a team. He still loves that feeling. He's been coaching this game a long time, and he's still waiting for that magical moment when it all comes together. The players at the top of their game, the breaks going your way, the weather cooperating, and the Hawks supporters in the crowd giving the team an extra push. This is the beginning of the push towards the State Championship. Last time the Hawks won State he was finishing his last year of college. Two years later, he took a teaching job at Hoganton and was named the Head Coach of the men's lacrosse team. In his forty-five years on this earth, he has been on the Hawks sideline for twenty of them.

Everyone huddles around Coach Blair. He is smiling, but all the players know there is an edge to that smile. Blair is a kind man, an understanding coach, but he doesn't tolerate laziness or stupidity. He seems calm and relaxed but everyone knows that he is as wound up and excited as any of them. He isn't big on long, extended pregame motivational speeches, so they don't expect a lot of rah-rah.

The players take a knee and are silent as Coach Blair looks at his team and asks them one question, "How bad do you want it?"

Ben instinctively responds, "Real bad!"

Coach knows his squad is ready to go and he only says two words. "Show me."

THE HAWKS SIDELINE EXPLODES into loud screams and cheers as they take the field. Coach Blair thinks to himself about how proud he is of these boys. He's going to have a hard time not being around them when he does eventually step down as coach.

The breeze rattles the broadcast booth and Hank Thomas. The metal contraption is more than a little rickety and Hank sometimes gets a little nervous if he thinks about how high up they are sitting. Heights don't bother Robbie.

"Hank, if that wind picks up a bit more, you and I could end up getting up close and personal with some of the players down there on the field. What do ya think about possibly taking a nosedive?"

Hank clutches the sides of his chair and scowls at Robbie Redbird.

"I'm trying to have a good time here, and you're making fun of me. That's an easy thing to do on a bad day, so how's about we focus on the game and the fact that it's an excellent day for lacrosse?"

Redbird is grinning from ear to ear. "That's why I like working with you, Hank. You know the game and you have a sense of humor, no matter what. As far as I'm concerned, any day is a great day for watching this game, and if Hoganton can shut down Dennville, it'll be an even better day."

Hank nods at Robbie and gets ready to kick off the broadcast. "Got your game notes organized? I don't want to have to carry you any more than I already do."

At the Henry grandparent's house, Gram and her daughter Laurie are sitting down in the living room. Game time. Joyce Henry is a short, solidly-built woman, barely five feet tall. Her curly gray hair still has a hint of the original black color. She clutches a cane that she doesn't really use in the house but likes to swing it around when listening or watching sports. Maybe it reminds her of her younger days. She played a lot of softball at local diamonds and hockey on frozen ponds with the boys. Maybe that's why she's so tough. That combined with her outspoken personality. Despite her age, she's a spry seventy-one-years young, and she is still an avid sports fan.

Laurie and Gram are the only two members of the Henry clan not in attendance at the state quarter final game between Hoganton and Dennville. The game is being held at Hoganton field and Gram is reluctant to go there. She has it in her head that after the dust up in the stands she was involved in years ago that she continues to be blacklisted to this day. The older woman still thinks about that day sometimes. If you're going to mouth off you better be ready to throw hands. Now, thinking back, she wouldn't change a thing. She is stubborn so no amount of persuading can change her mind about not going. Besides, it's pretty damn comfortable right here. Gram switches her cane to her left hand, then stretches over from her perch on the couch and turns on a small radio with her right hand. The station is pre-set and a familiar voice booms through the radio.

Hank Thomas has an easy delivery and his voice commands attention. "Here we are again, folks, with more unpredictable and exciting Hoganton lacrosse. This game is brought to you in part by Big Dave's Gas and Convenience. Remember, Big Dave's is the real deal. Now, Coach Blair has just charged up the troops, and we are set to watch the Hoganton Hawks take on the Dennville Mustangs in the Section Finals. This is a dance that seems to happen often at this time of year. These two teams have met at this point for the past two seasons and Hoganton has come out on top in those previous meetings. Hoganton boasts a 12-6 victory over Dennville earlier this season, but Dennville has improved a great deal since then. In many respects there is no resemblance to the team that lost to the Hawks, and they will undoubtedly be bringing their 'A' game against Hoganton as a berth in the State Semifinal is on the line. It's all or nothing today, and with the commotion in the stands right now, it seems like the fans are loving this matchup."

Redbird jumps in with his take on things; his job is to bring some color and analysis to the broadcast. "That first meeting was a one-sided affair, but Dennville has looked solid throughout the year since then and match up quite well against Hoganton. I don't think the Mustangs will be intimidated. Ball control, which the Hawks like to rely on, could be a problem for them as Dennville has one of, if not the best face-off specialist in the state in Jamie Holman, so Shane Smoke might be in for a long day. One way or the other, he is definitely going to have his work cut out for him."

Off the opening draw, Dennville wins the face-off cleanly and has a 4-on-3 fast break. The Hoganton defense slides, but the Dennville offense moves the ball crisply with two quick passes and a Dennville attack man finishes the play with a well-placed shot. 1-0 Dennville.

Thomas tries to keep the disappointment out of his voice. "A clean face-off win, a fast break, and the Hawks are down 1-0 just six seconds into this Sectional Final. Not something we anticipated, but then again Dennville is the team with something to prove today."

Gram listens intently to the call and waves her cane over her head with a surprised look on her face. "Whoa, they better wake up. Hope they ain't taking these guys too lightly."

Laurie's lips spread into a slight smile. She has become accustomed to the running commentary during games. The younger woman stays behind partially to keep her mother company but also because of the entertainment value. You never know what is going to come out of the older woman's mouth.

Laurie responds with, "Maybe they're just having a slow start, getting the kinks out. It happens sometimes. You know that."

Joyce Henry points the end of her cane at Laurie. "Well, they better get the kinks out soon or they'll get their asses kicked!" Then the pair goes silent, both women staring suspiciously at the radio as if it might be responsible for the Dennville score in some way.

A veteran player, Redbird provides the voice of practical experience, and he has seen variations of this story unfold on the field many times before. "Well, we said it off the top of the broadcast. Jamie Holman could make life miserable for Shane Smoke. The Hawks either figure out a way to compensate or they may end up on the short end of the stick."

The second face-off and Holman wins again, throwing the ball behind him to a teammate. Dennville controls the ball slowly, moving it up field. Dennville changes to put some offensive players on the field. They calmly move the ball around the outside, not attacking the net but taking time off the clock. Every second closer to that elusive win, they hope.

Hank holds his coffee cup down to make sure the steady breeze doesn't tip it over and blow it out of the booth. A lot of little things make a broadcaster's life difficult, and the weather is almost always one of them. "Dennville is playing a very patient game. Throwing the ball around the outside of the Hoganton end. They have made a few attempts at the Hawks net but are trying not to turn the ball over. They should be getting a stall call from the referee, but the officials are giving the Mustangs plenty of leeway before nailing them for stalling. That kind of a call would mean that Dennville would have to keep the ball in a more restricted area, making it harder to move the ball around the outside, making it easier for Hoganton to regain possession."

Coach Blair feels his heartburn coming back. He knows he's getting angry, but he can't help himself. It always starts with a tight feeling right in the pit of his stomach and then spreads. He knows what Sarah would say. "Calm down, Tim. It's only a game. It's not life or death." But he is an emotional man. The collar of his already snug shirt feels way too tight now, and he's finding it really warm, maybe he's even a little nauseous although the temperature is hovering in the seventies. It's early in the game to be blowing his stack, he knows, but the officials are just too damn slow with the call here. Coach Blair's throat feels a little raw but he bellows anyway.

"Come on, you guys! It's obvious what they're doing. Do your jobs! This isn't a pickup game here. That's a stall, not hard to see. Make the call." If you take care of the little things, the big things take care of themselves. Blair has always liked that line. He just hates taking care of all the little things sometimes. *Why can't everyone just do their damn job? Is that too much to ask?*

Weasel and Jordy have made the trek to the game. They both enjoy a good match where they get to let loose and yell to their hearts' content. The boys sit close enough to the Hawks bench to hear Coach Blair shout at the officials. Weasel picks up the last bit of Blair's rant, and he and Jordy begin chanting it in the stands. "A stall is a stall. Make the call!" Some of the Hawks fans pick up on it and soon dozens of spectators are chanting.

Robbie Redbird uses his elbows to pin down his papers in the breeze as he leans over to watch the action. The glamorous life of a radio broadcaster is not all it's cracked up to be sometimes. "So the stall call should be up by now, and you can see Coach Blair on the Hawks sideline really giving it to the officials to make the obvious call, which would force Dennville to keep it in the box. And as you said, Hank, making it tougher to take time off the clock. Even some of the fans have had enough and are letting their opinion be known. You can certainly see the frustration in the Hawks' defenders. They are playing a lot of defense, and man, take it from personal experience, I know that is exhausting."

A Dennville midfielder makes a move towards the net, and Ben Lucas puts a slash on him that is not worthy of a penalty but the referee throws the flag signaling an infraction anyway.

Sometimes you get the elevator, sometimes you get the shaft, thinks Hank. It's starting to drizzle a little bit, and Thomas finds himself seated right under a leak in the roof of the broadcast booth. Drops of water are hitting Hank on the top of his head and running down his nose. Shaking his head, he moves closer to Robbie than they both prefer. The booth is usually a little crowded and the two men have gotten used to that. Regardless, the show must go on, and Hank never loses track of the action. "Flag down on Ben Lucas for slashing. Don't know if that was a bit of a soft call. We have seen harder slashes than that go without being called a foul. Dennville still swings the ball around, but they will likely go to the net now that they'll be a man up even if they don't score. A Dennville midfielder takes a dodge down the right side against a Hawk short stick defender. He has a step and lets a low shot go. The shot is stopped by Devin Clarke as the referee blows the whistle and signals a Hoganton penalty to Ben Lucas. One minute for slashing and Dennville has good chance here to go up 2-0. We're getting a little bit of rain now but not enough to affect the play of either team I don't think."

Weasel looks over at Jordy. "Those fuckers see only what they want to see. They've got it in for us. Ben slashed me harder than that when we were ten years old." Jordy glances at the auburn-haired agitator but knows better than to say anything that would encourage him.

Robbie Redbird is not particularly enjoying the up close and personal smell of Hank's aftershave, but he wouldn't miss this game for anything. "The Hawks man down unit has done very well this year, but with one of your top defenders off in the penalty box it's gonna be tough to stop the Dennville snipers from getting a good shot off at the Hoganton goal."

Though Dennville is man up on a 6-on-5, they still use up as much of the clock as they can, killing most of the penalty before taking a shot. Just as Ben Lucas is released from the box Dennville finds a man open on the crease. He fakes once and wings the ball into the Hawks net, making the score 2-0. Coach Blair calls a Hawks timeout.

"What the hell is going on?" protests Gram, thumping her cane on the floor, peering at her daughter as if Laurie should have the answer. Tommy's aunt gives a little shrug. She knows how emotional her mother can get, especially when it concerns her grandkids.

"Relax, Mom, it's only the first quarter. They have plenty of time left."

Joyce Henry grunts, grips her cane a little tighter, and turns her attention back to the game. Maybe scowling at the little radio will help get the Hawks back in the game.

The rain has let up but is promising to stay around just to make things interesting. Hank smiles and with a deep breath shifts a few inches away from his broadcast companion. The leak in the roof has let up for the moment.

"Well, Robbie, Dennville scores just as the Hoganton penalty is released. Almost six minutes has gone by in this game and the Hawks have yet to get the ball in the Mustangs end of the field. Doesn't look like there's any secret about the Dennville game plan. They want to win the face-offs, slow the game down, and keep the ball away from the high-powered Hoganton offense. What do the Hawks have to do to counter that tactic?"

Redbird smiles and wipes his forehead jokingly, thanking Hank for the extra breathing room. "The Hawks are going to have to find a way to get some possessions on offense. The Dennville coaching staff knows Hoganton has some very good attack men in Flint, McCrae, and Henry, but if they don't have the ball, they can't hurt you. The Hawks have to find a way to win the battle at the midfield and come up with some ground balls."

As the team gathers around Coach Blair during the timeout, he does his best to settle the team down. The tightness in his stomach has spread to the right side of his chest and is making him extremely uncomfortable. The feeling is like an extreme muscle cramp that won't go away. Blair puts that out of his mind. It's not important now. Only the game. It's all about the game. He knows some of his players go into panic mode when things are not going their way. And that's always a problem.

"Okay. Everybody calm down and relax. Remember what I said. We play as a team and win as a team. We're only down by two shots and we got a lot of game left here. Obviously, they want to keep the ball in our end and slow the game down. So we have to make some adjustments and start getting a few offensive possessions."

Coach Blair tells his team the alignment he wants on the next face-off. The team comes together as Tommy yells, "Hawks on three... one, two, three!" and the entire team yells "Hawks" as loudly as humanly possible. They head out to take their positions for the face-off, but Tommy is surprised by something he sees. Coach Blair looks like he is having trouble breathing.

"You okay, coach?" Tommy asks.

Coach Blair responds through gritted teeth. "Yeah, I'm okay, Tommy. Now get out there and bury a couple for us," he says as he taps his player on the back of the helmet. Tommy jogs out to his attack position but glances back at Coach Blair and wonders if he really is alright. He has never seen Coach Blair out of breath like that. His face was red, but that's nothing unusual. It happens almost every game. Coach Blair reaches over for a water bottle and takes a quick drink, squirts some onto his face, claps his hands, and yells, "Come on now, Hawks, let's get after it!"

Hank Thomas slides a short note over to Robbie. It reads, "Let's keep things upbeat, Blair is a cagey guy and he knows what he's doing." Then Thomas fills in the radio audience on the Coach's change in tactics.

"Looks like Coach Blair is going with a Double Pole set on the face-off. He's got Troy Wilson taking the face-off with a long pole and Ben Lucas on the wing also with a pole. Shane Smoke is covering an attack man with a short stick."

Robbie Redbird smiles. "I like this move, Hank. By putting a long pole on the face-off even if he loses the draw Wilson can immediately try and strip Jamie Holman of the ball. Holman is great at winning faceoffs but he's not great at carrying the rock. We all know Troy Wilson can throw some nasty checks with that long pole, so Holman is going to have a tougher time moving the ball with Wilson hunting him down."

The players lean down for the face-off and again Holman wins it behind him, but just as he picks the ball up Wilson uses his long pole to give Holman's stick a huge chop, knocking the stick right out of Holman's hands. The ball is loose and Wilson picks it up, running up field and then circling back to pass it to a Hawks short stick midfielder.

Redbird gives Hank a thumbs up and continues on the positive theme. "That's exactly what the Hawks needed. Wilson comes up with the ground ball, and now he and Ben Lucas go back to the defensive end. Shane Smoke goes to the offensive end. Another long pole comes to the box, and the Hawks get settled with their offensive players on the field. Now that potent Hawks offense can do their thing and try to cut into the two-goal deficit."

The Hawks get the ball to Andy, who moves it to Steve McCrae, who passes it off to Tommy Henry. They swing the ball around in the Dennville end, getting all the Hawks players a touch of the ball. When the ball gets back to Andy Flint, he does a right to left split-dodge, getting a step on his defender. The Dennville defensemen slide as Andy passes to a cutting Tommy Henry, who catches the ball and fires it into the Dennville net. 2-1.

Hank silently pumps his fist in the air and has a hard time restraining himself from cheering into the microphone. "That's a little more like what we've been used to seeing this season. Flint to Henry and the Hawks are on the board."

Redbird decides to look ahead at strategy and how the rest of the game might play out. "I imagine Coach Blair will go with that same face-off alignment and have his squad concentrating on getting possession. The more they control the ball, the more Dennville's defense will have to try and slow down the slick offensive players of the Hawks."

Gram drops her cane in her lap and claps her hands together after hearing the call on the radio. "That's more like it! Atta boy, Tommy," she says with a big smile on her face. "Let's see if they can get on a roll now."

The Hawks use the same alignment on the next face-off and gain possession of the ball once again, setting up their offense in the Dennville end. After a few passes, a Hawks player fires a shot at the net, which is stopped by the Dennville goalie. He quickly passes the ball to a short-stick team-mate and the player runs up field towards the Hawks end of the field.

James Henry sees the play happening and reacts quickly by chasing the Dennville player. Just before crossing midfield, James runs down the player with the ball. The younger Henry swings his stick hard, making a loud smacking sound of metal hitting metal. The opposing player's stick is knocked from his hands and goes flying into the air. The ball falls to the ground and James is quick to scoop it up and darts the other way towards the Dennville net.

The Dennville players have all spread out from their own net, assuming the ball was going towards the Hoganton end of the field. James sees Andy standing in front of the Dennville net with absolutely no one covering him. James fires a long pass to Andy who fakes a couple times on a helpless goalie before depositing it into the opposing team's net. Both James and Andy have big smiles. The game is knotted at 2-2.

Hank has done the unmentionable – knocked his coffee cup over with java running all over the broadcast table. Robbie stands up quickly to get away from the runaway liquid and bumps his head sharply on the low roof. Hank pays no attention to the spillage or Redbird's pain. "Whooaaa!! Big time hustle play by James Henry, stripping the ball away from a Dennville player, scooping up the ground ball, and moving it to Andy Flint on the crease. And it's an easy goal for the Hawks!"

Rubbing his head, Redbird crouches down to get closer to his microphone. "Coach Blair has got to be happy with that exhibition by James Henry. He never gave up on the play, showing great determination to get the ball back for his team, and it leads to a goal for the Hawks. Great to see one of the younger guys step up and make a difference."

Gram waves her cane over her head with one hand and pumps her other fist in the air as she hears the broadcasters sing the praises of her younger grandson. "Alright, James! That's my grand boy! He's got my genes. He is tenacious. Go Hawks!" Laurie maneuvers back into the room with a couple of glasses of iced tea. She is careful to avoid Gram's cane, which is always on the move.

As the Hoganton sideline erupts after the goal, the whole team mobs James with fist pounds and pats on the head as he makes his way to the sideline. Coach Blair gives James a fist bump while saying, "Good job, kid," followed by a pat on the back of the helmet. Energized by James' superb play, the Hawks begin to take over the game at this point. They cruise to an 11-7 victory.

Hank Thomas smiles his "I told you so" smile, feeling happy that there is at least one more game in the Hawks season. "After a shaky first quarter, the Hoganton Hawks come away with an 11-7 victory over the Dennville Mustangs to win the sectional championship. The Hawks showed they can play solid defense tonight as they were in their own end more than they would have liked, but great games were turned in on the defensive side by Troy Wilson, Ben Lucas, and goaltender Devin Clarke. Hoganton will now move on to the State Semifinal, and in two weeks will play against the same squad that has ended their season the previous two years, their arch rivals the Orrtown Wildcats. Any last thoughts, Robbie?"

Redbird, still rubbing his head, turns his mike on. "'Resilience' is the only word I can think of for this team. Even after a bad start, it seems the Hawks always find a way to claw their way back. I don't know, but if the Henry boys are on their game, and James seems to be stepping up at the right time, with Wilson, Lucas, and Clarke playing like they are possessed, you just might see a few surprises in the coming weeks."

Hank Thomas makes a rolling motion with his hand in the air telling Redbird it's time to wrap it up. "Thanks, Robbie, for the expert commentary as usual. That's it for us today. Hawks lacrosse will be back on the air in two weeks when Hoganton takes on Orrtown in the State Semifinal. Until then, I'm Hank Thomas with Robbie Redbird. We'll have more Hawks lacrosse in just fourteen days. See you then."

Gram sits on her couch smiling as she turns off the radio. The iced tea is gone and her cane lies on the floor beside her. Joyce Henry beams with pride hearing that her grandsons played well and that the Hawks are moving on. Laurie gets up and turns on the TV to Gram's other favorite team, the New York Yankees. The score shows the Yankees are losing 5-2 in the bottom of the fifth inning to the Toronto Blue Jays, and the senior citizen simply says, "Damn it, you guys. Let's go here."

CHAPTER TWENTY-ONE

A BROKEN HEART

It seems like an odd thing to do, but Tommy has agreed to meet Hazel after the lacrosse game against Dennville. She said she wanted to talk with him while he is still experiencing the smile of the Creator. While he is feeling the good mind that comes with playing the Medicine Game.

Initially, Tommy was unhappy about this, thinking about how he would miss a night out with his friends. Maybe he'll meet up with them later. Spending time with the boys seems to ground him and make him feel better, at least temporarily, and he doesn't want to give that up. A night out with friends makes him feel worthwhile, like he is with people who actually care about him and can make him laugh. Being out at team parties allows him to feel like someone else. Someone who matters. The someone that he wants to be instead of being stuck with his own life. This life where he can't sleep at night, his fights with Jessica, with thoughts of suicide to get away from the depression and the feelings of worthlessness. It seems that no matter how hard he tries, people always want more from him. He even wants more from himself. So much more that the pressure is becoming unbearable and unsustainable. Jen had told him she would make a man out of him, but down deep Tommy knows that's impossible because he feels hollow inside. Even people close to him would not know how he views himself. He hides it well and has never trusted anyone enough to tell them. The joke is that there isn't anything to work with. That's why he decided to meet with Hazel. He wants to feel some self-worth. He knows he has to start somewhere. He feels smothered by his own life, each day stealing his breath away a little bit more. Hazel may be his lifeline. The only real option is to spend time with Wahiéntha. She may help him find a way out of the darkness that seems to follow him around each day. And he is tired of living in the shadows.

Candles burn in the little house by the stream. Hazel sits in her rocking chair with her dogs at her feet. Sorn, the big, intimidating German shepherd is really a big suck who only wants his belly rubbed. Leo, the Shih Tzu, acts suspicious by nature. With Hazel's influence, Sorn remains coldly polite but still a bit standoffish. He waits for clues before he becomes involved in most situations. Leo is nosey and tries to act tough. Perhaps because he is a small dog with a big ego – a dangerous combination. But Hazel has worked miracles with him, so after a few minutes Leo is nosing Tommy's arm in search of some of the attention. Tommy knows Hazel has a way with dogs. Increasingly, he understands how people can trust her.

Hazel Blackwater is an odd woman, though. She smiles sometimes when nothing seems funny. She asks questions that Tommy would never think of in a million years. She asks those questions, and then by the look in her eye, you can tell she expects an answer. A truthful one, not some bullshit thing you made up like you can get away with sometimes when teachers put you on the spot. *Hazel is an odd woman, but she has every right to be,* Tommy thinks.

The last time they talked, when Hazel's friend Jean was here, Hazel started telling Tommy the story of her journey. She calls her life a journey because she feels she is on a predetermined path. As we all are, she believes. Hazel says her life's path is to help people who are struggling. People like Tommy. Tommy's eyes went wide when she told him that. Tommy thinks Hazel's eyes are like pools of sadness. But somehow that sadness also has a sparkle and a quiet look of empathy. She doesn't appear to have much physical energy sometimes, but her mind is quick and those eyes always seem to be searching. Dark eyes that seem to look right inside you. Looking for your truth. Hazel's quiet voice pulls Tommy out of his daydream.

"One thing I remember about our last summer together was how hot those days were. Endless days of blue skies and sunshine. My brother Floyd and I used to spend as much time as we could outside. One of the things we liked to do was play a hunting game that we thought we invented, but I am sure most kids play it at one time or another. Sometimes we had friends with us, but much of the time it was just the two of us. There was a freedom in running and looking, stopping and listening, that to this day I have never been able to find again. Floyd and I had an intense connection from those early days, which I have since come to realize was exceptional. We were more like twins even though Floyd was two years older than my five years. Floyd was so good, so quiet at the hunting game. He could find me and touch me on the top of my head and then be gone, and I wouldn't even know he was there. He was almost magical.

"That beautiful summer ended in August. They came for us towards the end of the month. They said there was a court order forcing Floyd and me to go to boarding school. I remember the short, fat, white man who was an Indian agent and two tall, white officers. Their uniforms scared us. We didn't know what it all meant. We didn't know what boarding school was. It sounded like we were in trouble, like we had done something wrong. Our parents were given two minutes to say goodbye to us. The agent said we didn't need any belongings because we would be given everything we needed. My mother was crying. I was crying too. But Floyd and my father were quiet. I remember my father with his hand on Floyd's shoulder. I remember crying for Rake:ni, my father, as tears filled his eyes. My brother told me later that all he could think about was grabbing me and running. He said he was so sure that the agent would never be able to find us, that he knew where to hide. But he said it was our father's hand on his shoulder that kept him there. He didn't want them to hurt our parents if he ran. Imagine a seven year old thinking like that. Imagine a seven year old being forced to think like that.

"So, we went with them. The trip to the Martindale Indian School, everyone called it the Mush Hole, was the longest ride of my life. It was the last time I was ever with Floyd for any length of time. When we got to the boarding school, we were separated onto the girl's side and the boy's side. They cut our hair, they took our clothes away, and they gave us the school uniforms. They gave us English names. They assigned us numbers and that's basically all we were to them, just a number. I was number 38. First, they took us away from our homes, and then they stripped every familiar thing away from us. To them, we were just faceless children. We went from playing in the sunshine and sleeping soundly at night to spending all day in the school building and sleeping two to a bed. Jean was one of the first girls I shared a bed with. We helped each other survive those early days. I remember one night coming back to the dormitory after dinner and one of the older girls had hung herself from the rafters with a bed sheet. Jean and I hugged each other to sleep that night."

Hazel's voice stops then. The dogs are dozing on the floor with their eyes closed, the room filled with the sound of their breathing. Tommy realizes that he has been holding his own breath and slowly lets it out. Hazel closes her eyes as if to more closely examine the memory preoccupying her.

"The Mush Hole was really a hell hole. There was so little food, and we

...ngry all the time. The reason it was called the Mush Hole is because we were fed mush every day. To this day, I hate mush and will not eat it. Sometimes we got bread. One slice. No butter. A little pork fat smeared on the bread. That bread was a big deal to us. It's funny how little things like that stay with you for a lifetime.

"Several of the priests and nuns had special girls. Those girls sometimes got some good things to eat, but you never saw a smile on any of their faces. Like they were old before their time. The hardest thing to endure was not seeing my parents or my brother, and even though I knew Floyd was in the Mush Hole with me, I almost never saw him. Sometimes a glimpse of him in a line-up. Sometimes at the beginning or end of a meal. He was like a ghost to me. Him being there with me, though, made me feel safe.

"One thing I know for certain is that Floyd was a fighter. He had to be. I was told this later by some of the boys who knew him well. The Mush Hole wasn't a social club. You didn't make many friends, so most of the boys weren't close even though they went through a lot together. I think Floyd just wanted the other boys to leave him alone. Fights happened often at the Mush Hole, but Floyd never got picked on after the first few weeks because he was so good with his fists. Even the bigger boys steered clear of him because, even though they might be able to beat him up, it was just too much effort. The bullies just moved on to easier pickings. My brother's Mohawk name was Raweras. It means Thunder, and you could see why when he would fight. When we got to the school, they changed his name to Floyd. Floyd Blackwater. The priests noticed his fighting ability. They looked for boys like him to be the entertainment for themselves and some of the local people. They staged boxing matches once or twice a week, always late at night when most of the world was sleeping. They were human cock fights with kids. They made the boys box so they could place bets on who would win. The boys didn't have any choice. All of what I am telling you I wasn't there for. Floyd's best friend was a boy named Frank King. I spent time with Frank after we were both out of that place. Frank also had a fight the night Floyd was last seen alive. At first Frank didn't want to talk, but after a while I think he felt better sharing some of the memories he had kept inside, with me, even if they weren't good memories for us.

"Frank told me my brother was a good boxer. But the priests got frustrated with him always winning, so they started pairing him with bigger and older boys. Sounds like they wanted to teach him a lesson. He kept winning even against some older boys. Until one night. Frank said at the time Floyd was only ten, and the boy he had to fight was thirteen and much bigger. They were the last fight of the evening. It was pretty obvious the priests' message to all the boys was 'we control you and there is nothing you can do about it.' Frank had fought earlier and told me it was hard to watch Floyd's match. Floyd kept fighting even though he was hurt. He was knocked down many times and finally could not get up. At the end of the fight he had blood running down his face from a cut over his eye and from his nose. It was probably broken. Frank is pretty sure Floyd had broken ribs as well. When he was counted out and the other boys picked him up, he could barely stand and looked out on his feet. The priests didn't waste any time getting Floyd out of there. Frank said some of the men from the town were yelling at Floyd, mad at him because they had lost money by betting on him. Frank remembers one of the old white men, drunk and smoking a cigar, shouting at Floyd, 'You worthless fucking wagon-burner, you just cost me two dollars!'"

Hazel leans over and picks up Leo from the floor. She puts him in her lap and starts to pet him slowly and methodically. Sorn stands up and goes to sit beside her, leaning on her leg. Tommy doesn't know what to say. It feels like he should ask a question. He wants to know what happened to Floyd, but there's an awkward feeling in the room like you've walked in on someone in a private moment. Tommy decides to let Hazel continue her story. Or not. However she wishes. All he can do is patiently wait. He realizes there is no rush.

After a long pause, Hazel focuses her dark eyes on Tommy. She continues to pet Leo who has gone limp, asleep in her lap.

"I didn't find out what happened to Floyd for the longest time. He wasn't at meals. There was no sign of him. It seemed that no one saw him after the fight. Like he had just disappeared. Then one day a sister, one of the nuns who worked in the infirmary, took me aside. I think she took pity on me. There were some good people at the Mush Hole, just not enough of them. She told me Floyd was no longer with us, that he had passed while in the infirmary. She said he caught pneumonia after losing so much blood and being bedridden after the beating he took. When she said that, I suddenly felt all alone. And cold like the life had gone out of me too. As long as I knew Floyd was with me, I thought I could handle the Mush Hole. With my brother gone, everything felt hopeless. I know the sister was trying to be kind in her own way, but I don't believe anything she said. I don't think it was pneumonia or tuberculosis or measles or any other rotten disease that killed us kids at that place. I believe Floyd died of a broken heart. He had fought as hard as he could, and he just couldn't fight anymore."

"Why did you stay, Hazel? Why didn't you just run away?" The questions rush out of Tommy's mouth before he thinks. He doesn't mean to make Hazel feel any worse than she already feels.

Hazel's eyes look just a little bit sadder before she replies.

"Kids did try to run away, but the agents usually found them and brought them right back, not always alive. Some would get lost and die from exposure. But I think I stayed for Floyd in a way. I wanted to show him that I could be strong. That I was trying to be as tough as he was and make him proud of me. So that if I ever saw him again, he would pat me on the back and smile at me. I love my brother, and I miss him still. There is a hole in my soul. My heart is broken. In a way, Tommy, all our stories, our journeys, are about life and death. That's the natural way of things. If you are lucky and the Creator smiles on you it may be a long time before you have to deal with your death or that of a loved one. And by death I don't just mean the end of your physical body. Sometimes we suffer many smaller deaths throughout our lives because of the things that happen to us. Things that gradually kill our spirit. Things that upset us so much that we are tempted to end our physical existence. Sometimes the life sequence gets twisted. In my life, in the beginning, death came early. So, I feel this is what I am meant to do now. To talk with you, to share my experience, and to focus on what is meant to be regardless of what has happened to you. What happens to you doesn't have to shape you. You don't have to let the bad things make you into a victim for the rest of your life. I learned to see beyond what was happening to me and forward to where I was meant to go. There are some life lines drawn for all of us. You have to want to see them. The Creator doesn't want us to waste all the goodness that we come into this world with. But sometimes you have to step back. Step out of the mess that you might find yourself in. Then look ahead and move forward."

Hazel puts Leo down and stands up from the rocking chair, walking over to her little dining table. She very carefully lights another candle. The room fills with a pine smell. She smiles and turns to walk over to straighten one of the paintings on the wall – the picture of the young boy with the short haircut. Tommy knows who it is. He doesn't need Hazel to tell him.

"What I am about to tell you isn't to make you feel sad or to pity me. It is meant to show that horrible things can be overcome. You can change things even if there are many who want to beat you down so that you do only what they want."

The wind is picking up outside Hazel's small house and some tree branches are tapping on the window by the front door. Rain falls lightly on the metal roof. Listening to Hazel's voice, and with the dark outside, it seems to Tommy that the whole world consists only of this room. That time is fluid and on the move. Back to the past. Tommy can imagine Hazel as a girl with short, dark hair. In his mind, he can see that she had her sad eyes even then.

"One day, not long after my fourteenth birthday, Father Brennan complimented me on my schoolwork. Cheerful Father Brennan, always telling a joke with a quick smile and a laugh. He was a priest who spent a lot of time helping students, especially the girls. He never paid much attention to me until I was thirteen. This day he told me what a bright girl I was. Told me that he wanted to give me a gift to show his appreciation for how hard I had worked in his classes. I was happy that he was pleased because that was how we were taught. We just had a routine and discipline at the school, and we followed orders. So when Father Brennan said nice things to me, and when he asked me to take a walk with him, I thought it was a good thing. I didn't worry about anything really."

Both dogs are now lying on their sides, eyes closed. They have no worries in their world. But Tommy feels uneasy and uncomfortable. He has moved to sit in a chair at the table. He feels ugliness in the room. It comes from Hazel's words. He wants to do something to help her, but he knows he can't change a thing.

"I had no worries until he opened the door to the furnace room and gave me a sharp push inside. It was loud in that room and very hot. And how dirty it was. The floor was filthy, dust balls and cobwebs. Before I could think, Father Brennan put his hands on me. Now he had a pained smile on his face, his sweating face, as he pushed me down to the floor, pulling off my dress. He didn't say a word. I tried to push him away, then I screamed and screamed, but the furnace noise was so loud that no one could hear me. I'm sure this was not the first time this man had taken a young girl to this room. I can still hear myself screaming as he raped me. Sometimes even now I wake up from a nightmare where I can smell his bad breath hanging in the air around me. The pain he forced on me was a jagged thing, a tearing, urgent feeling that made me choke. Father Brennan was an older man, heavy, with jiggling fat on his body. The sweat was pouring off him, and it was so uncomfortable in that room. And I remember a smell coming off his body, a dirty, unwashed smell. Like something that wasn't taken care of properly. It made me gag. I remember watching his flesh sway back and forth as he grunted on top of me. That is an image I will carry with me for the rest of my life."

The candles flicker in the night air. Some heavy breathing emits from the sleeping dogs. Tommy feels frozen. Doesn't know what to say. Wants to be anywhere but here. Hazel looks at him with a comforting smile. She knows what she has told him could upset anyone.

"Jean and I have talked a lot about what happened to us at the boarding school. The one thing we both agree on is that the best thing you can do for your spirit is to face your fears. Running away from them – and that can be by drinking alcohol or using drugs to ease the pain – only leads to more problems. Why would you make it worse for yourself? Facing your fears can mean realizing that whoever or whatever has caused you pain has no control over your life now. That you can move ahead by leaving the past behind. Reject it entirely if you must. However you need to cope. You can learn from it, but you are under no obligation to repeat it. You make the choice. It is entirely under your control. It may not have been your life then, but it certainly is now."

Tommy slouches in the chair with his arms crossed, digesting what Hazel has told him. What she has revealed to him. But before he can speak, Hazel continues.

"That's as far as we will go on my journey today, Tommy. I will tell you one more thing. Father Brennan made me pregnant that day. I was a fourteen-year-old girl at the Mush Hole. And I had no one I could talk to. No one I could tell. Well, that's not quite true. I had Jean. I thank my lucky stars I had Jean. When we talk again, I will tell you more of my journey. But next time you should be ready to share some of your path so I can understand your past. So we can both understand who you are now."

Tommy fights back tears and anger as he thinks about a priest doing such horrible things to an innocent young girl. Thinking about Floyd dying in the Mush Hole with no family around him. Hazel puts her hand on Tommy's shoulder. Her touch makes him feel better.

Chapter Twenty-Two

THE RANCH

Tommy debates with himself whether he should go straight home after his session with Hazel. In one way, he feels burned out. He's not sure he's exactly in a party mood, but the game against Dennville still runs around in his mind as well. They had a bad start, and Tommy knows they can't let that happen during the next game against Orrtown. There are some things to talk about. It's like the truck has a mind of its own and Tommy finds himself on a familiar route, headed to catch up with the rest of the boys. After a tough game, you know, maybe stop in for a couple. The Ranch, as it is known to the locals, is a small establishment on the Rez that was a garage converted into a small bar where people come and enjoy a few drinks. Not a very big place, it can get packed inside with people lined up for a beer or just socializing and listening to music.

Weasel and Joey have found a spot in the Ranch to hang out. Weasel double fists a couple beers, always sure to order two because the wait for another could take a while. He swigs a drink of his brew and notices three familiar guys, all the same age as him, walking in and heading towards the bar. The first guy is average height, brown skin, thin build, and sporting what's known as a "Rez-stache" above his lip. Everyone knows him as Rez Dogg. He got this handle because people are pretty sure that he has never actually taken a step off the Sparrow Lake Rez even once his entire life. The second guy has crazy long black hair and is about 6'5" and 300 pounds. His real name is Todd, but because of his size everyone calls him Toddzilla. Just the sight of the third guy makes Weasel's blood boil. He is the same height as Weasel, about 15 pounds heavier with light brown skin, dark hair, and dark eyes. His real name is Evan, but thanks to Weasel, he's known simply as Boner.

It all goes back to seventh grade. Evan was a jerk to a lot of kids, but he always seemed to give Weasel and Jordy an especially rough ride. He constantly made fun of them and actually came up with the nickname "Salt n' Pepper" because of their contrasting skin colors. One day the teacher called on Evan to finish a math problem on the blackboard. When the twelve-year-old boy stood up he was sporting an erection, which may not have been so obvious to everyone until Weasel jumped up, gestured dramatically, and blurted out, "Hey look, he's got a fucking boner!" That's when Evan charged at him, and the first epic scrap between Boner and Weasel took place. According to Jordy, who was a delighted spectator in that ill-fated math class, the first tilt was a draw on account of that, while trying to fight, Boner was also trying to conceal the hard-on in his pants. Jordy has been keeping track of the confrontations ever since. According to his calculations, they have fought a total of 15 times with Weasel winning 7, Boner winning 5, and 3 called a draw.

Rez Dogg, Toddzilla, and Boner buy beers from the barkeep and make their way through the crowd. They walk by where Weasel and Jordy are standing. Boner and Weasel make eye contact. Boner stares hard at Weasel. "The fuck you lookin' at?" Boner snarls at his nemesis.

Weasel, his eyes never wavering, spits out, "A worthless piece a shit, that's what I'm lookin' at."

Boner grinds his teeth aggressively as he utters, "You wanna fucking go?"

Weasel stares back at him with a straight face and responds, "Why, you want some more welts on your fuck face?"

Boner hands off his beers to Rez Dogg and heads for the exit as partygoers begin to flood outside to watch what is about to go down. Tommy has just entered the building as people are on their way out. He sees Weasel stomping towards him. "Weasel, what the hell's goin' on?"

Weasel already has his game face on. "It's fucking go time." Tommy immediately knows what that means and follows him outside.

Dust ups are commonplace at the Ranch. You got a problem, take it outside. And most people do. Both combatants quickly lose their shirts and square off. They waste little time. Fists begin to fly. Thuds can be heard as both guys land punches and the crowd cheers. Weasel lands a solid right to Boner's jaw and he stumbles back. Weasel quickly tackles him as they hit the grass. Weasel climbs on top of Boner and starts raining down rights and lefts. Boner avoids and blocks many of the punches until a loud thud comes from a left hand crashing into Boner's right cheekbone. The crowd collectively oohs and aahs, knowing that Weasel has gained the upper hand.

Weasel grunts through clinched teeth as he lands more and more punches to Boner's head. "How the fuck you like that? Piece a shit."

Boner is now only trying to cover up and avoid more damage when Toddzilla pipes up, "Okay, that's enough," as a couple of guys start to separate the flyweights from each other.

Tommy steps between the two and starts to lift Weasel off Boner. "You got him, Weasel. I think he's done."

As Weasel starts to get up, he gives Boner a few parting words, "Wooooohhh, kicked your fucking ass."

Jordy tosses Weasel his shirt as he heads back inside to catch his breath and crush some more beers. Boner's buddies help him to his feet, his nose bleeding and right eye already starting to swell up as the crowd make their way back into the cozy confines of the Ranch. Jordy announces to everybody the updated count. 8, 5, and 3 for Weasel.

Nursing his injuries, Boner yells, "Fuck you, Jordy!" People in the crowd are buzzing, recounting the highlights of the spirited bout to anyone who showed up late. The crowd also knows that there is a good chance those two guys will be going at it again before the night is over.

CHAPTER TWENTY-THREE

DO IT FOR THE GUY BESIDE YOU

Tim Blair is still sitting in the living room long after his wife and sons have gone to bed. He told Sarah he would be right up, but it's been more than an hour and here he sits. *It's been a great day*, Blair is thinking to himself. A special day. In many ways he doesn't want it to end. The Hawks have beaten Dennville like he knew they would. The boys are on their way to the State Semifinals. Blair continues pondering whether he should stop coaching after this season. Just can't make a decision about that right now. Things are going so well. *Man, this Lazy Boy chair is extremely comfortable* and his whole body feels stiff. Feels like he played a lacrosse game today instead of shouting himself hoarse while coaching on the sidelines. What he wouldn't give to be twenty years old again. Well, that's not quite true. He loves Sarah and the boys. He wouldn't change that. Where would he be without them? What would he do without them? Maybe it's time for bed and everything will be a whole lot clearer in the morning. He knows his wife wants him to quit coaching. He doesn't want to disappoint Sarah, but he sure as hell doesn't want to disappoint himself either.

Blair knows the second and fifth stairs are the creaky ones, so he skips over those on his way upstairs. Slipping into bed, wearing his pajama bottoms and an undershirt, Tim tries to get comfortable. He doesn't want to move around a lot. Doesn't want to wake Sarah. He can't get comfortable because of shoulder tendonitis that flares up from time to time. He does a few stretches on his left shoulder. Fighting the pain in his upper body, Tim Blair somehow manages to put it out of his mind long enough to eventually fall asleep. The dream starts immediately.

Tim Blair stands on the sidelines at the State Championships. It takes him a minute to grasp that he is here. Everything seems larger than life. He coaches one of the teams at the big game. Not only at the big game, but the Hawks are ahead by three and time is winding down. Everything around him seems so exaggerated and colorful. The grass an outstanding shade of deep green. The black Hawks lettering on his jacket incredibly bold. And the sky, the deepest blue he can ever remember. Tim Blair feels amazed by the size of the crowd. The stands are overflowing. He can't believe that as a coach he is finally about to win a State Championship in front of this many people. He doesn't see anyone among the spectators that he recognizes, which seems odd to him. Usually more than half of any lacrosse crowd he knows on a first name basis. Time is running out on the fourth quarter and it is an unusually warm and glaringly sunny day. Almost too bright. Unreal in a way. He feels a sharp pain in his shoulder again. Just as the game enters the last few seconds, the excitement building towards victory among the Hawks players and the faithful fans, Tim Blair finally spots people he knows in the crowd. His parents and his older brother. The pain in his shoulder immediately becomes more severe and Coach Blair knows something is seriously wrong. Both his parents have been dead for years and his older brother Rod died of a drug overdose when Tim Blair was in his teens. Suddenly, on that hot and sunny day, Coach Blair feels very cold. *Why is it so fucking cold?* His whole body shivers. That's when everything changes.

Sarah wakes up in the morning with a little jolt. There is a lot on the agenda to get done today. She rolls over and listens for Tim's rhythmic, heavy breathing. There isn't any. She reaches out and touches his shoulder. It is cold.

"Tim?" she asks plaintively. "Tim?"

There is no answer. Intuitively she knows there will never be a response. Sarah's scream startles Konner and Keegan out of a deep sleep. The two boys are on the way to their parents' room when Sarah meets them at the bedroom door. Her voice is quavering and her eyes are red and moist, swollen with tears from her terrible realization.

"Boys, we have to go downstairs. I need to make a phone call."

SARAH WISHES SHE HAD THE LUXURY OF BEING ABLE TO BREAK DOWN. To scream and wail. To throw herself on the coffin of the man she has spent more than half her life with. But she can't do that. Sarah needs to keep herself together most importantly because her boys need her, so she keeps her spine stiff and comforts Konner and Keegan. Ever the loving mother. The responsible adult who knows what to do. Even if she doesn't.

There has been a steady stream of people through the Blair home. People wanting to pay their last respects to Coach Blair. Some stand for a minute as they file past the coffin and look down at Coach Blair's body, his big hands clasped at the waist. Some fight back tears and stand silent as if there are a few more things to say that they never had the chance to utter. Sarah is the last one to spend time with Tim. She stands alone in front of the coffin. There are no more tears left now. Sarah is wondering what might have been if Tim had been able to quit coaching. Cutting down on his stress might have prolonged his life. That's just a fantasy now. She understands that her husband really didn't have any choice. He had to coach the Hawks. He had to be a mentor to the young men of Sparrow Lake. That was an important part of what life was all about for him. Sarah can come to grips with that now.

She also understands something else. She faces the rest of her life with two young sons and no father or husband to help her. No partner to watch the boys grow into men. *Oh my god, what am I going to do*, she agonizes. *Tim was so strong and now I don't know if I can make this work anymore by myself.* Before her thoughts spin out of control and before she completely loses her composure, Sarah leans over, puts both her hands tenderly on Tim's hands, and kisses him on the forehead. This is the first time in a long time he won't tell her how much he will miss her. Tim was always such a romantic at heart. It's just so unfair. Sarah turns away from the open coffin. She can hear Tim's voice saying, "You are the love of my life. You know that, don't you?"

She wants to say "yes" out loud but instead just closes her eyes for a minute. There were always supposed to be better days to come. Now time has run out and she is not prepared for this. *Life is like that*, thinks Sarah. But no one told her about this. It was a secret kept from her.

Konner and Keegan are sniffling, wiping tears from their eyes with the palms of their hands as small children do. The boys stand still, watching the six pallbearers carry the coffin out of their family room where the wake had been set up. The weight is considerable, and the men struggle to get out of the front door and then gently slide the casket into the waiting hearse. For each of them it is a point of pride to be helping out Coach Blair one last time, they are honored to do it.

Many generations of lacrosse players mill around the Blair yard and home – word of mouth spread the bad news rapidly, and they are all here to pay their respects. More than one towering man has gently pulled Sarah aside to tell her that Tim was like a second father to him, helping him through some life crisis, how tough he was but how kind at the same time, how Coach Blair taught them to be good men. The coffin is piled high with Hawks' pennants and flowers.

For the people attending, the counters are crowded with food and drink, the fridge and freezer already full. Sarah's parents have arrived, and they will stay with her as long as she needs them.

Among all the familiar faces, Sarah spots Robbie Redbird and Hank Thomas. As the two men approach, she wonders if she will be able to keep it together for much longer. All these people with their soft words of condolence and sympathy. None of it will bring Tim back home where he belongs.

Hank Thomas isn't a large man, no more than average height with a slight potbelly. His fondness for doughnuts and coffee contribute to his weight, but he loves the combination too much to give them up. Hank has known Tim and Sarah for a long time, not as close family friends but acquaintances. Hank has the utmost respect for Tim Blair.

"Sarah, I was just thinking about something that Tim and I had talked about earlier this season. He told me that his philosophy was simple. He told every player that he didn't need superstars. He needed teammates. 'Do it for the guy beside you,' he used to say. Man, he was proud of his players and he told them so. He made personal connections with them and brought them together so the Hawks always seemed more like a family. I guess what I am saying is that maybe it's a small consolation right now, but Tim had such a tremendous influence on so many people that he really does live on in all of them. All his players became better at the game, sure, but they also became better people. He was a great guy and left us all a bit better. We'll all miss him."

Hank leans over and gives Sarah a gentle hug. "If there is anything Robbie or I can do for you, be sure to let us know. We'll be there for you."

Redbird nods his agreement adding, "Coach was larger than life. A real hero to many of us. The best kind of hero because he lived right here in our community."

All Sarah can manage is a tight smile. "Thanks for those kind words, Hank and Robbie. Maybe sometime if you get a chance to talk to Konner and Keegan, tell them those things about their dad."

Sarah takes a minute to notice all the former players her husband coached, all the lives he's touched. Maybe he didn't win that State Title he wanted, but his coaching career was definitely a successful one.

Finally, after the graveside service and the long drive home, Sarah has some time to herself. She goes into the master bedroom – only hers, now – and lies down on Tim's side of the bed. There is a comforting dent in the mattress, and when she buries her face in his pillow, it still smells of his cologne. Hugging the pillow to her chest, Sarah finally lets her protective shell fall away. The rest of her life stares her in the face now. Tears begin to fall down her face as she whispers, "I love you."

Chapter Twenty-Four
EVERYTHING IS GOING TO SHIT

Tommy heads out the door with his lacrosse stick, joining Weasel, Jordy, Ben, and Andy who are down in Jordy's Chevy. Jessica abruptly grabs Tommy's arm as he continues toward the car. Her long fingernails dig into his skin. "Tommy, stay here with me," she pleads. "My mom is gone for the night."

Tommy shrugs uncomfortably. "I'm leaving my truck here; Jordy will bring me back later. I just wanna be with the boys for a bit. Just chill out for a bit," he finishes in a rush. He knows he has to be with the guys. It's a way of coping for all of them, but Jessica's needy and wounded eyes make him squirm.

"When aren't you with them? It's bullshit, Tommy. If I was important to you, you'd stay. You should understand but you don't. Maybe you can't," says Jessica sharply with dark anger clouding her face. Without looking at her, Tommy quickly gets into the car. He has seen Jessica like this before. There is nothing he can say that will help. There is no talking to her in this state. The Chevy backs up and then accelerates away slowly, leaving her to sort things out on her own.

In her room, Jessica throws things around and lets out several angry screams. Each one more pain filled than the one before. She is in a rage and doesn't have anyone or anything to take it out on. Troubling thoughts crowd into her mind, crashing into one another.

Jessica lies down on her bed and slams her fists countless times into the mattress. Just as she stops, there is a light tap on her bedroom door. Her friend Torrie walks into the room smiling, cradling an eighteen pack of beer. "Was wondering if you felt like having a couple?" she asks mischievously. Jessica can think of nothing better to calm her down right now.

"Thank you! I need a beer," she says as Torrie tosses her a can. In one smooth motion Jessica opens it and takes several long swallows. Her phone beeps with an incoming text.

In Ben's back yard, the boys have their lacrosse sticks out and are tossing the ball around a bit before a game breaks out. It's a backyard session of lacrosse, played with an intensity and focus that Coach would have loved. Others show up to join them, and the game goes for hours with few interruptions. Players dropping in and dropping out. By the time they are done playing, it is too dark to see the green tennis ball.

They light a bonfire and sit, basking in the heat as they talk. A few of them are having beers, even though they know they shouldn't. They are joined by Ben's older brothers Dean and Derek. Derek is the oldest of the three Lucas boys.

"Man, can't stop thinking about Coach Blair. Gonna be so weird without him on the sidelines," says Troy.

"Now Jenkins is gonna be running the show. Guess we'll see how that goes," Andy adds gloomily. That thought depresses all of them. Jenkins has done nothing at recent practices to change his hard-ass image, and the boys believe the head coaching job will just turn Jenkins into a total dictator.

"It's gotta be so hard for Keegan and Konner. They're just little kids," Ben says, thinking of those two stricken little faces from the funeral.

"Yeah, that's awful," Tommy agrees. "Coach really loved those little guys, treated 'em so good."

Dean sums it up for all of them. "Coach is really gonna be missed – he was a big presence, a good influence on a lot of guys around here. Coach being gone leaves a big hole in this place."

This is too sentimental for some of them, and Derek pulls the conversation to a different topic. "And he was a tough motherfucker. You guys are too young to remember him when he used to party. I was just a young guy then and he used to get into his share of tilts at the bar. Coach could throw 'em pretty good. Actually, Tommy, maybe the best fight I ever seen was when Coach and your dad went at it one time. That was the longest scrap I've ever seen. I'd have to call it a draw. Holy shit, I'll never forget that one," Derek says eagerly, a look of pleasure all over his face at the recollection.

Tommy feels a bit startled. "Whoa, yeah, guess I could see that happening," he says automatically. Then he remembers the night that Marian and he went to sleep at Gramma's house. The blood on the snow and the wrecked pickup truck. Maybe it isn't so farfetched. He can't believe that Coach Blair ever fought Beau to a standstill. But then he thinks it's appropriate somehow.

Sitting alone on the far side of the bonfire, Shane is again texting away on his phone. His fingers are flying, incredibly intent on something, chuckling a little.

"Holster it, Shane. God, put it away for once. Always on your damn phone," Troy snaps. Troy doesn't think there is any room for that shit now, but Shane just doesn't care.

"Relax, relax," says Shane, waving him off. He keeps his phone out at the ready.

As the night wears on, most of the guys leave until only Ben, Tommy, Andy, Weasel, and Jordy are left. The bonfire is down to a bed of glowing coals, surrounded by fluffy gray ash. Staring at what's left of the fire, Tommy imagines if you look closely in the ashes you can see faces. He wants to see Coach's face, giving him a sign that he is alright, that he is in a better place. That doesn't happen. He doesn't see anything as he finishes the beer in his hand. Coach's sudden death combined with several beers and Jessica's anger… it all makes Tommy feel unstable again. Not sure of himself. Not sure what he should do next. So he reaches for another beer.

"I know Coach used to give me shit a lot – especially about how much I party. He used to call me into his office and tell me how much better a player and person I could be if I took things seriously. He didn't just care about me as a player. He cared about me as a person. I don't know a lot of people like that," Andy says wistfully.

Everyone goes quiet for a couple of seconds. Almost like a last-few-minutes-of-silence, for the departed. Coach Blair's passing is almost too much to deal with and everyone knows it.

"Well, I'm about ready to bounce. You guys need a lift?" Jordy asks, breaking the mood. He is the perpetual designated driver. As usual, they all need a ride.

As the others walk to the car, Andy waits for them to move out of earshot. Looking up at the sky, he says, "Gonna miss you, Coach," and solemnly pours out the rest of his beer on the fire. It extinguishes the remnants of the bonfire, and Andy heads toward the car.

Tommy is the last to be dropped off, and he is dreading the reunion with Jessica. He nervously wonders how upset she is or whether it has blown over. He hates living like this. You're never sure if the person you left earlier is going to be the same person you return to or a completely different personality when you get back. Jessica told Tommy once that something isn't quite right with him. *Well, that goes both ways,* he thinks.

Leaving his lacrosse stick just inside the door, he walks quietly to her bedroom and finds her asleep – no, passed out on her bed, fully dressed. Empties are scattered around the room and her cell phone is still in her hands. The TV is on, some trashy reality show, but she is dead to the world.

He quietly clears the cans to the side without waking her. Her cell phone flashes with an incoming text, and he gently eases it out of her hands, checking the screen.

I want you too.

"What the fuck?" hisses Tommy, scanning the conversation chain. It is lengthy with timestamps spanning hours. Jessica has been texting with Shane for most of the night.

What are you wearing?

Not much. Bet you'd like a taste.

Kiss your soft lips and run my tongue—

It takes Tommy a while to read all the messages as his vision blurs with rage. Reaching down, he viciously shakes Jessica awake.

"What the fuck is this?" he demands, shoving the phone in her face. "You were texting Shane the whole night? You fucking slut!"

It takes a moment for her to really wake up, and then she's screaming back at him, her face distorted and ugly.

"Fuck you, asshole!" she screams.

"So you text one of my friends and tell him you wanna fuck him? You fucking whore!" he screams, voice cracking under stress.

"Fuck you!" she screams back and lunges at him, fists balled up and aiming for his face. He ducks and covers, trying to avoid the frantic punches. Most of the punches hit Tommy on the top or side of the head. They hurt a bit, but they are mostly just pissing him off more and more, until finally his temper takes total control. Tommy grabs Jessica by the neck, picking her up and slamming her down on her bed. He wraps both his hands around her neck and begins to squeeze. Jessica's face turns red as she fights to breathe.

"Fucking bitch," Tommy says through grinding teeth.

Desperately trying to pull Tommy's hands off her neck, she barely manages to say, "Stop, please."

Instantly, Tommy has a flashback. He recalls pleading the exact same way with Jen to let him breathe as she tightened her hands around his little neck. He lets go of Jessica and stands up in shock, watching her gasp for breath, not believing what he's just done.

Jessica starts sobbing hysterically. Tommy pauses for a moment, and then bolts out of the house. Jumping in the truck, he punches the steering wheel, cursing and yelling. Everything is going to shit. He has a feeling that he just wants to leave it all behind. Starting the vehicle up, he peels out of the driveway, driving erratically.

No more than a minute after leaving Tommy glances in the rear-view mirror and sees the red flashing lights of a cop car. This night is like the horror show that never ends. Tommy pulls his truck over to the side of the road and puts it into park. Then he slowly lowers his head onto the steering wheel.

BEAU ANSWERS THE HARSH KNOCK on the front door with rising concern. Tommy isn't home yet and Beau doesn't sleep well when his kids aren't home. From the kitchen window he can see the police cruiser in their driveway, and he knows that this can't be good news.

"Evening, Beau?" politely asks the officer. Tommy stands next to him, looking like ten pounds of shit in a five-pound bag.

"Hey, Eric," acknowledges Beau.

"Beau, I pulled your son over tonight. Can you be responsible for him for the night?" asks the cop, not unsympathetically.

"Yeah," grunts Beau with disgust.

Beau knows the police officer from playing lacrosse together in high school and this is the only reason that Tommy is not sitting in jail.

"Okay, so my partner drove his truck. Here are his keys. Since he has no record and we've never had a problem with him before, I'm going to give him a warning. The rest of the officers will be informed of this and won't be so generous if it happens again."

Beau gathers the shreds of his dignity, inwardly storming. "Okay. Thanks, Eric."

"Have a good evening," replies the cop, returning to his car.

Tommy walks zombie-like into the house. Beau numbly closes the door, still unable to believe what's happened. In the kitchen, he confronts his son.

"What the hell happened?" he demands. "I can't believe you would do something that stupid – you know goddam well that I would come and get you if you needed a ride! Holy shit, you're lucky I know that cop or you could be really fucked right now!"

Tommy pours himself a glass of water at the sink and downs it, wearily resting against the counter.

"I got in a fight with Jessica and was pissed off so I decided to head back here," he says in a low voice, avoiding eye contact.

"What do you mean a fight?" A sudden nasty thought occurs to him and he stares at his dejected son. "Did you hit her?"

Tommy's guilty posture is answer enough for Beau.

"Goddammit, Tommy, all you've been doing lately is drinking, and now this? What the hell is wrong with you? It's time you stopped acting like an idiot," he lectures.

To his surprise, his son looks up sharply, staring him down like an enemy. "What – you're really surprised I grew up to be the same asshole that you used to be?" he sneers.

"The fuck you say?" Beau asks in disbelief, reaching for him. Tommy slaps his hand away and swings a furious punch at his father's face.

Beau ducks with the reflexes born of many bar fights and lunges at him, forgetting that Tommy is his son. All he sees is another man arrogantly challenging him. He drives a fist into Tommy's gut, knocking the wind out of him, and then before he can recover, he grabs his son by the throat and slams him up against the fridge. He pulls his fist back readying another punch and then, all of a sudden, Marian is there and yelling at him.

"Stop! Beau, stop!" she screams. And Beau does, his rage dropping to a steady simmer. He loosens his grip on Tommy but doesn't let him go.

"I don't know where you get all this anger inside you, but you better find a way to control it real quick or you're gonna really hurt somebody – or somebody is really gonna fucking hurt you." He releases Tommy and the boy slides down the fridge to sit on the kitchen floor.

With disdain, Beau turns his back on him and walks back to the bedroom with Marian.

As he sits on the floor, Tommy has a stunned look on his face. There is only one thought on his mind. He just doesn't want it to be this way anymore.

CHAPTER TWENTY-FIVE

THE RIGHT PATH

azel Blackwater's phone is an old, black rotary dial model. Her friend Jean jokes that Hazel bought it new and can't bear to part with it. It doesn't ring very often because Hazel likes to talk with people in person. She doesn't discourage anyone calling, but she believes you need to look someone in the eyes to see what is in their heart.

When the phone rings first thing in the morning, the jangling, jarring sound sets both dogs to barking furiously. Someone, a long time ago, set the phone's volume to maximum so when it rings the whole house is battered by the sound. Hazel has never turned it down. It doesn't seem to bother her. Sorn and Leo, however, are dancing around the front door getting ready to confront the intruders they expect to barge through the entranceway at any minute. Hazel puts down the piece of toast she was half-heartedly nibbling on.

Picking up the phone, she says, "Tommy, is everything alright?"

Tommy, wrapped up in his own dark thoughts, doesn't even think to question how Hazel knows it is him. "Hazel, can we talk again? Things aren't going so good."

Hazel feels a sudden chill as she speaks to Tommy. "I couldn't sleep at all last night thinking something was wrong. It so happens that I have some time this morning. I was going to do some sketching, but it's better that we see each other. We'll talk a bit more about my journey, but then you will need to talk about yours. It may be that we have more things in common than we first thought. I'll be waiting for you."

Tommy hears barking dogs as he hangs up. That, at least, brings a fleeting smile to his face.

Beau's truck comes to a stop outside Hazel's house. A metallic, grinding squeal sounds out as he presses the brakes. Beau Henry looks at his son who is lost in his own thoughts.

"I know this visit is important, and Hazel is one of the best people you can talk to. We are supposed to go over to Grampa's today to split wood, so give me call when you are ready to leave. I will pick you up later. And Tommy, what happened last night? That's not ever going to happen again, right?"

Tommy looks at his dad for a second, weighing whether to say what's on his mind or not. He decides to spit it out. "Guess we are a lot alike, huh?"

Beau's eyebrows go up mischievously. "That's what your mother says, and is she ever wrong when it comes to our family?"

Finally, a smile on his oldest son's face. They have been few and far between recently. Tommy feels a little less like shit when he sees the genuine look of concern on Beau's face. "Right, Dad, see you later."

There is an overturned canoe perched on the banks of the creek that flows behind Hazel's house. The small creek resembles a little river now, the water running high with all the recent rain.

Hazel holds onto Tommy's arm, not so much for balance but for the contact, the message it sends of support and presence. "I thought we might go for a quick paddle. I find it comforting to be on the water. You never know what you're going to see on the shoreline, so it's also a little bit of an adventure. Sightseeing right in your own back yard."

There are two paddles lying across the thwarts on the underside of the canoe, and as Tommy helps Hazel put the craft into the water, she tells him to take the bow position. *Better that way*, Tommy thinks. Hazel knows the water here. Hazel, however, is thinking something completely different. She wants Tommy to be looking out over the water, listening. And when he talks, it is better not to be looking at her, better that he be surrounded by nature, and hopefully seeing his place in it.

The current is not strong. Tommy finds that they have no difficulty maneuvering wherever they choose to go. Hazel remains quiet, and Tommy knows this is unusual. He glances back at her and she is smiling at him. Then she softly speaks, her voice blending in with the flowing sounds all around them. "Take some deep breaths, Tommy. Get comfortable. There is no better place that you can be right now. Just listen to what is all around, observing."

Turkey vultures are riding the thermal currents high above the creek and casting their shadows over Tommy and Hazel as they glide overhead. The birds forms are huge and seem to be moving in slow motion circles as if swimming effortlessly in the air. Tommy wonders what it would be like to be up there like them. Away from it all. The big birds are high above any threat that exists on the ground, but always watching.

The conversation picks up just where the last conversation left off. The way she talks creates a mood. It transports Tommy right back to Hazel's past. Like listening and watching someone's life playing out right in front of his eyes. He sees all the people Hazel describes in his mind. Feels her fear. There is a connection for him, as if Hazel and Tommy are two parts to the same whole.

"Did I ever tell you that I love babies? Newborns, toddlers, five year olds; they all have an aura of innocence and genuineness. Not much of that to be found in the world at large, as I came to find out later in my life. Anyway, there I was at the boarding school, still a child myself and about to have a baby. The nuns actually used to monitor the menstrual cycles of all the girls at the school so when my period didn't come, alarm bells went off. Jean of course knew before they did. She was the only person I could talk to. But we were both kids. What advice could we give to each other? What help could we be to each other? We hugged and cried. Jean was the only moral support I had. She suggested that we should both run away one night, but I was too scared. All of us at the boarding school had heard stories about girls who had become pregnant. Most of those young women lost their babies after *accidents,* we were told. The story was always that they fell down the stairs. Those girls didn't fall, Tommy. They were pushed. Jean knew one girl, Lydia, who was punched in the stomach and then pushed down the stairs. She not only lost her baby but injured her spine permanently. She was never able to walk upright normally again. We were told it was a punishment from God.

"When the nuns realized that I had missed two periods, they sat me down and interrogated me. I had no reason to lie to them, so I told them exactly what happened. I told them about Father Brennan and what he had done to me. Their eyes went wide, and I could tell they didn't believe me. Sister Mary Margaret was a tall woman. She was the one in charge. Had to be six feet and dressed in her black and white habit she was a very imposing figure. Looked a bit like an old crow. Me, I was the little sparrow. I was so scared I must have been shaking when she was looking at me. I can still remember Sister Mary Margaret's eyes when I told her about Father Brennan. 'Hazel you stop telling these lies about Father Brennan. You may go to Hell for this!' is all she said.

"So, the sisters took me away to stay at a convent where I lived during my pregnancy. That wasn't an easy time. They made me work and clean up to the very last day before I gave birth. I got bigger and bigger, but they didn't care how hard it was for me. They never said it outright, but I knew they were punishing me. The thing I never understood is that if you want people to change, to become better, is the way to do that by punishing them and condemning them to Hell? I don't think so. I think sometimes you need more chances to be able to find your way, your place in the world. But the nuns were having none of that. I was headed for my special place in Hell and nothing could change that according to them.

"When the labor pains came and I started giving birth, I thought that was going to make everything all right. But it was a hard birth and I remember lots of blood. When the child finally came, I thought that the fear and the ugliness and the condemnation by the sisters would all be worth it when I held my baby. But that didn't happen. You see, after all I went through, the scorn and the belittling and the discrimination, I never got to hold my son. I saw his face for a second. He was so precious and beautiful. And they took him away immediately and never brought him back. The nuns said he was sickly and that he had not lived, but that was a lie. Years later, after I had graduated from the school, I was told by one of my older classmates who helped the nuns that my son did not die, that instead he was put up for adoption and had a good home. I tried for years to find out where he was. I cried so many tears wanting to know he was safe. I wanted to just hold him once, to tell him that I loved him. But I was never able to locate him.

"All the things I felt then made me want to kill myself. I felt confused about my life. Was this really the way the Creator wanted things to be for me? I felt guilty because the nuns made me feel worthless, that I was a bad person and a waste. I was afraid for my future. I was grieving for the son I never knew. I was angry and I felt so helpless. I had no resources, no support. And I was so depressed. Today they might call it postpartum depression, but for me at fourteen, it was the end of the world. I didn't see a future. Life is not always kind; it's not always fair and you sometimes have to start over. But you have to realize that a particular dead end does not mean everything is finished. And there was one more thing that I found out much later. Because of that difficult birth I was not able to have any more children.

"That was the final insult. I had no baby to hold and I never would have any. I felt such heartache you cannot imagine. Then came years of alcohol abuse, attempting to create a world I could live in, as if the one outside of me had no room for me. I lost my way for a long, long time. I was sad and lonely and forgot the essence of who I was until a woman said she saw something in me. That she saw the good person I was inside. She helped me by teaching me our traditional ways, our culture, our language, our ways to heal. I had to relearn how to live, how to be a healthy person.

"One of those ways to be healthy for you, Tommy, you already know… lacrosse. You may not know it, Tommy, but when you play lacrosse, the Creator is smiling. And that smile will help you heal. You are full of anger, Tommy, and you can't keep that inside you. Let the game take that away. Let the game be your medicine. You can start with the healing it can give you and build on that. We can build on that. Life is so precious that you don't want to waste any of it. I can tell you that life goes by so fast. There is an old saying that goes something like this: 'Life is the flash of a firefly in the night. It is the breath of a buffalo in the wintertime. It is the little shadow which runs across the grass and loses itself in the sunset.'"

Hazel stops talking then and silently guides the canoe into a small inlet. Tommy realizes he has been holding his breath off and on while Hazel was talking. He feels bad for what happened to her but he also feels better in a strange way. Better because bad things happened to Hazel and she is still a good person. If she can live through it and find a way to heal herself, maybe he can too.

About twenty yards away a red fox intently digs around a fallen log. Hazel and Tommy sit in the calm water, watching. The fox has white on his chest and a white tip on his tail, and the dirt is flying. He stops for a second when his eyes flick over to the people in the canoe, but he isn't worried. He isn't receiving any danger signals from the pair, so he keeps working at the dirt, looking for his next meal. Then Tommy realizes Hazel's voice again, there in the background, flowing with the water all around him.

"This is where my journey pauses again. It's time for you to speak of the things you have inside you. Why that anger is there and what it is doing to you. But before you do, there are some things to know. If you want to heal and move forward, you have to start walking the right path. What is in store for you does not have to be anything like what has happened to you before. The Creator has patience while you find your way. He won't give you a challenge that you aren't strong enough to overcome. You will have all the strength you need. You just have to look within and then around you. It's your turn now, Tommy. Are you ready to start walking the right path? To start your healing journey?"

There is hesitation in Tommy's voice. "I want to. I just don't know where to start?"

THE TRUCK IS FOLLOWING A FAMILIAR ROUTE on the way to Tommy's grandparents' house. Beau turns the radio off, which is uncharacteristic of him because he loves to listen to music.

"I see so much of me in you," Beau says stiffly, but then there is a sympathetic tone in his voice. "I know how hard it is to control your temper sometimes, but drinking will only help you lose your temper quicker. You understand?"

"Yeah, I know," says Tommy. He pauses, but stumbles into the question that he's been wanting to ask. "Dad, Derek told us how Coach Blair used to drink and get in fights back in the day. And he said you two actually fought with each other once. I can't even picture that. You both seem so different now. How did you guys change? I mean, how did you go from the way you used to be to the way you are now?" Tommy knows he's taking a chance asking the question. Sometimes Beau can turn moody on a dime and that usually ends the conversation. But not this time.

His father takes a big breath. "He told ya 'bout that, huh? Well, Tim and I were a lot alike when we were younger. Both of us drank too much, and we both had bad attitudes. I guess it was just bound to happen sometime. But we just grew up and realized that we were better off trying to be good fathers rather than trying to be tough guys. And I think we both respected each other more for the changes we were able to make in our lives than for anything else. I know for me, the way I was able to change was for you guys and your mother. I knew that if I didn't change, I would lose my family, and to me, no amount of partying was worth that."

"But how were you able to just quit drinking? I mean, we live on the Rez and it just seems like everybody parties around here. Isn't it really hard not to drink sometimes?"

"Can't say it was easiest thing I've ever done, but I had help from a lot of people. Just like you, I had so much anger in me. Drinking was the way I dealt with it, and it caused me to do a lot of things that I ain't proud of. I knew I had to find a better way to deal with what was inside me.

"I guess the first time when I really knew I could quit is when I went to see Hazel Blackwater and asked her for help. She took me way back into the middle of a big open field. She told me that she was going to burn some tobacco and the smoke from the tobacco would carry my thoughts to the Creator. When the tobacco began to burn, I asked for guidance to help me be a better person, a better husband, a better father. I asked him to help James. To give my little boy the strength to fight the cancer that was inside him. I said I would never touch another drop of alcohol again. After a lot of pain, a lot of tears, and a lot of strength, James beat cancer. And the way I see it, I'm just holding up my end. So, to answer your question: no, it's not hard for me to leave the bottle alone. Not anymore," he finished, voice choked with emotion as they pulled into Grampa and Gram Henry's driveway.

CHAPTER TWENTY-SIX

A CURVE BALL

G rampa and Gram Henry depend on a fireplace and wood stove to heat their home, and upstate New York winters can burn up a lot of wood. The spring and summer months are used to stockpile wood for the winter. Wasting no time, Beau grabs an axe and begins reducing the larger logs of cut wood into more manageable sizes. Tommy splits the smaller pieces with an axe, stacking the wood neatly in the woodshed.

The work lasts until the sun is just about to go down. Beau heads into the house to see if his mother needs any help in the kitchen. Grampa Henry sits under his favorite shade tree as Tommy walks over and takes a seat beside him. Doug Henry does not split wood anymore – not because he doesn't want to, but because his kids told him he no longer needed to. His kids and grandkids handle the work because they think a whole lot of physical labor is not a good idea for someone is his late seventies. Doug Henry has been busy his whole life. He worked on his father's farm and then attended Martindale Indian School from grades seven to twelve. He joined the U.S. Marine Corps and spent several years overseas. When he returned home he spent years driving big rigs, making deliveries for a local company while running his own farm. He's never been someone to put his feet up and watch the world go by, so it's understandable that he has a hard time sitting around and relaxing in his retirement.

Doug Henry takes a great deal of pleasure in watching his grandkids play sports. He loves the competitive nature of sports, especially lacrosse. Grampa Henry didn't have time to play organized sports when he was a kid and worked so much that he missed a lot of his own children's sporting careers, but he makes sure to attend as many of his grandkids games as he possibly can. The only sport that Doug Henry was able to take up in his youth was boxing. He got started at Martindale and continued when he was in the military. He was a natural at it, and he liked the discipline and physical training involved. He tried and still tries to instill the same kind of discipline in his kids and grandkids.

As Tommy sits down beside his grandfather he receives a broad smile of appreciation for the work he has done today.

"So, how things going, Tommy?" the older man asks.

"Ahhh, not too good, Grampa," Tommy shyly responds.

"Your dad said you're going through a rough patch right now, but honestly it might get that way from time to time as you grow up, so you better learn how to deal with it," advises the senior Henry.

"I just don't know what to do. Everything just feels so messed up," says Tommy. "I get mad fast, and I don't know why. Maybe I get that from Dad."

Doug Henry watches his grandson carefully as he talks, noting the body language. Tommy's clenches his fists and digs the toe of his boot into the ground as he talks.

"I don't know about getting your temper from him, but I can tell you that your dad wasn't always angry. In fact, he was a pretty happy kid. He went through some tough times and is much better now than he had been for a long time."

Tommy unclenches his fists and gestures towards the house. Laughter faintly drifts out and the appetizing aroma of roast chicken wafts on the breeze. "Really? Most things I remember is him being pissed off all the time and me getting yelled at."

Grampa Henry has always talked to his grandchildren as if they were kids. And they have been children up until now, but he can see Tommy is growing up. That maybe he's progressed beyond the simple explanations that younger people would be satisfied with. So he decides to try a different approach.

"Well, I can only tell you what I think."

Tommy sits up straight when he hears his grandfather say this. There is a serious tone in the older man's voice that Tommy recognizes. That tone usually means it's time to listen.

"You never got to meet your Uncle Donnie. He was gone long before you ever appeared, but I think your dad's anger problems all go back to losing his brother. Beau really looked up to Donnie. He couldn't do anything wrong according to Beau, and he was always trying to be like his big brother. And maybe your dad never really got over his death."

Tommy sits on the edge of his seat. He knows his grandfather is talking serious stuff, and there should no interruptions. Tommy had been told his Uncle Donnie died in a car accident, but that was all he knew.

"The night Donnie died, the boys were out front of the house playing ball. Both kids had good arms, but Donnie had a cannon. He had serious interest from some college scouts and might have been on his way to a baseball scholarship. He sure was one smart and talented kid."

Doug Henry's eyes grow a little watery, and Tommy has to look away. How would his dad have been different if his brother was still alive? What kind of a life would Donnie have had? Would he have played pro ball and made millions of dollars and changed everyone's life? Tommy sits quietly with his thoughts while he waits for Doug Henry to compose himself.

"Anyway, the boys were playing catch. It was getting dark. Spitting a little rain. I had told them to come in the house and get ready to settle down soon, but they just wanted a couple more minutes. I think Donnie was trying to show Beau how to throw a curve ball. I got some of the story out of your dad a few days after the funeral. Apparently, Beau had thrown a couple of pitches that had started to curve and he wanted to try a couple of more to get the hang of it. Donnie was always game. He would play ball forever. Anyway, Beau threw one that got away from him, maybe because it was raining, and Donnie had to run after it into the ditch by the road. Nobody saw the two pickup trucks booting down the road. They were flying, both with no lights on, and the one in front, fishtailing, swerving all over the place, and it lost control. I think, according to Beau, that Donnie did see the truck coming at the last second, but it was too late to get out of the way. The first vehicle hit him going at about eighty miles an hour, and Donnie must have been thrown fifteen feet in the air. No one can survive that kind of impact. Donnie died right there in front of the house with Beau holding his head up and trying to talk to him. Whoever was driving didn't even take their foot off the gas. They had no intention of ever stopping. Just going like bats outta Hell. I hope that's where they both are right now. Beau couldn't see much with the dark and the rain, but he knows there was one guy in each truck. Later on, the police found two burned trucks in different spots. No way of saying for sure if they were the ones, but it makes sense. The cops never were able to come up with any leads and no one has figured out who was responsible after all these years."

Doug Henry's voice trails off and he stops talking, then swallows hard.

He pulls a cloth handkerchief out of his back pocket and slowly wipes both his eyes.

"So, your dad thinks if he hadn't made that wild pitch that Donnie wouldn't have run out by the road, and I think you get the picture. Doesn't matter what people said to him. I think he feels responsible. He's been carrying that with him all these years. Blames himself. Never mind that there were two idiots out there driving like maniacs. Anyway, that's when your dad started to get out of control, and it just plays out from there. I watched him get into trouble more times than I care to remember. Fighting with people, sort of like he was suspicious of everyone, thinking maybe they were the ones driving those trucks. The booze certainly didn't help, but I think it's all about guilt that he didn't need to have. He was mad at the world and just wanted Donnie back, I'm guessing. Well, we all did. It took a long time to accept his death. I'm not sure Beau ever has. I don't know how those killers could go through life with the death of my boy on their conscience. Less than human, maybe, in my estimation."

Doug Henry stops there with the handkerchief motionless in his left hand. He seems lost in thought, and Tommy knows enough not to say anything. Grampa Henry has always seemed like a larger-than-life character. Now he seems a little more down-to-earth to Tommy. The older man lets out a big sigh.

"Tommy. Sooner or later in life, you're gonna get knocked on your ass. It happens to everybody, and when it does, you have to decide if you're staying down or if you're gonna get up. You've got that Henry blood in you, so I know you're gonna get back on your feet. That's something I learned from boxing. It's okay to get knocked down; you just have to get back up."

Doug Henry is smiling, sitting up straight as he tucks the handkerchief in his back pocket. Tommy had never really seen his Grampa talk this way. It's obvious now, though, that the old man wants to change the topic.

"Did I ever tell you about how I started boxing? It wasn't a sport that I knew anything about as a kid. That is until I went to the Mush Hole."

Tommy has heard his Grampa talk about the Mush Hole before, but he's never gone into much detail. It's not every day the senior Henry wants to talk a whole lot. Tommy knows he has to take advantage of it.

"What was that place really like, Grampa? I can't imagine anybody ever making kids go there."

Grampa Henry's eyebrows are bushy, a little wild, the way some older men let them grow, like they have a mind of their own. He raises his over-grown brows in surprise when he hears Tommy's request.

"Not really something I like to talk about Tommy, but I'll tell you a few things. Number 9, that's the number they gave me when I got there. That's why your dad always wore number 9 when he played lacrosse. Didn't know that, did ya? Your Gram's number was 24. That's the number your Uncle Donnie used to wear when he played baseball. We were supposed to be at the Mush Hole to get education. Honestly, the only two things I learned while at that school was how to fight and to never trust anybody. They had a boxing ring set up in the basement of the school. Just rope tied around four pillars and the priests used to set up fights. Some of the big wigs from town would come to place bets on us. If you did good, you didn't get in trouble, but if you didn't do well, you might get the strap or miss a few meals. There was one priest, Brennan… I would have loved for him to get in the ring with me just once when I got older. But that guy didn't have the parts to mess with anyone that could fight back. Sometimes the fights were really mismatched. I saw some kids have to fight that weren't old enough, weren't big enough, weren't experienced enough. And they got hurt bad. A lot of us got hurt bad at that school, not just in the ring."

Tommy feels baffled by his grandfather. How could such a gentle man have so much violence in his past?

Grampa Henry stares off into space. Tommy had heard his grandfather talk a little bit about the Martindale Indian School before, but Doug Henry has usually sounded so bitter about his experiences that any talk of the Mush Hole has been short-lived. Today, though, his grandfather sounds almost nostalgic.

"The main goal of that place was to strip you of your identity, your language, your culture. Goes back to that old saying: 'Kill the Indian, save the man.' First thing they did was cut my long hair. Gave me a buzz cut. When I spoke any Mohawk words they held me down and stuck needles in my tongue. I learned quickly to speak English and never utter a word of our language. I barely remember any Mohawk at all now. We weren't allowed to believe in the Creator. We had to become Christians and attend mass. They wouldn't even let us play lacrosse because it was considered a cultural game. They only let us play baseball at recess. Worst thing was what the priests would do to us at night time." Grampa Henry pauses a moment before saying, "This is getting me a little worked up and I promised Joyce that I would watch my blood pressure."

As Tommy listens to his grandfather talk, he is preoccupied with a thought, an ongoing feeling about his Grampa's experiences. Is it possible that even though he tried his hardest to be a good parent that some of the bitterness and anger that Doug Henry experienced during his days at the Mush Hole got passed down in the family?

Tommy asks a question, "But didn't they teach you how to read and write and get an education and stuff?"

Grampa Doug nods his head "Yeah, I learned how to read and write, even got a high school diploma. But you know where else you can go and come out with a high school diploma? Prison. Only difference is people in prison are forced to go there because they committed crimes. The only crime us kids committed was being born Haudenosaunee."

Tommy has one more question, "Grampa, how come my dad never had to go to the Mush Hole?"

Doug Henry gives Tommy a blank stare. "That place was closed down by the time my kids were old enough to go to school. But let's put it this way, Tommy. If your dad had gone to the Mush Hole, I wouldn't be here. They would've had to kill me to get any of my kids in that fucking place." Tommy has never seen that look in his Grampa's eyes before, but it's the same look he has seen many times from his father Beau.

The senior Henry stands up at this point, signaling that the conversation is at an end. Except for one more thing. "Just remember, Tommy, if you ever have something bothering you, you can come to me. I don't have all the answers, but I've got a few of 'em."

Tommy knows the old man is treating him as an equal. It's an odd feeling, but it makes Tommy feel like he's not alone in the world. That somebody other than his buddies has his back.

"I will, Grampa."

The sun has set now and a chill lingers in the air. Grampa puts his hand lightly on Tommy's shoulder and smiles. "C'mon, your Gram's probably got dinner ready." says Grampa as they start to walk towards the house.

Gram Henry has prepared chicken and dumplings to thank them for their hard work – meat and dough smothered in peppered gravy that everyone loves. With the smaller number of family members present for this meal, they all fit around the modest kitchen table. Beau and Tommy are especially hungry and dig into their plates in a way that makes Gram Henry beam. She has little patience for picky eaters or vegetarians. One of her favorite lines is, "If you ain't hungry, you ain't working hard enough."

CHAPTER TWENTY-SEVEN

THAT'S FUCKED UP

Tommy sits alone on the bleachers at the Hawks' game field, thinking about everything, when he receives a text from Jessica. She wants to talk with him for the first time since their big fight. He agrees, and within ten minutes she pulls up in her mom's car.

As she gets out of the car, Tommy watches her bashfully, wondering how badly he hurt her. She looks tired, hunched into a zip up sweatshirt and jeans, hood drawn up. But there is purpose in her walk, an aggressive energy that Tommy has seen before. It always worries him.

Looking at her, he feels deeply ashamed. He can't believe what happened. He can't believe he allowed it to happen. He knows better, even if Jessica doesn't.

She plunks herself down in his vicinity, but a good-ways away as if having him in her personal space is too much to handle. Her eyes are the same – lustrous like polished mahogany, shadowed with long-straight eyelashes. There is some glassiness there now, too, he realizes as he studies her face. Jessica has obviously had a couple of drinks; Tommy smells the alcohol. Maybe to add to her courage. Maybe because she can't help herself.

He can't think of what to say, so he says nothing. Jessica breaks the silence first.

"So, what are we going to do now?" she asks abruptly.

Jessica feels torn when she sees Tommy. She wants to hug him, but at the same time she wants to curse him and lash out at him. There have been times throughout their relationship when she thought Tommy was the only one for her. More recently, all she feels is disappointment and anger when she looks at him.

"I don't know what to say," he admits.

"You don't really care about me, do you?"

Tommy can sense what's coming and readies himself for the storm. They have fought often in their relationship. More bad times than good?

Tommy can't really be sure what the ratio is at this point, and he doesn't know why it's been that way. He's often wondered about Jessica and her relationships with the men in her life. It seems to him like Jessica continuously looks for something that isn't there. He heard stories about her relationship with her ex-boyfriend – how he would cheat on her and when she drank she would beat him up. She admitted before to having trust issues. Tommy knows Jessica didn't really grow up with a father. Her dad, Rob Wolfe, died after a fall while ironworking when she was only five. Her mom, Vicky, has had to carry the load of raising two young daughters while working full-time at a Rez daycare. Tommy knows that some things can really fuck you up. He can't imagine what he would be like without both his parents in his life.

"My family would be mad if they even knew I was talking to you. They think you're a piece of shit and a bad influence on me. They told me the best thing I could do for myself is stay away from you, permanently," she confides.

"Yeah, I bet," he replies.

"I know I shouldn't have been talking with Shane, but you weren't even paying any attention to me," Jessica begins in a rush, tears pooling and starting to fall. "I wanted to be with you. I needed you. But you were out with your friends again – like always."

"Were you with him?" Tommy asks, voice almost breaking.

"No, that was the first time we had ever texted each other – and all we did was text. I shouldn't have done it, but you had no right to do what you did either. You crossed the line," she finishes defensively with all the dignity she can muster, wiping her eyes on the sleeve of her sweatshirt.

"I know. It was wrong. I'm sorry about that."

"I hate that the whole damn Rez knows what happened. People are calling you a woman beater and everybody's talking about it. I'm just embarrassed – people stare at me and everyone keeps asking me stuff I don't want to answer."

Tommy winces and lets out a sigh as he recalls a line in the text messages he read on her phone. She said to Shane: "I wanted to go all the way last time but was afraid of getting caught." So Tommy knows she's lying. Maybe they didn't fuck, but they still hooked up behind his back. He imagines the argument that will happen if he calls her out on it. Instead, he doesn't bother.

"Well, you know how this place is. They got nothing better to do than talk about other people."

"It's like a bad dream that I keep thinking I'm going to wake up from," persists Jessica. "It doesn't even feel real."

"Yeah, feels the same way for me – like a nightmare," Tommy agrees, and she nods knowingly but then her face hardens.

"I think it's a nightmare that has to end. Remember when I told you I thought there was something wrong with you? I still think that. Tommy, I don't want to waste my time. I don't think you're ever going to change. You're just one of those Rez lacrosse fuck boys who want to party and screw anybody they can."

"What are you saying?" asks Tommy, not surprised by her edgy and combative tone.

"I mean that you may not be a complete loser yet, but after you put your hands on me, I don't think I can trust you anymore," she clarifies. Tommy doesn't know what to say. He wants to defend himself. He wants to tell Jessica what he sees in her. Somebody who has problems that she's not facing up to. That she may not even be able to recognize in herself. Tommy feels helpless. He has recognized things in himself that he knows he needs to change. He just doesn't want the backlash that would come if he told Jessica there are things she needs to change as well.

She looks at him with something more like contempt in her eyes now. "You're not ever going to fucking grow up, are you? Maybe you think too highly of yourself. Maybe you just need some help, but I can't waste my time with you anymore. I'm better than that. I have more self-respect than that. Everybody is saying you're a loser and you're lucky to not be in jail. All I know is I don't want to be your victim anymore. So don't call me again, Tommy. I want to move on with my life. It's over. We are over. We should have been over a long time ago. I deserve so much better."

The tears slide down Jessica's cheeks again. The fact that she is crying somehow takes the edge off her harsh words. Tommy doesn't hear a lot of truth in what she is saying. He senses more push back, more looking to place the blame. Tommy doesn't say anything. Jessica gets up to leave, wiping her eyes, and Tommy can see that more needs to be said but struggles for the right words.

"Jess, I never wanted to hurt you," Tommy manages. She stops and faces him. He can see rage in her bloodshot eyes.

"Yeah, well, I have trouble believing that. Go take a long hard look at yourself in the mirror. You may not like what you see."

Tommy feels a little weak, like he's coming down with the flu. He knows it is from sheer exhaustion in dealing with Jessica. He watches her go, passing Andy and Ben who have come out to the field to find Tommy. He didn't go to school today, and the whole Rez is buzzing with varying versions of what happened between Tommy and Jessica.

Andy and Ben plop down next to Tommy.

"You okay?" Ben asks kindly.

"Yeah, I'll be okay." *Eventually*, he thinks.

"Missed ya at practice today," continues Andy, sliding a sideways glance at him. Tommy shrugs and manages a half smile.

"Yeah, I just don't know if I could be around Shane right now and not snap," he finishes.

"Fucking Shane," mumbles Ben. "I wanted to fucking cross-check him in the throat today at practice. Fucking asshole! I mean what he did is gotta be like the biggest scumbag move in all of sports. How could somebody do that to a teammate?" he demands, warming to his subject. Tommy finds himself getting emotional.

"I don't know, man. I just feel so fucked up right now. Lacrosse is where I always went to forget about everything. No matter what was going wrong, I could go to the field and forget about that shit. I mean, I like lacrosse and I always have, but what I love most about it is you guys – being around my friends, people that I trust, just having fun. But now, a teammate stabbing me in the back? I never saw that coming. I don't know if I even wanna be around the game anymore. It'll just bring back all the bad fucking thoughts that I'm trying to forget. Wouldn't be fun anymore."

"I know how you feel about being able to forget everything when you're playing. Hell, I don't even know what to do with myself away from lacrosse. Probably why I drink so much," Andy suggests in a flash of insight.

Tommy grins. "Yeah, maybe."

"I know right now, Shane's the one guy that you don't want to be on the field with, but there are twenty-three other guys who need you out there with them. Especially me. I play this game for my friends too, ya know," he explains.

"Yeah, I know."

As the guys continue talking, a small gray car pulls into the parking lot, and as it gets closer, the boys notice the driver is Jen. The same Jen who repeatedly molested Tommy when he was a child. She looks different now. Her face appears rough and worn from the years of drugs, alcohol, and hard living Jen's been through. As the car nears, she recognizes the boys and gives them a wicked smile as she takes a last drag of a cigarette and flicks the butt in their direction. Though her face has changed, she still has the same piercing glare coming from her dark, cold eyes. Jen does a slow U-turn and drives back across the parking lot heading out the way she came. The image of Jen is menacing to Tommy even after all these years.

"The fuck is that bitch doing back around here?" asks Tommy.

"Slut's probably just cruising around looking for some dick," says Ben disgusted.

Jen moved away years ago after her father married a woman from another Rez on the other side of the State. This was good news to Tommy when he was a child, but she did resurface back around Sparrow Lake every once in a while to visit family. Fresh fuel for the fucking nightmares that hold Tommy so tight sometimes he can't breathe, unable to sleep at all some nights. Hazel has helped him talk about it, has helped him feel his way out of a dark corner, but he is a long way from starting down the path Hazel talked about. He's not sure if he'll ever be ready for that.

As Ben watches the gray car leave the parking lot, he confides something that stuns his friends. Ben's head hangs down as he talks into his chest, his voice so low that the Tommy and Andy can't be sure they've heard him right.

"When I was a little kid, that girl used to babysit me, and she'd stick her hand down my pants and grab my nuts."

The other two guys look at Ben with looks of shock, and Tommy finally breaks the silence when it actually registers what Ben is telling them.

"Did she do more than that?"

Ben looks at Tommy, and in a calm, serious voice simply says, "Yeah."

Tommy sees the emotion in Ben's eyes as he looks down at his feet. He is in deep thought, and Tommy knows far too well what his friend is thinking and feeling.

"She did the same thing to me. She was my babysitter too."

Ben looks up and sees the seriousness in Tommy's face and knows he's not kidding.

Andy shakes his head in disgust hearing what had happened to two of his best friends. "That's fucked up," he sympathetically remarks.

And that's as far as they take it. All the guys know that a barrier has been broken. That if Tommy and Ben need to talk about Jen again there will be sympathetic ears.

As Tommy, Andy, and Ben walk down the bleachers, Weasel and Jordy drive up in Jordy's dad's truck. For a change, Weasel is driving – and the sight triggers Tommy's memory. It is Jordy's birthday, so Jordy must be drinking for once, and indeed, as they get closer, Tommy spots a bottle of whiskey sitting next to the talkative, grinning Jordy. He reaches in and fist pounds Jordy.

"Happy birthday, kid," he grins and Jordy laughs.

"Thanks, buddy. Have a birthday drink with me?" he offers, holding up the bottle.

For a moment, Tommy can already taste it. But then he remembers.

"Nah, taking 'er easy, man," he replies awkwardly.

Andy nods. "Yeah, me too."

"I need a fucking drink right now," says Ben as he grabs the bottle for a quick blast.

"Glad someone's having a shot with me," says Jordy jokingly, having a shot himself.

"Your old man let ya borrow his truck?" Andy asks, admiring the pickup. It's a massive upgrade from Jordy's little shitbeater of a car.

"Yeah, man. He's been pretty cool lately. He's been on the wagon for a while now. Him and Mom seem pretty happy for a change. It's kinda weird, but it's my birthday, so I can have a few tonight," he finishes in a flush of excitement.

Driver or not, Weasel is enjoying a massive blunt. The redhead is almost totally obscured in a cloud of smoke.

"Hey, Tommy, I see Shane out – you want me kick his ass? I know it'd be easy – that douchebag's never won a fight in his life," he says, an unholy grin lighting up his face. Weasel loves a worthy cause to get into a dust up over.

"Nah, your hands are too valuable, Weasel. Don't bother hurting 'em on that fuck face," reassures Tommy, smiling at his enthusiasm. It's good to have real friends.

"Yeah, you're right," says Weasel, rolling a second blunt for later. "My hands are valuable."

"Fuck that noise!" interrupts Jordy. "I see him, I'm gonna fucking drop him!" he insists. Tommy grins. Jordy is already well on his way – not drinking means he has little to no tolerance for hard liquor.

"Hey, you have fun tonight, alright, buddy?" Tommy says to Jordy, humoring him. "You're a good friend – thanks, man."

"You know what, Tommy? I'm proud to be your friend; you too, Andy; and you, Ben. Not you, Weasel. You're a fucking dink," he finishes, grinning at his driver. They all crack up, but Weasel pretends to be pissed.

"What the fuck? I'm driving you around for your birthday and you're just giving me shit. See what I gotta fucking put up with?" he demands, throwing his hands up in the air in mock protest. Jordy laughs and takes another belt of his whiskey.

"Alright, I'm gonna go let 'er roll tonight. Catch ya later!" whoops Jordy, and Weasel takes the cue to drive away. Both guys are wearing some of the biggest smiles Tommy has ever seen. It makes him feel good just to look at the two party animals.

"I love those fucking guys. They can always make me laugh," Tommy says, smiling after the truck.

"Yeah, me too," says Andy.

CHAPTER TWENTY-EIGHT

A HELL OF A PARTY

Y ou can say a lot of things about "Nasty Nate," but one thing you can't say is that he doesn't know how to throw a party. His house is rocking tonight: a good DJ, speakers blasting, and the dance floor packed full of people well on their way to being wasted. Those who aren't into dancing are playing various drinking games or scarfing down food in the kitchen.

Weasel is a master at beer pong. He always says if you want to be good at something you have to put in the hours. Weasel's ability for sinking the ball in the opponent's cup is uncanny, so the other players have quit the game leaving the field to the self-proclaimed champ and Jordy. They hang out by the table, finishing up the beers and chatting. When a fresh group of people enter the crowded house, the boys give the room a once over casually, and then suddenly Weasel freezes.

Chantel. She is wearing tight blue jeans with a white top showing off ample cleavage, and her full lips are outlined with dark liner and filled in with a pale, frosted pink. Her eyes smolder under an application of liner. Her lush body exudes an easy, practiced sexuality that makes Weasel feel like a kid with a massive crush on his teacher. Fuck, he wants her.

He nudges Jordy. "Aww man, there's Chantel. Damn, she's hot. I been wanting to fuck her for years!" he agonizes.

"Guy, she's married and like ten years older than you. She won't give you the time of day, kid!" Jordy snorts.

Weasel downs the last swallow of his beer. "Doesn't mean I can't give it a shot," he replies confidently. "I've been whacking off to that for years!" With this poetic assertion, he makes his way through the crowd, stopping in front of Chantel and her posse.

"Hey, Chantel. How you doing tonight?" he asks, smiling.

Chantel gives him a cool glance, but then smiles slightly. "Oh, hi. Weasel, right? Hey, could you do me a favor and get us some drinks?" she purrs, casually indicating her group. They are her friends, not her husband's – so Chantel knows they won't say nothing about nothing.

"Sure, if you dance with me when I get back," counters the cocky, red-headed kid, and she laughs at his nerve. Now with any luck, the kid might have a dick to match those balls.

"You're cute," she purrs. "Maybe we'll dance if you tell me something first?"

"Sure."

"What's your real name? I feel weird calling you an animal."

"But I am an animal," he suavely boasts. Seeing her raise an eyebrow, he hastily backtracks. Maybe he has gone too far, too soon. "My real name is Melvin. Melvin Monture."

"Melvin, huh?" she replies, lips curving in a leering smile. "Hmm, maybe we'll just stick with Weasel."

"I'd like that. Okay, I'll be right back with your drinks," he promises, scooting off into the crowd. Chantel's friends roll their eyes, but they know the side benefit that free drinks are free drinks. Hard to argue with that.

In the kitchen, Jordy chats avidly with several guys he hardly knows. Whiskey has loosened his tongue to the point where he is friends with everyone – except Shane, who he is still dimly planning to kick the shit out of if he sees him. As he laughs at a joke, someone behind him taps Jordy on the shoulder. It's Nate, as in Nasty Nate, the host of the party. He got that nickname back in his high school days when he was one of the best point guards in the area.

"Hey Jordy, waz' up, kid? I see you're boozing tonight," said Nate sociably. "Having a good time?"

Jordy is beaming. "Yeah, man, it's my birthday, so I'm sampling tonight. How about you boys have a shot for my birthday?" he invites, offering them his bottle. Nate takes a shot, passing it to his boys for their own swigs.

"Hey, man, you really wanna have a good time, how 'bout you try some of these," he suggests, offering Jordy some small white pills. "On the house; happy birthday."

"Thanks, man! Appreciate it," Jordy beams, taking the pills. Without hesitation, he downs all three of them, washing them down with more whiskey.

The drug dealer chuckles, elbowing one of his boys. "Shit, my man ain't playin' around tonight – he's out to have a good time. Alright bro, I'm gonna go check the bittie situation in this place. Have a good one, playah," he smiles, patting Jordy's shoulder. They move off into the crowd, looking for more customers.

The night takes on a frenzy of its own with a feeling of ever-increasing excitement. The dance floor is jammed so full that there's hardly room to move, and the sweating DJ keeps pulling out one excellent dance tune after another. Weasel and Chantel grind on the dance floor as she works her voluptuous ass with some obvious passion into his pelvis.

A fight breaks out on the dance floor and suddenly the couples clear to the side allowing the two men some space. The music abruptly cuts out as the DJ scrambles to protect his equipment. The biggest guys in the house pull the fighters away from each other and throw them out the front door. One of the impromptu bouncers turns back to the DJ and yells, "Turn that shit back on!" and the crowd cheers, oozing back out onto the dance floor.

Weasel finds Jordy still in the kitchen.

"Hey, I'm going with Chantel and her friends. You wanna come with us or are you gonna chill here?" he asks. Jordy is the happiest drunk Weasel has ever seen, grinning from ear to ear. The birthday boy sobers up slightly as Weasel's words sink in.

"Fuck off, you serious? Don't tell me you're gonna hit that!" he exclaims in admiration. "That's cool as shit if you do."

But Weasel knows drunks aren't predictable, having been there himself too many times to count. "I don't know what's gonna happen, but she says her husband is outta town… so damn right I'm gonna try and nail this girl. The truck is unlocked, but I'm taking the keys with me, okay?"

"Yeah, man, don't worry about it. I'll be alright. Go take care of business," he smirks, cracking up at the thought of Weasel fucking a woman all his boys have lusted over. Only Weasel. The last thing on Jordy's mind is getting behind the wheel. He has no intention of going anywhere. He's having a good time.

"Okay, have fun. Catch ya later," says Weasel breezily, heading out of the kitchen to find Chantel.

WEASEL AND CHANTEL ARE DROPPED OFF at her house where Chantel manages a fairly civilized goodbye to her friends. By the time they're inside her front door, they are groping each other. He presses her up against the wall, mouth eagerly seeking hers. She is fully on board, reaching down to feel his cock through his pants as she sucks on his lower lip.

The girl is pleasantly surprised. He might even have a bigger dick than her husband's. "Mmmm, feels like you've got a nice cock," she whispers into his ear. "Let's see if you know how to use it."

Grimly thinking of his "fight" with E, Weasel blurts out before thinking. "Just hope it still works."

Chantel freezes, momentarily thrown off. "What do you mean?" she demands.

Weasel realizes his error in a flash. "Nothing, don't worry about it," he reassures her, reaching around with both hands to grab her firm ass. Weasel then kisses and nibbles on Chantel's neck as she lets out a soft moan. He will be pulling out every move he knows in order to impress this woman.

Shuddering with pleasure, she disentangles herself and kneels in front of him. She pulls his dick out of his pants and notes its girth with satisfaction. She's a size queen, and this one will fit the bill nicely. "Seems fine to me," she says, running her tongue up and down the underside. Weasel shivers, but manages to cope.

"Oh, yeah, never lets me down."

She runs her hot tongue over the head of his cock, and it's too much for him to wait any longer. He ushers her down on the floor of her hallway, undoes her jeans, and pulls them off her long legs. He reaches into her bra to fondle one of her heavy, full breasts. Their first fuck happens on the living room couch; the second on her bed; the third half on and half off her bed.

As she drifts off to sleep in a pleasured haze, Chantel wonders why she hasn't been screwing younger men all along.

As Weasel drifts off with a dazed but ecstatic expression on his face, he wonders if his life will ever get any better than this very moment: falling asleep in Chantel's bed, cuddled up to her soft, warm thighs and ass.

Even after one of the best and most tiring nights of fucking in her life, Chantel is a light sleeper. Her eyes pop open at the sound of her husband's car pulling into their driveway. Without a second thought, she shakes Weasel.

"Get the fuck up," she hisses. "My husband's home – hurry up!"

"What the fuck?" mutters a groggy Weasel. He feels like he pulled a muscle – several of them in fact. Does a dick have muscles?

"Go through the window!" she insists, and he sits up, bare-assed and panicked. She tosses most of his clothes out the bedroom window, cleaning up with a speed that bears testament to some measure of practice.

Weasel manages to grab his jeans and slip them on before she can chuck them out with the rest of his outfit. He follows his clothes out the window, and Chantel quickly adjusts the bed sheets and pillows trying hide any evidence of sexual activity. Weasel gathers up his clothes from the ground, tucking his underwear in his pocket.

She spares a moment to watch Weasel's skinny little form run across the back yard wearing only jeans and shoes.

"A weasel with a dick like a horse," Chantel mutters, shaking her head and jumping into the shower to wash off all the traces of her adventure with the auburn-haired cocksman.

On the far side of some trees, Weasel stops to get dressed. He's grateful that his phone didn't get left behind, and he dials Jordy.

"Come on, Jordy, pick up; you'll definitely wanna hear this," he grins. The phone rings and rings, but Jordy doesn't pick up. Weasel is disappointed but sympathetic – Jordy undoubtedly has a massive hangover and is probably still sleeping it off. Weasel hightails it over to the nearest road, and starts to walk with his thumb out eventually catching a ride back to the house where the party was held. They drop him off at the end of the laneway and he walks up, spotting Jordy's truck still pulled off to one side of the driveway.

The house is still standing, but the yard is a disaster zone – bottles, cans, and empty cigarette packs scattered across it. One of the front windows is boarded up with plywood. Weasel shakes his head happily. "Must have been a hell of a party."

He gets up to the truck and spots Jordy, passed out in the passenger seat. Weasel smiles. *Poor Jordy, that boy needs to slow down his drinking until he gets used to it.*

Weasel hops in on the driver's side.

"Yo, Jordy, wake up," he grins. "You gotta hear this one. You would not guess where Chantel has a tattoo!"

Jordy doesn't move.

"Aww, all partied out! Trying to sleep it off, huh?" he says, starting up the truck. The engine turns over loudly, rumbling like an old man with lots of phlegm in his throat.

Weasel reaches over to shake Jordy. "Come on, man, wake up!" he insists, shaking him hard. Jordy slumps over in the seat and falls sideways, his head bouncing off the passenger side window with a sickening thud.

A cold thought hits Weasel head-on all at once and he shrieks in shock, frantically trying to wake his friend.

"Jordy! Get the fuck up, man! Jordy, c'mon! No, don't do this!" he yells, shaking him and hoping for Jordy to open his eyes. "No no no, Jordy! Wake up man, c'mon, Jordy. Jordy!!"

CHAPTER TWENTY-NINE
BITCHIN' AND MOANIN'

As the casket is lowered into the ground, Quinn Harris' uncle Reg Harris, who is a faithkeeper, speaks in Mohawk to the people gathered to say their last goodbyes to Jordy Baker. A few of the people there know the language, but many do not. All remain respectfully quiet, and everyone feels comforted by the sound of his words flowing over them like a soft, warm breeze.

Reg then switches to English. "There comes a time for us to go back to where we were made – Mother Earth, back to the clay. The Creator will grab hold of this matter and take care of the spirit now."

When he finishes and the casket has finished its slow descent to the bottom of the grave, most people start to disperse and thoughtfully walk away.

Jordy's parents remain standing next to the grave. Shelby's face is a tragic image of loss. Harry remains expressionless as tears roll down his face. Shelby has never felt this kind of pain in all her life. Parents aren't supposed to outlive their children. While Jordy was alive, Shelby could still think of the three of them as a family. Now she isn't sure what is left.

Sidling up to the grave, Weasel grabs a shovel and sticks it into the earth, filling it with dirt. When he tosses the soil on the casket, the hollow sound makes his shoulders hunch and stiffen.

Tommy, Andy, and Ben each grab a shovel and begin to cover the casket with dirt. The hollow sound fades as more dirt covers the top, and they work briskly. The whole scene is surreal – Tommy half expects Jordy to wander up and grab a shovel himself.

Once the earth is piled high on the burial plot, the bouquets of flowers are laid on top. Staring down at the wash of color the flowers make in the otherwise bleak landscape, Weasel shakes his head and mutters, "I can't believe this."

"Did his family ever hear back from the doc about what happened?" asks Ben.

Weasel's face tightens. "I found out he took some X at the party. Doc said that the combination of the X and the amount of booze might have just made his heart stop. Maybe he had some sort of heart condition? They don't seem to know." The others nod soberly, but Weasel is haunted. If only he'd stayed at the party.

"You know he'd never miss any of your games," he tells the others, an unbearable pressure squeezing his heart. "It didn't matter how far away it was – he'd find a way to get us there. Sometimes I'd be hungover and not feel like going, and he'd drag my ass outta bed and make me go with him." The others nod, but Weasel has more that he needs them to hear.

"He really liked being around you guys. So many people used to pick on us when we were kids – we didn't fit in anywhere, but you guys always stuck up for us whenever we needed you. That's why he would drive all the time – he'd do anything for anyone of you. He loved you guys." The four boys stare silently at the pile of dirt and flowers. Tears begin to stream down all their faces. They will miss their friend.

❑❑◆❑❑

USED TO ALWAYS BE THE SAME TWO GUYS sitting in an old aluminum boat with the ancient Mercury outboard, the motor that sometimes starts and other times acts like a piece of shit. Harry Baker bought them a long time ago, in another lifetime, but he doesn't have any use for the boat now. For Harry, once upon a time, fishing used to be a good excuse to cut out and have a few drinks. These days he doesn't need an excuse. So most often it was Weasel and Jordy dropping a line and Weasel drinking some beers. Maybe a little cannabis between them. But Jordy's not here today. And he won't be here tomorrow. That leaves Weasel staring at the boat and the water feeling reluctant to go out on his own. It just wouldn't be the same.

Weasel asks Tommy to come fishing with him only one day after they laid Jordy to rest. Tommy doesn't go fishing often, but he doesn't want Weasel to be alone.

So, today it's Tommy and Weasel on the lake. The old anchor holds them in one place, more or less. There's no current or wind to speak of near this part of the Sparrow Lake shoreline. Lots of rotting, submerged logs and weeds growing in the relatively shallow water. Ideal for bass.

Tommy can get a little bored if there's no bass action, but Weasel has endless patience when he has a line in the water. His orange hair creeps out from around his gaudy hat. The man likes colorful things and his headpiece is no exception.

"You're fucking going to scare the fish away with what you're wearing," Tommy flicks up his sunglasses for emphasis and squints at his fishing partner in the bright sunlight.

Weasel's hat is blue with a black brim, an almost psychedelic contrast with his hair. Three words stitched on the front of the hat.

"Who wears a hat like that?"

Weasel carefully lights up a joint, takes a long drag, and holds it. His eyes bulge out of his head before he expels the smoke in a steady stream from both nostrils.

"It has occurred to me that you're jealous. You wish you had a lid like this one, but you don't, and maybe you aren't even sure you would have the guts to wear it if you did have one."

"If you think I would ever contemplate wearing a hat with 'Playboy Talent Scout' written on it, you must have some brain damage from the extensive partying you have conducted over the years."

Tommy has been complaining to Weasel on their way over to the lake. About life in general, but also how Beau Henry is such a hard-ass and is always on his case. Tommy starts in again on the boat. "My old man was bugging me about what we were doing today. Asking if I was coming fishing just to booze. Fuck, he gets on my nerves."

For reasons of his own, Weasel has heard enough of it. "You know what, Tommy? I'm sick of your shit. Always fucking complaining about your dad. My dad's too mean to me. My dad's always bugging me about what I'm doing. I don't even know what the fuck my dad looks like! He sure as hell don't give a fuck about what I'm doing. Just be happy you have a fucking dad!"

Weasel's outburst stuns Tommy, who is rarely so serious and always looking to have a good time. So much so that his words seem out of place to Tommy. Advice that should have come from some deep thinker, not Weasel. Not the party guy who gets kicked in the balls and dropped by his former girlfriend. Not the loudest spectator at Hawks lacrosse games. Not the guy who mouths off to bouncers twice his size. *Shit, who's he think he is?*

"Weasel, why don't you stick to being an asshole? What the hell do you know about me anyways?"

Weasel stands up in the fishing boat, which is not recommended at any time. The boat rocks back and forth as he emotionally waves his arms over his head. But no words come out of his mouth. He takes a last puff from the roach and then flicks the sparking remnant like a daytime shooting star, arcing into the water. Tommy can't be sure but the redhead's eyes look moist. Tommy thinks it must be from the smoke.

"Fuck you, Tommy! You are one of the luckiest assholes I know, and you never stop crying about how tough you have it, how your dad is always watching over your shoulder, and you never think you're good enough for him. Never realize how good you got it because you're too busy bitchin' and moanin'.

"You know the difference between you and me, Tommy? You're going to do things with your life. You know why? Because your dad and your mom will make sure you have every opportunity. Hell, my dad didn't even stick around long enough to see me fucking born. My mom did her best, but life's not fair, Tommy. Who's going to look out for me? Well me, and maybe some of you guys if you're around, but it's mostly me, and it used to be Jordy. Well, not anymore. I loved that guy. Jordy was one of the few people who seemed to care about me. Now he's gone, and I'll never see him again. And the person I'm supposed to be telling this to is my dad, and he's not even fucking here!"

Now there is no question that those are tears coming out of Weasel's eyes. Streaks of moisture glisten on his cheeks as he sits down and takes a deep breath. But he's not finished. "You know why I used to spend so much time at your house when we were kids? Because I wished your dad was my dad. Someone to teach me how to play lacrosse, take me fishing. Hell, keep me outta trouble. Sure could've used that growing up around here. So you have an old man who's worried about what happens to you? Boo fucking hoo. Far as I know, that means your dad loves you. Could be a lot worse. But what the fuck would I know about it, right? You should be the happiest prick around here far as I'm concerned. Personally, I think you've got it so good it just about makes me sick. In fact, I feel like puking right fucking now."

Tommy's thinking about what Weasel just said. He did make a lot of sense. Maybe Tommy needs to hear this.

Just then, a splash of water appears out where Weasel's worm has been minding its own business. Weasel's line goes tight and starts to pull the fishing pole out of the bottom of the boat where it had been abandoned in the heat of the moment. The redhead leans precariously to one side, reaching for his escaping pole.

Tommy slides closer to Weasel and grabs his fishing pole and hands it to Weasel. "Well, you're the luckiest fishermen I know. Fucking asshole."

CHAPTER THIRTY

IT'S JUST A GAME

The Black Bear Diner is a favorite local eating spot with lots of booths and tables and even a couple of prized window spots looking out onto the main street. Red and white plastic tablecloths and a menu that has lots of burger options with some daily lunch specials. Today, you can get a toasted western sandwich with chicken noodle soup for $5.50. Even includes coffee. Breakfast all day if you want it. Ben considers it fine dining and drags Tommy, or whoever he can convince to go with him, every chance he gets. It's a seat yourself place, and Ben eyes one of the booths by the window. The previous customers have left, and the remainders of their lunch still sit on the table. French fries wearing ketchup and gravy that someone didn't have room or time for.

"That's what I like about this place. You always get enough to eat. Fills you right up," Ben comments cheerfully to Tommy. He's anxious to get seated so he can place his usual order, get the ball rolling. He wants the window seat, but he'll have to get it cleaned up first.

"Do you think we could get this table?" Ben points and then smiles at the server, a young woman delivering an order of food to another table. She is at least ten years younger than any other waitress in the establishment and stops to appraise the two young men standing in the entrance, blocking the doorway. Tommy stares at a sign that says, "Eat here or we'll both starve."

"Megan" reads the server's name tag with a hand-drawn happy face beside the name. She is also wearing a small smile. Perhaps shy. Perhaps small because she is just tired of being on her feet. "If you guys will move out of the doorway, I'll clean the table for you in a minute. You're not in a rush, are you?" Another weak smile.

Megan stands about five foot seven, bright-eyed with long hair to her shoulder blades, a lighter shade of brown, closer to a golden color. *Like brown sugar,* Tommy thinks. Delicate, almost fine features with a small beauty mark on her left cheek. He gets the impression Ben knows her, but he can't remember ever having run into her before. He sure would remember that face.

Megan swiftly removes the plates from the table and wipes it clean. Leaving menus on the table, she says, "If you want to look at the specials, they're on the chalkboard. I suspect you already know what you want, though." Her eyes roll over to Ben, who is seated and hasn't made any move towards the menus. "Be back in a minute."

Tommy checks out the specials while at the same time watching Megan walk away. "You know her?"

"Yeah. From the crowd my brothers used to hang out with. Megan Walker. She's a year older than us. Her mom is from Sparrow Lake but she married a white guy. Grew up in Huntington. Went to school there. She started going out with this dude who is really possessive so nobody around here has seen her much since then. Some big shot. He got a scholarship to play baseball somewhere out of state. Not sure why she's back working around here."

Tommy can hear a different tone in Ben's voice with that last line, but he doesn't know why or what to make of it. The sign on the wall above the cash register says: 'Today's menu: Take it or leave it." Tommy thinks he'll go for the fish and chips.

"Okay, guys. What fantastic meals do you have planned for yourselves? Do you want to start with appetizers?" Then Megan smiles as if she has just cracked a knee slapper of a joke. Tommy looks at Ben. Ben acts as if he hasn't heard Megan's attempt at humor and immediately launches into his order. "Chocolate milk, large, two double bacon cheeseburgers with the works, except for no onions but a side of onion rings. French fries come with that right? And coleslaw. A small coleslaw. The creamy slaw is so good here, but you don't want too much."

Megan's laugh rests frozen on her face as she listens to Ben's shopping list. She jots down a few notes and then turns to Tommy. "Are you just going to watch the show or did you want to order something too?"

"Fish and chips and a Pepsi. Thanks." Tommy looks at Megan's arm as she writes down the order. Specifically, the bruise on her left arm. Megan looks up suddenly and catches Tommy staring. She self-consciously folds her arms. Looking into her eyes, Tommy feels a little jolt. Like he's been caught spying over the neighbor's fence into their back yard. "Waitressing.

It can be a contact sport," Megan says abruptly. She then turns on her heel and heads to the kitchen.

Ben is a little puzzled. "What was that all about?"

Tommy suddenly isn't feeling very hungry anymore. "Man, I don't know. Shit is just screwed up for me right now. Everywhere I look it seems I see things that aren't supposed to be there. That I'm not supposed to see. I'm just happy to close my eyes at night sometimes."

Ben feels worried about Tommy. "You're not eating enough. Lack of food will do that to you. I just think you need to crush a good meal."

Tommy cannot stop watching Megan standing at the order counter. They lock eyes once when she glances back in their direction before taking some food to another table. From Tommy's vantage point, he can see everyone leaving and entering the Black Bear. The place seems popular with all ages. The older people spend more time eating and talking. The younger people eat faster, talk more quickly, and leave sooner.

Tommy is snapped out of his mini daydream by Ben's lunch order hitting the table. The cheeseburgers are like twin peaks glistening with grease and cheese. Slices of crispy bacon are being smothered by the cheese. There is a small mountain of French fries on the side of the platter. A satellite dish of onion rings is right next to the large soda fountain style glass of frothy chocolate milk. The modest bowl of coleslaw looks like an afterthought.

Ben wears the broadest smile humanly possible, and he pulls the plates closer to him like a poker player collecting his winnings. In comparison, Tommy's fish, chips, and Pepsi look like a Weight Watcher's order.

"You guys enjoy everything? Ben, I know you will. Let me know if you need anything else," Megan puts some extra napkins on the table. Tommy nods and smiles.

"Megan, this is Tommy by the way. A good buddy of mine and fellow excellent lacrosse player." It's as if it just dawned on Ben to be polite instead of being totally obsessed with his food.

Megan looks at Tommy with some exceptionally sparkly eyes, quite possibly green. "Nice to meet you, Tommy. A word of advice: don't get between Ben and his fork. It could be fatal." She touches Tommy's hand lightly and then heads over to start cleaning up a vacated booth.

Even though they have vastly different amounts of food, Ben and Tommy finish their meals at approximately the same time. As Ben sits there holding his stomach, Tommy takes the opportunity to go to the washroom before heading out.

While he's waiting, Ben decides to wave Megan over on impulse. "You know if you have some time on your hands this weekend, you might want to come and check out our lacrosse game this Saturday. We win this one and we're going to the State Championships."

Megan eyes Ben like a creature from another world, but then a thought crosses her mind. She does need to do some different things to get her life back on track. Even if just for a little while. "You know, Ben Lucas, I just might do that. On one condition: you have to win."

Ben laughs and hiccups at the same time. "I'll talk to Tommy about that. We just might be able to arrange something along those lines."

After paying, and as they are heading out the door, Tommy pauses to read one more dorky restaurant sign. This one says: "In case of emergency, pay your bill and run." He may come back to the Black Bear Diner sometime, but certainly not for the restaurant humor. As they are standing on the sidewalk outside the diner, letting their eyes get adjusted to the bright sunlight, Tommy sees Megan and a guy with dark hair talking in the parking lot. The conversation is obviously a heated one and not going well, but that's not what bothers them. The guy is gripping Megan by the arm. Her left arm. The argument is cut short when Megan pulls her arm away and stomps back into the restaurant through the back door. Ben and Tommy give each other a curious look before they leave.

CHAPTER THIRTY-ONE

TENSION

Tommy feels like one of the walking wounded. As if dealing with the deaths of Coach Blair and Jordy wasn't enough, add the whole ordeal with Jessica to the list. That would be enough to tip any normal person over the edge. But somehow, that's not the icing on the cake for Tommy. No, not by a long shot. Now he has to deal with having to continue to play on the same team as Shane. Shane's face makes Tommy itch to punch it, but he's trying to keep his cool. But when Tommy sees the dipshit standing in the locker room laughing with one of the other players, cool goes out the window. Something about that laugh, that smirk on Shane's face, flips a switch in Tommy. He walks over to Shane and gives him a firm, aggressive shove on the shoulder. "The fuck you laughing at?"

Tommy feels the blood rushing to his face. He knows what's coming. He has been there plenty of times before. How many underhanded things has Shane done behind his back? Not just to Tommy, but to all the other guys too. He couldn't care less that he and Jessica are done, but Shane broke a locker room code, which makes him a complete asshole.

Shane has a thunder cloud of a frown on his face as he turns to face Tommy. Before he can open his mouth to respond, Tommy's fist crunches solidly onto his temple. Nothing remains of the frown on Shane's face, just a wide-eyed look of fear. Shane has always been the type to mouth off and talk tough, but he's had his ass kicked plenty of times on the Rez. He knows if he actually tries to fight Tommy, he'd get fucked up, so he does his best to try to scurry away as some of the players break them apart.

"You've always been such a little bitch, Shane. Fucking pussy."

Coach Jenkins doesn't see the punch up, but he yells into the locker room for everyone to hurry up and get out to the field. Everything calms down and players quickly put their gear on. Out of the corner of his eye, Tommy notices Shane winces as he puts his helmet on over the egg already forming on the side of his head.

Tension ripples through the team, and as a result, more bad stuff rolls out from that. Shane does his best to stay as far away from Tommy as physically possible. The players are flailing around out on the field, missing easy passes, taking bad shots, just generally screwing up. Coach Jenkins is not anywhere close to being a Tim Blair. The same team that adored Coach Blair is the group that loathes Jenkins, and that makes the coach just a little more bitter than he is on a normal day. He knows what they think of him, but Coach Jenkins is the man now. He's in charge. No teenage know-it-alls are going to run his team. No sir.

He blows the whistle. Long and loud. In a way that just has to irritate anyone within earshot.

"Let's go, pick it up ladies!" he barks. "How 'bout we catch some of those passes here for a change? Offense!"

The drill continues, but it's clear that nothing is being learned. In other words, it's a complete waste of time. Jenkins sees a lot of anger directed toward Shane and wonders what the boy did to piss off the entire team. Teenage boys – you just never know what's going on unless you're on the inside looking out. Sighing, he gives the whistle a short, quick blast, calling them in.

"Offense, you're getting killed out there. Take a knee," he orders, and they do.

"Our next game is the State Semifinals. That's a big deal. If the team that showed up here today shows up again tomorrow, we're gonna get our asses kicked. It's too late in the season for a pep talk. I can't fix things with another practice. You either have it in you now or you don't," he says flatly. "You've got tonight to fix whatever is wrong. Think about it. Ball hunt, then pack it in. Ben."

Ben leads their cheer.

"Hawks on three… one, two, three, HAWKS!" they yell, but it sounds a little scraggly with no one sounding terribly convinced. Jenkins supposes that's only fitting – he's not so convinced either. *Fuck, Tim,* he thinks. *I can understand why you had a heart attack after years of coaching these prima-fucking-donnas, but they're not gonna get me.*

The players have their helmets off and jog around the field rounding up any stray lacrosse balls. As Tommy goes to join them, Coach Jenkins calls him over, his face is pinched with a grim look.

"Tommy, quite honestly these last couple practices are the worst I've ever seen you have. Now, you might think you're a good player, but this was godawful. You better get your head outta your ass real quick or it could cost us a State Title. You wanna be responsible for that?"

Tommy glares at him, pissed off enough not to try and hide it. He tries desperately to control his anger but struggles.

"You understand me?" demands Jenkins, taking a step closer, unflinching.

"Yeah," Tommy grits out, eyes dark with fury.

"Good," says Jenkins evenly, turning his back to Tommy abruptly and walking away.

Tommy glares at Jenkins walking away. His temper seethes in full flare, making him see red, but for a change, he is both conscious and ashamed of his impulse. Coach Jenkins may be an asshole, but he only has to put up with him for a little bit longer. That's not something he can change. His own anger, on the other hand, is something he will have to deal with for the rest of his life.

CHAPTER THIRTY-TWO

A SAFE PLACE

When the boys get home, James takes off to his room to do his homework. He likes sports, but he is also a studious kind of guy who takes pleasure in getting good grades. Tommy knows he'll never be as smart as his brother, and that's okay. Anything James achieves academically makes Tommy proud too.

Tommy drops his bag in the hallway and stands there motionless. He can't decide if he feels nervous or beyond calm. It could be he is just tired from the practice and dealing with Coach Jenkins. He feels like he is drifting, detached from his body. There is a lump in his throat, and all of a sudden, his mouth is dry. Then he knows that he is feeling more than fatigue. It's that sense of not being any good that always seems to creep back into his life. He and Hazel have talked about feeling empty. Where it comes from. Something that Hazel understands. That Tommy is beginning to understand as well. Hazel thinks it starts with Jen's abuse of him as a child. The wounds and scars left on him to grow up with. For the briefest moment he reflects back to his last session with Hazel. He can remember parts of it practically word for word.

"Tommy, you are on your healing journey now. That journey will bring you many good things, believe me. Part of the healing will be talking to your parents about it. When you talk with your parents, you need to feel that you are in control and that you are in a safe place. You choose the time to share and their job is to listen. This isn't about them. It's about you. But only when the time is right."

"Mom? Dad? Can I talk to you both for a minute?" he asks, hearing himself say the words but not recognizing his own voice. He knows that now is the time to talk as he enters the kitchen.

Marian hears the odd tone in Tommy's voice and pauses, part way between the sink and stove with a pot of water. She is making spaghetti for dinner, but suddenly she doesn't feel hungry. Tommy rarely says he has to talk to them, and Marian instinctually knows something is up.

Beau sets down the newspaper and intercepts his wife, setting the pot on the counter for her. Together, they sit down across from Tommy. Beau puts an arm around his wife.

"What's wrong?" Marian asks, the wrinkles around her eyes deepening.

"I got something I have to tell you," begins Tommy desperately, searching for the words. Marian closes her eyes, a variety of nightmare scenarios running through her head.

"It's okay, Tommy, you can tell us," says Beau.

"It's not gonna be easy to hear... something bad happened to me. It was a long time ago. When I was a little kid," he begins. And then it starts to gush out of him all at once.

"When I was like six or so, someone used to hurt me. It was our babysitter, Jen. When she first started to touch me, Jen told me it was just between us. That it's just a game. That we were only playing and that everything was going to be lots of fun. But she said I couldn't tell anyone, that what we were doing was our secret. If anyone found out, bad things would happen to me and to James. She said if I didn't want to play anymore then she would see how James liked the game. I just wanted to protect him from her so I didn't say anything. I was just a little kid. I didn't know what any of it meant, so I didn't say anything to anybody. And it happened again and again and again. So many times that it started to feel normal. I just never knew how to deal with it, and I thought now you should know."

Tommy is unaware that he's clenching both fists on the table as he talks. His voice has gotten louder and more agitated. At first Beau and Marian stare at their son, wide eyed, but then in unison they both reach over to quiet Tommy's hands. Tommy begins speaking again but much calmer this time.

"When I knew that I could talk with Hazel, she told me that I hadn't done anything wrong. Hazel understands what I feel, and she told me that part of healing is telling you. Letting you know and letting you try to understand. Sometimes when I do things, I just lose control. I know better, but I just can't stop. But I want it to stop, and I'm asking you to just try and understand."

Tears squeeze out of Beau's eyes as he remembers Tommy as a tiny little kid stuck to Marian's side, desperately clinging to his parents. *I don't want you to go.* But they'd gone. They'd gone out many times, leaving the boys with that girl. Not knowing.

Marian can't believe what she is hearing, that her little boy has been abused right under her nose and she never suspected a thing. She thought that Tommy was a typical kid not wanting to be left with a babysitter, not that he was afraid of who he was being left with.

By the end of Tommy's confession, all three of them have tears in their eyes, but the tears feel cleansing. There are some small smiles too, because now they realize that they are in a new place. A healthier place.

"I don't know where we go from here, but just know I love you both." Tommy watches his parents closely, holding his breath, waiting for a reaction.

Marian continues squeezing Tommy's hand. It seems like she doesn't ever want to let go. "We love you, too, Tommy," she says softly as she and Beau move to hug their oldest son.

Chapter Thirty-Three

FLOW OF THE GAME

"**W**hat is it that you don't understand? I just want to play baseball. It's what I'm good at, and that's all I want to do. I know I'm good enough to play pro ball and nothing is going to stop me from doing that." Ryan has a look of disgust on his face as if he is dealing with an unnecessary inconvenience.

"That's what I have to concentrate on. Not you, not being in a relationship. Nothing is getting in the way of my career. Fuck, Megan, grow up. This is the real world, not some fairy tale land where people play house and everyone lives happily ever after."

Ryan clutches Megan's left arm with his right hand. He is hurting her, and she jerks free of his grasp. Her voice quavers a bit with the sickening emotion she is feeling but trying not to let get in the way. "I thought we had a future, but I'll be fine without you, Ryan. Maybe you're the one who needs to do the growing up."

Ryan McDowell isn't happy that this is how things are playing out. He's the All-American kid, tall and handsome, success written all over him. He is used to having things his own way. At college in Ohio, the coaches are all high on Ryan and his fastball. He's a rising star. Another year or so and they say it's likely he'll be ready to sign a pro contact. The Show. He might get to play in the bigs. He's got stars in his eyes. Damn it, he is going to be a star. That's why no hometown girl can be allowed to have a stranglehold on him. No complications. Megan Walker, cute as she is, can't be allowed to derail his career before it's really even started.

"We're going to have to call it quits then. You just aren't being reasonable. I've told you before we'll try and keep this long-distance thing going, but if you're hell bent on having things your way, and me coming back here, then I'm sorry to say it's all over."

Megan struggles with the tears in her eyes, but she is determined not to let them fall. She is seeing a side of Ryan that is ugly. This is not the guy she first fell in love with. Not the Ryan that told her she was the best thing that had ever happened to him. Not the Ryan that told her he was going to make sure they stayed together no matter how far away they were. That their relationship was different and always would be. It's the Ryan she is now learning to hate.

The parking lot outside the Black Bear Diner isn't busy. Just a few cars, not too many people around. It doesn't seem like there is anyone to notice that two people are ending their lives together before they even really got started.

-◻-◻◆◻-◻-

HANK THOMAS AND ROBBIE REDBIRD are having a hell of a ride with the Hawks this season – there's never a dull moment in lacrosse. Just when you think you have a team figured out, they go and do something that turns conventional wisdom on its ear. So here they are in the playoffs. Hank's wife wouldn't agree with this, as she's sat through too many lacrosse games, but Hank still can't believe that his beloved Hawks have made it this far. He only wishes Coach Blair was alive to see it. Tim deserves to be here. He worked so hard to be here.

Switching his headset on, Hank starts the radio broadcast. The thrill of it almost makes him chuckle out loud but he limits himself to a grin instead.

"We're all ready to get the State Semifinal rolling here in Orrtown, and once again the Hoganton Hawks are doing battle with their arch-rivals, the Orrtown Wildcats. This is sure to be high school lacrosse at its very best. We're looking forward to an intense, hard-fought battle between two teams that are evenly matched, and on top of that, they don't much care for each other," he finishes, a massive understatement at best.

"I'm with ya on that one, Hank," agrees Robbie. "There is no love lost between these two schools; the last meeting was a very physical battle and we can probably expect more of the same today. Orrtown has had the Hawks' number in the last few meetings, and again with a berth in the State Final on the line, I think we're in for a dandy lacrosse game today."

Megan Walker and her friend Carli Thompkins sit among the capacity crowd at the Wildcats' field who have come to see two good teams butt heads and decide who punches their ticket to the State Finals. Everyone is talking, an expectant buzz in the air.

Meanwhile Weasel, Doobie Thomas, and Greg Cosay sit in a smoke-filled Dodge Ram pickup in the parking lot. What Weasel can really appreciate about Greg is the fact that he can lay his hands on his dad's truck occasionally. Weasel doesn't miss a Hawks game if he can help it, but transport isn't guaranteed since Jordy passed. Drugs can be an issue too, but Doobie has that covered this time. Orrtown is not Weasel's favorite place. It's a grimy old industrial town, big-time rough around the edges. Kind of place where you don't have to look for trouble. It most often finds you if you hang around long enough, especially if you have a Rez mailing address. So the boys always make sure any trip to Wildcats country is a quick in and out. That doesn't mean you don't enjoy the visit as best you can.

"This shit is good, Doobie, but I do not understand why you like these flavored rolling papers."

Weasel considers himself a purist and prefers his skins bland, the way nature intended people to smoke. Rum flavor has its place, but that's in a twenty-six-ounce bottle or a shot glass according to Weasel. Doobie sucks the last of his joint and flicks the roach out the truck window.

Greg chimes in, "I read somewhere that variety is the spice of life. Let's live a little, Weasel, and relax. The Hawks are gonna take this one. They're due. Way overdue."

Doobie looks through the slits of his eyes with a half-smile. "I didn't know you could read, Gregory." Nobody laughs or reacts to Doobie. It's like Greg and Weasel didn't hear him. He's used to that reception. Doobie just keeps on smiling.

Weasel's eyes are a little bloodshot, but he is ready to rumble. He opens his door and starts to step out.

"Let's go get some good seats. The Hawks won't know what to do if I'm not barking orders from the stands. This is the Semifinals and the boys may be feeling the pressure. I gotta get 'em fired up. Let's go."

Megan wasn't sure about coming to the game after Ben's invitation, but she decided to go based on just needing to get out and do some different things. Clear her head a bit. Also, her friend Carli is a very down-to-earth person who loves doing new things. Carli's philosophy? "Why the hell not check out a lacrosse game? I don't know the first thing about the sport, but I do know it's got cute guys running around, wearing shorts, trying to beat each other up. It's worth a look, don't you think?" Carli has a great sense of humor and Megan loves to laugh, so that's why they're in the stands behind the Hoganton bench.

Megan's relationship with Ryan is over. It feels like so much wasted time. Megan laughs to herself thinking about what her mother used to say about those Rez lacrosse guys. She always warned Megan about them and how they only cause you heartache. *Well how about those baseball players, Mom? Maybe you should have warned me about them, too.*

While Megan remains preoccupied with her thoughts, Carli actually enjoys the game, the crowd, and life in general. For her, it's all about having a good time. "Which one is Tommy and which one is Ben? Can you tell from here?"

Megan is squinting at the program. "Ben is wearing number seven and Tommy is number nine." Carli is wearing a sly smile. "Maybe they could hear us if we yelled their names. Give them a little encouragement." It seems a little bold to Megan, but both girls decide to give it a try. First number seven slowly turns, and smiles and then number nine bashfully follows.

THE BROADCAST BOYS obviously know what they're talking about and their assessment of the game is dead on. The match becomes physical right from the opening face-off as the teams are big, fast, and extremely athletic. Defense is the name of the game today. Both teams are extremely confident in their own end, throwing good stick checks and damaging physical hits often causing turnovers. The goaltenders are the last line of defense, the backbone of each team, making clutch stops one after the other, and keeping the game scoreless. The fans remain on the edges of their seats as the Wildcats try to pummel the less-organized Hawks into submission, but the Hawks refuse to be intimidated. This game has all the makings of a classic confrontation that will go right down to the wire.

"We're nearing the midway point of the first quarter and neither team has been able to get on the scoreboard," Hank Thomas says with an undercurrent of surprise creeping into his voice. The Hawks have a good goaltender, but the defense tends to let things slide and get a little loose. No goals against is a good thing, but the no goals for is also a by-product of Coach Jenkins' conservative offensive system that the Hawks players hate.

The players feel like he tries to make them into robots, doing everything by the book, like most of the teams they play against. Just seems to be a waste of their individual talent. Coach Blair let them do what came naturally to them, using their skill to light up the scoreboard, but it's obvious on the field that Coach Blair isn't around anymore.

"Both teams have played smart and tough in their own end," approves Robbie Redbird. "And when someone has been able to get a good shot off, these goaltenders, among the best in the state, have come up with the big save."

The three guys, Weasel, Doobie, and Greg, have been sitting relatively quietly up to this point. Not much to clap or yell about. Weasel is starting to feel the frustration. He doesn't play organized lacrosse anymore, hasn't for a long time, but he is still competitive in everything he does. If he's a spectator, then he's damned well going to make his presence known.

"Let's go, Hawks! You guys are sleepwalking. Come on, O, get us on the board here."

Some people in the crowd are eyeing Weasel suspiciously. Nobody wants to sit next to a loudmouth. A big man with a beer belly and shaggy, shoulder-length hair, wearing greasy camo pants and a Miller Lite ball cap starts to get up but a woman sitting next to him grabs his arm.

Then the flow of the game changes because of some great individual efforts. The Hawks get the ball into the Wildcats' end. Andy has the ball behind the net with a long stick defender covering him. He drives right with only his right hand on his stick, using his left arm to deflect the defenders' checks. He gets the defender chasing him and quickly rolls back, driving left and swiftly switching his stick to his left hand. As Andy rolls back, Tommy cuts to the front of the net. Andy sees him and throws a slick back hand pass right into Tommy's stick. Tommy catches the ball and immediately fakes toward the far side of the goal, making the goalie lunge the wrong way as he stuffs the ball into the top nearside corner.

Tommy and Andy sprint to each other, celebrating the goal as their other teammates join them. Shane runs up to Tommy with his fist out for a bump… and Tommy cuts him dead, turning away towards Steve, James, and Quinn.

"Andy Flint with a beautiful back hand pass inside to Tommy Henry who makes no mistake putting it in the cage to put the Hawks up 1-0," cheers Hank.

"Great dodge and feed. Those are the kinds of finesse plays we've come to expect from Andy Flint, a pinpoint pass to Tommy Henry who knows exactly what to do with the ball when he gets an inside look like that," analyzes Robbie, always looking to add a little extra color and insight to the broadcast.

When Tommy scores, both Carli and Megan jump to their feet and cheer. Megan notices she's standing shoulder to shoulder with an older woman with long, white hair in a single braid. She applauds and smiles. The woman looks at Megan as they are sitting back down. "You're Megan Walker, aren't you? I know your mom Michelle. How is she?"

Megan can't help but be drawn to the woman's aura. She seems to ooze friendliness and safety at the same time. Looking at her, Megan feels calm, almost tranquil even in the middle of the rowdy lacrosse crowd. Megan hasn't ever met anyone quite like her. "My mom is good. I'm not sure we've met, though. You are...?"

Hazel stretches her arm out and both women clasp hands gently for a moment. "I'm Hazel Blackwater. I've known your mother since she was a baby. I also remember you as a baby. You were a cute child, and you've turned out to be a very beautiful young woman. I've always loved babies, kids, watching them grow up. How about you?"

Megan feels a little taken aback by the question and her green eyes focus on the action on the field. She says the first thing that comes into her head. "I guess I do too." Megan is not quite sure why she said that, but just then the roar of the crowd at a second goal interrupts their conversation.

The Wildcats and Hawks begin to trade goals back and forth. The lead changes hands several times. It's a seesaw battle, but neither team is able to open up more than a one goal lead.

With 5:48 left in the fourth quarter, the Hawks are on the good side of a 7-6 score. Their defense causes yet another turnover and they clear the ball into the Wildcat end. Coach Jenkins calls a timeout, and the team goes to the sideline and gathers around Coach Jenkins.

He spells it out for them, scarcely able to believe that they haven't fucked things up more than they have. Maybe they'll manage to play like a team the rest of the way. Jenkins gathers the squad, telling them how he wants the rest of the game to go.

"Okay. Six minutes left: slow the play down, move the ball around, and take as much time as we can off the clock. I don't want them to get the ball back for the rest of the game. Even if we get called for stalling, just keep it in the box – don't go to the net, don't shoot."

That directive brings a few looks of surprise. The natural inclination of the players is to keep playing the way that got them the lead in the first place. Go to the net. Put the ball in the cage every chance you get. So, of course, someone has a question for the good Coach.

"Ain't there too much time, Coach?" Tommy asks. "We can go to the net if we get a good match up, right?"

"No, are you fucking deaf, Henry? I said kill the fucking clock and we win this thing," he insists. Coach Jenkins is a very conservative, defense-first oriented coach, which is a boring contrast to what the lacrosse players from how Sparrow Lake are used to playing.

Tommy looks sideway at Andy, who just shrugs his shoulders. The coach has spoken. The play starts, and the Hawks move the ball around the outside trying to waste as much time as possible.

Hank nods as the players maneuver – it's pretty clear what Coach Jenkins wants them to do: play it safe these last few minutes.

Weasel is standing up, watching the play like he's scrutinizing a virus under a microscope. He has a sour look on his face. "Are you serious? Trying to kill the clock already? They can't win if the ball is in their net. Let's go here!"

"The Hawks are moving the ball around the outside, trying to take as much time off the clock as possible. The Orrtown bench is yelling at the official, looking for a stall call. And the ref raises his arm and signals a stall. That means the Hawks are going to have to keep possession of the ball inside a more restricted area in the offensive end. If they go outside of the box, Orrtown will get possession," warns Hank.

The ball comes to Tommy, who is chased by his defender and pushed right to the edge of the restraining box. Tommy is narrowly able to tip toe the line and avoid going outside the box, which would give Orrtown the ball. Tommy moves the ball up top to Quinn Harris.

After a pick inside, Andy has a short-stick defender guarding him as he catches the ball on the left wing. When Andy gets the ball, he sees he has a mismatch and so does Tommy.

"Go! Go to the net!" bellows Tommy, breaking into a run. On the side-lines, Coach Jenkins is ready to blow a gasket.

"No! Keep it outside!" he yells, wishing he could take a stick to the outside of that Henry kid's head. Maybe that would get his attention.

The Orrtown defense sees the mismatch and are able to get a switch so a long stick defender is back covering Andy.

"Whoa! Don't see that too often. Andy Flint had the ball, was covered by a short-stick defender and didn't take him to the cage, choosing rather to keep the ball outside and chew up more clock time. Coach Jenkins was yelling from the sidelines not to take his defender," Hank remarks.

"Don't know if I like that call," Robbie skeptically admits. "Still a lot of time left on the clock and they already have the stall call against them. Maybe the best one-on-one dodger in the state with a good match-up and you don't let him go to the goal? Might have missed a chance to make something happen and possibly go up by two. I hope that doesn't come back to haunt them."

"The Orrtown defense also saw the mismatch, though, and were quickly able to pull a switch to get a long pole defender back on Flint," Hank reminds Robbie.

The ball goes behind the Orrtown cage to Steve McCrae. As he catches the ball the goaltender comes running out of his net to help the long stick defender on Steve. They double team him. They have the Hawks player hemmed in as he runs to try avoiding them, but the long stick defender is able to hit McCrae's stick and knock the ball to the turf. The goaltender picks up the loose ball, and Orrtown is able to clear it out of their end, getting the ball to their offense in the Hoganton end. After a good possession, an Orrtown midfielder dodges a Hawks short-stick defender from up top. The defense slides to help their beaten defender. The Orrtown player throws it inside to a player left open and he puts the ball in the net, tying the game up at 7-7. At the other end of the field, Tommy and Andy look at each other both shaking their heads in disgust knowing that the Jenkins strategy just cost them the lead.

Fuck sakes, Tommy thinks to himself.

Weasel is up on his feet again. "Come on, Jenkins, you're killing us. Take the handcuffs off, coach!"

"Big face-off coming up here as we're locked at 7s with 2:34 remaining," Hank calls out.

"The Hawks really need one here. They have been led offensively today by Andy Flint with three goals, Tommy Henry has two, and sophomore Quinn Harris, who has really come on late in the season, also adding two.

But they need at least one more if they wanna move on to the State Title game," Robbie warns. He loves the Hawks, but he knows their penchant for screwing things up at the last minute – and this would certainly qualify if they can't come back.

The face-off is a mad scramble, but a long stick mid-fielder for the Hawks comes up with and gives the ball to Shane, who carries it into the offensive zone. The ball is moved around, and Quinn dodges from up top and passes to Tommy. Tommy lets go a shot that sails wide, but Andy is closest to where the ball went out so the Hawks keep possession with 1:37 remaining.

The ball is jockeyed around, and again the ball is up top. Shane dodges one short-stick defender and takes a shot. The goalie gets a piece of the shot and the ball is loose on the ground. There is a vicious scramble to get possession of the ball, and Tommy is successful with 49 seconds left on the clock. He moves the ball to James who passes behind the net to Andy. Andy dodges to his left, drawing two defenders to him. He rolls back to his right and passes to Steve McCrae, who is now behind the net. Steve dodges to his right as Quinn calls for the ball. Steve passes in front of the net to a cutting Quinn Harris, who catches and shoots all in one motion.

The ball goes in, and the crowd explodes out of their seats, screaming themselves hoarse. The Hawks lead 8-7 with just seconds on the clock.

"Quinn Harris! Quinn Harris has scored!" yells Hank into his mike, beaming from ear to ear. "And the Hawks lead 8-7 with 23 seconds left!"

"Both teams are out of time-outs; if Hoganton comes up with this face-off, they should be able to run out the clock. If Orrtown gets possession, they will have to quickly go to the goal," cautions Robbie.

Off the next face-off, there's another wild scramble for the ball and Orrtown comes up with it, only 16 seconds left on the clock. Hank and Robbie are holding their breaths, intent on the distant players.

An Orrtown short-stick player gets the ball, and the Hawks rush back to defend their goal. The ball is moved to an attack man who passes into the middle, and the pass is caught by an Orrtown player who shoots, desperate to beat the clock.

Devin Clarke makes a stick save and runs behind his net. With five seconds left, he lofts the ball all the way to the other end of the field as the clock runs out and the horn sounds to end the game.

Weasel, Greg, Doobie, and many others have been standing and applauding during the last few minutes of the game. Weasel is almost beyond words. Almost.

"Hawks fucking rule! I can taste the State Championship now. C'mon, boys, let's get out of this dump."

The fans are ecstatic and red Hawks pennants are being waved all over the field. It's been a long time since the Hawks pulled something like this off. Time to celebrate.

Hank and Robbie are backslapping each other and cheering along with the rest of the fans. Eventually, Hank recovers himself enough to finish the commentary.

"Devin Clarke with another save to end the game… and the Hoganton Hawks are going to the State Finals!" he triumphantly bellows.

As the spectators begin to leave the stands, Megan and Carli find themselves walking out with Hazel. The three of them stop to congratulate some of the Hawks players who haven't yet left the field for the dressing room.

Ben has a broad smile on his face. "You see, Megan? I told you Tommy and I might be able to arrange a win if you came to the game."

Carli is laughing at the comical expression on Ben's face. It's a look of sheer delight coupled with a frown that tries to make a serious point. While Megan talks to Tommy for a minute, Carli gets up the courage to ask Hazel something that has been bothering her since the three of them were chatting in the stands during the game.

"Hazel, are you one of those new agers? Like a hippie sort of? No offense, but you seem like you might be into meditation and yoga and all that stuff."

Hazel flashes a quick smile in Carli's direction but never takes her eyes off Tommy and Megan. "Carli, I'm not a new ager. If anything, I'm what you might call an old schooler. I believe in connections, that everything is connected. Sometimes you just have to figure out how and why."

IT'S SAFE TO SAY that after the Hawks win the match over Orrtown and sail into the State Finals, there are few sober people among Hoganton's lacrosse fans as well as the Sparrow Lake Nation's lacrosse community. Parties extend throughout the night, and none of the twenty-four Hawks players have to buy their own drinks. They are heroes. For tonight.

Harry Baker, however, is not a hero. He's just a quiet drinker cruising down a gravel Rez road in a pickup truck as the sun is beginning to rise. The pickup that his son Jordy died in. Since Jordy's death, Harry has not been sober very often. Sometimes he falls asleep long enough to wake up and start remembering, but a few beers help chase the memories away. Or at least dulls them so they don't hurt as much. Sometimes, when he's very drunk, he sits in the truck and talks to Jordy.

Harry drinks a beer as he pulls into his driveway. There's a mouthful left, so he finishes it and tucks the bottle into a case with the rest of his empties. The case is full of them, though he doesn't really remember drinking them all. He turns off the ignition and stumbles out of the truck, tears swimming in his red-rimmed eyes. He's thought about getting rid of the vehicle, but he can't bear to sell it – it's his last connection to his son.

When he walks in the kitchen door, Cash is waiting for him, whining anxiously and bumping up against Harry's unsteady legs.

"Quit it, boy. You're as bad as an old woman," he teases the dog, ruffling his ears. The dog wags his tail but continues to look around uneasily. Harry looks up from undoing his shoes, and notices that something is different.

Shelby's coats and shoes are gone. All of them. Her grandmother's antique rocking chair that usually sits by the window. In the kitchen, her favorite coffee mug. All missing.

He walks to the bedroom, and the sight confirms it for him. Their closet doors are open, and her clothes have all been removed. Only his are left, taking up a lonely third of the closet. All of her toiletries have been scooped from the bathroom. Most of the family pictures on the walls are gone, although she'd left him a single family shot from three years ago. It sits on their dresser, across from the bed.

Shelby had put her foot down that day and insisted that they get a family picture, and so she'd dragged Jordy and Harry to a studio. A bored female photographer had them pose in front of a blue background, reminding them over and over to smile. Jordy sat in front of and between his parents, white teeth gleaming against his deep brown skin. His black hair was due for a haircut, but he looked happy. Jordy almost always looked happy.

Shelby looked very elegant in a tailored blouse and long skirt, the deep blue of her shirt setting off her dark eyes and black hair. Harry couldn't read her expression, then or now.

Harry remembers he was half hungover in the picture, but he stood as straight as possible, an arm around his wife and a hand resting on his son's shoulder. His eyes were a little bloodshot, his grin goofy, and his shirt rumpled, but at the time, he'd thought he'd pulled it off.

He could see later that he hadn't fooled anyone.

Sitting on his bed, holding the picture, Harry breaks into body-convulsing sobs. First, he loses Jordy and now Shelby. Cash comes over and places his massive head on Harry's lap. Harry pets Cash's head and realizes the Rottweiler is the only family he has left.

Chapter Thirty-Four
WHAT THE FUCK

Back at school on Monday, Tommy and Ben are killing time by hanging out at their lockers.

"Only one more to go," says Tommy, stating the obvious, closing his locker and popping the lock back on.

Ben nods, but there is impatience in his voice. "Yeah, man. I just wanna get through these last few practices and get to the game. State fucking Title game!" Ben replies, picking up his backpack. He can't quite believe they've made it this far, especially with everything that has happened.

"You talk to Andy at all?" Tommy shoots the question at Ben with raised eyebrows.

"Yeah, he said he's staying straight 'til after the game."

"Good. Well, I gotta get to class. Later." As Tommy heads off in the opposite direction for Math class, he pauses, feeling someone staring at him from behind. It's Jessica, about to enter a classroom. She gives him an awkward look but manages a small wave before heading to class. The two of them have not spoken since the blowout on the bleachers, and Tommy has a gut feeling that there is too much animosity now for them even to be friends. It's a relief to be honest. Especially with himself. Tommy knows he's struggling with his issues, but Jessica has her own problems that she'll have to figure out someday as well. Tommy knows from listening to Jessica talk, especially when she's had a few drinks, that she misses her dad. Feels abandoned by him, really. Even through no fault of his own. She has never gotten over losing her father when she was just a little girl. Jessica's mother Vicky was so busy keeping the family together that there was no time for another man in her life to be any type of father figure for Jessica and her sister. She always saw it as unfair and cruel that she lost her dad. Her sadness could quickly turn to anger. Anger that would cause her to lash out at Tommy sometimes.

-ロ-ロ♦ロ-ロ-

ANDY SLOWLY DRIVES his father's truck out of Hoganton, creeping back towards Sparrow Lake. He had not been able to keep his promise to the guys. He had gone to visit Tara at her apartment, but instead of going straight home, he stopped at a little hole in the wall bar where he figured no one would recognize him. He thought he would only have a couple of drinks, but it turned into quite a few more. Andy reaches a stoplight and when the light turns green, he makes a right-hand turn. Doing his best to keep the truck steady, he takes the turn too tight and nudges the curb as the truck's back wheels ride up on the sidewalk. Andy gets the truck steady and keeps cruising down the street, hoping nobody saw his mishap. Just as he comes to the edge of town, he sees flashing lights in his rearview mirror. As he pulls the truck over to a stop, he thinks, *Fuck, why didn't I just go home?*

The officer walks over to the truck as Andy rolls the window down. "You been drinking, sir?"

"Just a couple," states Andy.

Andy feels nervous. He knows there is no way the officer doesn't smell the booze on his breath. As Andy goes to step out of the truck, his foot slips and he stumbles. If the cop had any doubts that Andy was hammered before, he doesn't now. The cop grabs Andy's wrist.

"Okay, buddy. You're under arrest," the officer says, reaching for his handcuffs.

Andy yanks his wrist away. "Fuck off," he growls really not thinking straight.

The officer then pushes Andy against his truck in an attempt to subdue him. In his drunken state, Andy starts flailing his arms in a vain attempt to get away. The cop throws Andy on the ground, pins him, and almost effortlessly gets his wrists into the handcuffs. Andy lays on his stomach with his hands cuffed behind his back, thinking about just how much shit he's in now. *What the fuck?*

-ロ-ロ♦ロ-ロ-

THE NEXT DAY, Tommy and James arrive at school for morning classes only to get pulled into a huddle with Ben, Troy, and Clarkie.

"What's up?" asks Tommy.

"Andy got arrested last night," Ben says soberly.

"Got pulled over coming back from a bar. Now he's in the Hoganton jail. He got into it with the cop, and it sounds like he ain't getting out in time for the game," Troy adds, and Tommy's heart sinks to his shoes. How the hell could they play without Andy? They were fucked.

"Coach Jenkins is talking to a lawyer in the office, trying to figure out what's going on," says Ben, just as Quinn Harris joins the group.

"Coach wants to see the captains in his office," he announces. So, Tommy, Troy, Ben, and Clarkie head to the office.

"You guys may have heard, but Andy got arrested last night. This is Mr. Kaline, the lawyer Andy's family hired to represent him. Mr. Kaline has explained to me that Andy's been charged with multiple offenses and may not be able to play in the State Championship game for a variety of reasons," he finishes, lip curled in disgust.

"Can't he be like, bailed out?" demands Clarkie with more than a little hysteria in his voice.

The lawyer perks up. This is where his expertise comes in. Even if it doesn't help much. "The Hoganton police chief is flatly not letting him out until Mr. Flint can see the Judge, who is conveniently not seeing anyone until Monday. The arresting officer said Mr. Flint took a swing at him, so he has been charged with driving while intoxicated and assaulting a police officer. I am trying to get him out of custody, but it doesn't look possible to have him released within forty-eight hours, in time for the game."

Coach Jenkins holds up a hand as the rest of the boys begin to ask a barrage of questions. "Look, guys, I don't need you to argue Andy's case. I just called you in here to let you know what the situation is. Now, Mr. Kaline is doing what he can, but if Andy got himself into this mess, then that's his problem. We have to be ready to play the State Final game without him."

The guys leave the office, shocked.

"Man, we're gonna have to play our asses off now," mopes Troy sadly, knowing just how difficult the game is going to be with Andy in the line-up, never mind playing the game without him.

CHAPTER THIRTY-FIVE

A SECOND CHANCE

The sign says: "Visitor parking this way." Tommy follows the direction and wheels the truck into the first available space. His head pounds like a drum with an intensifying headache and no aspirin. That's not a good start to his first time hanging out with Megan. He's talked casually with her a few times, but this is the first time one-on-one. See what happens. Maybe his head feels like splitting because he's taking things too seriously. He should loosen up. Sometimes a drink helps do that, but he's not drinking. He promised himself that. Not that he's quit alcohol totally, but he's just a little sick of it considering everything that has happened recently. That's what he's telling himself anyway, and it's easier that way.

The campus isn't large. Ralston College can't have more than a couple of thousand students at most, and it's located outside of town in the countryside, so it has a very casual atmosphere. Students walk in all directions, but there's no hustle and bustle. Tommy likes that. He can take a breath and feel a relaxing vibe all around him. The throbbing in his head lets up just a little as he swings the truck door open and steps out.

"Tommy Henry, what the hell are you doing here?"

The voice is familiar, and when Carli Thompkins steps into his line of vision, Tommy smiles right away. Carli is a laugh, a fun person to be around, and Megan's best friend. They both go to Ralston, so Tommy wonders if it's just a coincidence that Carli is in the vicinity.

"I'm picking up Megan. There's a band that I know playing at a bar in Ralston, so we thought we could check them out together."

Carli stands right around Tommy's height, strongly built with blunt cut blonde hair to her shoulders. Her attractive, lightly freckled face looks like she is always ready to break out into a smile, and that's not far wrong. She reaches over and gives Tommy's arm a little slap.

"You be gentle with her. She's been through a lot recently. Her ex was a jerk. I don't want her to get hurt again." Carli smiles but Tommy knows she isn't joking.

"Maybe you could join us later. Keep an eye on me. Make sure I'm not another asshole." As Tommy is saying this, he's hoping Carli will laugh. He wants Carli on his side.

Carli does laugh, finally. "I just might do that. Who's the band?"

"It's a bunch of guys who have been around forever. They're called 'The Breeze.' They do a lot of classic rock covers with a little bit of blues thrown in. But I gotta get moving or this will be over before it gets started. See you later?"

"Maybe. Say hi to Megan." Carli continues smiling, but Tommy has received the message loud and clear.

The Alward is a bit of a dive, but the atmosphere doesn't bother Megan or Tommy. He's seen worse, and she is more intent on people watching and soaking up the atmosphere.

"Drinks?"

They have a small table about halfway back from the tiny stage. Tommy wonders how they cram a four-piece band in the limited space. He just knows it's going to be loud. They've got a little while before the band comes on, so they're just settling in.

Megan laughs. "Drinks? I'll have a double. Actually, a glass of ice water and a ginger ale would be fine."

Tommy starts to ask her if she's serious, but then thinks better of it and just heads to the bar. As he is getting the drinks – a large Pepsi is his poison of choice – the band's roadie starts the mandatory, "Check, check," with the microphones. It's kind of funny to think The Breeze has a roadie now. The guys used to hump their own gear and even wrote a song about it. Tommy just shakes his head.

Back at the table, Megan stares in disbelief at Tommy's glass. "Rum and coke. I didn't picture you as that sort of guy."

Tommy shakes his head and takes a sip. Smacks his lips. "No, it's just straight Pepsi. I'm on the wagon for a bit. See how it goes, you know? Maybe I'll turn into an AA counselor. That could be my career. Already know a few people who could be clients."

Megan chuckles as she uses her straw to spin the ice cubes around in the ginger ale. "I'm taking a break from it, too."

An awkward silence fills the air between them. Tommy wants to ask her why she's not drinking, but just then the band hits the stage. There isn't going to be any more talking for a while as the musicians crank up one of their favorites. You might call it their signature tune. Tommy has heard it so many times he knows all the words by heart. It's "Come and Get Your Love" by Redbone.

Tommy doesn't want to let Megan's last comment go, so he leans into her ear and basically shouts over the thumping music "Why are you taking a break from drinking?"

Megan drums her hand on the table in time to the beat. She stops and leans over to Tommy's left ear. "You shouldn't drink while you're pregnant. It's not healthy for the baby."

All of a sudden Tommy isn't hearing the band's hypnotic rhythm any more. He's not sure he's heard Megan right. The music is being squeezed out by the racing thoughts in his head. *What the fuck?*

TOMMY REACHES OVER and turns off the truck's ignition. It's relatively quiet now on campus except for some music coming from one of the student residences. There wasn't much serious conversation at the club because the music was so loud it sucked up most of the available air waves. Even during breaks, it was a real party atmosphere with loud clubbers having a fun night out. In retrospect, maybe The Alward wasn't the best place to go to get to know each other better. Tommy and Megan had decided not to stay for the last set because she has an early class in the morning.

"Tommy, I guess one thing I've been thinking about since you and I have been talking is… what really happened between you and Jessica? Lots of things get said. Maybe you can tell me. That's if you want to. No obligations."

Tommy has been looking for a way to talk with Megan about Jessica and now has his chance. He can also read between the lines. He knows what no obligations means. If he doesn't want to talk about his ex, then he might as well kiss Megan good bye. And he wouldn't blame her. All the gossip that flies around a small community can get out of hand. Tommy knows he is no saint, but realizes that he has to come clean with Megan.

"Our relationship was up one day and down the next. That's about the only way I can describe it. We got into way too many arguments, too often, that mostly ended badly. I think jealousy was a problem for both of us.

You're going to ask me if it's true that I put my hands on her? Yeah, it is. Was I provoked? It doesn't matter. It was one of the biggest mistakes of my life. We didn't part on great terms, but I think Jessica has some things she needs to work through. Same with me. I know I have a bad temper, but I'm working on it. I know it's a big problem, but I'm trying to deal with it."

Megan watches Tommy's face intently. He knows that and wants to meet her green eyes, but he has something else to say before he can do that. "This might sound strange, but I think that everything happens for a reason. I know we don't know each other that well, but I believe everyone should have second chances. Who knows? Maybe you're my second chance. If that doesn't sound too weird."

They look into each other's eyes now as Megan leans over to give Tommy a quick kiss on the cheek. Before she pulls away to get out of the truck, Megan whispers in his ear. "Maybe I need a second chance, too. See ya, Tommy."

CHAPTER THIRTY-SIX

GOOD MIND STRONG HEART

Weasel misses a lot of things about Jordy – shit, they'd known each other since kindergarten. But one of the things he misses is Jordy having a car and always being sober and willing to drive. He never had to worry about that after Jordy got his license. Now the State Title game is on the line tonight, and here he is flat on his ass. Stranded, Greg couldn't get his dad's truck this time, so the boys have no vehicle to get to the game. His phone beeps, and he glances at the screen.

"Shit, everybody either has no room or can't find a ride themselves! Kraze just texted me looking for a ride," he complains. Kraze is short for Krazy Kirk. They call him that because he talks so much nonsense about sports. He thinks he's a genius at fantasy football, but really his head is so far up his ass he can't even acknowledge that he's never actually won any of the many leagues he plays in. Weasel is hanging out on his mom's porch with several acquaintances, trying to score a ride to the game. None of them are having any luck.

"Shawn just texted me for a ride too," gloomily reports Doobie Thomas. His real name is Dwayne, but nobody uses it.

"Shit! No fucking way I'm missing this game," Weasel declares, standing up. He heads into the house and loudly opens and slams the fridge door. His mother is in her room in the back of the house – probably watching TV.

"Hey, Ma! We're outta milk! I'm gonna take the car and get some more!" he bellows, heading toward the door.

"There's milk in the fridge – I just got it two days ago!" she yells back. Weasel opens the fridge, grabs the mostly full carton of milk and begins pouring it down the sink.

"Nope, it's all gone!" he calls as the last of it gurgles down the drain.

"Well, take that money on the counter and grab me some smokes too," she replies.

"Okay," he calls, scooping up a ten dollar bill along with the keys off the counter. They're in business. He exits the kitchen and grabs the guys. "Let's go."

"Shotgun!" whoops Greg, heading toward the passenger's side. Doobie and Danny Onions grumble, but they pile in the back. They know Greg can be a dick sometimes, so it's better he's in the front with Weasel. Weasel doesn't tolerate any shit, unless it's his shit.

Weasel glances at the gas gauge and cusses. The son of a bitch is running on fumes. "Shit, how much money you guys got for gas?"

They dig through their pockets and come up with a combined jackpot of $35 in crumpled bills.

"It's a four-hour drive – that might be enough to get us there and halfway back," Greg remarks from the passenger seat.

"We got room for one more. Text Shawn and Kraze – see if either of them has money to chip in for gas," orders Weasel, driving toward the Rez's gas station.

He puts in $35 worth and pays. When he gets back in the car, he gets an update from his crew.

"Shawn just texted me back and said he's got money for gas," announces Danny Onions from the back seat.

Weasel smiles. "Good. Kraze gets on my fucking nerves anyway."

He pulls out of the gas station and heads toward Shawn's house. "Text Shawn and tell him we'll be there in a bit."

"Hey, Kraze just texted me back. He said he doesn't have any money, but he's got a lot of weed," informs Onions.

Weasel hits the brakes. He executes a perfect three-point turn and heads in the opposite direction. "Sorry, Shawn. Tell Kraze we're on our way."

THERE'S A KNOCK ON THE LOCKER ROOM DOOR as the Hawks start getting into their pre-game gear – shorts and T-shirts. It's early, but Tommy's been expecting this, and he opens the door to chat briefly with the person before turning back to the roomful of players.

"Let's go, guys! Outside," he calls, and they all get up quickly and follow him to the middle of an empty field. Everyone feels a little nervous. The State Title match is an away game hosted at the Walkersville facilities.

Hazel Blackwater and Reg Harris are waiting for them in the middle of the empty field, where Reg has made a small fire. Hazel and Reg have a special bond as Hazel has taught Reg a lot about his role as a faithkeeper for the people of Sparrow Lake.

The players gather around, faces solemn.

Reg's face is anything but solemn. He smiles broadly and looks each player in the eyes, one at a time. "I'm here to help prepare you for what is about to come. First of all, I want to remind you what this game means to all of us. This game you are about to play is a gift from the Creator and is to help our wellbeing. This game was given to us to heal, not to harm. When we play this game, we entertain the Creator. When we play this game intensely, but fairly, the Creator smiles and blesses us with our good health. Lacrosse helps cleanse our bodies and clear our minds. I'm going to ask the Creator to watch over your mind and body, that he keep players from both teams free from harm. I'm going to ask him to help remove negative thoughts. I'm going to request he give you strength and to cleanse anger from you. I'm going ask you be allowed to play this game with a good mind and a strong heart, the way it was meant to be played. As the tobacco burns, the smoke carries our thoughts to the Creator. So I want you to think of all the things that have caused you pain, made you angry, and this will help rid you of those things that are holding you back from your good mind," he concludes, opening a small pouch and gently tossing tobacco into the fire. He begins to speak in Mohawk.

As he does, the players remain quiet, staring intently at the burning tobacco and the rising smoke. They all have thoughts that need the Creator's attention. Tommy thinks of Andy sitting in a jail cell and missing the biggest game of his life. He thinks about the knife lodged firmly in his back at the hands of one of his own teammates. He fondly remembers Coach Blair and how proud he must be with them making it to the State Title game. Megan and the child she is carrying flash through his mind for a second. He feels a warm connection with her. He thinks of how he misses Jordy's smiling face and the ache in his heart. He can feel tears forming in his eyes and does his best not to let them fall. *Why does the world have to hurt us so bad sometimes?*

Then Tommy thinks about today and what everyone on the team has been striving for all season. The State Finals. You've got to put everything else out of your head now. You have to play with a good mind and a strong heart. The way it was meant to be.

The smoke trails a bit thicker now, rising, soaring it seems, with a mind of its own. Hazel has her eyes closed listening to Reg's words. She knows how hard it can be to let the bad things go. She also knows how good it can be. Hazel hopes the boys can feel that too.

A TREMENDOUS ROAR EMITS FROM THE CROWD as the Hawks burst through a banner and sprint out onto the field, whooping and hollering. The adrenaline pumps through them, and the players are feeling charged up. Many of their fans have made the four-hour drive from Hoganton, and the stands shake under the roar of approval from the Hawks side, red pennants waving madly. The Hawks fans are still outnumbered though, which doesn't bother Weasel in the least.

"Tender is Swiss cheese; he's full a holes!"

The goaltender for Walkersville is a big kid with long hair flowing out from under his helmet, and Weasel has decided he's going to try get in the kid's head. A group of Walkersville fans look over, shooting daggers in Weasel's direction. The Rez's mouthpiece is in fine form today, though, and considers heckling one of the highest art forms.

The Walkersville media booth is a slick operation, much more high-tech than the one at the Hawks' home field. Hank Thomas and Robbie Redbird are torn between grudging admiration and their natural competitive dislike of the Bulldogs. Settling into a comfortable chair by the controls, Hank resigns himself to admiration. Even the coffee is a notch above. He elbows Robbie, indicating that he is about to begin, and the second broadcaster grabs a chair next to him. They have a fantastic view of the field.

"Here we go, folks! This is another edition, a very special edition of Hawks lacrosse. Today's contest is brought to you in part by the Black Bear Diner. This week featuring the Black Bear cheeseburger blue plate special. Remember there is nothing finer than the Black Bear Diner." Hank is in his element. No place he'd rather be. "The Hoganton Hawks and the Walkersville Bulldogs are about to go head to head for all the marbles. The 2003 State Title is up for grabs today. This is Hoganton's first trip back to the State Final in twenty-two years, while Walkersville are the three-time defending State Champions."

The two teams line up for the "Star-Spangled Banner." Their faces are intense, so serious that some of them seem to be scowling as the National Anthem ends. The first ten players from each team line up for instructions from the refs. Once the refs lay out the ground rules, the teams shake hands in a customary gesture of sportsmanship. The atmosphere is so tense that the buzz of the spectators in the stands crackles like a whip of electricity in the air as the two teams get ready to play what will be, for many of them, the biggest game of their lives.

Andy hunches over, feeling the pressure of the cruel finger of fate in his jail cell. What happens when Hoganton gets to the finals for the first time in twenty-two years? Andy ends up in a jail cell, unable to play or even watch it from the sidelines. He can't stop thinking that all he had to do was go straight home. Andy was having a really hard time with the loss of Jordy, and he thought a couple drinks might help. Turns out they didn't help anything.

One of the guards is apparently an ex-lacrosse player and has the radio tuned to the sports station covering the game. The well-known voices of Thomas and Redbird fill the air, and with the roar of the crowd Andy can't decide if this constitutes torture, or whether he's grateful to be able to hear it as it happens.

"The big story for the Hoganton Hawks is they will be without All-American Andy Flint. Some personal legal problems are preventing him from being here today. So that's a large piece of their offensive game gone from the line-up. The Hawks will attempt to compensate with sophomore James Henry stepping into the starting role on the attack. Henry has some experience, but the question is whether he can fill Flint's rather large shoes," says Hank. On the drive out, he'd noticed that the police chief's house had been egged by diehard Hawks fans.

"Flint is a big loss for the Hawks, and they will have to find a way to run their offense and put up some goals without him. Good teams find a way to win when adversity strikes. Now we'll see just how good, and deep, the Hawks really are," Robbie analyzes.

Walkersville gains control of the ball on the opening face-off, and after a good offensive set, punch one in to make it 1-0. They are known for a relentless, hard-hitting style. They have a proud tradition, and they aren't about to let anyone take their title away easily.

After the second face-off, the Bulldogs easily score again, making it 2-0.

The Hawks double down, and pick up the next face off, working the ball around the field and just trying to get on the board. Steve McCrae takes the ball behind the net and manages to dodge his guard. Turning sharply, he fires at the net – just as a Walkersville defenseman crashes into him. The goalie is cat-like quick and deflects the ball with a foot, leaving it lying in the open, up for grabs in front of the cage.

Tommy picks it up, swiftly throwing it at the net as a defender knocks him to the ground with a punishing hit. Walkersville isn't dicking around – they are absolutely fanatical about defense. The goalie makes an unbelievable save, lunging up off the ground and jumping to catch it in his stick. *They're fucking ninjas*, thinks Tommy, springing up to chase after the ball. The goalie rockets a pass down to a breaking Bulldogs midfielder, who is on a 4-on-3 fast break toward the Hawks net.

The Hawks gallop after them, and the Walkersville player with the ball passes to a teammate, who passes off again. The third man in drills it, and the ball is buried in the Hoganton's goal.

"Walkersville's All-American goalkeeper makes two great saves, then throws rope to a teammate, starting a fast break. Walkersville cashes in to make it 3-0 early in the first quarter. It seems like the Bulldogs are able to score at will," says Hank, trying to remember to count his blessings. At least the Hawks made it to the State Title.

"Come on, Tommy, put the ball in the stinkin' cage!" yells Coach Jenkins from the sidelines, face like a thunder cloud. It's turning into a shit show, and Blair is no longer here, unable to share the blame. Jenkins thinks, *If we lose, it ain't my damn fault.*

"The way Walkersville is controlling the ball, I don't know how many scoring opportunities the Hawks are going to get. They need to make the chances they do get count," says Robbie.

In his distant jail cell, Andy can hear his teammates fucking up. Already 3-0 in the first quarter? He starts to beat his bed with his fist and swear. "Fuck, fuck, fuck sakes!" He flops down on the bed, almost wishing he had just gone home that night so he didn't have to listen to this shit.

The Hawks get the ball, and Quinn Harris drives down the wing. James rushes up to set him a pick, and their defenders switch, but not quite fast enough. Quinn flips the ball back to James, who fires a streaking shot into the top corner of the net. Finally, they are on the board.

"Quick shot there by James Henry to break the Hoganton goose egg and trim the deficit to 3-1. Maybe that can get the squad going," reports Hank, beaming.

"Nice shot by James Henry off a sweet little flip pass from Quinn Harris. That's the kind of play the Hawks need more of if they're going to have any chance against this very tough Bulldogs defense," adds Robbie happily.

The Bulldogs score the next goal on a man up from a foul by Ben to extend their lead to 4-1. Hoganton answers back with a goal from Tommy, set up by a nice feed from Steve McCrae. But Walkersville retaliates with two more goals, one on a foul by Troy.

Late in the first half, Tommy has the ball and tries to go to the net. He is held by his defender and draws a foul. Steve McCrae scores on the man advantage and the half ends 6-3 for Walkersville.

The Hawks fans have become more and more subdued as the first half played out. This is not the kind of outcome they had been hoping for today. Carli and Megan sit not too far behind the Hoganton bench and have done their share of cheering, but even they are feeling a little worn down by the Bulldogs onslaught.

"Seems like the field is tilted towards the Hoganton end," comments Carli drily. She is doing her best Robbie Redbird imitation. "I think the second half might be a little different. The Hawks don't want to get spanked in the Championship game so guys like Tommy Henry have to step up."

Megan has a grin on her face. "Since when did you become a lacrosse expert?"

"Expert at many things, sweetie," Carli throws that remark at Megan, waiting for a zinger comeback.

But instead Megan changes the subject. "Isn't that Hazel two rows back? Let's go join her. Maybe she can tell us how this game is going to turn out."

In the locker room, Coach Jenkins goes ballistic on the entire team. He reams them out while they sit, slouched over and demoralized.

"What the hell is going on out there?" he bellows, his narrow face turning a reddish purple. "Defensively, Ben, Troy, we can't win this game if we keep taking stupid penalties! Clarke! Have you made a save yet? I don't think so – every shot they've taken has either missed the cage or gone in it! Are you a fucking goalie or a dodge ball player?" he raves, as Clarkie's jaw tightens. Jenkins continues, veins popping out on his neck and forehead.

"We're getting killed on face-offs and ground balls! I don't even know what the hell the offense is doing! Tommy! I thought I told you to get your head out of your ass! I didn't come here to get my ass kicked! Maybe you did, but I sure as hell didn't. You fucking guys better fucking wake up for the second half!" he finishes with his eyes flashing fire. Then he storms out of the room without looking back and slams the door.

There is stunned silence for a moment.

"Thanks, Coach, real fired up to play now," says Ben. It breaks the tension a bit. There are a couple of small laughs, but they're all still pretty quiet. A good coach is supposed to motivate you to turn things around. Trust Jenkins to make a bad situation worse.

Tommy stands up, wishing that Coach Blair was here. He feels like an imposter, but someone's got to say something. The Coach was always the Man in these situations. He knew just what to say. What buttons to push. How could anybody replace Coach Blair?

"Guys, maybe we don't agree with everything Jenkins just said," he starts diplomatically. The others chuckle.

"Maybe we don't agree?" Ben huffs.

"One thing he was right about is we are making mistakes. But mistakes happen. That's part of the game. But we pick each other up after mistakes! We're a family; I know we are because I care about you guys like you were all my brothers, every fucking one of you. Maybe this season didn't go the way we all expected. We don't have some people here with us – we don't have Coach Blair, we don't have Andy," he leans in, voice intense.

"But you're still fucking here! We're still in the game. And your brothers, sitting right beside you, they're still here! One thing I learned this year is that it's okay to get knocked down; you just have to get back up! When you get knocked down, are you the kind of man that covers up like a fucking coward? Or are you the kind of man that gets the fuck up and starts swinging back!? I know you're the kind that gets up swinging, and you better fucking believe the guy next to you is too! Now that team out there just knocked us on our ass. Are we gonna get the fuck up?" he asks, heart pounding.

"Fucking right we are!" snaps loyal Ben, lunging to his feet. This sentiment is echoed by the others.

"Let's go fucking swing back! It's our turn," yells Tommy, and then they storm back out onto the field.

Hazel Blackwater is looking thoughtful as she prepares to answer Megan's question about the game's outcome. "This might sound like heresy coming from a Hawks fan, but it's not really important who wins and loses today. It's more about what all the individual players, like Tommy, find out about themselves. The game resembles a test in many ways. A test that can be passed or failed. If you play with all the right intentions and with the pure natural talent you have then nothing but good can come out of it. Does that answer your question?"

Megan has been hanging on every word. She feels there is so much knowledge buried in Hazel and wishes she could spend more time with her. "It does answer my question. It just wasn't the answer I expected."

Hazel's eyes are looking directly into Megan's. "If you embrace the unexpected, you will never stop learning. A wise woman told me that a long time ago. I have always lived by that and it has never taken me down the wrong path."

The Hawks come out a whole different team in the second half. They throw big hits and battle for every ground ball. Their enthusiasm is infectious, and they stay fired up, cheering each other on as their fans roar from the stands. Quinn scores the first goal of the second half, and James follows it with another, bringing the score to a close 6-5 for Walkersville. Staggered but further motivated, the home squad pull off another goal to bring their lead back to a more comfortable 7-5.

The Hawks refuse to give it up, even when Walkersville scores again, making it 8-5 with 7:20 left in the fourth quarter. Troy strips the ball from a Walkersville midfielder and turns it into a fast break with his long pole. The defense doesn't slide to him, and he fires an exuberant high shot past the goalie, scoring. Tommy is next to score, off a pass from Shane with 3:26 left on the clock.

After the goal Tommy walks over to Shane, holding his fist out for a bump. They haven't spoken since the texting incident with Jessica. Shane looks at him for a moment before reaching out for a solid fist bump.

"Nice pass, now go win that fucking face-off," urges Tommy.

Shane nods. "Fucking right," he agrees, running to the face-off area.

Shane wins the face-off and starts a fast break, flipping the ball to Tommy, who passes to Steve. Steve shoots and scores, tying the game at 8-8. There is a little over three minutes left.

"I don't know what adjustments were made at half time, but the Hawks came out on fire and have battled all the way back to tie the game at 8-8," exults Hank, practically dancing in his seat.

"They have definitely played typical Hawks ball this entire half," adds Robbie.

In his distant jail cell, Andy is screaming himself hoarse, cheering for his teammates. "Come on, boys, you got this! Come on!" he yells, grinning from ear to ear.

On the next face-off, there is a furious scramble for the ground ball. A Walkersville player controls it, but he is pushed from behind by a Hoganton player... and the ref throws his flag. It's a foul, and Walkersville goes on a man up situation just when the Hawks need every player they've got. The Hawks' defense does its damnedest to keep Walkersville from scoring, but just as the penalty runs out, a Bulldogs attackman manages to punch one past Clarkie. The score jumps to 9-8, and now there is only 1:49 left on the game clock.

Shane again battles to win the face-off and flips the ball to James. James passes to Steve, who is lurking behind the net, and Steve tries to dodge his defender. The Walkersville defender refuses to budge, sticking like glue. In desperation, Steve hurls the ball to Tommy for a shot at the net.

Tommy has a moment where he dodges his guard, and he takes it, jumping high to shoot on net from a full jump. Then time seems to go in slow motion. The crowd standing and cheering, the other players watching, Tommy's heart, his good heart, pulsing one slow beat at a time. Then all of a sudden, in real time, the ball screams through the air, rifling past the goalie with ease. He's tied it with 1:27 left. There is bedlam in the stands, everyone on their feet.

"Tommy Henry ties the game at 9 with a great righty jump shot!" yells Hank, standing up in the broadcast booth, beside himself with excitement.

"We knew we'd be treated to a heck of a lacrosse game today," says Robbie warmly as he puts his hands on Hank's shoulders and gently pushes him back down into his seat. "Neither team has disappointed. We have a little over a minute left to decide who takes home the State Title. This next face-off is huge!" he grins.

Weasel pumps his fist and gives Greg a high five as he turns his attention back to the Walkersville goalie. "I've seen coupons that save more than you, tendy!"

"Yeah, you need 'em, ya bum," a Walkersville fan yells back at Weasel.

"I've heard better chirps from a dead bird, buddy!" Weasel spouts back. "What are you the Reservation's redheaded step-child?"

"It's auburn, ya jackass!"

People in earshot of the lively conversation give a chuckle, and the two guys give each other a lengthy stare before they turn their attention back to the playing field. Greg is sitting beside Weasel as he giggles and shakes his head, wondering if the auburn hair agitator is going to get a brawl going in the stands.

In his jail cell, Andy is going nuts. "Fucking right, Tommy!" he yells, punching his fist in the air.

Shane and a grim-faced Walkersville player set for the face-off. The Bulldogs can't believe that this train wreck of a team is this close to taking the Title from them. The draw is won by the Walkersville player behind him, but Shane hits his stick to keep him from picking it up. They battle for the loose ball, but it gets picked up by another Walkersville player and swiftly moved to their offensive players. They move the ball around, and eventually a Walkersville player fires an outside shot that goes in past a horrified Clarkie with 32 seconds left to make it 10-9 Walkersville.

The stadium echoes with cheers from the Walkersville faithful.

The Hawks are stunned but must compose themselves if they hope to tie the game back up. Off the next face-off, Shane wins it back, and Troy Wilson comes up with the ball. Troy runs it over the midline, and Coach Jenkins calls timeout with 23 seconds left to play.

"Okay, 23 seconds left in the game. Hoganton gets possession and calls timeout," reports Hank breathlessly.

"They're going to draw up a play and try to tie this thing up. What a game this has been!" says Robbie.

The Hawks return to the field, and a Hoganton player has the ball at midfield as the ref blows the whistle to start the play. Shane tries to dodge the short stick defender but turns back and passes back up top to Quinn Harris, who dodges right, rolls back, and dodges left. The long pole defender stays with him, not allowing him to shoot, so Quinn passes behind the net to Steve. As Steve catches the ball, James and Shane set a double pick on Tommy's defender. Steve dodges left from behind the net. Shane cuts towards the net as Tommy runs out to the wing. Shane is covered inside, and Steve passes to Tommy. Tommy catches the ball and let's go a high, hard shot that has the top far side corner pegged. At the last second the Walkersville goaltender raises his stick up in desperation and just manages to get a piece of the ball. It's enough, and the deflected ball sails just over the crossbar and out of play. The clock winds down, time runs out, and the horn sounds, signaling the end of the game.

It's all over. Tommy drops to his knees as the Walkersville players swarm their goal keeper in victory.

"The Walkersville goaltender gets just enough of Tommy Henry's shot to keep it out of the net and secure another State Title. Walkersville takes it, 10-9 over the Hoganton Hawks," says Hank. He's disappointed that his guys didn't win, but it was a hell of a game!

"What a finish to a classic battle," adds Robbie. "The Hawks have no reason to hang their heads. They fought back from a deep hole early in the game and should be extremely proud of the effort they put forth this entire season."

In his cell, Andy is lying on his back on the cell bed, hands under his head. He stares blankly at the ceiling. It is all his fucking fault – at least from his perspective. And he can't even say he's sorry. Locked behind these bars with just his thoughts. Maybe that's what they mean by cruel and unusual punishment.

Weasel and his crew are already out of their seats and heading towards the exit as they get pelted with jeers from the Walkersville fans. Weasel simply sticks a finger in both ears and keeps walking. He doesn't want them to know they are getting to him, but they are. He's pissed, and he knows he better get out of there before he does something stupid.

On the field, Tommy is still on his knees as James walks over, picks him up, and hugs him. The rest of the Hawk players in that end of the field console him and pat him on the helmet. It's hard to lose something that seemed so close. Both teams line up to shake hands with the exception of Coach Jenkins, who is seen stomping back to the locker room.

"That guy's real classy," mumbles Ben.

The teams are lined up as the State trophy is awarded to the Walkersville captains and the Bulldogs take a victory lap while the Hoganton Hawks make their way to the locker room.

Tommy does not go into the locker room right away. He sits down on the players' bench, watching as the Walkersville players celebrate with the State Title trophy. He sits for a long time all by himself. He's wanted that trophy for so long. Dreamed about it. Now it's never going to happen. It's hard to move. Most of the stadium has cleared out when the team equipment manager and Ben come walking out of the locker room to Tommy.

"Wish I'd stayed out here with you; Jenkins was just giving everybody shit. It's all he's good at," Ben grunts in disgust.

"I don't really need to hear anything that dickhead has to say," says Tommy evenly. He knows that if he has to hear another one of Jenkins' verbal tirades, he'll have a hard time keeping his own temper in check.

"Sorry, Tommy, but I need your jersey," interrupts the equipment manager. Tommy lets out a long sigh.

"Never thought it would be so hard to take it off," he jokes, pulling the jersey over his head and passing it to the manager. Ben sits down next to Tommy as the equipment manager heads back to the locker room.

"That was a quick four years, huh?" says Tommy.

"Yeah, but a damn good four years," reminds Ben.

Ben puts his arm around Tommy as they walk toward the locker room.

⬛—⬛◆⬛—⬛

THE GAS MILEAGE ASSESSMENT the boys made turns out to have been a little generous. Thirty-five dollars worth of gas has gotten Weasel and his entourage to the game, but not much farther.

On the trip home, Weasel pulls into a small gas station just outside of Walkersville, heart pounding. He turns the car off and gets out, leaving the keys in the ignition. The gas attendant is watching him suspiciously from the window of the convenience store, and Weasel does his best to look casual.

He begins to pump gas into the empty tank and starts whistling to cover his nervousness as the dollar total racks up. There is just something about Weasel that makes most people automatically suspicious – and with Weasel, it is generally a justified belief. The pump clicks to full, and Weasel replaces the nozzle, starting to saunter toward the convenience store. The attendant relaxes, turning away to answer a customer's question.

Greg twists the keys in the ignition, and Weasel jumps in the car, flooring it as they peel out. The angry gas attendant comes running out of the store, yelling and waving his arms after them as they speed down the road with the driver's door still open. Weasel manages to close it after they are firmly back on the road, and they hightail it towards the Rez.

TOMMY GRADUALLY FINDS HIMSELF FEELING BETTER, surprisingly okay for having just lost the biggest game of his life. As he changes into his street clothes, his ears pick up the sound of crying. He turns, and sees Tim Blair's youngest son, Keegan, sitting on a bench. The little guy is sobbing like his heart is about to break, his brother and grandfather trying to console him. Tommy heads over to him and kneels down in front of him.

"You gonna be okay, buddy?" he asks sympathetically.

"I wanted you to win!" Keegan bursts out. "My dad said you were gonna win this year. I wanted you to win for my dad," cries Keegan, his tear-stained face wearing disappointment all over it.

Momentarily, Tommy is at a loss for words. Then it comes to him. "Hey, did you see that trophy the other team was holding up after they won?" he asks Keegan. The little guy nods sadly.

"Just think; someday you're gonna be holding that trophy over your head. And you're gonna do it for your dad, right?"

"Yeah," says Keegan, brightening a little.

"Well, if you're gonna win a State Title someday... you'd better get practicing," Tommy advises him, and hands him one of his own lacrosse sticks. The little boy takes it, and his eyes light up as he runs his hands over it. His brother Konner crowds in for a look, and Tommy hands him his other stick, feeling light as air.

"You'd better get practicing, too," he tells Konner, and Konner grins.

"Thanks, Tommy," says the boy's grandfather, reaching out to shake Tommy's hand. The two boys are already running out of the locker room to show Sarah their new sticks.

"Mom! Tommy gave me his stick!" hollers Keegan, waving it over his head.

"Me too!" yells Konner, not about to be outdone by his little brother.

WEASEL AND HIS BUDDIES ARE HEADED HOME, smoking the last of Krazy Kirk's weed. They've elected to take the back roads to avoid cops. Weasel feels mellow, and it isn't just the weed. He's been there for his friends, and he was glad. They might have lost, but they hadn't sucked, and that was the important thing. Jordy would have loved it.

An unpromising thud rattles the car, and they begin to coast, despite Weasel's best efforts. "What the fuck?" exclaims Weasel.

"Something must be fucked with the tranny," comments Danny Onions. Danny is an amateur mechanic and even when mightily buzzed can still diagnose most car ailments.

The car rolls to a stop, still running. Weasel cycles through the gears, but can't get it to move forward. In desperation, he tries reverse... and the car begins to move backward.

They are about a half hour from the Rez. Weasel turns the car around, and begins driving home backwards, slowly. He is grateful they're on the gravel country roads and not the highway.

Jordy, I bet you're laughing your ass off at this, he thinks, white-knuckling the steering wheel.

Chapter Thirty-Seven
ENJOY THE RIDE

The team might have lost the championship game, but many of their diehard fans are still loyal and want to find a way to show their appreciation for a spectacular effort. When the Hoganton Hawks pull into the school parking lot in the team bus, family and friends are waiting for the players. At least a hundred people cheer them off the bus, slapping shoulders and pulling them into hugs. It has been a heck of a season, and the real fans are not going to hold a final loss against them. Truth be told, many are surprised the Hawks got as far as they did. As each player steps off the bus, they are immediately met with a firm handshake from Chief Gary Williams, a Hawks alumnus.

Beau and Marian are waiting for their sons – even though Tommy's truck is still in the parking lot and the boys don't need a ride home. Marian wants to hug her boys and tell them again that it's okay that they didn't win; they are proud parents, no matter what. Tommy and James played well, and in the end, that's all you can really ask.

After the parents and James head out for a celebratory dinner, Tommy hurries toward his truck. He just wants to go home. Before he can open the tailgate, Tommy notices a car pulling into the school's driveway... in reverse. Of course, who else? It has to be Weasel.

The ginger fireplug backs the car up to Tommy and rolls down the window.

"The fuck are you doing driving like that? Just showing off?" Tommy asks.

Weasel grins cheekily. "If it's got wheels, I can drive it. Damn, good game, man – thought you guys had 'em," he says, shaking his head remorsefully.

"So did I," replies Tommy.

"Doing anything tonight?" asks Weasel hopefully.

"Nah, think I'm gonna lay low."

"Well deserved. Proud a ya, kid. You did good. Hey, can I borrow a few bucks?" he asks casually. "I told Ma I'd bring her back some smokes."

Like hell you did, thinks Tommy, but digs his wallet out anyway.

"Sure, man, here," he says, handing him a bunch of small bills. It's Weasel – he can't say no.

"Thanks, man, out!" he grins, driving away in reverse.

Tommy chuckles as he tosses his gear in the back. He starts the truck up, enjoying the powerful roar of the engine, and heads out to the main road. He'd love to know the real story behind Weasel's new driving style. Maybe he'll get it out of the little troublemaker later.

ON A SIDE ROAD NOT FAR FROM THE SCHOOL, Scott Davis and his old lacrosse teammate Lance Bennett are booting along in Scott's car, his pride and joy. A 1970 Chevrolet Chevelle SS with a 427 V-8 and 450 horses. An old school muscle car, blue with white racing stripes. They are laughing as Scott floors the gas pedal making the powerful engine roar and the car jump. Not a fucking care in the world. The men have raced down this road hundreds if not thousands of times before. *Anyway,* Davis is thinking, *we're the fucking 1981 State Champions. Never been anything like us before and won't never be again.*

Lance has had enough beers to be introspective, but not enough to be buzzed. At least not like Scott is buzzed.

"I don't know why, but when we're cruising like this, I still think about that night sometimes, you know. Sometimes it's all I can think about."

Scott looks scornfully sideways at his old buddy while holding his bottle almost to his lips without taking a drink. *Man, not that again. Am I the only one who can leave that shit in the past?*

"You're not going to start raggin' on about that again are you? We've been through this shit before... it was years ago. Nobody ever found out. Drink your fucking beer and forget about it."

Scott has one hand on the wheel and the other raising the beer to his lips as he continues to talk about the game. The pair has been powering back the ale during the game in the hopes that the Hawks' pathetic play might be improved by the alcohol haze. No dice. Once a bunch of losers, always a bunch of losers.

"I knew those guys weren't gonna win. They got no heart," Scott sneers, taking another swig. His mouth is numb from the alcohol he's consumed and now the beer tastes like water.

Lance remains quiet for a moment, but then ignoring what Scott had to say, carries on with his own train of thought.

"All I'm saying is that if I had to do it all over again, I woulda stopped to see if he was okay, maybe taken him to the hospital. He was only seventeen. He didn't deserve that, Scott. Christ, we were only fourteen, just kids. Sometimes I have nightmares about it. Plus I always wonder what Beau would do if he found out."

Scott crushes the gas pedal to the floor in anger causing the Chevy to surge forward, slamming Lance back into his seat.

"If we stopped, we would have went to fucking jail. Enough with that shit, Lancer. Nobody will ever find out as long as you shut the fuck up about it."

Scott downs his beer, rolls down the window, and throws a lazy hook shot with his left hand. The bottle shatters against a road sign.

"Oh lefty, still the best fucking sign man around! Grab me another one," he orders, and Lance reaches around his seat, trying to locate a fresh soldier in the cooler. He knows or at least strongly suspects there are more in there, but he can't find any.

"I can't reach 'em," he grunts as he strains, reaching.

"For fuck sakes, man!" snaps Scott. He reaches behind the passenger's seat with his right hand, trying to find another of the long-necked beverages. He can't feel any of them either, and he glances away from the road quickly to try and figure out what the hell is going on. He sees the bottles have fallen on their sides, and he lunges to get his fingertips down into the cooler, scooping one out. *Got it!*

At the same moment Lance shouts, "Look out!" as he braces his hands on the dash. Scott looks up just in time to notice they've swerved onto the wrong side of the road and oncoming bright lights are headed right for them.

In the other vehicle, Tommy only has time for a startled exclamation. "Shit!"

The vehicles collide head-on, the smaller car thrown off to the side of the road. The car flips, landing on its roof with the sound of crushing metal and cascading broken glass. On the road, the truck's front end is folded up, and coolant leaks out onto the road. The alarm blares briefly then abruptly cuts out as the truck loses power.

The road is dark with only the Chevelle's headlights to illuminate things, and no one is moving in either vehicle. It is deathly still.

Chapter Thirty-Eight

CONNECTION

Marian and James are sitting next to each other in the waiting room. Beau, Marian, and James have been taking shifts sitting with Tommy. The hospital allows only one person at a time in the patient's room. James tries to distract himself with the battered, out-of-date magazines. He notices a story about a grizzly bear attack and flips through the pages.

Many rooms and a maze of hallways away, Tommy lies unconscious, propped up in a hospital bed. Bruises and stitched gashes cover his exposed skin, and a number of machines bleep and chirp as they monitor his vital signs and occasionally dispense pain medication in an IV drip.

Suddenly, Tommy begins to open his eyes, and he wakes feeling confused. This isn't his room – where are his posters? He peers out of bleary eyes and recognizes his father's face. Beau, through his own exhausted, half-closed eyes, snaps fully awake, sitting upright in his bedside chair.

"Tommy? You there? Can you hear me, Tommy?" he asks urgently. No one has been able to tell him whether Tommy's brain will be okay when he wakes up – concussions are "tricky," in the words of the doctor.

"Yeah, Dad, I can hear you," croaks Tommy. God, his throat is dry. He tries to move to find some water, and all of a sudden everything hurts. "Oh shit," he whispers, freezing to let the pain dissipate.

"What hurts? Your hip?" asks Beau worriedly.

"No, my shoulder. Check that, my whole body," he mumbles. "Water?" he asks, and Beau gets up and grabs him a Dixie cup of water on the bedside tray, positioning a straw so that Tommy can drink with little effort.

"Try not to move, okay? You've got a lot of parts that will hurt if you move. You broke your collarbone and your wrist. You've got some pretty bad damage to your hip and knee, too," Beau summarizes. "The doc says you have a severe concussion – you've been out for almost two days."

"Two days? They say anything about how long to recover?" asks Tommy.

Beau hesitates. "You mean play lacrosse?" he clarifies.

"Yeah."

Beau's face is grim as he addresses his athletic seventeen-year-old son. "I'll be honest with you, Tommy. Doc said you'll need surgeries on your knee and hip just to walk normal again... and with the concussion, they don't know if some brain damage may have happened," he says slowly.

Tommy seems alert and sensible, but Beau dreads that there will be some sort of residual damage that will only come to light later or Tommy might just have a relapse. "He said it would be a long time, maybe not ever. Tommy, I'm just happy that you're awake – I couldn't care less about lacrosse right now and neither should you," he adds.

"When can I go home?" asks Tommy, finding his own voice dim and raspy.

"Doc said after you wake up, they would have to monitor you for a while before you can leave, but it shouldn't be too long. A couple of days, maybe, I don't know. You've had a lot of visitors come to see you. Ben, Troy, Weasel, Andy even came straight here soon as he got out of the clink. And Megan and Carli have been here a lot. I have to tell you those two have senses of humor like I've never seen. They can make almost anything seem funny. Megan has been sitting with you a lot. She did tell us you that the two of you have become close, and that she's expecting a baby. A baby that isn't yours," Beau says, grinning but trying to look serious as Tommy blushes.

"She told you that, huh?" he asks weakly.

"I'm sure it's a story for another time. We'll have time to talk about that later. Right now, I have to go find your mother. She's just happy you're alive, and she's gonna be even happier when I tell her you're awake. I better go get her. She's out in the waiting room with James. Don't go anywhere," he teases, leaving the room.

"Ha ha," croaks Tommy. He turns and notices that there's a picture on the nightstand – a color photo of him and Megan standing in front of the library on the Ralston Campus. Carli insisted on taking it, saying it was the magic hour for photography and that she could make Tommy and Megan look like a couple of movie stars. Sure enough, Megan's light colored hair looks golden, beautifully backlit by the setting sun. She smiles broadly with her arm around Tommy, her green eyes twinkling. They look good together. They look connected.

Chapter Thirty-Nine

PATIENCE

Time passes slowly for Tommy in the hospital. Despite the original thought that he might only have to be there for a couple of days after recovering consciousness, he stays there for another week. The doctors want to make sure that he is well on his way to recovery before he leaves. That doesn't make it any easier for him. He has a steady stream of visitors, but for a guy who is used to being active and not standing still very often, it is torture. Tommy's not a big reader. He reads some books, sure, but not one after the other. Television, sure. Listening to music, sure. But what about the other twenty hours in the day?

Then Grampa Henry comes to visit. Doug Henry is still five foot ten inches of lean muscle with just the slightest hint of a pot belly. He is seventy-four-years old but barely a wrinkle intrudes on his handsome face. His light brown eyes look out over a nose that has a slight curve in it, but that comes with being a boxer back in the Marine Corps. He claims he doesn't have a favorite grandchild, but he sure does love to watch Tommy play lacrosse. Tommy is pretty sure that Grampa Henry remembers every play of every game.

When he walks into Tommy's hospital room, he's wearing his usual outfit. It never varies unless he's going to a funeral or maybe a wedding. A ball cap pulled down over his short, wavy gray hair. Jeans and buttoned up flannel work shirt with his same old worn out work boots. He crunches Tommy's fingers in a handshake that says he might be older but not to underestimate him. A little whiff of cigarette smoke follows him to Tommy's bedside.

"Maybe we can go out fishing when you get out of this place, Tommy. Everyone says you got to take it easy for a little bit."

Tommy isn't feeling too optimistic with all the pain and the restricted mobility he's experiencing. In fact, he's worried that the good part, the best part of his life, might be over. He doesn't know how well he'll be able to walk. The idea of going away to college and playing more lacrosse has disappeared. He's worried. And Grampa wants him to go fishing? Tommy feels so clumsy that he's more likely to fall out of the boat and drown in the lake.

Tommy grins at his grandfather sitting in the hospital chair by the window. Grampa Doug has a good sense of humor, and Tommy knows he's just trying to cheer him up. Life has turned everything upside down now. Tommy wouldn't mind going fishing actually. He's never gone much because he has always been so busy playing sports or getting in shit with his friends. The time on the boat with Weasel was the first time he went fishing in a couple years. James, on the other hand, spent much of his childhood summers in the boat with his Grampa Doug. Those two really had a special bond, especially when James was sick as a kid. Tommy's not much of a fisherman, never had the patience for it, but right now he can think of nothing better than spending some time on the lake with his Grampa.

"Yeah, I want to go fishing. Not sure when that will be, but that's something I can look forward to."

Doug Henry moves to Tommy's bedside chair and examines some of the get well cards sitting on the small end table. "Everything is going to work out, Tommy. You'll just have to have some patience. Though I know you ain't got much. Another thing about you that reminds me of your dad," says the elder Henry shaking his head.

"Well, just wanted to say hi and check up on ya. I'm supposed to meet up with the old boys for coffee. They'll want to know how you're doing. I'll tell them you're practically ready to start running around again."

"Everybody around the Rez probably still mad at us 'cause we didn't win State," mutters Tommy.

Grampa Doug stands up slowly with a couple of joints cracking as he pulls himself to his full height. As he heads towards the door, he looks over his shoulder at Tommy. "Well, that's the thing about some people around here. They ain't happy unless they're mad."

As Grampa Doug leaves the room Tommy thinks to himself for a second, and laughs quietly. "That's so fucking true."

A̶MES PUSHES TOMMY IN A WHEELCHAIR, and it gives Tommy a weird ꜱense of déjà vu. He remembers James being the sick one not so long ago. ꞵeau pulls up to the exit in his double cab truck and James helps Tommy ꞈut of the wheelchair and into the front passenger seat. The slow climb is ꞏmbarrassingly difficult for Tommy, and he has to pause partway through ꞏo let the pain subside and to catch his breath.

James waits until his brother is secure in his seat before loading the ꞷheelchair and hopping in the back. As they leave the hospital's parking ꞈot, Tommy questions. "Did you see my truck at all?" he blurts, almost ꜳfraid to ask.

James shakes his head. "Oh man, your truck is totaled. Seen it at Martin's Ⲧowing."

Tommy's heart breaks a little. It was his first vehicle. A lot of stuff ꞕappened in that truck. Lots of memories. Beau notices Tommy's down-ꞓast expression and hastens to reassure him. "The other driver's insurance ꞓompany is going to give you money for another vehicle. They already ꞇuled that it wasn't your fault," says Beau.

Another thought occurs to Tommy. "Who was driving the other car?" ꞕe asks. He doesn't remember anything from the accident.

"Scott Davis. Lance Bennett was with him," says Beau soberly. "Nei-ꞇher one of them made it."

They're all silent for a moment. He doesn't feel downright sorry for Ⴝcott Davis, but he does have some sympathy even after all the pain he has ꞓaused Tommy. After being a high school lacrosse star, his life went pretty ꞗuch downhill. Tommy doesn't want that to happen to him.

Tommy comes back to reality as their truck passes the big "Sparrow Ⴑake Nation" sign. He's home. That means a lot. More than he thought it ꞷould.

Beau clears his throat. "Tommy, you should probably start thinking ꜳ little bit about what you wanna do, career-wise. I know you just got ꞈut of hospital, but it's never too soon to start thinking about it. I mean ꞷou'll always have your job at the hardware store, and you know your ꞗother and I will always be here to help you guys. Have any idea what ꞷou might wanna do?"

As Beau finishes his question, the truck passes by a very lived-in look-ꞏng house. It's a little rundown but six pre-teen boys are trampling down ꞷhat is left of the grass in the front yard, engaged in a furiously competitive lacrosse game.

"Oh, we got one," James says as two of the young boys have dropped their sticks to exchange punches before wrestling each other to the ground. Tommy smiles as the other boys try separate the two combatants .

"Yeah, Dad. I've got an idea."

Chapter Forty

THE CREATOR SMILES

Reg Harris, alongside Hazel Blackwater, is blessing the Hoganton Hawks in their new stadium with pungent-sweet tobacco smoke rising up toward the clear blue sky. He is speaking Mohawk, thankful for this game, this moment, and at the same time asking the Creator for safety for all the players. Tommy Henry, head coach of the Hawks, stands beside the players, who are without their helmets and gloves. His assistant coach, Ben Lucas, nods solemnly. It is a fitting way to begin, especially for this final game of the season.

They've come a long way in two years. It still feels surreal to be the coach – several of the players were on the team with him during their freshman and sophomore years. Now Tommy's in charge, and he understands all too well the frustrations that made Coach Blair pull his hair out.

Reg finishes speaking, and Tommy thanks him with a handshake and Hazel with a heartfelt hug, before she heads back toward the stands. She whispers in his ear, "Remember, Tommy, follow your path. Be happy." The players head back to the locker room to put on the rest of their gear as Tommy and Ben stay out on the field at their home bench area.

It is a full house for the State Title game, and the Hawks' side overflows with everything red and black – sweatshirts, pennants, and homemade signs.

High up in the stands, Marian and Beau along with Megan and her eighteen-month-old daughter, Jordon, are just settling into their seats. Megan's mother, Michelle, is also part of the entourage. Carli Thompkins is there of course, keeping everyone laughing with her "boys in shorts" lacrosse observations. Megan and the curly-haired toddler are the focus of Tommy's new life, and he still can't believe how lucky he is to have these two ladies by his side. Tommy turns away from the field to look up into the stands. He can feel the overwhelming waves of excitement coming from the fans. Strangely, for him at least, with the game about to start, he feels calm. Then he catches sight of his family members and waves. Everybody, including Jordon enthusiastically returns his gesture.

Tommy and Megan's relationship has developed gradually, but intensely, into a strong emotional bond based on the growing feelings they have for each other. Megan has watched and helped Tommy recover from his injuries. They've had long talks about life and the future as Megan's pregnancy advanced and Tommy got back on his feet. For Tommy, the partying has all but disappeared. He no longer feels the need to get wasted to be able to accept himself. Part of that acceptance has come as a result of Tommy being able to open up to Megan about his childhood trauma. How it plagued his life. How it almost cost him his life. He was also able to confide in Megan all the details of his destructive relationship with Jessica. Not just what happened, but also what he has learned about how to be more in control of his life. About not letting other people and other experiences control him. There is so much less anger in Tommy now. Much of what he has to say Megan can easily relate to as well. Ryan McDowell is just a fading memory for her now. Both Tommy and Megan knew ultimately that they were headed for new lives and decided that the timing was right for them, that they wanted that new life together. The three of them. One of the biggest parts of that new life is the little girl named Jordon who Tommy loves as his own daughter. Megan and Jordon have somehow given Tommy the freedom to be the person he wants to be, that he is meant to be. And Tommy seems to complete the circle for Megan and her daughter. He is now the manager at the hardware store, and Megan plans to return to college to finish her degree.

Up in the announcer's booth, Hank and Robbie couldn't be happier. Two years ago, they'd watched with extreme disappointment as the Hawks came close but failed to capture the Title. Now, in the new Timothy Blair Stadium, they have another shot. A shot at redemption.

"Hank Thomas here once again for another installment of Hawks championship lacrosse as the Hoganton Hawks get ready to do battle with the Walkersville Bulldogs for the 2005 State Title. This is a rematch of two years ago when Walkersville won a 10-9 thriller," he grins, reveling in the tense, happy excitement of the moment. He has butterflies, damn it, and he's not even on the field. It is games like these that make the grind of the season all worthwhile. Hank has watched, and called, too many lacrosse games to count. The big ones never get old. And Hank knows he's lucky to have Robbie with him to back him up. It's all about teamwork.

Robbie Redbird is waiting to pick up the narrative thread as usual, feet propped on a low stool as he surveys the turf field. Hoganton has finally joined the modern lacrosse world, and it makes Redbird feel like today just might be the day. The day the Hawks will capture that elusive State Title. Robbie doesn't want to say it, doesn't want to jinx it, but just maybe all the stars have aligned.

"First year Head Coach Tommy Henry has got these Hawks believing in themselves, and I expect another great game between these two talented and tough teams," says Robbie breezily. No one can accuse this head coach of being out of touch with the players – two years ago he was on the field himself.

"Tommy Henry took over the vacant coaching position following the resignation of Coach Adam Jenkins following a dreadful 7-8 season. Since then, the Hawks have radically altered their philosophy going back to the high octane, unpredictable offense that former Head Coach Tim Blair was known for. The Hawks have an unblemished 17-0 record and their worthy opponents, the Walkersville Bulldogs, have also seen a season without any losses. Going into this final game, we have two teams with undefeated records – there can only be one winner at the end of the day, though, so this should be a nail-biter from the get go!"

Tommy spots Grampa and Gram Henry arriving to sit with Tommy's parents Beau and Marian. Joyce Henry had stubbornly refused to go back to the old lacrosse field, but as she put it, she hadn't been kicked out of this new stadium... yet.

Further down the stands, Shane and Jessica arrive and find their seats. Both of them sip from cups of rum and coke that they snuck into the stadium. As they sit down, Shane's phone buzzes with an incoming text. Shane turns away so Jessica can't see his phone as he types his reply. Jessica tries to look over his shoulder to see his phone to know who he is talking to.

"Who you texting?" she sternly asks.

"Just my brother," Shane grunts.

Then Jessica's phone buzzes with an incoming text, and she turns away from Shane to read and reply to it.

"Who you texting?" he asked with his eyes sharpening.

"Just my sister," remarks Jessica, noticeably annoyed.

Up higher in the stands, Hazel sits with her friend Jean and notices Shane and Jessica bickering back and forth.

"Is that Tommy's old girlfriend, Jessica? You know her?" Hazel asks, using her lips to point towards the young girl.

"Yeah, that's her, and yes, I know her through her mom," Jean replies curiously.

"She's hurting, can see it in her eyes," Hazel says, tilting her head as she watches Jessica.

"You think so?" asks Jean, also looking in the young girl's direction.

"After the game, do you think you could introduce us? I'd really like to meet her," Hazel asks, a small smile coming over her face.

Weasel, Andy, and Troy, with his girlfriend and young son sporting a red Hawks sweater, are seated much closer to the field. Even in a sea of Hawks red, Weasel's orange-ginger hair stands out like a beacon. Tommy gets a lump in his throat when he realizes that he still automatically looks for Jordy. Andy struck a plea bargain with his charges. He plead guilty to driving while intoxicated and resisting arrest, and he served eight months in jail. When he got out, he enrolled at a local junior college, but that didn't last a semester. He was able to get a job with Troy ironworking, and they play some Sr. club lacrosse when they can. Weasel has had a number of odd jobs over the last little while. Still doesn't like being told what to do, so he never seems to get along with any of his bosses. And he still manages to have himself a good time on the weekends.

The loudspeaker booms overhead and Tommy returns to the moment.

"Now entering the stadium, the Walkersville Bulldogs!" bellows the announcer, and the team jogs out onto the field in a double line, whooping and hollering as they gallop to their net. Their many fans cheer, wearing green and gray while waving a sea of small flags. The Bulldogs and their fans are used to winning. They expect nothing less from the boys today.

"Now entering the stadium, in their traditional way, the Hoganton Hawks!" calls an announcer from the loudspeakers, and the crowd hushes.

The Hawks appear at the entrance to their locker room, lined up in twos and led by Quinn and James. The boys are solemn as Quinn breaks into a traditional chant known as Standing Quiver Dance. Quinn's voice echoes throughout the stadium as his teammates join in. They shuffle, dancing in the traditional stomping steps of long-gone warriors, and the crowd watches transfixed. When they reach the midline of the field, they break into a sudden sprint for the net, where they give their proud Hawks cheer. The crowd roars its approval.

"Please welcome a special presentation from the Sparrow Lake Nation Dancers," comes the announcement over the PA system. Six Mohawk dancers have centered themselves on the field, dressed in gorgeous, brightly feathered native regalia. The music starts, and the dancers leap into action, whirling and dancing in time to the traditional Smoke Dance. In the stands, Hazel Blackwater smiles triumphantly. This is how the Medicine Game should be honored.

When the music finishes and the dance ends, the crowd is wildly appreciative, cheering and yelling like the State Title is already in the bag. The dancers collect themselves and gracefully leave the field.

"Will you all please rise and remove your hats for the playing of the Star-Spangled Banner?" echoes through the stadium as the crowd gets to their feet. When the anthem finishes, the starting ten players for each team make their way to center of the field for the referee's instructions.

"Here we go! It's the Hawks versus the Bulldogs to see who is the best high school lacrosse team in the state!" yells Hank, almost beside himself with excitement.

The teams do not disappoint from the outset. Both are fired up and eager for victory; both have that combination of passion and discipline that makes for a drawn-out pitched battle where every second counts. Both teams are loaded with experienced and talented players. The fans are living the game moment by moment with them, the constant roar of the crowd impressively loud and not restricted to goals or saves. Tommy just hopes he can keep his players focused. You don't want to get too far ahead of yourselves. Just do the stuff that got you here. All the little things. The crowd loves their players, and is showing them heartfelt appreciation in the only way they know how.

Tommy feels emotionally drained, but Ben is there to back him up, both of them keeping their Hawks focused. They congratulate the players on every good play, keep them on track and focused on their end goal. Ben concentrates on defense, his specialty, and coaches them intensely throughout. Tommy directs most of his attention toward the offense – Quinn Harris and Steve McRae are the offensive leaders, and even the stingy Bulldog defense can't entirely keep them from scoring.

In the fourth quarter, Steve takes the ball behind his net and is able to shake his defender. He then dishes the ball to James who winds and fires a high hard shot. The Walkersville goalie is having a great day in net and makes a stunning save, corralling the ball in the webbing of his stick. The goalie fires the ball to his Walkersville teammates, and they take the ball to the Hawks end. In the stands, the very same woman who had berated James years ago at the hardware store is in fine form, constantly yelling irritating advice.

"Come on, Henry, put the ball in the net!"

Tommy immediately turns around a little pissed, wanting to see who made the remark. Just as he looks up he hears a responding comment.

"Sit yer fat ass down and shut the hell up!"

Tommy spots all five feet of Gram Henry standing and pointing at the woman who had yelled at her grandson. She is gritting her teeth, trying to restrain herself. Joyce Henry glares at the woman with intense anger. The heckler is more than a little intimidated and takes her seat amongst a little laughter from nearby spectators. Beau and Grampa Henry both smirk trying hard not to bust out laughing. Lacrosse may be the Medicine Game, but it's a serious affair to Joyce Henry. Tommy turns back to the game with a satisfied smile. He knows his grandmother can handle what's going on in the stands.

With 1:27 left in the game, Hoganton has a tenuous 11-10 lead. Walkersville gets the ball into the Hoganton end, and the Bulldogs head coach calls a timeout.

"1:27 left in regulation and the Hawks are clinging to a one goal lead. Walkersville has the ball in the Hoganton end of the field and they call a timeout," announces Hank for the benefit of those listening in via radio.

"The Bulldogs' coaching staff is drawing up a strategy, hoping they can tie this game up. In the meantime, the Hawks' coaches are trying to make sure their defensive guys are ready for anything Walkersville might throw at them," Robbie reports.

He really hopes that the Hawks don't blow it again – Hank may finally snap. Robbie knows that wouldn't be pretty.

Ben pulls the defense players around him, face tense. This is it. Crunch time.

"I want a long pole on 19," he orders. "We know what direction each player wants to dodge. Take away their strong hands and make them dodge with their off-hand. Nothing inside! Take away any easy dump passes inside. Out on their hands, and don't let them wind up for a clean shot. They do have some guys who can fire the ball," he admits, worried. That is a massive understatement – the Walkersville Bulldogs are unnervingly competent in all areas of the game. This is why they are the defending champs.

"Come on, D!" cheers Tommy. "Let's go win this thing right here!" he proclaims, and the players return to the field, newly invigorated.

When play resumes, Walkersville controls the ball, swinging it around the outside. The Hoganton defense continues doing their job to the utmost, keeping the Bulldogs from getting an easy shot at net. All they have to do is run the clock out, and they'll have won it all for the first time in twenty-four years.

Frustrated at the Hawks obstruction, the Bulldogs take an outside shot that completely misses the net. They don't get a goal, but they manage to keep possession. Furious at being contained, they try another outside shot that also misses. The crowd constantly roars in frenzied excitement as the clock keeps ticking down the seconds.

After the second missed shot, a Walkersville attack man picks the ball up from the endline, swiftly dodging left before heading right. A Hawks defender is hot on his heels, urged on by the taste of an impending victory. The Bulldog attacker runs behind the net, skimming as close to the crease as possible in order to shake his pursuer. The Hawks player follows, but catches his cleat on the netting, stumbling almost to his knee. The Walkersville player takes his half-step advantage and darts toward the goal. Another Hawk is there, almost instantly, sliding to prevent a one-on-one shot. But the Bulldogs' player swiftly passes to a teammate who has just cut in front of the net. The second Walkersville player hurls the ball, and it hits the back of the Hawks' net, scoring a goal with a scant 13 seconds left on the clock. It's all tied up.

"Walkersville ties it up with 13 seconds left! Hoganton was 13 seconds away from winning the State Title, but now they must score once more for them to walk away champions," Hank agonizes. Thirteen seconds? What can you do with thirteen seconds? In the fast-paced game of lacrosse, thirteen seconds is plenty of time.

"Just 13 seconds left and both teams are out of timeouts. So whoever wins this next face-off is going right to the net to try and win it," says Robbie, patting Hank's shoulder sympathetically, trying to settle him down a little bit.

Tommy consoles his boys – the player whose stumble led to the goal is particularly downcast. "It's okay, guys. It's okay. We're still winning this thing. Keep your heads up! Keep battling! It's a long way from over."

They listen, but they are still subdued. Everyone feels exhausted, but they know they have to go the extra mile.

The next face-off is not won cleanly by either team, and they battle for it at the midline. A Walkersville player comes up with the ball and throws toward the Hoganton net, hoping that one of his teammates will pick it up and score for a decisive win. Instead, one of the Hawks catches it and takes it out of their end just as the clock runs out on regulation time. The game is still tied.

Tommy calls his offense over, and directs their attention to some quick strategy he's mapped out on their whiteboard.

"If we win the faceoff, this is what we're going with."

High above the crowd, Hank shakes his head. "Ladies and gentlemen these two teams have put on quite a show today and 48 minutes just wasn't enough to get a winner. We are going to sudden victory overtime. The next team to score wins the State Title."

The Hawks are still plotting their next moves. "Steve, your first look is inside. If it's not there, you'll have Quinn coming down the wing James, you're on the other side by the net. You gotta back the cage up if we miss the net."

The teams line up for the face-off, and Hoganton wins the draw. The crowd continues with non-stop cheering. The Hawks settle down and throw the ball around the outside, sending it to James, who throws it behind the net to Steve. Steve dodges left and rolls back right. Two Hoganton players set a double pick inside for Quinn, who gets free of the defense and is suddenly open. Steve whips the ball to him, and Quinn catches and releases in a single smooth motion, firing right at the Bulldogs' goal. The panicked goaltender lunges, and the ball thwacks off of his glove, deflecting away from the net. It skips through the air and suddenly out of nowhere a stick lunges to catch it. It's James Henry.

James cradles the ball for a breathless instant before hurling it at the empty corner of the cage. The ball settles into the back of the net. It's a goal. Not just any goal, but a game winning, playoff winning, State Championship winning marker. There is no bigger goal a high school player can ever score. And the hometown crowd goes berserk.

The stadium shakes with the deafening roar of approval from the crowd. Decades of pent-up frustration released in a single play. People are hugging and jumping up and down as the Hawks grab each other for a joyous group hug. James gets mobbed, tackled to the ground by his teammates in a pile of red and black jerseys.

Tommy and Ben hug each other. They never thought they'd ever see this day. Running over to the stands, they high-five Weasel, Troy, and Andy who are beside themselves with excitement.

Over the roar of the crowd, Tommy's ear catches a woman's voice. "Tommy, Tommy!" it calls, and he turns to see Megan walking towards him holding Jordon. Jordon is grinning and kicking her feet excitedly, curly black hair framing her cute face. He grabs her for a tight celebration squeeze.

"Tommy!" calls James, and he turns. James tosses him something, and Tommy catches it, realizing what it is.

It is the white, shiny, game-winning lacrosse ball. Obeying a half-remembered memory, Tommy turns to where his parents are standing next to the field. Beau has his arm around Marian as they admire what their two sons have just accomplished.

"Dad!" calls Tommy.

Tommy tosses him the ball. Beau catches it easily with one hand.

He stares at it for a second and then glances over to his sons, revealing a slowly surfacing smile. Pride is written all over Beau Henry's face.

Hazel Blackwater watches the scene from high above in the stadium stands, Tommy Henry surrounded by the people he loves. A satisfied smile spreads across her face as she thinks, *Now, Tommy, now you're on the right path.*